6 Caledon Street

D. Wells has written four books, with 6 Caledon Street being her first full length novel. She hopes to write many more. She lives with her family in East Anglia, but has also lived in Kent and overseas in South Africa. She lists reading, coffee and good food as some of her favourite things.

6 Caledon Street

By D. Wells

This edition published 2018

ISBN-13: 9781090526083

D. Wells has asserted her right to be identified as the author of this work

This book is a work of fiction. Names and characters are the product of the author's imagination and any resemblance to actual persons, living or dead, is entirely coincidental

Cover Design by Angie Zambrano

Dedication

To my little monkeys for allowing me the time to write this novel.

Contents

Prologue

5th February 1907

Nanny sighs deeply as she lifts the pail of water from the copper bath. She struggles with it to the fireplace to reheat the water for our water bottles. Her face is red and angry and she's sweating rather unattractively. I write this as I sit and watch her, from on top of the dresser in the kitchen, where our food is prepared.

I am the daughter of the Master of this house, and I wouldn't usually be permitted entry below stairs. However, life has become somewhat extraordinary of late and the rules are no longer enforced so stringently.

The scullery maid was recently let go and with Housekeeper sick in bed once again, Nanny has rather found herself put upon. She is running the kitchen as well as looking after my two younger brothers (I am far too old to be looked on in such a manner. I have just turned fourteen). I know Nanny is unhappy about this. Her bedroom is next to the room where I am tutored and I heard raised voices the other day. She was complaining to Housekeeper of the extra burdens placed upon her to which Housekeeper coughed and spluttered in reply. There is nothing for it, Nanny must take on the extra duties while the staff situation is so woeful.

I wonder how long she will last. I also wonder how long my father's financial worries may continue. I am not consulted in these matters, but I have ears and take it upon myself to be aware of the fortunes, or misfortunes, of my own flesh and blood. I have always had a curious nature.

Father first spoke of his concerns last year, when forced to depart with several staff members. This act seemed to buoy us for a short while. But recently we have said goodbye to almost all. Only Nanny, Housekeeper and my tutor remain. Father was particularly sorry to say goodbye to the butler, of whom he had shared many interesting talks with over the years. Mother departed with her lady's maid not long after and she was equally affected.

None of this has passed me by unnoticed. But I do not know the particulars as to why, nor as to what might come next. I worry my tutor might soon go. This pains me greatly and I wish it not so with all my heart. Without my education I have little options. I am expected to marry well; a woman of my station always will be. But I have dreams above and beyond the simple joys of running a home. I have seen and heard and even smelled the tide turning for young women around me. There are jobs. Opportunities not before on offer. I may not be expected to require a profession, like those belonging to a lower class. But I desire it, nay I crave it. If I was to lose my tutor, my dreams will be swept away as well, and that is my deepest and most troubling fear.

Chapter One

2015

The early morning sky was lit with streaks of gold, magenta and rose. Threatening grey wisps of cloud hung menacingly in the distance, with a rapidly quickening breeze bringing them ever closer. But the weather could not shake Sarah Miller's good mood. She sat on a bench, on the common opposite, nursing a travel mug full of coffee, and watched the grand Edwardian house in front of her. She felt a flicker of peace.

In just over a week she would be moving in to the converted flat on the top floor. She felt the stirrings of exhilaration. This was all part of her new life; a cleverly honed strategy she had implemented just a few months before. Leaving behind her painful past, Sarah had crafted a three-step project, commencing with the new job she had started almost four months ago.

The second step consisted of the move which was now upon her. Tired of sharing with a housemate (a stark contrast to the many years of being too scared to be on her own in the house), Sarah knew she'd never be able to fully move on until she had her own place again. But it had required the new job, and the increase in salary, to be able to pull it off.

Step number three was by far the scariest. Sarah didn't really know how it would play out. She didn't even know what it would consist of, what it might look like. She only knew as much as the header she'd written in her diary: Let it go.

She watched the violet grey clouds sputter ever closer. A slight damp to the air alerted her to the likelihood of rain. Spring seemed to be taking its time to arrive, with winter clinging on for dear life with its icy fingernails.

Sarah looked forward to the spring and then summer evenings at her new place. Walks on the common. Picnics with her best friend Izzy and family. Sitting on the small roof terrace with a glass of wine. It was one of the reasons she had grabbed the flat with both hands.

*   *   *

"So, this is the lovely and spacious living area-cum-kitchen," said Angel, the enthusiastic and bubbly rental agent.

Sarah nodded numbly in agreement. When you had seen what felt like a hundred flats in barely a week, Sarah felt a nod was the best she could muster. Even though she had instantly loved the location of Caledon Street and the building itself, she simply had no energy left to try and match the enthusiasm of the woman standing opposite.

The four hours of sleep probably hadn't helped either.

It had been weeks since the last broken night, but the previous evening it had swept in with force and left Sarah awake at two in the morning. It was always two.

She tucked her short dark bob behind her ears and tried to pay attention to Angel's sales spiel.

"As you can see, it has been lovingly restored to include genuine Edwardian period features. You'll notice the fireplace, which works by the way, and the elegant striped wallpaper which was common of the time."

While wallpaper, especially striped, wasn't usually Sarah's thing, she couldn't help but be impressed. Damask with gold gilding gave it a sumptuous look, offset with the magnificent fireplace and repaired ceiling rose which adorned the ceiling. The restoration was subtle, combining modern features with those of a hundred years ago. It was, in short, stunning.

Sarah managed a decent attempt at a smile while simultaneously suppressing a yawn.

"This is nice," she managed, once she'd got her reflexes under control.

"Oh yes, this place won't hang around long," Angel confided with a knowing tone.

Sarah had heard that sentence in the last week more times than she cared to count.

"Can I see the rest of the place?" she enquired, keen to hurry the viewing along. She desperately needed to crawl back into bed.

Angel, her long auburn hair sashaying across her back, led Sarah through the rest of the flat. It was spacious and surprisingly light and airy. The bedroom was a good size and also decorated in a subtle Edwardian style. Next to the bedroom and off the main living area was a small but sufficient bathroom. A slim shower unit had been squeezed into the right-hand corner, with a toilet and sink to its left and the bath on the opposite wall. Simple white tiles were accentuated with a soft yellow-gold feature wall.

Sarah liked it. The flat was by far the best option she'd seen. At least this one was decorated tastefully with the space and light she liked and needed. And it was clean. A major improvement on some of the dank, dark, small properties she'd had the misfortune to view.

"And the *piece de resistance*," Angel exclaimed happily, almost clapping her hands. "Is the wonderful and recently restored roof terrace," she paused for dramatic effect and waited for Sarah's reaction.

"Wow," Sarah managed to express.

"It really is," Angel was practically squealing now and Sarah couldn't help emit a short laugh as she followed the agent onto the roof.

It was accessed behind the kitchen area, through a door she had presumed was just for storage. Left of the large bay windows, the door opened up to a short flight of stairs, which the two women began to climb. Another door at the top led Angel and Sarah onto a small, yet pleasant, space which overlooked the garden below and the tall hedgerows lining the property.

Sarah could see the roofs of neighbouring houses, pleased that none overlooked the space. It was effectively private. A few pots with plants would go a long way in creating a very nice little haven.

Feeling a bubble of excitement Sarah followed Angel back down. She looked over the flat with a brief glance. The living space, which wrapped around the kitchen, became the dining area, where the impressive bay windows stood. The bedroom and bathroom were off the living space, with generous storage cupboards in between the two rooms. It was ideal.

"So, what do you think?" Angel asked, grinning as if she already knew Sarah's answer.

Sarah opened her mouth to speak, before being cut off abruptly by the sound of Bach's Mass in Minor B coming up through the floor.

Angel's confident gleam turned into a look of panic. "Um, that's just the neighbour below. Moved in a few weeks ago. She's a piano tutor and apparently a former concert pianist... isn't that wonderful!" It wasn't posed as a question, but more a statement of fear.

Sarah felt like she was getting nearer the truth. Angel had clearly been having a hard time renting the place out, with piano music interrupting her viewings and scaring weaker hearted candidates away. Sarah had thought the flat was too good to still be available.

She listened quietly for a moment. The melodious tones drifted upstairs, punctuated by Bach's trademark technical composition. Sarah placed her head on one side as if mulling on a response. Angel grew increasingly nervous beside her and started playing with her fingernails.

Sarah lifted her head, gave her first genuine smile of the morning and boldly exclaimed, "I'll take it."

*　　*　　*

That had been nearly a month ago already and Sarah was itching to get the keys. Next Saturday was the day and she sat, delighted, as she watched her new home through the emerging sun rays. Step two was nearly complete. Step three was a terrifying unknown and she hoped step two would keep her occupied enough that she wouldn't need to attempt the next one for a very long time.

Chapter Two

"Aargh," Izzy groaned as she clumsily sat up on the exercise mat. Sarah beside her suppressed her own moan of discomfort as she pulled herself back into a normal human position, and out of one of the numerous Pilate contortions they'd endured the previous half hour.

The break of Christmas and New Year had taken its toll on their fitness regime and both women were out of practice. Not to mention Izzy's late festive surprise. She was eight weeks pregnant.

Having confided her news to Sarah (waiting until twelve weeks was never going to work. Izzy simply couldn't hide such a huge secret from her friend), Izzy now wondered if doing Pilates was such a sensible idea. Already the tell-tale signs of parental guilt crept up on her before she'd even got through the first trimester. *Did I just hurt the baby?* The doctor seemed to think it was fine to do Pilates, but what if he's wrong? What if I cut off circulation and starve my child of much needed oxygen? I'm a terrible mother!

She thought she'd have been used to it by now. But that wave of guilt obviously planned to gained momentum and become a giant tsunami now she was carrying her second child.

Izzy, still panting and sweating slightly, pushed back her ash blonde hair from her forehead, and mused for a moment on her pride and joy. Henry, her beautiful blue-eyed, cherub-looking little angel. Two years old and already growing up too quickly. Exhausting. Utterly exhausting. But so worth it.

Now she was about to enter uncharted territory. Two children. How it would logistically work Izzy had no idea. She could barely get her day organised with just the one. Two seemed an impossibility. Not to mention the 'big plan'. How was having another child going to affect *that*?

As much as she loved her little boy, and equally loved being at home with him, Izzy craved something of her own. So much so, that at the end of the last year she had feverishly jotted down weird and wonderful ideas that she hoped might translate into her very own business. All she had to do was pick one idea and go for it. To do what was necessary. Study, take out a loan, sell on a market stall; whatever option suited the idea she chose. There were only two problems with the plan. Firstly, she hadn't the foggiest which idea she liked best (nor what she actually really wanted to do). And secondly, she'd found out she was expecting again.

Not one to be put off, Izzy decided she'd still pursue her dream. Pregnancy didn't have to change that. She wanted to one day be considered one of the best business women in the country. To start small and build an empire. It was so tangible she could almost taste it. She just didn't know what *it* was. And now this crazy mother guilt was going into overload, threatening her plans, before she'd even had the first antenatal scan.

Was it right to start a business now? Would the stress and hours and workload have a negative impact on the unborn child? And what would happen after the baby was born? If the business was successful already, she wouldn't be able to take maternity leave. What emotional turmoil might that cause the infant, only to reveal itself years later and turn her child into a delinquent? The questions, and the guilt, was relentless.

"Izzy?" A voice interrupted her thoughts and it took a while for Izzy's eyes to regain focus and notice Sarah sitting in her field of vision.

"Mmm," she muttered as if she had just woken from a dream. Which she kind of had.

"Izzy," Sarah repeated, a flicker of laughter in her voice. "You're staring into space again."

Izzy inwardly cringed. It was a habit. She had always been like it and Sarah had always found it amusing, in an endearingly fond way. The women were well suited as best friends. Completely different in personality, but with a total tolerance of each other.

Sarah, the sensible level headed one, with a creative flair toned down (and kept in control) by sheer practicality, versus Izzy, completely spontaneous and creative to the point of being a distraction. Always with a new idea or crazy scheme.

Izzy knew Sarah loved that about her, but for once she wished she could be more like her best friend and a little less, well, *Izzy*. Just a bit. Just until she'd sorted out this dilemma and put a firm step forward in making her dreams a reality.

"So, excited about the move?" Izzy abruptly changed the subject, suddenly feeling dangerously close to tears. Stupid hormones.

Sarah helped Izzy up to her feet and nodded vaguely as they headed out of the Pilates studio.

"Sure," she replied. "I can't believe it's only two days away. It just seems," she paused briefly as she chose her words. "It just seems a little overwhelming, all this change at once. I'm only just getting used to the job and now the move on top."

"But I thought you were ready for all that?" Izzy exclaimed, a stab of alarm coursing through her. "You said you were ready?" She instantly felt protective of her best friend. She'd been through more than anyone deserved to endure.

"That's it, Izzy. I *am* ready. I think it is just a reaction to how my life is moving forward. It's been static for a long time."

"No..." Izzy began.

Sarah gave her a withering look. "Yes, Izzy. Let's face it. My life has pretty much been on standstill for the last six and a half years. Not by choice. Just... just the way it has turned out."

The resignation always hit Izzy in the gut. Every time. Sarah had had no choice but to accept her circumstances. There wasn't even much sadness any more, at least not on the surface. Sarah just appeared resigned. Resigned to the loss, the grief, to the half-lived life ever since.

Izzy would give anything to see Sarah happy, truly happy, again.

"But you must be excited about being in your own place? This new flat sounds incredible," Izzy said, deliberately sounding enthusiastic. She was in investigating mode. The last six years she'd taken the unofficial role of checking up on Sarah and making sure she was all right. Izzy had managed to keep it discreet. Sarah had no clue.

"It is," Sarah replied shortly, knowing exactly what Izzy was up to. She'd been aware of Izzy's probing for a long time. The woman simply didn't know how to be subtle. "And I am excited. You don't need to worry about me Iz. I'm a grown woman and I can cope."

Izzy adopted a look of pure innocence. "I'm not worried," she stated, unconvincingly.

They made their way across the car park and approached Izzy's sky-blue Ford Focus. It wouldn't have been Izzy's first choice. Wildly unsuitable cars (when having a family to consider), such as the shiny red convertible she'd instantly fallen in love with on the forecourt, were more her thing. But seeing as Will held the purse strings, and being the more sensible of the two, he'd ended up getting her the perfect suburban family car. Another reason to own her own successful business, and gain some much-needed independence, Izzy thought ruefully. She could buy whatever car she liked then.

She unlocked the Focus with an efficient beep of the remote and the two women climbed in. As Izzy started the engine, she looked over at her friend of fifteen years. Sarah held the same familiar expression she'd adopted a while back. One of utter concealment. She wasn't about to give the game away easily. Izzy knew more probing was needed.

"It's okay to feel a bit unsettled, nothing wrong with that," Izzy said as breezily as she could. "You've had a lodger a long time too. The thought of your own company might seem daunting at first."

Sarah sighed and turned to her friend. "Izzy, stop. You don't have to worry about me," she started.

"I'm not!" Izzy cried indignantly. "I just," she continued, "want to make sure my best friend is okay. You're going through some major changes and I know, with having a full-on toddler, that I've not been there as much as I should have."

"Izzy, I've got to make these changes at some time. And if I can't handle a new job and a new house at 33 years old, then I really don't stand much chance in life, do I?" Sarah said this last bit with a feeble attempt at humour, but Izzy saw through it straight away. The woman was straight up terrified.

And it was no wonder. Sarah had put off the inevitable for so long that it was bound to tie her up in knots. Inside at least. On the outside she was doing a good job pretending that all was fine.

"I'm excited about the house Izzy," Sarah said simply.

That much at least was true. Sarah was looking forward to her new home. It was a great find. Former concert pianist and all. But the actual thought of the move was keeping her awake at night. And Sarah didn't like being awake at night. There were too many bad memories associated with the wee small hours.

The move was daunting. Not just because Sarah had put it off for so long, but that it meant she'd had to pack up and say goodbye to the house she'd spent the last eight years of her life in. Her life had been extremely different when she had first moved there. When *they* had first moved there.

Her blue-green eyes felt the all too familiar prickle of tears stab the surface. She had to keep herself under control. She hadn't allowed herself to cry in front of Izzy for two years. She knew Izzy would be the least likely person to judge. But Sarah just couldn't risk it. She couldn't risk isolating and losing yet another friend, all for the price of a few tears.

They drove in complete silence for awhile, Sarah getting her emotions under control and back behind the mask where they belonged, and Izzy still concerned but knowing when she was beaten, trying to figure out a safe topic they could discuss.

"How's Will and Henry?" Sarah broke the silence first.

"Good," Izzy ploughed into one of her favourite subjects, relieved that the tension in the car had dissipated. "Will's, well Will. He's going clay pigeon shooting this weekend with his father." Her eyes rolled dramatically.

Sarah smiled. Will was from an extremely well-off family, which was completely the opposite of Izzy's upbringing (well not completely. Izzy had enjoyed a comfortable lower-middle-class-semi-detached-three-bed-house-family-with-a-dog-and-car, type of upbringing. But compared to Will's childhood, you'd think she had grown up on a sink estate. It seemed to be his parent's impression of her at least).

Izzy tolerated that side of her husband's life and Will was a sweet, slightly bumbling, character who wouldn't hurt a fly and tolerated Izzy's own eccentricities, so she didn't complain. Even if they did argue more over political differences than domestic issues. Their opposing beliefs had caused the first year of marriage to be a rather dicey one, especially given the general election which inconveniently fell within the first twelve months of their nuptials.

Henry, their son, had done little to enamour Will's parent's to Izzy. In fact, they were horrified, realising all too late that Will was indeed committed to this woman and now they had the child to prove it. Henry being an absolute Will mini-me somehow did nothing to improve matters. At which point Izzy simply gave up trying.

Henry was adorable. Izzy loved his constant dribbling chin and red cheeks, the flop of blonde hair (so much like his father) and toothy grin. Her heart swelled with pride and her eyes filled with tears whenever he said something cute, learned a new skill, or was simply just being him. She was a besotted mother, she knew, yet the exhaustion, sleep deprivation, and sometimes sheer boredom of being at home was causing her to enjoy those moments a little less. She felt a bit trapped, if she was completely honest.

She shook the thought from her mind and focused her attention on the road. She was blessed to be his mummy and delighted to be able to be at home with him. So what if she spent most of her day lacking adult conversation, or if her house was in a constant mess, or if she hadn't had an unbroken night sleep in two years?

She *knew* how blessed she was, really. But she also knew that she needed something else in her life and fast. Especially with a new baby on the way. She choked back a bubble of panic rising in her throat and gave Sarah a brief glance.

Sarah was looking straight ahead, her expression giving nothing away. Izzy knew it was self preservation. But why Sarah felt the need to put barriers up with her best friend, she had no answer. It hurt, but what Sarah was going through was far worse, so Izzy never pushed it.

Sarah watched the greying sky jar against the constant moving smudge of red and amber car lights. It was hypnotic and helped her relax. Memories had, all of a sudden, come flooding back and Sarah fought to suppress them.

"It's been *three* years," Sarah remembered the whispered voices at a work party. "I know it's sad, but her mood just brings down the office." Sarah had listened in shock and indignation. She'd deliberately tried to keep her personal life out of the workplace, but her anniversary the week before had resulted in her crying at her desk. Obviously, it had made a few colleagues uncomfortable.

Izzy's baby shower also came to mind. "It must be so hard for Izzy, what with being pregnant and having a widow as a best friend. She must feel like she has to watch everything she says. I wonder if Sarah's truly happy for Izzy?" That one had hurt badly and sent Sarah into a downward spiral which took weeks to recover from.

But the worst comments, by far, came from friends. At a summer party Izzy and Will had thrown, just before they'd found out they were expecting Henry, Sarah had arrived with school friend and her second bridesmaid Gemma.

Gemma, long dark hair with hazel eyes and fluttering eyelashes was a stunner and instantly had the attention of the room. Sarah hadn't minded at all, simply glad the attention (and sad, sorry faces) was off her for once. But later that evening, Gemma having drunk too much wine began to regale the room rather loudly on the woes in her life. And Sarah's life too.

"My friend Sarah," she said to her dance partner, her voice carrying the other side of the marquee. "Is so sad. She lost her husband right, but it's been *four* years and she won't even date other guys. How sad is that? I mean, none of my relationships have lasted four months and I don't want to still be single in my thirties, but she was married too young anyway...."

Gemma was very drunk, not making sense, and could barely remember her comments the next morning, but the damage had been done. Sarah forgave her; she wasn't one to hang on to grudges or welcome the heavy crush of bitterness, but it drove a wedge in their friendship that never really recovered. When Gemma moved away for work six months later, they didn't keep in contact.

There were other incidents equally painful, but the friends and acquaintances who simply didn't know what to say and kept their distance due to their awkwardness were just as bad. She'd lost a few friends that way. So, on the whole, she kept her barriers up. Kept her feelings to herself. It was better for everyone that way.

*   *   *

"Sarah!" Will greeted her enthusiastically as they arrived at Izzy's home and walked through the door.

"Will!" she replied in matching tones and accepted his welcome embrace. They'd seen each other just two days before, but that was the wonderful thing about Will. He always showed appreciation for the things he cared about. Family, friends, beer, that kind of thing.

"So, what did you two girls learn tonight?" he asked. That was another wonderful thing about Will, Sarah mused. Most people would be offended by those kinds of comments, but with Will it was endearing.

Izzy rolled her eyes. "I learned to not eat a whole pizza before an exercise class. Is that a good enough answer?" She was used to her husband's slightly off skew questions.

"Perfect," he said with a smile, nuzzling her hair lightly with his lips, his arm reaching around her shoulder. Izzy rolled her eyes again but leaned into him and gave a contented sigh. Feeling slightly uncomfortable but warmed at the same time, Sarah averted her eyes and took a seat at the kitchen table.

"Mmm, drink anyone?" Will snapped back to attention and with a flourish opened the fridge, gesturing toward the vast array of beverages lined up inside.

"Henry asleep?" Izzy enquired. Will nodded and Izzy's eyes lit up, "great, a glass of wine then please." It took a brief second until the realisation dawned. Her face fell.

"I can't, I'm pregnant. Just an orange juice then."

"Um, me too," said Sarah, desperately wanting a glass of wine, but not wanting to rub salt into the wound.

Sarah loved the warm environment at Izzy and Will's. Their house was a converted barn on the outskirts of town. Refurbished with a modern twist, it still boasted traditional flourishes of its long defunct working farm heyday. The land, now carved up and sold with neat new builds in its place, once contained a large farmhouse and the barn in which they now sat. All that remained of its heritage was the barn and a slightly larger than average mature garden.

It was a successful and attractive conversion. A stunning galley kitchen, with large fireplace and Aga taking centre stage, led into the comfortably sized living space, the roof of which contained original beams. Upstairs were three spacious bedrooms, a family bathroom (with a massive freestanding bath) and a modern addition of an en-suite to the master bedroom.

The cream walls throughout contrasted beautifully against the dark wooden beams and Izzy had deliberately kept the smattering of colour to a minimum, accentuating each room. The living area had soft gold and duck egg blue scatter cushions, a theme replicated in the ornate gold mirror above the second fireplace, and the duck egg lampshades and artwork.

Upstairs, the main suite enjoyed a splash of red, from the stunning wall length artwork of poppies in bloom, to the red vases Izzy herself had made during a pottery 'phase'. Henry's room was typical for a two-year-old boy; blue silhouettes of vehicles were painted onto canvas and hung at different heights across the walls. The same pattern was printed onto his curtains, as well as the cushion resting on the nursing chair, which hadn't been sat on in quite a long time.

It was a homely place and one of the few where Sarah always felt peaceful. It was inexplicable really. What she had lost was now in full display around her. Family, husband and wife, the future she'd thought she'd have as her own, but instead of hers it was Izzy's. And yet, she still felt comfortable here.

She drank her orange juice in contemplative silence as Izzy and Will filled each other in on their day. Will had been Alex's best friend. Despite completely different backgrounds and upbringing, the two men had become instant mates when they met in Halls at University. Sharing nothing more than the same sense of humour had been enough to cement their friendship.

It was soon after dating Alex that he'd introduced her to Will. Izzy had happened to be there at the same time and Izzy's interest in Will was immediately sparked. It had taken him an agonisingly long time to get his act together and ask Izzy out. That was typical of Will though. No malice, just a lack of awareness of what was under his nose.

Alex had been very different, Sarah thought. He was never one to wait around when he knew what he wanted. Always one to grab life with both hands, he had wasted no time asking Sarah on a date. She hadn't even finished paying for the drink she'd ordered. Stood beside each other at the bar they had literally only said hello to one another, swapped names and a couple of witty remarks, while she waited to be served. Her surprise at his over confidence was almost entirely to blame for her instant acceptance.

He had been very good looking too. A great smile, attractive laughter lines (despite only being in his mid twenties; he always had an easy grin on his face), short dark hair and blue eyes, he was one of the most attractive men she'd ever met. Admittedly it had helped her make the first spontaneous decision in her life. And one she hadn't regretted for a day since.

Even with all that had happened. She never regretted it.

Chapter Three

Moving day arrived. After weeks of anticipation Sarah was simply glad the wait was over. The boxes were packed and picked up the day before by the removal van. She'd spent the night at Izzy and Will's with the keys to the new flat tucked safely in her overnight bag.

Once again sleep had evaded her, but expecting it she'd made preparations. At three am Sarah sat at her friend's kitchen table, a mug of warm milk and a magazine to hand. It was all she could do to keep distracted from the volcano of nerves threatening to erupt through her body.

Now, at nine, a far more reasonable hour, Sarah was dressed, fed and joined by her best friends. She was about to embark on a new phase in her life. Sarah felt the key in her pocket, as they left the comfort of the converted barn. It felt almost like a formal ceremony, some sort of initiation, as quietly they made their way to the cars. No words were exchanged, just hugs and small smiles.

As she drove toward Caledon Street, with Izzy and Will following on behind, Sarah felt her anxiety growing.

She still felt the move was the right thing to do. She knew she needed to take this next step. She'd been proud of the quick progression from step one to step two and had felt, just weeks before, that she'd achieved so much already. But the reality of the new life she was sculpting was becoming all too real.

Driving into the heart of town Sarah's mood picked up slightly. The anxiety was still present, but just as the grey clouds were parting to reveal the strong vibrant rays of the morning sun, so was Sarah's heart lifting with the feeling of promise. This was a chance for a new start.

The flat was by far the best she'd seen and knew she could be happy there. Furthermore, it was all part of the road she needed to walk. Alex had been dead nearly seven years and she had been trying to move on for a long time.

Circumstances, mingled with grief, had prevented Sarah from taking this step before now. Failed dates, focusing solely on her career, and even unreliable housemates, had all contributed to Sarah's reluctance to move on. But more than that, Sarah knew, was the myriad of emotions that had kept her static. The feelings of failure, guilt and loss over the sudden death of her husband and even more so over the dreams that had also had to die, had taken over Sarah's life. All to a point where she had been unable to take a step in the right direction.

Turning thirty had been the first shift in mindset. Sarah had always imagined she'd be a mum by then, especially as having married at the young age of twenty-six. The fact that she was, in reality, single and nowhere near going on a date with anyone, was enough to scare her into thinking of the future. But the heavy grey fog wasn't ready to lift. Only another three years later did Sarah finally feel enough of a panic to start to turn her life around.

She hated knowing that everyone felt sorry for her. That her work colleagues and friends looked on her in pity whenever there was a 'plus one' occasion. When friends had married and subsequently had children, Sarah was always the last to know, so great was their fear that she'd crumple into a ball and sob at her own misfortune. Izzy was the only one to buck that trend and Sarah loved her for it.

She no longer wanted to be pitied or to be the cause of hushed voices and sympathetic looks. She no longer wanted to be the reason friends drifted, nor the reason some grew frustrated with her for not having the audacity to move on already.

The reality was that Sarah had accepted her fate a long time ago. She missed Alex every day and knew she still loved him, yet she no longer sat on the kitchen floor crying her heart out, nor struggled to get out of bed in the mornings. She had long ago given up the urge to hide in her house, curtains drawn, excluding herself from the world. Instead she had channelled her energy into establishing a career and building her remaining relationships with friends and family. The fear that she was still single and far from having the children she'd always wanted had never left her, but it simply had not happened yet and she couldn't change that.

But she could put her plan into action and turn her life in a new direction. One with hope. One where she would no longer be pitied or feel uncomfortable. One where new dreams could be made and fulfilled.

*　　*　　*

Will unloaded the last of the shopping bags from the car and began the climb upstairs. On the third and top floor stood Sarah's new flat. The movers had already been and left the boxes, and while the women began the unpacking process, Will slipped out and stocked up on some much-needed groceries for Sarah.

"Thanks, Will. You're a star," Sarah poked her head around a particularly large box, crammed full of cushions and linen.

"No problem. We've got a bit of fruit, some essential twiglets, beer and..." he rummaged at the bottom of the bag for a moment, "ahh, teabags."

Izzy exchanged glances with Sarah. "It could have been worse, I guess." Rolling up the sleeves of her chunky fisherman style grey jumper, her hair tied messily with a purple sparkly scrunchy, she turned to her husband. "Anything practical, you know, like milk for the tea?"

"Oh, yea of little faith," Will exclaimed, waving his arm in the direction of the other two shopping bags. Neither Izzy nor Sarah had noticed them, so engrossed in their unpacking.

"Milk, sugar, eggs, coffee, bread, cheese, a bit of cooked ham, toilet rolls, cereal...."

"Let me know how much I owe you," Sarah began, standing up from behind the towering box.

"No, our treat," Will waved his arm again.

Sarah gave him a stern look. "No, Will, I asked you to get some shopping for me. I don't expect you to pay for it."

Heading over to her purse on the kitchen counter, and before Will could insist, she pulled out a few notes and waved them in his direction. "Is this enough?"

Will nodded mutely and took them, slightly subdued. He'd obviously wanted to make a kind gesture, and Sarah felt momentarily guilty, but quickly composed herself. She was done accepting people's well thought intentions. At least for the reason of being a widow. Will still had that haunted look in his eyes whenever he did something kind for her, as if the death of his best friend was his fault or the widow left behind, his responsibility.

"Great, we can get takeaway for dinner then," Izzy said happily. Now her morning sickness was abating slightly, Izzy was delighted to indulge in food again. And junk food, even better.

Sarah pushed her red bandanna further on top her head and brushed some packaging snow off her black sweat shirt. "No need Iz, my mum is going to drop something off for us."

Pippa, Sarah's mother, was well known for her delicious meals and Izzy's eyes lit up.

"What time has the babysitter got Henry until?" Sarah asked, turning her attention back to the box of seemingly endless linen.

"About ten this evening. She goes into double time after that."

"Thanks for taking off your Saturday to be here. Especially as it means you're away from Henry so long."

"No, that's a pleasure," Izzy replied quickly. "No, really it is. It's nice to have a break."

"With that in mind I'll get on with making some tea. I'm sure there's some chocolate biscuits in here somewhere," Will said idly as he returned to rummaging through the bags of edible goods.

Ten minutes later they sat on Sarah's sofa, the plastic wrapping still wound tightly around, swinging their legs and enjoying cups of tea and cookies. Sarah was pleased by their progress and could already imagine herself living here. It gave her the sense of peace she had been missing on the drive over.

Her phone rang and she made a grab for her pocket.

"Darling, it's me. I'm here already. A bit early I know. But I can come and help."

Sarah smiled broadly, "Mum's here."

Izzy returned the grin, already daydreaming about what meal Pippa may have cooked up.

Sarah dashed downstairs, while Izzy and Will sat in companionable silence. When you had a toddler sometimes silence was the best gift of all.

"What an interesting building," they heard Pippa's voice before she'd even reached the second staircase. "Edwardian or Victorian?"

"Edwardian, the agent said," Sarah replied, her own voice more muffled and less prone to carry like her mother's.

"I thought it was difficult to get permission to convert them into flats these days," Pippa mused as she studied the tasteful fabric wallpaper in the hallway.

"Angel, the agent," Sarah clarified, "mentioned it was done in the sixties. Apparently, my landlord had them restored and redecorated more sympathetically, but decided to keep the separate apartments. I don't know why."

"Well, it's charming for flats, I must say. Nicely done," and with that Pippa stopped abruptly on the stairs and kissed her daughter on the forehead. "Well done. I'm proud of you."

"But I wasn't the one who did the place up," Sarah joked, knowing full well what her mother was referring to, but trying to deflect the sudden emotion welling up inside.

Pippa had spent many years silently praying and hoping. Seeing her daughter's grief and the long years that had followed nearly destroyed her. But she had remained strong for Sarah's sake. Sarah had needed that strength when her own was so depleted. Pippa longed for the day when Sarah truly moved on, but today was a good start.

Entering the flat, Pippa looked around in further appreciation. "Very nice, Sarah."

Spotting Izzy and Will on the sofa, Pippa threw open her arms. "And my favourite children from another mother," she exclaimed happily. Both Izzy and Will couldn't help grinning like idiots as she somehow managed to envelop both of them into a warm and ferocious hug.

Pippa was the kind of mum everyone wanted. Elegant, with mid-length reddish brown hair, bright piercing blue eyes and stylishly dressed, she still managed to exude a cosy homely feel. Despite the neat as a pin clothing Pippa was an avid gardener and loved nothing more than hours spent in the garden, planting herbs, sowing veggies or designing attractive flower beds. She loved baking and cooking even more, and from as long as Sarah could remember, Sarah's friends had always wanted to hang out at her house. Especially on the days Pippa made her famous breads or rich puddings.

Having worked hard, establishing a catering business from scratch with Sarah's father, they'd sold up two years before and now enjoyed early retirement. Not that either Pippa or her husband David had slowed down. She now supplied cakes to a deli as a part time 'extra' to keep her busy, as well as growing mountainous volumes of homegrown fresh herbs to local restaurants. David, Sarah's dad, had his own pursuits too. Mainly to do with racing cars on circuits and fixing up vintage cars. He might have been pushing sixty, but he certainly wasn't about to admit it.

"Um, we were just wondering what dinner you brought with you," Izzy stammered, not wanting to appear hasty or rude.

Pippa laughed and handed Izzy the bag she was carrying.

Izzy peeked inside, lifted her head and said in awe, "Lasagne!"

"With homemade garlic bread and a fresh, straight from the garden, salad," Pippa elaborated, with a complete absence of ego. "Oh, and a lemon cheesecake for dessert."

Sarah smiled wryly at Izzy and Will, who both stood staring at the food with silly grins on their faces. Her mum's food had that effect on people. Pippa, either not noticing or subtly ignoring their reaction, continued to look around the flat. She stopped short at the bay windows and looked out over the view into the garden.

"Very nicely done," she mused, almost to herself. "The landlord has clearly put in some extensive work. If I'm not mistaken these bay windows are brand new."

"Really?" Sarah replied absent-mindedly. "I hadn't really noticed."

"Yes. They look like originals, but I think that's just to be in-keeping with the rest of the house, but they definitely look new to me." Pippa thought for a moment. "I'd imagine it was a bit poky in here in centuries past. Possibly just an attic originally."

Sarah nodded as she unpacked another box. It wasn't that she wasn't interested in the heritage or history of the building, it was just that her mum tended to be a little obsessed with anything historical and Sarah had learned to block out most of it. It was a skill she'd developed as a child and still came in handy.

"Have you met the landlord yet?"

"Hmm? Um, no. Why?"

"I'd be interested to hear what work was done and how they restored the place. It must have been fascinating work."

"Sure," Sarah crossed over the living area to the kitchen and flicked the kettle on. A cup of tea was the best way to distract her mother. She busied herself with the tea bags and quickly rinsed out a dusty cup she'd found in a box.

"Maybe I'll meet him soon. I know," Sarah said playfully. "Give me a list of your questions and I'll ask him when I see him."

Pippa fixed her a look of a mother not impressed, but couldn't help be amused by the sparkle in Sarah's eye. She knew her daughter was teasing her.

"Oh, don't you worry about that Sarah. I'll have a list drawn up immediately. I can think of twenty questions already... no, twenty-one," Pippa could give as good as she got.

Sarah stirred the tea for her mother and smiled as she handed it over. "It is a nice place, isn't it," she sighed happily. The feeling of peace was back and she hoped it would stick around.

"It is," Pippa replied simply, looking intently at her daughter. This was a small hint that the tide was turning for the better. Pippa had glimpsed it a few times lately and it was like a rainstorm after a drought; refreshing and full of hope. She took a sip of her tea to stop from grinning like an idiot and embarrassing her daughter. Or even worse, to chase away that spark of happiness that was beginning to rebirth inside Sarah.

*   *   *

A whole day of unpacking, endless cups of tea and biscuits and a scoffed lasagne, dessert and all the trimmings, and the five of them (Sarah's father had joined them later on) were lying on the carpet exhausted.

"That was simply the best meal I've ever had," Will said happily, looking up at the ceiling rose with his arms resting on his stomach.

"I feel sick," Izzy said with a grimace.

"Sorry Pippa, it's not your food. Well, it kind of is...."

"You have a good excuse," Pippa waved the potential insult away with a flick of the hand. Izzy had told her their pregnancy news during the afternoon, when she'd needed to slip away to the bedroom for a quick nap.

Izzy was about to thank Pippa for her understanding, when she suddenly leapt to her feet. "Sorry, need to go," she shrieked and disappeared through the bathroom door.

"Well, that's the first time my food has ever made anyone sick," Pippa gave a good-natured sigh and sat up. "Right, I think we'd better make a move, once we've made sure Izzy is okay."

David nodded in agreement but didn't shift. He was exhausted after a morning at the track, followed by unpacking all afternoon. Factor in his wife's food, which he'd had more than his usual sized portion of, and he simply wanted to stay where he was and fall asleep.

Sarah looked around the flat from where she was laying. There was still a lot to do, but she could comfortably manoeuvre between the furniture and the boxes that remained. The bedroom had been more or less completed; the bed, wardrobe and bedside table were in place and her clothes packed away on hangers. All her essential toiletries and towels were unpacked in the bathroom and all the major appliances adorned the kitchen. She could actually envision the flat finished.

The bathroom door opened and Will looked up with a sympathetic expression.

"All right my love?" he asked tentatively.

"False alarm. I think," Izzy answered, her voice small and with a distinctive grey look to her pallor.

"You want to head home? It's nearly nine," Will asked softly.

"I think I'll just sit still for ten minutes, just to make sure."

Pippa and David finally made their goodbyes and headed out the door a few minutes later. Giving Sarah a bear hug, David whispered "well done" as they headed out into the night. Sarah smiled in return and hugged herself as a wintry chill swept into the hallway from the open front door.

She made her way back up the two flights of stairs and joined her best friends. Izzy was looking a little better, her complexion beginning to return to normal. Will was checking his phone quickly before gathering up their belongings.

"You don't mind if we head off, Sarah?" he asked with a trace of guilt.

"Of course not," she replied lightly, "you need to get back to your boy."

"Bed more like it," Izzy stated. "I'm exhausted. Not to mention the quicker I get to sleep the quicker the nausea will go away."

Sarah saw them out the door with big hugs and kisses and waved them down the pathway. Returning upstairs for the second time, Sarah once again looked around her new home. She had been scared of this moment. Once all the busyness had subsided and people left, she was nervous of what remained. Just her. Just her and a long night ahead.

She tried to compose herself. This was a new house. Maybe she would sleep better here than at the previous house where all the bad memories were attached. Or maybe those memories would just follow her wherever she went.

Shaking herself from the depressing train of thought, she tried to focus her mind on positive things. This was a new start. She had a lovely flat, in a nice area, with a busy job to return to on Monday morning. The past was done. It couldn't be changed and Alex wouldn't be coming back. It had been over six years.

There was no time limit to grief. She had accepted that. She knew it could hit her full force again at any moment, rendering her paralysed for weeks if not months at a time. And yet she also knew in her heart that the worst was passed. This was a new start and she couldn't deny the flickers of excitement and hope that emanated from that thought. She just needed to embrace it and step out in faith.

She made her way to the bathroom and quietly dressed for bed. Sheer exhaustion of the day was catching up with her. Even if she couldn't switch off emotionally to sleep, her body had certainly had enough. She just wanted to lay down in her comfortable bed again.

Turning the lights off in the living area and checking the door was locked, Sarah made her way into the bedroom. Her first night in her own place. The bed looked inviting with its cream duvet, overlaid with turquoise and silver embroidered swallows and flowers. She climbed in and lay her head on the matching pillow, reaching to turn on her lamp and then across the bedside table to retrieve her novel. Finding her place, she turned the pages and began to read.

She was shocked, when hours later she woke to realise that that was the last she remembered, and that she'd slept the whole night through.

Chapter Four

"Want toast Mummy," a little voice awoke Izzy from the wonderful dream she was having. Something to do with winning an award for something vague, as well as a nice big cheque and expensive bottle of champagne. It was already fast becoming a blur.

"Hmm?" she replied, eyes still closed, hoping the little voice had already given up and gone back to bed.

"Toast Mummy," came the answer and Izzy inwardly sighed as she forced her eyes open. She looked over at Will, who was typically still fast asleep and snoring slightly. Lying next to her, as close as possible, breathing slightly onto her cheek was her tousled hair, blue eyed toddler.

"Morning Henry," she said. He looked up into her eyes and gave her a heart-warming grin. "Toast?"

"I'll get up in a minute," Izzy replied. She turned her head slightly to read the clock on the wall. It was just after six am. She groaned. "You see Henry, it's not breakfast time just yet."

Trying to reason with a toddler was a futile act, she knew, but it was worth a try.

"Why don't you cuddle up to Mummy for a little while, hmm?" She could already feel herself slipping back into a cosy state of unconsciousness. She barely dared to breathe as she waited to see if her ploy had worked. Henry lay still and quiet and she silently began to congratulate herself.

"Toast Mummy. Now, peese."

Izzy knew her day had officially started.

*   *   *

Sarah gave a deep sigh of satisfaction as she drew in the first mouthful of coffee. The intense flavour mingled with its exotic scent and sent her taste buds and nerve endings tingling. Her one vice, coffee, had proved a powerful and even seductive ally after years of sleepless nights and exhausting starts to the morning. Despite having slept well the night before, Sarah almost couldn't bear the thought of missing out on that first cup of the day.

The bay windows were flung wide open, letting in the new day sun. Winter was finally melting into spring and the freshness of the air was no longer painfully icy, but rather cold with a hint of fragrance dancing through it. The new buds would soon emerge on the trees and after that the flowers would burst into full bloom. It was Sarah's favourite time of year and the open windows symbolised her desire for spring to be ushered in fully.

She sat at her oak dining room table and stared contently out the large windows. From her position she could see the tips of the trees and hedgerow which lined the garden. Beyond that was a great expanse of sky; light periwinkle grey, with wispy white clouds scattered across the horizon.

She liked that from this angle she couldn't see what was happening on the ground. It was her own little haven, separated from the busyness of life below. It was just her, the sky and nature. Nothing else mattered.

Suddenly her reverie was disrupted by the sounds of Tchaikovsky. Her resident concert pianist was back. Sarah smiled broadly as she raised her coffee cup to her lips. The scene was now perfect, her relaxed Sunday morning complete.

A knock at the door quickly dispersed that feeling. Reluctantly leaving her coffee on the table she made her way across the flat. Wondering who it could be at nine am on a Sunday morning, Sarah opened the door to a complete stranger.

"Hi, sorry to bother you so early, but I thought I'd better introduce myself sooner rather than later," the stranger said. He had sandy blonde hair, blue eyes which held flecks of grey and a warm welcoming smile.

"Oh," was all she could manage. She hadn't a clue who he was or what he wanted.

"I'm Dermot Matthews," he said in a slight Irish lilt. He reached out his hand, which she shook tentatively. "I live in the ground floor flat."

"Oh, I see. Well that's very nice of you to come and say hello. It's good to know my new neighbours are friendly."

He looked awkward for a minute then nodded. "Yes, especially in a building so small. We're bound to bump into one another. And, you're Sarah Miller, right?"

"How do you know that?"

"Well, that's the thing...." the awkwardness was back, and Sarah began to feel a prickle of alarm. How exactly did he know her name and ought she be worried?

"I'm not just your neighbour. I'm your landlord too."

Shock, mingled with disbelief, hit Sarah somewhere in her gut. No wonder the flat hadn't been let when she'd viewed it, especially at such a good price in a good area. If the concert pianist downstairs didn't scare you off, discovering that you'd be living under the same roof as your landlord would.

Angel, the letting agent, had clearly learned through hard experience and kept the information to herself. Obviously, she wasn't as innocent as her name suggested. Or perhaps she was even more desperate to let the place as Sarah was to fulfil the second stage of her plan.

"I know this is a bit of a shock," his voice broke into her thoughts. "I only found out yesterday that the letting agent had forgotten to inform you of the arrangements."

Huh, thought Sarah. Sure, she had forgot.

"But don't worry. I'm a fairly laidback landlord. No strange curfews or checking up on my tenants," he said, a slight smile on his lips. He was trying to reassure her. It wasn't working.

"I'll be handling most of the day to day stuff. You know, simple DIY jobs and the like. The agents will pass on any queries and make decisions when to get professionals in. I've done rather a lot of DIY in the past, so I'll handle most of it," seemingly aware he was beginning to ramble he stopped talking and looked at Sarah expectantly.

She didn't know what to think. Partly horrified that her landlord was not only on her doorstep (literally in this case) as well as being present to fix things around the flat (she was hoping for a professional hands-off approach, dealing only through the agent) and partly relieved that her landlord was of similar age and seemed a fairly reasonable guy (though you could never really tell), Sarah just stared, mystified, at him.

"I'm sorry," she managed eventually. "As you can see, I'm a bit shocked. I had no idea."

"Right," Dermot said, looking awkward as he put his hands in his pockets. "Um, there's obviously been a gross lack of communication with the agent. I'll talk to them about it. And like I said, I'm not an ogre of a landlord. I intend to be as relaxed as possible. Just ask Greta, she'll vouch for me."

"What? Who? You said 'intend'. Does that mean you've never been a landlord before?"

"Nope. First time. But I've owned the property awhile and Greta been here two months already." Ahh, the concert pianist, thought Sarah.

Sarah's heart sank as the severity of his words hit her. He was an amateur landlord. He'd never managed a property before. And he was clearly green if he thought they'd all live in peace and harmony under the same roof. What happened when one complained of noise against another, if there were parties (not that Sarah had many of those), or large groups of friends visiting? Would they all be so chummy then? What happened if the plumbing, or similar, started to pack up? Would the tenants be hit with a huge bill, or find their rent increasing to cover the escalating costs? As unethical as it was, Sarah had heard plenty of similar horror stories before.

"Okay, I'll do that. I'll speak to Greta," she was aware she sounded brisk, but it was all she could say to stop herself panicking. What had she gotten herself into? Was this a huge mistake? Had she progressed from stage one to two too quickly?

"Yes... you do that," Dermot looked thoroughly unsure and Sarah instantly felt guilty. He was clearly trying his best and seemed harmless enough. It didn't stop her worrying if he was up to the job though.

"Well, enjoy the rest of your Sunday. If you need anything I'm around today, but otherwise you'll have to go through the agents. I'm trying to prevent people knocking on my door every time a light bulb blows. But you're still welcome to come and knock if you need a cup of sugar. I guess those are the differences between being both tenant and landlord. I don't want the two to become confused."

Sarah tried to smile encouragingly as she said goodbye, but her spirits sank a little lower. The chances that the two roles wouldn't get tangled and muddled were slim. In her experience, as a landlord to her previous lodger, it was difficult to maintain rules and authority in your own house, let alone between three separate apartments. Perhaps the separation would make it more professional, but Sarah had a sneaking suspicion that wouldn't be the case.

Coffee cold and with Greta having finished the symphony, Sarah looked around the flat with new eyes. She really hoped this wasn't a big mistake.

*　　*　　*

Izzy stared at the list in front of her, perplexed and a little concerned. She'd spent the best part of an hour, during Henry's midday nap, writing down all the possible career paths she could feasibly consider. It was extensive.

The problem was that she was interested in a lot of things. She'd spent her twenties dabbling in ceramics, training in beauty therapy, making jewellery, organising overseas adventure trips for her and her friends, working in a gym, doing the first module of a physiotherapy course (she'd stopped to have Henry) and selling scented candles. She had worked in shops, bars, clinics and from home. She certainly didn't lack the ability to work hard. She just hadn't found the definitive profession, the one that would keep her interest.

One thing she had ascertained, as her furrow deepened upon perusal of the list, was that she was creative and she liked to help people. It didn't exactly narrow it down, but it was a start.

She sipped her now cold decaf tea and ran her eyes down the numerous rows again. Every option seemed to prove an issue. If she went for the creative route, she'd have to find something easy and non-time consuming to make it financially viable. But she liked the idea of being self-employed. Starting slowly, with a young baby in tow, was also appealing.

Then again, if she went the 'helping others' route, she'd have to train up, get qualifications, and put in the long hours to establish herself, right from the start.

As she contemplated this, she heard a small cry from upstairs. Henry was waking up from his nap and it was time for Izzy to slip back into Mummy mode. The decisions would have to wait.

She collected him from his bedroom, his warm body snuggled against hers and his cute button nose buried into the crook of her neck. Still sleepy, he murmured incoherently and wrapped his arms around hers in a vice like grip. His hair smelled of baby products and Izzy surreptitiously sniffed his blonde locks as they came down the stairs.

Will was entering the kitchen from the back door, having spent the morning in the garden attacking the now unkempt plant life. It was allowed to grow wild during the winter months, yet despite not a lot of growth due to often freezing temperatures, it had become rather unruly. Not much of a gardener herself, Izzy was happy to leave it to Will, who with a beer or hot beverage in hand, found the task rather therapeutic.

On the stove a large saucepan of minestrone soup was simmering and Izzy, planting her young son in his father's arms, focused on ladling up the lunch into bowls. She had invited Sarah to join them, but had received a text message to say that she couldn't make it. Still slightly worried for her friend, what with going through such a huge adjustment, Izzy vowed to phone her as soon as they'd eaten.

"Guess what Daddy found Henry?" Will asked, Henry lifting his gaze in sudden interest. "About a dozen snails, all slimy and gooey and hiding in our plants." He traced his fingers across Henry's hand in imitation of a snail's walk. Henry shrieked in delight and wriggled in his dad's arms.

"Then I discovered a wet, slippery toad, who hopped toward me with a plop, plop, plop." Henry shrieked again and grabbed Will's face in his hands, and gave him a slobbery kiss. "Yes, Henry, a bit like that."

Izzy smiled as she saw the look of adoration on her husband's face. Watching the two of them together made her swell with pride and contentment. For a brief moment the worry of what she was meant to do with her life subsided. All that mattered in that moment was their closeness as a family. That was what life was really about.

"After lunch you can come and help Daddy. I've got a little spade for you and you can dig for worms."

"Ucky worms," Henry blew a raspberry in indignation. His little face screwed up in distaste and he quickly wriggled off his father's lap.

"Well, that suggestion went down well." Will said good naturedly.

"Here you are, get some hot soup in you. It's freezing out there." Izzy handed the bowl of soup over and ladled some into Henry's Thomas the Tank Engine bowl. "Maybe Henry shouldn't join you in the cold."

"He'll be fine if he's wrapped up warm."

"Easy for you to say. I'll be the one at home nursing him if he gets sick."

"Well, let's go out for a drive then. Get him out of the house a bit. It'll give you a break from entertaining him and he loves being in the car."

Izzy grimaced but tried to hide it. The motion of the car made her morning sickness worse and she didn't want the thought of it to spoil the soup, which up until now she'd been craving.

"What love?" Will had obviously noticed.

"Just a bit queasy. Perhaps you ought to take him out on his own. I'd like to phone Sarah anyway. It's the first day on her own in the flat and I'd feel like a complete failure of a friend if I didn't at least check in with her."

"As long as you're sure. You seem to miss out on all the fun lately."

Izzy suppressed the sudden sigh of frustration bubbling inside. Those were her exact feelings, yet she felt she couldn't express them. She had so much to be thankful for, was so blessed, that she felt guilty for feeling like life had become rather less fun.

"Yes, well I am pregnant. It is the first trimester after all. It'll get better," she said, trying to convince herself. She sat with her family and lifted a spoonful of soup to her lips. It tasted nice and the all too familiar pang of nausea was thankfully absent.

She tried to relax and enjoy the inane conversation. Henry was jabbering away in his own little language and Will nodded along encouragingly. She felt a curious and disconcerting mixture of contentment, combined with feeling separate from what was going on around her. Her mind kept trying to shift back to the list, now tucked into her diary on the sideboard. The potential of a business idea within its pages, gave Izzy a swoop of hope, which she desperately needed. She was tired of feeling like she was treading water. She needed a focus away from her life as a mum and wife. She loved being those things dearly, but something was missing. She needed a plan. She needed purpose.

*   *   *

"Hey, just phoning to see how your first day is going," Sarah heard her best friend's voice as she picked up the ringing phone.

"Not bad. I've just got in from the farmer's market down the road. I bought fresh chocolate cupcakes," Sarah teased.

"Urgh, I'm off chocolate," came the disgusted reply.

"Wow, what's that like?"

"Almost as bad as puking three times a day for weeks on end."

Sarah wasn't sure whether to laugh or sympathise. It wasn't always easy to read Izzy's mood.

"So, how's it going really?" Izzy's voice cut into Sarah's brief contemplation.

"Fine actually," Sarah moved over to the sofa and sat down. "I slept all night, though I think the busy day yesterday was responsible for that."

"Well that's great."

"I definitely appreciated the sleep, I can tell you. And I've just taken it easy today, I haven't touched a box."

"Good girl. And what about the crazy pianist? Have you heard anything more from her?" Izzy had found it amusing that Sarah, so straight laced in many ways, would actively choose an apartment where her peace and quiet could be so readily interrupted.

"Just briefly this morning. It was nice drinking coffee, watching birds out the window, and listening to the music. She is really very good."

"You sound like an old lady."

"Yeah, well maybe I need a little calm and escapism in my life."

There was a slight pause, during which Sarah knew Izzy would be worrying.

"It's fine Iz. I just mean that I'm craving the laidback environment I think I'll get here, over the craziness of work." Sarah's job as a copywriter for an agency could be frantic. She loved it, but there was rarely time to switch off during the working day. She needed that oasis of calm away from it all.

But the fact that Izzy's thoughts had slipped straight to Alex didn't escape Sarah's notice. Even after nearly seven years, Izzy was still overly protective and sensitive to Sarah's feelings. Most would have, and often had, given up any attempts of sympathy, believing it was time for Sarah to 'move on'. Not that Sarah hadn't, in her own way, but people's unrealistic expectations of how long grief should last, or indeed what it should look like, had resulted in plenty of misunderstandings.

Sometimes Izzy's concern felt a little claustrophobic for Sarah's liking, but she never said anything. She didn't want to scare Izzy away or create an awkward atmosphere between them. It was better to just let her get on with it.

Deciding to change the subject, Sarah turned the conversation to what had been bothering her all morning. Her new landlord.

"I met Dermot Matthews this morning. He's my new landlord," she explained. "Turns out he's living in the ground floor flat and is a bit of a novice when it comes to managing tenants."

"Eek," came Izzy's helpful response.

"He seems a nice enough guy. I just hope I'm not going to regret this."

"How old is he?"

"About our age. Maybe a few years older. Definitely no more than mid thirties."

"Single?"

"Why?" Sarah asked, a note of suspicion creeping into her voice. Izzy was known to try and match-make occasionally.

"Oh no, nothing like that," Izzy knew exactly what Sarah was thinking. "Just that if he's young and single he might actually be a good landlord."

"How do you figure that?" Sarah laughed.

"Well, he won't have family responsibilities or time constraints getting in the way of him replacing a broken washer. Plus, he's our age and better able to relate to you. He's not some fuddy-duddy who doesn't have a clue about the modern busy lifestyle we lead."

Reluctantly, Sarah admitted, Izzy made sense.

"But what about the lack of landlord experience?"

"Is he going through an agency?"

"Sort of. He wants to do a lot of the DIY stuff himself, but I'll be dealing directly with the letting agent, not him."

"Well that's good then. See, he does know what he's doing. He's clearly thought that through. He obviously doesn't want you and Piano Lady knocking on his door all times of the day and night."

"That's pretty much what he said. Just more politely. And her name is Greta, not Piano Lady."

"Cool, well that's sorted then," Izzy was clearly losing interest. "By the way, we need another girl's night out. When are you up for it?"

"What, even when you have morning sickness and can't drink?"

"Uh, yes. I still need a night out you know. I might be pregnant but I can still have fun, thank you."

"Okay then..." Sarah carefully sidestepped Izzy's slightly overheated hormones, "what have you in mind?"

Chapter Five

Dermot Matthews stared down his arch nemesis. It had been months since they'd last seen each other. A smile played at the corner of his lips as he stood, leaning on the door frame, arms folded and looking down. There, leaning against the radiator, as if in imitation, was the object that caused so much trouble.

Calling it an arch nemesis was perhaps too strong. The reality was more of a love-hate relationship. Dermot regularly swung between the two emotions, especially after a long absence. This was one of those moments.

The bike stood silent and looked innocent enough. He knew the first time back on the bike was going to be painful. And the second and no doubt the third. It hadn't been long ago that he'd participated in cycle races and rode cross country for miles on end. The buzz had been exhilarating, meeting nature head on with a competitive spirit; riding over acres of lush green landscape with vast blue skies stretching out like a canvas overhead.

But the last year had fled past at breath taking speed, full of the busyness of work and life and Dermot had found no time nor energy for mountain biking. The motivation it required, to get up early before a hard day's work, despite whatever weather was flung his way, was at times too easy to resist.

Much rather a comfortable bed, before a sixteen-hour day graft restoring his pet project, and an early night after such a gruelling task. Life had pretty much ground to a standstill during those hectic months. And now, when he finally had the spare time, Dermot just hadn't quite managed to throw himself back into the intensive training.

He could have started slower. Perhaps getting back into riding at a leisurely pace. But that wasn't his personality. He liked goals. He liked projects that would terrify most other people. It was how he had become a successful property developer, how he continued to look for opportunities that would overwhelm even he. It was what motivated him. So, with that in mind he couldn't resist signing up for a cycle race in just six weeks time.

Spurred on by his friends down the pub, Dermot had literally signed the dotted line with little hesitation. Despite having not sat on the bike in over a year, Dermot suddenly had a focus again. Work was okay, interesting if not riveting. The nine to five job was a welcome change from recent years. But the thrill was missing. A small step perhaps, but having the race to focus on would bring a little excitement back into the mix.

Giving only a half-hearted sigh, the tingle of anticipation diluting his reluctance somewhat, Dermot stepped forward and took the handle bar. It was time.

*　　*　　*

Sarah approached the building she now called home. Key in hand she smiled as she unlocked the grand front door. Only a week had passed since moving in, but she already felt comfortable here. The last traces of doubt and apprehension had faded during the previous seven days. She had been sleeping well and now, fully unpacked, Sarah felt rested and settled. With the weekend upon her she looked forward to kicking off her heavy winter boots and relaxing.

Stepping into the hallway Sarah immediately noticed the carpet. Big ugly blotches of dirt made their way across the floor. Small flecks showered the lower walls and radiators. Sarah gingerly stepped over the offending marks toward the stairs. Hoping whoever was responsible was going to clean up, but preparing to do the job herself, she heard a door click behind her.

Dermot stood there shaking his head. "Aargh, what a mess."

Noticing her, his head snapped up. "I'd somehow forgotten how muddy a bike could get. Probably because my last house had a conservatory that I shoved the thing into. No nice new carpets to ruin there."

"So, where's the bike now?" Sarah asked, amused by his sheepishness.

"Sopping wet on the kitchen floor," he grinned back. "Now to work my magic on this lot."

He lowered his gaze again and emitted a quiet sigh. He was not looking forward to this. Furious with himself and equally with the bike, for potentially ruining a carpet that had only been bought three months before, Dermot rubbed his stubbly chin in frustration. He didn't have the first clue how to lift the stains.

"You can use white vinegar and baking soda to clean that up," Sarah commented, guessing the reason for his sudden pensiveness. "I have a homemade cleaning solution that'll work. Just white wine vinegar, baking soda and water. Works a treat."

It sometimes came in handy having a domestic goddess as a mother. This was one of Pippa's favourites and one she'd diligently taught her daughter to make.

"Just vacuum up the loose bits and apply the solution. Wait a few minutes and scrub with a damp cloth," Sarah recited, feeling like she was in a cleaning advert. She smiled self consciously.

"Really? Wow. Are you sure I should be putting vinegar on the floor?"

"Got to be better than mud."

"True," he mused. "Right. Let's give it a go," he looked up apologetically. "I mean, I'll give it a go. Obviously, I don't expect you to help me. It's my mess."

Sarah raised her eyebrows. She sensed an undercurrent of begging, but he was clearly too embarrassed to ask. Deciding to put him out of his torment she slowly nodded. "Okay, I'll go fetch it."

*　　*　　*

Twenty minutes and two applications later, the carpet was looking normal again and Dermot was looking stunned.

"I can't believe that worked."

"Thanks for the vote of confidence," Sarah teased, getting up from the floor where she'd been gathering up the spray bottle and cloths, which now resembled dirty rags.

"It just sounds so... unlikely. Just three ingredients, two of which sit in your kitchen cupboard all year round. I'm amazed."

"Well, you learn something every day," she said, shrugging. She was dying to get herself into a warm relaxing bath and shake off the busy work week. Scrubbing the floor hadn't been part of her plans for the evening.

"I owe you," Dermot said, sensing her change in mood. "No really..." as she shook her head. "I kind of forced you into the situation. It had nothing to do with you. I do feel bad."

"Dermot, really there's no need. Happy to help. Besides, I've got to keep on the right side of my landlord," she joked.

Having said goodbye Sarah made her exit up the stairs and into her flat. She headed straight for the bath, grabbing the new novel she'd bought from the bookshop near work. Time to relax.

But a few hours later and Sarah found herself tossing and turning in bed. Sleep alluded her for the first time since the move. Despite the unwinding bath and a welcome glass of wine, Sarah had yet to enter the land of slumber. Aware that it was still evening, and that the night's entirety stretched before her, she continued to lay in bed hoping to tempt her body into a state of sleep.

It didn't work. Nor did the eleven chapters of the novel she subsequently read. Nor staring at the ceiling. As it approached two am her thoughts began to darken and the familiar prickle of anxiety stabbed at her body and mind with increasing intensity. Sarah immediately tried to distract herself using methods she'd learned in bereavement counselling. Closing her eyes, she breathed deeply, in through her nose and out through her mouth.

She focused her thoughts on one scene alone, the one she used each time. The picture began to build up in her mind. A meadow, with tall wild grasses and purple, pink and white flowers. The vast sky was always blue with a delicate smattering of cloud. A slight breeze danced through the willow trees which nestled in one corner of the meadow. Hanging over a fast rushing stream, tendrils of the willow trees playfully tapped the water's surface. The stream itself moved quickly and elegantly. Cascading over small rocks and boulders the water provided a musical harmony alongside the buzzing of insects and hum of the warming sun. Dragonflies; metallic purple and blue, hovered majestically at the water's edge before basking on the banks in the warmth. It was a peaceful place. Yet each element was in constant motion with one another.

Sarah felt her body relax as the meadow developed in her mind. She found herself walking among the long grass, sweeping her hand carelessly across its feathery tips. Birds sang in the trees in the distance. Their songs rose in unison and perfect melody. Creation around her was alive and thriving and glorious. It was her favourite place in the whole world.

It was a real place. Somewhere she had spent many hours, not just in her mind. A place where she and Alex had used to come to walk, to share picnics, to sit and watch the beauty around them. There they'd exchanged dreams and laughter. It was a place she had yet to visit since his death and had become locked into her thoughts instead.

The betraying thought of Alex cut through her relaxed mind like a knife. Sometimes she could envision him there and it simply added to the picture she was creating. Other times the vision would be too much and she would find herself thrown out of her peaceful state. Tonight was one of those nights.

Opening her eyes reluctantly she looked up at the pitch-black ceiling. The anxiety had thankfully passed but she knew she would not sleep. Getting up, she grabbed the blanket off the end of the bed, and made her way to the living room. Only four hours later, after finishing her novel, was she able to crawl sleepily under her covers. Ignoring the first bird calls of the new day, she closed her eyes tightly and fell into an exhausted sleep.

*   *   *

Three nights later and things had barely improved. Exhausted at work and feeling emotional at home Sarah desperately needed something to break. Fending off her mother's probing questions, when Pippa had called to invite Sarah over for dinner, she knew she couldn't keep up the pretence much longer.

On that fourth night, bored of sitting on the sofa or at the kitchen table in the wee small hours, Sarah had a brain wave. Digging out the thick mountain jacket she'd used to wear during hikes with Alex, she pulled it over her shoulders. Taking a freshly brewed cup of tea, Sarah opened the door to the roof terrace.

A blast of frigid air hit her full on, as she prised open the outside door at the top of the staircase. Not forgetting it was still March, Sarah pulled out gloves and a hat from the pockets of the jacket and slipped them on. Finding a natural seat on a low wall which formed the lower part of the roof, Sarah sat down. The jacket padded her backside, for which she was grateful, as a thin layer of frost was forming on the concrete.

The view in front of her was astounding. The night sky was a deep purple. Amber grey threads of smog layered the horizon beyond, with the odd twinkling star erupting through the density. The slight rustle of trees mingled with the occasional hoot of an owl and bark of a fox. In the distance she could hear the faint rumbling of motorway traffic, never ceasing despite the hour. But the roads below were silent and peaceful.

Gripping the cup of tea with two gloved hands, Sarah watched nature's display before her. The longer and more intently she stared the more stars she could spot. Occasionally aeroplanes flew overhead and disrupted her avid attention, but she didn't mind.

Sarah was not aware how long she sat there, but eventually the cold catching up with her, she reluctantly made her way back inside. Yawning before she'd even reached the staircase, she hoped that the fresh air would help her sleep.

Making her way down the staircase she noticed something for the first time. A small hatchway, not unlike one you'd find in the ceiling, stood vertical on the wall. Curious, Sarah pushed it slightly and felt it ease, but not open, beneath her fingers. Wondering whether it was extra storage space, or entrance to an attic, or boringly just the fuse box (which she hadn't made any effort to locate yet), the fleeting thought was soon forgotten as she approached her bedroom.

Suddenly overcome with tiredness Sarah sunk down on her mattress and quickly fell asleep. She didn't wake again until the alarm pierced the calm.

*   *   *

Dragging his bike through the door for the second time that week, Dermot felt little to congratulate himself on. Getting back into cycling was sheer hard work. Every muscle screamed with indignation as he'd cycled the several miles through town. He couldn't believe how unfit he'd become, despite months of DIY and restoration work he'd mostly done with his own two hands.

The reality was he was no longer cycling fit and time was against him. He was running out of weeks until the race.

Having learnt his lesson after the first training session, Dermot had taken to cleaning his bike outside before bringing it in. The thought of having to beg Sarah for her cleaning solution again was an embarrassment too far.

Entering his flat he saw the red light flashing on the answer machine. Hitting the play button, he poured himself a large glass of juice as he listened.

"Mate, it's Max. You up for five a side tomorrow night? Oh, and we're going to be hitting the mountain bikes on the weekend. I've found a fifteen-mile trail to get us going on Saturday. Let me know."

Dermot groaned loudly. A fifteen-mile trail off road was usually well within his capabilities. At least it was within his capabilities a year or two back. Now, with his body so sore and his lung capacity not yet recovered, it seemed too big a challenge. But he knew he needed to do it. Whether purely to save face or whether his competitive spirit was making a comeback, he knew he couldn't say no.

$*$ $\quad$ $*$ $\quad$ $*$

Sarah touched the indented panel again. Curiosity had stopped her sleeping that night. It made a refreshing change to the usual reason. But if it was an obstacle to her sleeping, it needed to be vanquished.

Pushing the panel, tentatively at first, it once again moved beneath her hand, but didn't open. Pushing harder the second time Sarah felt it resist and she realised it was locked or stuck. She let out a sigh of frustration. She hated seeing a job half done. She knew she'd never sleep now with the absence of a satisfactory answer. She didn't usually consider herself neurotic, but Sarah wondered if sleep deprivation had sparked a new character trait.

Frustration mounting, she pushed on the panel one last time, as she turned away in apparent defeat. Fully prepared to storm down the stairs back into the living room, she paused as she felt the panel suddenly give way. Nervous that she may have damaged something, she took a quick look. The panel was now wide open with the full lock still attached. It was an old lock, as was the frame holding the panel. It had weakened over time, pulling away with the entire panel and leaving a rectangular hole where it had once secured the door.

Beyond the panel it was dark and Sarah, nervously lifting the torch she'd brought with her, tried to peer inside. The narrow shaft of light revealed a large area and Sarah realised she'd discovered an attic. Reaching her hand inside and around for a light switch, she quickly swiped it out again. The fear of faulty wiring or large spiders was of equal concern.

Using the light of the torch she slowly stepped inside the space. Not one to be frightened by dark small spaces in the dead of night (spiders were an entirely different matter), she hunched over and made her way through the room.

It was dusty and looked long forgotten. Seeing no obvious sign of arachnids, except for old decrepit looking webs, she moved forward more confidently. The attic space was mostly empty and contained no natural light.

Sarah reached the end of the darkened room and surveyed its entirety. The only contents were several scraps of hideous looking carpet, perhaps kept there as spares by the previous owner, and a small collection of innocuous looking items next to them.

A box, no bigger than a shoebox, stood on top of the pile, with a few books underneath and bizarrely a pair of old-fashioned boots. A small white and blue oval shaped trinket box lay next to the pile. They were all incredibly dusty and Sarah wondered fleetingly if they had belonged to the original inhabitants.

She carefully reached down and wiped away some of the dust from the shoebox. It came off in layers and revealed a plain surface. There was no writing nor label and Sarah wasn't sure if she should look inside.

But knowing she couldn't leave the attic with such a mystery behind her she decided to lift the lid. Inside the box lay two small notebooks and an elegant old-fashioned fountain pen, the ink long dried up. Beside the notebooks, which were each covered in a beautiful deep red satin, was a delicate hair pin and an old black and white photograph. The hair pin had small porcelain roses on top, with minute white flowers nestled in between.

The photograph, upon closer inspection was actually a picture cutting from a newspaper. It was of a woman, serious and poised, and wearing what Sarah suspected was either Victorian or Edwardian clothing. She was facing the camera in a formal pose.

Realising she'd just created more mystery: the identity of the woman in the picture and the content of the two notebooks, Sarah reluctantly replaced the lid. She would need to do some more investigating in the morning, starting with Dermot. But for now, she hoped upon hope that the new mysteries wouldn't persist in keeping her awake.

Chapter Six

"Okay, shall we take a look then?" the Sonographer asked.

Izzy gave a nervous, tight smile in response while Will sat beside her beaming. All the feelings of Henry's first scan came to mind. Was the baby healthy? Would they find a heart beat? What if nothing was there? They were mingled with the bubble of excitement that Izzy realised, with a jolt, was the first she'd even felt during this pregnancy. A stab of guilt hit her in the gut.

It wasn't that she didn't want another baby, she had just become so consumed with the desire to find her purpose in life that she hadn't had time to appreciate the situation in front of her. She hadn't stopped to revel in the miraculous little life growing inside. The guilt burned deeper and a flush reach her cheeks.

Attempting to return her attention to the ultrasound screen in front of her, Izzy chastised herself. This baby deserved more than that. She endeavoured to make more effort to focus her thoughts on her children, even the one who'd yet to be born, and less on her own needs. And yet somewhere inside, somewhere less obvious than the location of guilt, that didn't feel quite right either.

"Well, we have a heartbeat. A strong one at that," the voice of the Sonographer filtered into Izzy's thoughts. Will squeezed her hand tightly in his exuberance.

Izzy stared transfixed by the image in front of her. The white, fuzzy nondescript shape squirmed against the brown-black background. The same delight she'd felt at Henry's first scan circled her now and she took a deep breath of relief. Relief that the baby was healthy and relief that she felt that initial wash of love sweep over her, as it had last time.

The usual checks were made. The baby had all limbs and all digits but it was far too early to identify the sex. Prior tests of Izzy's blood pressure, urine and weight had all come back fine and Izzy and Will left, hand in hand, clasping the grainy picture of the child growing in seclusion inside her.

The journey home was at first a quiet and reflective one. Both awed into silence, they kept shooting glances at the photo sat on the dashboard. At odd times they'd catch each other's gaze and smile. As Will drove home, where Sarah was babysitting little Henry, Izzy found her voice.

"What do you think it's going to be?" she asked, her voice almost a whisper.

"It already is, isn't it?" Will said, his forehead crinkled in confusion. Izzy whacked him on the arm. "You know what I mean," she stated indignantly. He grinned over at her.

"I know, you're just too easy to wind up sometimes," he replied. "Personally, I don't know. And I don't care. I'm a dad again. That's all that matters."

Izzy felt a sudden pang as she wished she could feel as calm and assured as her husband. It was enough for Will to be content to be Dad. Why couldn't she feel the same about being Mum? She reasoned that Will had a career already, he already had all his boxes ticked. She was left hanging, watching the world go by and wondering where her own place in it was.

She knew that Will had been attracted to her because of her spontaneity, something so far removed from the lifestyle and characteristics he'd grown up with. The regimented existence in his parent's home, followed by the comparative freedom of university life, culminated in meeting the (often flighty) woman of his dreams. It had been a real eye opener and a refreshing change of course.

But now her spontaneity seemed to be her downfall. Izzy was creative and now she wanted to create something all her own, beyond the four walls of home. Beyond all she had created as a wife and a mother, which she felt deep down should be enough (and would be for many) and yet she knew it simply *wasn't*.

It was no longer just a job she was after. Anyone could achieve that. There was something deeper happening, a deep sense of dissatisfaction that was eating into her daily thoughts and causing havoc and distraction. She didn't understand the root of it, or even what it was, but it was there and wasn't going away.

Pulling the list of career ideas out of her bag (she had started taking it everywhere with her) she flicked through the multiple pages yet again.

"What's that?" Will asked, innocently enough. But she knew him better than that and could sense his deepening curiosity.

"My list of business ideas," she stated simply. It was no secret between them and she wasn't about to start lying now.

Will looked perplexed but kept driving. "What?" she asked, at his expression. He shook his head as if thinking better of it, then sheepishly turned to Izzy.

"I was just thinking whether now is such a good time, what with the baby coming." Seeing her eyes narrow, he quickly explained himself. "You're due in

September. That's not that long away. I'm just saying why don't you wait until after the baby? Start up something early next year, once the newborn months are over."

She knew what he was saying made sense, yet she still saw red. It was okay for him. He already had a job he loved. Why should she keep putting off what she wanted to do? But then, at that thought, sweet Henry popped into her mind and she gasped at the guilt coursing through her. Why had he been relegated to such an insignificance in her life, compared to that of a career? And why did the two need to be pitted against each other? She felt ashamed that she could be so selfish. But at the same time indignant that there need be a choice.

Other mothers worked. She herself had a job (the most recent in a long line of many) shortly before she fell pregnant with Henry. Why hadn't she found something to stick to? Why had she, in yet another flight of fancy, quit all work and study to have her son, rather than take maternity leave?

Because, she realised, she simply hadn't known how she'd feel. There was nothing wrong with being at home full time, she knew that, but she hadn't banked on the strong desire to have something else that she now had. And once again she wondered at the source of it, and a small spark of alarm made her consider that perhaps she actually wanted an escape. Perhaps she wasn't cut out to be a mother after all.

A prickle of heat spread through her body fast and she tried to swallow the ball of tears trying to erupt from within. The terrifying reality that she might be struggling with the whole parenting thing threatened to send her spiralling. All parents struggled, she knew, but suddenly her fears and doubts seemed larger than everyone else's put together.

She looked down at the list again, through blurred tears, and wondered what the truth was. Did she really desire a career or was she simply trying to escape the mundanity that had crept into her existence?

*   *   *

Henry reached out his chubby hands and placed them on Sarah's cheeks. He pushed his hands inwards and Sarah responded by blowing a raspberry. He gave a deep belly laugh and threw his head back in hysterics. They'd played the game for over ten minutes and she hadn't yet managed to distract or tire him from it.

The sound of tyres on gravel entered Sarah's consciousness and she gazed out the window. "Daddy and Mummy are home," she said to a delighted Henry. He wriggled in her arms until she had no choice but to put him down and fast as lightning, he made his way to the front door.

Henry shrieked as Will's arms came around the open door and scooped up his son. Izzy followed close behind, kissing Henry on the forehead, with a subdued and distracted expression on her face.

41

Sarah's heart sank. Was something wrong with the baby?

"Thanks for looking after Henry, Sarah," Will said, his usual jolly self and Sarah relaxed slightly. Will would never have behaved normally had there been anything wrong. Yet, she looked toward her best friend and noticed Izzy wiping away a tear. Confused, Sarah waved away Will's thanks good naturedly and approached Izzy.

"Iz? What's happened?" Izzy noticed Sarah's worried eyes and concern. She handed Sarah the scan picture and smiled a brave smile.

"The baby's fine Sarah. Happy and healthy."

"And you?"

Izzy sighed. "I'm just so confused at the moment Sarah." She sat down heavily on the edge of the sofa, instantly regretting it as it jarred her already aching muscles. She shrugged off her coat and checked to make sure her husband and son had left the room. "I'm worried I'm a bit depressed." It sounded almost comical to say it, even though it was far from a laughing matter.

Sarah looked at Izzy with her head to one side. "What makes you think that Iz?"

"It's just this whole job list thing. It's all I can think about. I'm obsessing about it all the time and I can't even enjoy being at home with Henry, and I've barely thought about the baby at all! I feel like I'm trying to escape my reality, and the more I can't the more desperate I feel. What do you think?"

"I'm not a Doctor or a Counsellor Iz. Maybe go see one if you're worried," Sarah replied carefully. "But I must say you've always been a bit like this."

"I have?"

"For as long as I've known you. You've always tried to figure out what you want to do next. Trying out different jobs, signing up for courses. Just trying to find where you slot in. That's not a bad thing," Sarah hastened to add, seeing Izzy's distraught expression. "You're creative. You like lots of different things. You're *good* at lots of different things. Maybe you just haven't found your passion yet? Or maybe, you are one of the few who can do anything and everything, just because you throw yourself into it and excel.

Perhaps having Henry is the first time you've actually struggled and not sailed through. Maybe that's why you're feeling the way you do, because it's easier to control a job than the uncertainty of being a mum?"

"You think so?" Izzy's eyes lit up.

"Look..." Sarah said quickly, backtracking. "I'm not making a diagnosis here. I'm just saying it's a possibility. You're a great mum Izzy. Maybe you do need something more, a job, whatever, or maybe you are just feeling unsure because being a mum is... well, hard. But perhaps you should see someone professional anyway?"

There was a brief silence and then Izzy started to laugh.

"What?" Sarah asked, incredulous.

"That's the cheapest counselling session ever, Sarah!" she said, throwing her head back in hysterics. "Although, you missed out the bit about me being pregnant, therefore subject to a whole volley of crazy emotions, including the depressing ones. Cheered me up a bit though. Thanks."

"Um, that's okay," Sarah replied, confused not for the first time by Izzy, the emotional roller coaster. "Are you sure you are all right?"

"Yes. What you said makes sense, but I need to think it all through. Don't worry, I'm fine."

"You know you can call me if you need to talk. Any time. I'm awake half the night anyway."

"Really? Since when Sarah?" the sharp tone in Izzy's voice alerted Sarah to her best friend's constant concerns and misplaced feelings of needing to protect her. Probably why, subconsciously, Sarah chose not to share too frequently.

"The last week," she admitted.

"A whole week?" Izzy's eyes grew big and Sarah hated that the easy, happy expression that had been on Izzy's face two minutes before was now wiped clean. A deep furrowed frown of concern stood in its place.

"I thought you only had odd nights these days?"

"I do. Usually. Izzy really, it's nothing to worry about. I think it is just part of getting used to a new house."

"Why didn't you tell me Sarah? This isn't normal. Not these days. I hate to think of you up all night and on your own."

"Okay, I'm sorry I didn't say anything," Sarah threw up her hands in submission. "But I've been dealing with it. I've kept myself occupied and the anxiety isn't worrying me."

She wasn't about to admit to her attic excursion the other night. She hadn't yet managed to get hold of Dermot, who seemed to have been away the previous couple of nights, but she'd sneaked a look inside the box once again, only just resisting the urge to read the notebooks before she'd had a chance to check with him.

Izzy stared at her, clearly trying to decide if Sarah was telling the truth or not. A minute or so passed, and convinced that Sarah didn't carry that all too familiar haunted look whenever sleeplessness and anxiety were mixed, Izzy dropped the subject. Sometimes it was best just to let live.

*   *   *

Sarah left an hour later, fed up on homemade casserole as a thank you for looking after Henry, and drove back into town. During the remainder of the day she tried catching Dermot at home. She wasn't quite sure what was stopping her from opening the notebooks, after all Dermot nor anyone else needed to know. But something held her back, Ultimately the belongings in the attic were his property, in his house, and she knew she'd feel guilty if she didn't, at least surreptitiously, find out whether it was okay to go through them.

Finding no one at home once again, Sarah, feeling slightly deflated, made her way up to her own flat. Greta was busy at the piano and Sarah enjoyed the soft tinkle of music as she made herself a cup of tea. As she sat and took the first sip there was a knock at the door. Heaving herself out of the comfortable position she'd buried into, Sarah made her way across the floor.

"I realised I still owe you for helping me out the other week," Dermot said, as she opened the door wide. Holding out both hands in front of him, Sarah noticed the two bottles of wine protruding from each.

"White and Red. I don't know which you prefer, so I bought both," he grinned and Sarah smiled back as he handed them over.

"You really didn't have to," she began.

"But I did and it was deserved. You saved me from having to order a whole new carpet."

"That's a bit dramatic. It was only a bit of mud," she teased.

"Yeah, which I had no idea how to clean off. Give me a run-down Edwardian town house and I can work miracles. But a carpet and a splodge of mud and I haven't the foggiest."

"Well, if it wasn't for my mum, I'd have no clue either," Sarah admitted. "Do you want a glass?"

"Sure. Ah, but which bottle?" he asked.

"To be honest I like both. It depends on the weather. I find white is preferable in summer, red on colder days."

"Definitely a red day then," he mused.

"Agreed."

She took two glasses out of the cupboard and poured, completely forgetting about her newly brewed cup of tea. She was thrilled he'd turned up out of the blue as she'd now have the chance to find out about the attic.

She handed a glass to Dermot, who was already sitting on the suede sofa, looking at home. His dark blonde hair was wet. He was clearly just out of the shower and his blue eyes were striking against his grey blue shirt. Sarah joined him on the sofa, only then noticing the steaming cup of tea on the table beside her.

"Sorry, did I interrupt?" he asked, noticing the beverage too.

"No, it's fine. I much prefer the glass of wine," she smiled. "Thanks for this," she said, gesturing the wine in her hand and toward the other bottle on the side.

"Just a small token of appreciation. Which I'm now drinking," he realised, almost sheepishly.

Sarah laughed loudly and felt a small tug of self awareness. How long ago since she'd really laughed, because something was funny, and not out of simple fondness for a friend. Even Henry, with his endearing giggles, had not moved Sarah to such a carefree laugh like Dermot did now.

Shaking off the disconcerting thought, Sarah brought herself back to the present.

"Were you away this weekend?" she asked. "I just mean that I needed to ask you about something, but there was no answer at your door."

"Oh, yes. I went off-road biking with some friends and crashed at theirs. Easier than lugging a bike and God knows how much mud back home with me. Thought I'd save the carpet from any more indignity."

Sarah suppressed another laugh and focused her thoughts.

"What was it you wanted to ask?" Dermot's voice cut through her reverie.

"Oh," she started. "Nothing serious. I just... I just wanted to ask you about the attic."

Dermot looked confused for a moment then turned his head toward the stairwell leading to the roof terrace. "Oh, the one up there? Is there a problem?"

"Not really. Well no, not at all actually. It's just that I discovered it by accident the other evening and I wondered about the old dusty items still in there. Did they come with the house?"

Dermot sat up a bit straighter and rubbed the stubble on his chin. "I'd forgotten about the attic. Yeah, when I bought the place, it was in the details of the property. The lady I bought it from said there were some old items that she'd found in the attic, when she had the house converted into flats. All she mentioned were some 'original artefacts', so to speak, and that it was up to me what I did with them. She obviously didn't think there was much value in them. She told me to keep them or sell them. To be honest, I'd forgotten about it until now. Anything interesting in there?"

"A few personal items that look pretty old," Sarah confessed. "But there's also some diaries or journals. I haven't looked inside them," Sarah shifted uncomfortably, unsure of how to ask her next question.

"What?" Dermot said, having noticed.

"Sometimes I have difficulty sleeping and I, well I don't even know why I'm telling you that, but I wondered if you'd have a problem with me looking through the diaries if I found myself awake in the night again?" she knew she had said it clumsily, but Sarah really didn't know how to ask without it sounding strange.

"I guess so..." Dermot mulled over his answer. "As long as you don't smuggle them out to go on some antiques show. They belong to the property remember?" he said, half joking, but a hint of uncertainty to whether she was trustworthy or not.

"Don't worry," she said, in what she hoped was a reassuring tone. "They won't go anywhere. I'm just fascinated by the history, that's all," she shook her head with a smile. "I guess I'm more like my mother than I thought."

Chapter Seven

Sarah was almost disappointed when she slept well that night. Then the following night and every night through the rest of the week. She had been secretly hoping that she'd have at least one night to search the belongings in the attic and start reading the contents of the notebooks. She could have just read them in the daytime, after all Dermot had been happy for her to go ahead. But for Sarah, being alone and up when everyone else was sleeping could be lonely. In some strange way the promise of what was in the box was a welcome distraction and a potential form of companionship.

However, as the week drew to a close Sarah's patience started to slide. There was a growing temptation to pull out the box from its hidden and dusty corner. Why she even cared didn't concern her. It was an unknown. A mystery. Something to discover. Not to mention a break from the ordinary.

Saturday morning burst into being with a chorus of bird song. The lightening dawn left the surrounding buildings in silhouette. Sarah stirred from another good night's sleep and opened her eyes to see a shaft of pale light shining through the curtains. After the lack of sleep of the previous week she finally felt rested again. The thought of the box in the attic immediately came to mind as she woke and made a decision.

Reaching out of bed for her dressing gown, she threw it on and scouted around the lightening room for her slippers. Digging them out from under the bed she put them on and headed out to the kitchen. While the coffee pot hummed to life she made her way up the little staircase. Opening the small hatch, she folded her petite frame inside and approached the pile of items in the corner. Sweeping the trinket box and shoebox carefully into her arms she made her way back downstairs.

A few minutes later, sipping her coffee, she tentatively picked up the little blue and white trinket box. It was smaller than her palm and difficult to open. Practically shredding her fingernails, she slowly prised open the lid. Inside was a brooch, its dimensions filling the entirety of the box. She carefully took it out and studied it. It was delicate and beautifully ornate, silver with a turquoise face. She ran her finger over it and it felt smooth like a shell. Overlaid the turquoise were exquisite and minute silver flowers with tiny pearls set into the centre of each. Tarnished due to its age, it was nevertheless a gorgeous and breathtaking piece of jewellery.

Despite its apparent decadence Sarah wondered if it belonged to a child. The pin on the brooch was short and the lack of precious diamonds, rubies or other valuable stones suggested the jewellery might have belonged to a child. The trinket box itself had a blue and white picture of a young girl, on the beach, with her hair in pigtails and tied with ribbons.

Sarah cradled the brooch carefully in her palm for a few moments, wondering on the story behind it. What had happened to the child this had belonged to and why had something so precious been left behind by the family? Or had they died here and the jewellery forgotten? So many questions ran through Sarah's mind. She wondered if Dermot would know more of the back story?

Her gaze fell onto the shoebox and she thought of the notebooks. Quickly but carefully replacing the brooch in the box, she reached for the dusty and decrepit cardboard container. Noticing the hair pin inside she brought it out for closer inspection. The flowers on the pin were crudely carved and the pin short in length. Again, she wondered if the owner was a child.

She placed it back in the box and removed the two notebooks. They were identical in size and colour, so Sarah had to open each to work out which to look at first. Pleased to see what looked like diary entries, rather than scrawled notes or shopping lists, Sarah located the very first entry.

5th February 1907

Nanny sighs deeply as she lifts the pail of water from the copper bath...

Sarah sat down with her coffee and read on.

*   *   *

Within minutes Sarah was fully immersed and captivated. She expertly ignored the shrill ring of her mobile phone, lying just feet away on the kitchen counter, focusing her attention instead on the neat as a pin handwriting in front of her.

14th February 1907

It is St Valentine's Day today, a holiday I am not yet privy to, according to my dear father who wishes me to remain innocent of all male attention. Once I am out then he will welcome and encourage the flatteries of a gentleman seeking my hand. Until then, I am expected to pretend this day, nay romance itself, does not exist in any shape or form. I do not mind. I have more to mind than marriage.

My tutor must despair of me at times, revelling as I do at the opportunities an education is beginning to provide for my sex. Although it is his job to educate me, I suspect he thinks it not worth the trouble, seeing as I'll no doubt be married off in less than five years.

Yesterday I regaled him with tales, indeed talking of nothing else, of what I'd read of the Mud March last week. He looked horrified as I hastily recalled the details I had seen in father's newspaper. The article had covered the suffragette's march through the cold and damp London streets with banners and rosettes, calling for a right to a vote. Women of all backgrounds, titles and education stood together in unity. My father labelled it a 'laughable public spectacle', but my heart was swollen in pride at the bravery I had read.

Now my tutor thinks me a radical, of that I am sure. I don't believe I am (or perhaps, given my station in life, I am indeed considered such), but I do believe in pursuing my dreams. Come what may.

Sarah was startled back into reality by the phone ringing again. Tempted to ignore it a second time, she instead shook herself and reached for the phone. She rarely ignored phone calls anymore, especially when someone was so insistent on contacting her. She couldn't risk missing important or even bad news. It was a habit that had formed six years ago.

"Hello?"

"Hi Honey, it's Mum. Just checking you're still coming for dinner tonight?"

Sarah let out a breath of relief she hadn't even realised she was holding. She almost let out a laugh at the triviality of the phone call.

"Yes Mum, tonight's fine. Shall I bring anything? I've a spare bottle of wine." One of Dermot's thank you gifts had miraculously avoided being opened.

"No, just yourself love. See you at 7."

Sarah disconnected and looked over at the notebook, still open on the sofa. She desperately wanted to carry on reading, to discover more of the life held within the pages. The era, the politics, the plight of the girl were on one hand utterly foreign, yet everything somehow resonated.

Here was a girl facing uncertainty, a new chapter in history where women were recognising their rights and life was changing. Here was a girl who feared her dreams would never be realised, for reasons Sarah had only read hints. But Sarah could relate. She could understand the dreams under threat. Hadn't her own been vanquished at Alex's death? Hadn't it taken over half a decade to start carving new dreams and step out into them? What had happened to this young girl? Had her dreams been realised or had she found herself married off as soon as she was old enough?

Sarah picked up the notebook eager to find out, but a loud knock at the door distracted her. Placing the journal almost reverently back in the shoebox, replacing the lid and for some reason unknown to herself, hiding it in a kitchen cupboard, Sarah went to open the door.

"Long time, no see!" Tessa threw her arms out in welcome and bounded in the flat, not unlike a human version of Tigger.

Wearing a long purple coat with enormous buttons and a faux fur trim, black bootleg jeans and large chunky burnt orange beaded earrings, Tessa looked as eclectic as ever. Her long strawberry blonde hair looked immaculate despite the cold weather conditions outside. Her bright blue eyes were identical to Alex's and Sarah embraced her sister-in-law with enthusiasm and a sudden spasm of emotion.

"It has been long," she sniffed, despite herself. Alex's kid sister Tessa hadn't always seen eye to eye with Sarah. The two opposing personalities didn't complement each other like Sarah's and Izzy's. Instead they had, in the past, regularly wound each other the wrong way. But as Tessa matured into a young woman (she had been a precocious 16-year-old when Sarah first met her) they began to get along better. Tessa's legendary outbursts and flippant attitudes had never completely gone away, but had mellowed as she hit her mid twenties.

"Nearly a year, can you believe it?" sang Tessa in the sing song voice she often used when trying to appear over casual. Immediately alert that this wasn't just a day visit, Sarah decided to tread carefully.

"Of course, I was out visiting Steven in Australia for some of that, otherwise I'd have come sooner," Tessa continued. Sarah ignored the fact that Tessa had been back for six months.

"How was your time with Steven?" Sarah asked, referring to Alex and Tessa's brother who'd moved down under four years ago. Alex's death had hit him hard and he'd reacted by getting far away from all the memories they'd shared.

"Good. I needed to get away. The guy I'd been seeing was driving me nuts."

"And Steven himself?" Sarah asked, flicking the kettle on. Tessa had a habit of making each conversation about herself.

"Yeah, he's well."

Realising she wasn't going to get any more detail than that, Sarah changed the subject. "How did you know where I live? I only moved in a few weeks ago."

"I saw the postcard you sent Mum and Dad with your change of address," Tessa explained vaguely. Sarah knew she'd need to be patient if she wanted to learn more. It was never wise to try hurry Tessa. She worked to her own timetable.

"This is a nice place," Tessa mused, looking at the wallpaper in admiration and bending down to run her finger over the tiles in the fireplace.

"I like it," Sarah replied simply. "Tea or coffee?"

"Anything stronger?" Tessa joked.

"Not this early in the day." Sarah suddenly felt like Tessa's mother, a feeling not unknown in the past, and resented it. It was a familiar pattern that never seemed to change.

Tessa was already unbuttoning her jacket and threw it on the sofa. For the first time Sarah noticed she was carrying a large handbag; large enough to be used as an overnight bag and her heart sank. The thought of becoming her sister-in-law's babysitter, combined with the fear of having a witness to her sleepless nights sent a chill down her spine. She was just getting her life under control, after years of pretending she already had. She didn't need someone upsetting the cart nor realising she'd been a complete fraud the whole time.

Sarah hadn't spoken of her husband's death to family or friends for two years. She had given the illusion that she was past the fear and loneliness that threatened her on a daily basis and had deliberately put on a front, so that others wouldn't feel uncomfortable. The only one who saw through the facade was Izzy, but despite her thinly veiled attempts to check up on Sarah, she didn't raise the subject directly.

It was just easier this way. No one could tell Sarah how long she could expect to grieve. Her grief counsellor had told her that grief was cyclical and there was no time frame for it. On one hand Sarah *had* ceased to grieve. Alex was gone. He'd been gone a while and nothing was bringing him back. Life moved on. Friends married, had babies, got promotions, gained their first grey hairs. His face and laugh and characteristics were now a vague memory, tucked within the photo albums that she rarely allowed herself to view. But she wasn't depressed. She wasn't crying out for something that couldn't be retrieved. She had accepted what had happened.

But it didn't stop the pain. Nothing would, except perhaps time which couldn't be quantified. She just didn't want to be exposed for pretending. She knew if Tessa got a whiff of the truth it would get back to the family within minutes. Sarah would be faced by questions and sympathy and the seemingly obligatory pity. She didn't want to go backwards. She'd fought hard to keep pushing forward, sometimes feeling as though she were walking into a gale force wind. Not much ground had been gained, but it was progress nevertheless.

Coughing nervously, Sarah tried to keep her cool. "Why are you really here Tessa?"

Tessa's eyes widened before visibly composing herself and gave a laugh. "To see you of course. Why so suspicious? Can't I come and visit the closest person I have to a sister?"

Sarah folded her arms indignantly. "The truth Tessa," she stated firmly.

Tessa had the decency to look sheepish. "Um... can I just stay tonight? I can bunk with a friend tomorrow, but they're out of town tonight."

"Why don't you stay at your parent's? They have the space. I've only got the one bedroom here."

"Oh," Tessa thought a moment. "That's okay, I'll sleep on the sofa. It looks comfortable."

Sarah's heart managed to somehow sink further.

"Mum and Dad are... um... busy too," Tessa continued as she sat down on the sofa and tested out its softness.

"Out of town busy?"

"It's their anniversary."

"Their anniversary is in June, Tessa." Sarah was beginning to lose patience and busied herself in making two cups of tea before she said something she'd regret. Clearly there was something more serious behind this visit, and the fact that Tessa wasn't welcome at her own parent's home was worrying.

There was silence as Sarah handed one of the cups to Tessa, who took it without making eye contact. Sighing, Sarah took the armchair opposite and fixed her sister-in-law with a firm gaze. "Tessa, you can either start telling me the truth or you can find somewhere else for the night."

Screw Tessa's timetable. This was Sarah's house and she didn't want trouble.

A flicker of concern flashed across Tessa's features and she bit her lip. "I just need to lay low for a bit."

"Why?" Sarah raised her voice, her frustration fast reaching boiling point. She didn't lose her temper often but Tessa was one of the few who could spark the fire.

"Don't worry it's nothing illegal," Tessa spat defensively. "I broke up with Kris and Mum and Dad said I couldn't stay with them because I need to face up to my so-called problems."

Tessa made a habit of dumping men as soon as she'd got bored of the relationship and often straight after they'd fallen head over heels for her. Sarah couldn't exactly blame her parents-in-law for such a reaction. Last time a relationship had failed Tessa ran off to Australia to Steven, and half a dozen times before that her parents had been expected to pick up the pieces and welcome their adult daughter back into their home.

Tessa still had some serious growing up to do. Now it seemed to be Sarah's turn to take her in. She guessed she should be grateful that it hadn't happened sooner.

"What happened?" she asked, her tone softening a little. For all she knew this Kris could have been a monster.

"I liked him Sarah," Tessa's voice grew small and she reminded Sarah of the teenager she'd been when they first met. "I mean really liked him. More than any of the others."

Sarah managed to stop herself rolling her eyes. She'd heard this before.

52

More than once.

"He's so smart and intelligent and he treated me so well," Tessa continued. "We were only dating a few months but we'd already talked about marriage."

Blimey, thought Sarah. This wasn't like the other times after all. Tessa had never felt that way about anyone before.

"I think I just started to get a little scared. I love him, I really do. And I want to marry him."

"Then what's the problem. Keep dating a while, then get married. You can do it," Sarah added with a grin.

Tessa shook her head vehemently. "I can't. It's just... it's too much Sarah. He's better off finding someone else to do all that with. I'm not a good bet."

The silence that followed hung tangibly in the air and Sarah mulled over Tessa's words. She wasn't sure how genuine Tessa was being, but one night to clear her head wouldn't hurt. Unfortunately, she suspected one night was going to prove a massive understatement.

"Okay, you can stay the night. But just one night Tessa. I mean it."

Tessa gave a squeal of delight, out of keeping with her sullen mood, and Sarah instantly began to regret her decision.

"Thanks Sarah. I'll behave, I promise. So, what are we going to do tonight? I can treat us to a take away."

"Actually, Tessa I have plans, sorry." Sarah remembered the meal at her mum and dad's. She wasn't about to invite Tessa along. She felt mean but there needed to be strict boundaries where her sister-in-law was concerned.

"Oh, well that's okay. I'll watch a film, get a take away, maybe run a bath. I need to relax," Tessa said, already making herself at home.

Sarah's gazed flicked over to the kitchen cupboard where she'd placed the shoebox. She'd need to find a better hiding place. With Tessa's instant over-familiarity Sarah felt suddenly uncomfortable leaving something precious in such an easy to find location.

Chapter Eight

Arriving at her parent's house Sarah switched off the car engine.

The forty-minute drive had been a welcome escape from the day. Tessa had quickly settled into the flat, leaving endless used mugs and bowls scattered everywhere. Her clothes had been laid out across the length of the dining table and her toiletry bag pushed Sarah's own toiletries perilously close to the edge of the sink in the bathroom. The TV had stayed on all afternoon, turned up loudly as soon as Greta had started playing another melodic tune on the piano.

Sarah had eventually escaped up onto the roof terrace for some peace. But that had lasted barely ten minutes when Tessa's head popped around the outside door.

"Oh, wow. This is great. You could throw parties out here. Small ones," she amended as she studied its compact dimensions.

Grateful to have plans for the evening, Sarah soon made her escape. Now having arrived and breathing a sigh of relief, Sarah turned off the headlights and exited the car. She was looking forward to an evening spent with her mum and dad and her mum's great cooking.

"Hello, my darling," David opened the front door and embraced his eldest. Sarah sunk into his chest and allowed him to squeeze her tightly until it hurt. She used to hate that. Nowadays she appreciated the physical contact and the affection behind it.

He led her into the 1930s house he shared with Pippa. They'd downgraded the family home when Sarah's brother Jason had moved out five years ago. Now living in a two-bed bungalow, tastefully updated and decorated, with a large garden and garage and workshop to suit both their needs, David and Pippa had found a comfortable place to see out their retirement.

The village of just 4000 was nestled amongst fields and farms and was quintessentially English. Sarah loved visiting, not just to see her parents, but to enjoy the escape from city living.

"Come through," Pippa called out from the kitchen. "Make yourself at home."

David fixed Sarah a drink while she kicked off her shoes and plonked herself down on their ridiculously comfortable burgundy sofa. Taking the glass of red wine from a proffered hand, Sarah took a deep sip and closed her eyes. She opened them a minute later to be greeted with a look of amusement from her father.

"Hard day?"

"Something like that," Sarah mumbled. She still wasn't sure what to make of Tessa's sudden arrival.

Pippa entered the room holding a ramekin of warm oven-roasted nuts. Sarah took a few and returned to her wine.

"Anything we could help with?" Pippa asked casually, with a quick glance at her husband.

"Tessa arrived on my doorstep this morning," Sarah decided to come right out with it. Prolonging the story was just too painful. "She's going through another break up and apparently it's my turn to endure the fall out."

"She wants to stay?" asked Pippa, horrified. "What about her own place?"

"It sounds like she was staying with this guy," Sarah replied. "Tessa's asked to stay one night. It's not like I have the space for her to stay longer. But we all know what she can be like. Besides just the one day has been exhausting. Looking after Henry last weekend was less tiring."

"You're just going to have to be firm with her," David spoke. "You've only just moved into your own place and it is too small for guests. Don't be too scared to tell her to leave when the time is up. She's a grown woman, she can handle it."

Sarah scoffed and swallowed the last mouthful of wine.

"Another?"

"No Dad, otherwise I'll have to stay here the night. Oh, that's not a bad idea," Sarah's eyes lit up and Pippa laughed and stood up.

"Okay, I'm dishing up in five minutes."

*   *   *

Making her way quietly upstairs at just gone midnight, Sarah opened the door to her flat. She hoped the late hour would mean that Tessa was already fast asleep and that she herself would be tired enough to just crash.

The evening had been great. Just her and Mum and Dad. They'd eaten well, reminisced over family memories and anecdotes and even chatted briefly about Alex. Their fondness for their late son-in-law brought a smile to Sarah's lips. He had charmed her parents just as he'd charmed her and they were devastated when he died. It had been nice to discuss him and the memories they'd all shared. She hadn't felt comfortable to do that with anyone in a long time.

By the end of the evening Sarah was tired and spent. She very nearly accepted her mother's now serious offer of a bed for the night. But aware that Tessa would be expecting her, Sarah made the reluctant decision to head back. Listening to the late-night chilled music on the car radio had proved therapeutic, and Sarah arrived home more relaxed than she'd expected.

But upon hearing the low buzz of the television as she opened her door, her mood threatened to change again. Tessa was sat up watching a film, with another collection of plates and mugs scattered around her.

"You're back," Tessa croaked. She was getting choked up by a soppy moment in the film and she sat engrossed.

"Yeah, sorry I'm late."

"Have a nice time?"

"Wonderful. But I'm officially exhausted, so I'm off to bed." Sarah had taken out a couple of new novels from the library so she'd have plenty to read in case she couldn't sleep.

"Watch with me. It's only just started," Tessa asked, slightly pleadingly.

"I can't handle late nights like you," Sarah feebly protested with a white lie, but found herself sitting down next to Tessa anyway. The tell-tale signs that she wouldn't sleep were revealing themselves. Her now alert brain and the million questions she still wanted to ask Tessa about her dramatic appearance, spun round her mind distractedly.

When the first advertisement break came on Tessa jumped up and grabbed a large bag of crisps from the kitchen counter. Sarah noticed an empty one already on the floor. It was a wonder Tessa stayed so slim.

"Want some?" Tessa asked, bounding back onto the sofa with far too much energy for the time of night.

Sarah cringed. "No thanks. I feel sick if I eat this late."

"Old lady," Tessa teased.

"You must have found the shops then?" Sarah asked, noting that aside from the crisp bags, cans of cola and sweet wrappers littered the floor.

"Hmm, found out the secret you're keeping too."

"What?" Sarah started, wondering how on earth Tessa had come across the shoebox now hidden in Alex's old holdall in the bottom of the wardrobe. Would Tessa openly admit to snooping?

"Downstairs," Tessa explained. "The cute Irish guy living on the ground floor. He gave me directions to the shops. The mad piano woman was out, so I knocked on his door next."

Sarah felt a sharp stab of fury. This was the woman, who just that morning, had claimed her heart was broken by the man she wanted to marry. Now she was hitting on Sarah's landlord.

"He's no secret," Sarah tried to control the anger in her voice. "I just didn't think you'd be interested in my neighbour so soon after a break up."

Tessa looked briefly amused, then appeared subdued and turned her attention to the returning film.

"I just thought him cute, that's all. It's not a crime to notice a handsome man is it?"

"Tessa," Sarah began, shaking her head, before giving up. She had already written the night off, there was no point spending it angry.

Her thoughts turned to Dermot. The poor man would be eaten alive by someone like Tessa. If she chose to pursue him, he'd be in serious trouble. She was pretty, and no doubt would turn his head. But he couldn't be expected to know what Tessa was like. All this proved another reason to have her moved out by morning.

Sarah saw it as conducting a personal service. Saving men from Tessa's clutches before their hearts got broken. She briefly wondered as to why she might care and concluded that an unhappy Dermot meant an unhappy landlord. He might even blame her for bringing Tessa into his life. That seemed reason enough as far as Sarah was concerned.

*   *   *

She woke with a crick in her neck, having fallen asleep skew on the armchair, upright and with her slippers on. The TV was still running in the background, showing reruns of some 1970s sitcom Sarah couldn't identify.

Next to her Tessa lay across the sofa, a pillow under her head and Sarah's favourite blanket draped over her body. Typical, thought Sarah. Tessa had a look of utter peace and contentment on her face, while Sarah ached all over.

She looked up toward the bay windows. Its curtains hadn't been drawn the night before and sunlight flooded through in a torrent. Realising it must be quite late, Sarah turned her gaze in the direction of the kitchen clock. It was 10 am.

She padded over to the kitchen and prepared the coffee maker. She'd need her coffee extra strong this morning. As soon as Tessa woke, they'd have a heart to heart about her staying there and what the next step was. Sarah longed for her own company again and felt heartened by the revelation. It wasn't just the whirlwind that was her sister-in-law. Sarah was actually enjoying having her own space.

Realising what a major step forward it was, Sarah couldn't help congratulate herself. It was a small victory, but a victory indeed.

Tessa stirred on the sofa and made a grunting sound. Sarah smirked as she prepared the mug of coffee and contemplated turning up the television to get Tessa to wake up properly. It seemed unfair that Tessa sleep on while Sarah was already up.

Banging the spoon against the side of the mug, accidentally on purpose,

Sarah placed the coffee on the small table in front of the sofa and gave a cough. Tessa stirred again but refused to open her eyes.

"Coffee," Sarah said softly, then repeated again a moment later, firmer this time.

"Hmm," moaned Tessa, still keeping her eyes shut.

Suddenly an eruption of Beethoven's ninth symphony interrupted the relative peace of the flat and Tessa opened her eyes in fright.

"That woman!" she exclaimed, and held her hands over dramatically to her ears.

"I love Greta," Sarah murmured to herself and returned to the kitchen.

"There should be a law against playing piano on a Sunday morning," Tessa stated and sat up, grabbing the coffee and gulping it down. "Good thing I don't have a hangover, or I might be tempted to call the police."

"Well, you only have to put up with it for another hour or two. You'll be going to your friend's later, won't you?" Sarah asked hopefully.

Tessa nodded hesitantly and Sarah decided to push on. She could Tessa's mind working. She was preparing her excuses already.

"I'll give you a lift if you need. It'll save you some money on public transport."

"Thanks Sarah. I'll need to phone Shannon and check. She was a bit hazy on a decision. It might not be a good time for me to stay there."

Taking a deep breath to calm herself Sarah sat back down on the sofa.

"Tessa, you can't stay here. There's not enough room. It's probably not even allowed in my lease. Dermot might chuck me out."

"Why would he do that?" Tessa enquired, and Sarah instantly wished she hadn't brought his name back up.

"He's my landlord Tessa."

"Oh. Well he seems reasonable enough and seemed quite happy to meet me yesterday. I told him how I was staying with you and he seemed fine. Maybe he was okay about it for another reason?"

Sarah felt a twinge of annoyance and suppressed it. "What about Kris? What are you going to do about your relationship with him? Because," she carried on before Tessa could interrupt. "If you're already moving on to the next guy, there's really no need for you to be staying here right? You can move closer to work. I'm sure you've friends who can put you up until you've got your own place?"

"Oh Sarah," Tessa wailed. "I can't face him yet. His friends are my friends and they're all taking his side and no one likes me anymore because I've broken his heart."

So now the truth is coming out, thought Sarah ruefully. She sighed as the realisation of Tessa's words hit their mark.

"So, you've nowhere else to go?"

"Nope," Tessa sniffed.

"Right." Sarah replied, feeling there was nothing else left to say.

Chapter Nine

The doorbell rang incessantly. Red and amber lights flashed hypnotically and blinded Sarah's vision. The noise of radio static grew to a crescendo and Sarah put her hands over her ears and cried out. A blur of black shadow interrupted the glow of the lights and Sarah spun in each direction trying to find an escape. But her only scenery was the small grey room she stood in, the door in front of her, with the noise and light beyond, and nothing behind her.

She began to sob as she realised what they were there for. What they were coming to say. The lights grew stronger and blinded her even more so and yet she found her gaze drawn to them. It was inevitable. She couldn't hide from the message they were bringing. She had to hear it again and again, always repeated in a monotone but with the words hitting harder than a sledge hammer.

Tentatively she reached up to open the door, tears falling profusely down her cheeks, and she braced herself for what she knew was coming.

Suddenly, bolt awake and pouring in sweat, Sarah sat up in bed. The dream, one she had suffered from for nearly seven years, was as real and terrifying as ever. She used to dream it every night. It was one of the reasons she had stopped sleeping. It was one of the reasons fear had crept in. It had been a long time since her last dream. She couldn't remember how long exactly. But certainly months.

She realised she was shaking and took a few deep and steadying breaths. It was still dark outside, but a bird could be heard practising its flawless notes for the chorus due to erupt shortly. At least she'd made it through most of the night, she told herself. Waking up earlier, especially around two am, when she'd originally received the news, would have been far worse.

She closed her eyes, the imprint of the lights still flashing behind her lids, and continued to breathe slowly. She whispered a little prayer someone had taught her at grief counselling; an old lady called Joan who'd lost her husband of sixty-two years. It gave Sarah immense comfort as she recited it quietly and she felt the horror of the nightmare recede.

Now fully awake and unable to leave the bedroom, due to Tessa sleeping on the sofa, Sarah switched on the bedside lamp and read. But the novel in her hands could not take her mind off thoughts of Alex.

She remembered the argument they'd had just the week before his death. How she was angry that his work had excluded her from the business awards event that would mark his last night on earth. Of course, she hadn't known that at the time. She was instead indignant that she would miss out on such a prestigious event, especially when the Director's wives were all going. Except that Alex wasn't a Director. He was senior in his sales division, but clearly not high up enough to get a plus one invite.

It shamed her now to think how cross she'd been. How annoyed she was at the unfairness of all the partners who supported their loved one's as much, if not more, than the wealthy wives at the top of the ladder. If she'd known what would happen next, she wouldn't have been at all concerned by the supposed unfairness of it all. Nor would she have let him gone to the awards at all.

"Right. So, I'm meant to feel guilty because you weren't invited?" Alex said, as he practised his cravat tying skills in front of the mirror. He wasn't doing a very good job of it, but Sarah wasn't about to step in to help.

Sarah paced the bedroom, in her cream dressing gown, having just got out the bath. He'd told her about the awards as he took out his black morning suit and asked her to get it dry cleaned. She'd shrieked in joy at the thought of choosing an evening dress to complement his suit, which made him look incredibly handsome, and was already dreaming of her hairstyle when he'd broke the news. He'd been told in the morning meeting that it was for staff only. Except for the Directors of course.

She was furious. It was more the way he said it so casually, as if it were no big deal, than the snub itself. The thought of spoiling herself and having a wonderfully glamorous evening out, far from the norm of everyday life, was plummeted into oblivion in a split second.

She knew it wasn't Alex's fault. It wasn't anyone's fault really. But it had flicked a switch somewhere inside and she'd taken it out on her husband. Accusing him of dashing her dreams, he'd responded in his classic patient tone and it infuriated her even more.

"You could have at least told me in a kinder way," she stuttered, trying to think of a reasonable excuse for her reaction. "It was cruel to tell me the news first, without the bit about no partners, and let me get all excited. You only added the bit about no partners afterwards."

Alex lifted his eyebrows in the mirror. "So, by your reasoning, I should have structured my sentence differently, and because I didn't, you're now pissed at me. Did I get that straight?"

She only just resisted throwing the alarm clock at him, the closest thing at reach, and instead grunted angrily and stalked out the bedroom. They had gone to bed angry at each other that night and only Sarah's sheepish sorry over breakfast had broken the tension between them. Alex apologised too and Sarah, still disappointed over the invite, decided to let it go.

It wasn't a huge fight but now Sarah wished it had never happened. Those ten hours of anger were ten precious hours she had had left of Alex and they got wasted.

Back in the present Sarah put her novel down and wondered what to do. She was wide awake and while a greyish hue was starting to penetrate the black sky, it would be a while still before she could reasonably disturb Tessa. Her mind fell upon the shoebox hiding in her wardrobe. Without hesitation she jumped out of bed, retrieved it, and had the notebook out in record time. She found the next entry and began to read.

16th February 1907

My tutor is to leave our home. I write this with a heavy heart for I know he will not be replaced. Father will allow him to stay while he awaits a new post, so I can only seek solace that he may still be with us a few weeks yet. My lessons were cancelled this morning as he was allowed to consider his news. Father came to inform me himself, so concerned that I be fully aware that my studies will soon approach an abrupt end. I bit my lip to stop tears from falling as my thoughts comprehended my future.

Without a further education my choices are limited. I will remain here in the house, until I am out and then I shall marry. Should father permit me to attend a college at the given age, I may still have a chance at a different life. But I am not allowing myself to hope so vivaciously. Only sheer pity will bend my father's will to allow this, and he is not a man known for his empathy.

17th February 1907

The housekeeper is complaining. I have heard ranting each time I enter the kitchen. With Tutor still taken to his room, my lessons cancelled yet another day, I am left with little to do in the house except to wander. Mother would love nothing more than for I to assist Nanny in looking after Alfie and Freddy. I cannot think of anything worse.

My own emotions are not dissimilar to Housekeeper's. She is beside herself that yet another staff member is to leave our household and she fears she is next. I am also saddened as I lose an education that I'll struggle to replace. But I also fear what all this can mean. There is clearly no money. My father, a successful businessman, has been quiet of late regarding his proud achievements. I fear that his fortune is on the wane and what a predicament that'll leave us in. My two brothers will not need for a tutor yet. They were born far later than I and are still content to receive the attention of Nanny, over the school education they'll embark on in the next few years. Only after that will they require a tutor and perhaps our fortune will have turned for the better.

But what of me? I will be of marrying age before then. If there is no fortune it might dampen my appeal to potential suitors. Not only is my education and future career at stake, but my chances of marriage may also become woeful. What will happen to me?

I feel like screaming as loud as Housekeeper.

Sarah sat staring at the page, wondering again what had happened to this family. The passion of the 14-year-old girl within the pages startled her. She had not been sure of anything at that age, yet this unnamed girl knew exactly what she wanted. How unfair, Sarah thought, that she had so many obstacles in her path. Sarah didn't know much about Edwardian times but it seemed clear that the women didn't have many options in life.

Wanting to know more, and more importantly to *understand*, Sarah prepared to visit her mother, the walking history encyclopaedia.

*   *   *

"Morning Sarah. I was hoping to run into you."

Sarah wheeled round, already halfway out the front door, to face her landlord. She dreaded what he might say. Perhaps he was furious that she had a guest who was clearly not budging any time soon, and as a result would be contravening the lease agreement? Or perhaps he wanted Tessa's phone number? Either was feasible.

"Oh, hi Dermot," she said as breezily as she could. She tucked a loose strand of dark hair behind her ears and straightened her work blouse and skirt, feeling a bit like she had been called into a meeting with the boss.

"I was just wondering about the items in the attic," he said and Sarah felt relief, yet a new stab of concern at the same time. "Did you check them out?"

"Um," she pondered, wondering if she could lie. Deciding it simply wasn't worth telling fibs, she filled Dermot in on what she'd found. "Only the jewellery, and maybe the hairpin, looks like it could be valuable," she said.

"Hmm. But those notebooks and books could also have value in them. If one is a first edition or out of print. And the notebook might appeal to a collector."

"So, you are thinking of selling them then?" Sarah asked, her heart sinking.

He gave a reassuring smile. "No, not any time soon. But I would like to take a look at them sometime. I'm a bit vague on the laws regarding whose property they would be considered. But perhaps we could try track down the original owners? Of course, if they're as old as you say, it'll be pretty difficult. Either way, we should investigate further."

Sarah's heart soared, firstly by the thought of tracking down the family that had captured her fascination, but secondly by the mention of the word 'we'. Such a reaction shook her and she forced down a sudden ache in her chest as she swallowed. Just thinking what it could mean threatened to bring her out in a panic. She smiled at Dermot encouragingly and tried to get her thoughts on track.

"That would be great. But... there's no rush is there? I'm just a bit busy at work and with Tessa staying too. But I'd love to be involved with investigating."

She liked the idea of trying to track down the family, especially the girl. But she wanted to finish reading the notebooks first. With all the distractions of late, that might take a while.

"Sure, no rush. Oh, and Tessa; she's a character," Dermot grinned.

"Yeah, she can be," Sarah wished she hadn't brought her up. "She's only staying a few days, I promise. She just broke up with someone and has nowhere else to go." She thought it was only right, and perhaps even her duty, to tell him about the ex.

"No problem," he carried on grinning, giving nothing away.

Admitting defeat, Sarah made her excuses and left the building. She didn't want to be late for work.

*   *   *

Six hours later and thoroughly fed up with copy, branding and concept meetings and the seemingly impossible task of creating a tag line for a difficult new client, Sarah was more than relieved to receive a phone call from Izzy.

"You've been scarce," Izzy admonished down the line.

"Blame Tessa," Sarah replied simply. She had informed Izzy by text of all the recent drama surrounding her sister in law.

"Does that rule you out for Pilates tonight?"

"Probably Iz," she said apologetically.

"Great!" Izzy enthused. "I'm too exhausted. Can I come around this evening instead?"

"Yes," Sarah instantly perked up. "Tessa might be there, but we can still have a good time. Shall I order in some food?"

"Of course," laughed Izzy. "I don't have morning sickness any more. Buy lots of food and I'll bring some too."

The phone call and promise of Izzy's visit got Sarah through the rest of the afternoon. Becca, a junior copywriter was the only interruption. Approaching Sarah's desk, Becca, six foot and willowy blonde, bent over the edge of the desk over Sarah's petite frame. She was wearing a fitted white blouse with gold stitching and a tight grey a-line skirt. It wasn't dissimilar to Sarah's outfit, but Becca's extra length complimented the cut beautifully. Only 26, with girl-next-door looks and model proportions, Becca really seemed to have it all.

"Sarah, we," she waved in the direction of colleagues Sadie and Verity, "thought that an evening out, just the girls from the office, was well overdue.

You've been here months and we barely know you yet. Besides it's been so long, we wanted to go out anyway."

It sounded a little like a back handed compliment, but Sarah recognised Becca was just covering herself in case the answer was no.

"When were you thinking?"

"Friday night. Just the girls though. No partners and certainly none of the men from the office."

"Fair enough," Sarah grinned.

Becca filled her in on the details and made her way back to her desk. Sarah smiled quietly to herself as she tidied the cluttered surface in front of her. It was the first time she'd been invited out by work colleagues, bar the quick drink in the pub at the end of her first week. There had been lots of questions then, mostly surrounding the job itself, but a few personal ones had crept in to. The inevitable 'are you in a relationship' and 'do you have children' cropped up and Sarah had answered honestly to each. She just hadn't happened to mention the dead husband. The fact that she was single was information enough. She didn't want to create an awkward atmosphere, so had kept her personal details to a minimum.

As a result, she hadn't been asked out much by colleagues, but she couldn't blame them. They would all gossip at lunchtimes (if they weren't chained to their desks with a looming deadline) and discuss relationships. Sarah had nothing to add to that, so kept herself to herself. Being in a senior position, compared to Becca and the majority of the office, had helped. She wasn't expected to sit and join in the camaraderie. But nor did she want to become left out. She hoped the night out would readdress the balance.

Returning home that evening, Sarah threw her bag and coat on the table and looked around. There wasn't as much mess as she'd feared. A few cups stood on the kitchen counter and a change of clothing was haphazardly thrown over the back of the sofa. Tessa had obviously been on her best behaviour, grateful that Sarah had let her stay on. It wasn't a situation Sarah was happy about, but she hadn't the energy to face it now. She'd give Tessa a few more days and then contemplate phoning Alex's parents to see if they would change their minds and take in their wayward daughter.

The flat was quiet and Sarah wondered if Tessa had gone out, but soon heard the cascade of water from behind the closed bathroom door. Desperate for the loo, she hoped Tessa wouldn't be long and distracted herself by flicking through a magazine.

Over twenty minutes later and Tessa strolled out, white towel wrapped around her and another lopsided on her head. She saw Sarah and smiled the peaceful smile of someone who'd just had a wonderful shower. Sarah felt a twinge of jealously as she rushed to the toilet. She could do with a nice relaxing shower herself, but there was no doubt that Tessa had just drained the entire boilers contents. There'd be no more hot water tonight.

"Izzy's coming around tonight," Sarah shouted amongst the steam and smell of shampoo.

"Really? I haven't seen Izzy in years. What's she up to?"

"Busy having babies," Sarah said fondly. "Pregnant with their second."

"Rather her than me," came Tessa's flat response. Sarah didn't need to see her face to recognise that Tessa was fibbing and no doubt thinking of Kris.

"Will you be in or out this evening?" she enquired cautiously. She really wanted time with her friend without the sister in law hanger on. She loved Tessa, but could only take her in small doses.

"I was going to stay in, but then I had a phone call from this gallery owner guy," Tessa explained, absent-mindedly going through the kitchen cupboards, as Sarah re-entered the living room.

"Gallery owner?" Sarah asked perplexed. She didn't know Tessa could paint.

"There's an opening tonight for a new exhibition and he invited me along. I think he was worried no one would show up. His gallery Drago's has only been open a few months."

"Sorry, but how do you know him?" Sarah interrupted, feeling like details were being left out of the conversation.

"Oh, I used to work with him." Tessa worked in a deli and coffee bar. "He hated the job, so I encouraged him to leave and pursue his dreams."

This was typical of Tessa. Never one to think of the practicalities or finances, Tessa often gave advice on a whim. She also took her own advice, often leaving a wake of broken hearts in her midst.

"The exhibition is on all week. You should try and go. He's worried if he doesn't get some good sales, he'll have to shut down."

"I'll try be there," Sarah promised, feeling completely sorry for the guy. "What are you looking for anyway?"

Tessa was still rummaging around the kitchen, not really looking properly inside at the contents, but clearly trying to discover something.

"My handbag. I'm sure I left it here somewhere."

"In the kitchen cupboards? Seriously?"

"Stranger things have happened."

Sarah gave Tessa a look and moved over to the bay windows. The early evening sky was darkening quickly and the trees in the garden were already in silhouette. Birds flew as if in a panic to reach their destination for the night.

"Ah, found it!" exclaimed a voice behind her. "Now Cinderella can go to the ball."

Rolling her eyes, Sarah turned around in amusement. "So, Cinders, does that mean you'll be back before midnight?"

"Hardly," Tessa scoffed and entered Sarah's bedroom to dress.

Desperate for some peace and quiet and thoroughly looking forward to the evening ahead, Sarah took out the pre-prepared boxes of curry from her shopping bag and switched on the oven.

*   *   *

"So, how are you really coping with your sister-in-law?" Izzy asked, with a mouthful of curry. Izzy had briefly bumped into Tessa as she arrived.

"Izzy!" Tessa had exclaimed and given her a perfunctory hug and kiss on the cheek, before running out the door. Izzy hadn't even had a chance to reply.

"Not too bad surprisingly," Sarah replied. "Although I'd love to know how long she's going to be around for. Sharing space in a one-bedroom flat is not fun. But Tessa herself hasn't been the nightmare I'd feared," she admitted.

"And this Kris guy. Where does he fit in?"

"Only she knows and she's not revealing much. It's hard to know with Tessa if any relationship is ever really serious. She's never been known to stick with a guy long and Kris is no exception. The only difference is their friends seem to have taken his side. Tessa's on her own."

"And you're stuck with her."

"Not quite. I'm going to phone Keith and Lauren in a couple of days. Surely they can't refuse their own daughter?"

Izzy wasn't so sure. Having been spoilt rotten as the youngest and the only girl, Tessa spent much of her life getting her own way. Perhaps her parents had finally realised their precious little girl needed to stand on her own two feet for once. It was long overdue.

"Anyway, enough about Tessa," Sarah interrupted Izzy's train of thought. "What about you? You were so low last week. How are you really doing Iz?"

"Better," Izzy replied matter of fact. It was the truth. Talking to Sarah had helped and she spent the week concentrating her attention on Henry, instead of spiralling into her own confused thoughts. She was still no closer to answers, or the direction forward, but taking the week off the stress had been welcome and needed. She could put off decisions for another time.

"Sure?" Sarah double checked. Izzy smiled. She was used to being the one concerned about Sarah and now they'd switched roles.

"Sure," she grinned and took a large and loud bite of poppadum. "Now it's my turn. How's things really for you? The job, the new house. I want to hear it all."

With their roles reversed back to normal Izzy instantly felt more comfortable.

"I'm enjoying the house," Sarah mused through her own bite of poppadum. "And I feel like I'm turning a corner at work. I got invited out with the other girls."

"Ah, a night on the town, I'd forgotten what that was like. We still need to organise our own, don't you forget."

"We will. Now you're past the morning sickness it should make the evening more pleasant for both of us," Sarah grinned.

"That's for sure," Izzy looked down at her food, suddenly reminded how disgusting it would have tasted just a few weeks ago. "So, what else have you to tell me?" she switched topic, knowing Sarah's tendency to turn a conversation away from personal issues.

"Nothing much," Sarah shrugged. She was tempted to tell Izzy about the notebook, but knew her best friend wouldn't cease nagging to see them herself. Sarah wasn't ready to share her secret with anyone yet. It was odd, but it was like the notebook was just for her. She already felt connected to it and the story within. She didn't want anyone else knowing its content, not while she was still discovering it for herself.

"Oh, come on," Izzy wailed. Sarah was far too guarded for her own good. "No more terrible dates? No dreadful bosses? What about the landlord?" she suddenly remembered.

"Dermot is actually fine," Sarah said. "He's been very professional so far, so I think we're in the clear."

Infuriated by the lack of information Izzy sat back and studied her friend. Sarah never revealed exactly how she was feeling, but her expression *did* reveal that she was holding back.

"Is he good looking?" Izzy found herself asking. Sarah's expression didn't flinch but Izzy noticed a slight, split second, narrowing of her eyes.

"I suppose so. Tessa certainly thinks so anyway. She's already after his number." Sarah's face remained neutral and her eyes revealed that she felt comfortable, back in safe waters. Izzy wanted to scream. When would her best friend stop hiding behind the mask?

"So, not interested yourself then?" Izzy asked before she could think better of it. At one stage Sarah had been open to discussing her love life. Having taken a while to date again, Sarah had gone through a stage of going out for dinner, or for coffee, with various guys. Just a few, and none of them had lasted past the first few dates, but Izzy had felt excited for Sarah, believing her to finally be moving on.

But almost as fast as it had begun it stopped again. And Sarah had stopped talking about it. Sensing that her friend simply wasn't ready, Izzy had not pursued the topic. It hadn't been long before it became a taboo subject and one they rarely discussed. Well, it was now time for change, Izzy thought. Maybe she was just feeling bolder with the pregnancy and more likely to speak her mind. But whatever the reason Izzy wanted answers and to prompt Sarah into sharing her life with her again.

Sarah looked surprised by Izzy's direct questioning. "Why would you think that? Just because he's single and lives in the same building? I guess that would make it more convenient," she gave a half laugh.

"I'm just curious," Izzy shrugged. "I haven't heard you mention any guy since that date with Dylan."

"Don't remind me of that," Sarah grimaced and Izzy fell about laughing. The date had been organised by a friend at Sarah's previous job. Not one to usually agree to a blind date, she had been worn down by Kate's insistence that she knew someone perfect for her. Sarah reasoned that she hadn't been on a date in over six months and hadn't even come close to organising one since. So, she agreed.

It hadn't initially been a disaster. They met in an informal setting, a local Tapas bar with bright orange décor and Latino music blaring. When he arrived, she was pleased to see that he was pleasant looking, with an athletic build, green eyes, fair hair and a charming smile. He seemed pleased to meet her too which she took as an encouragement to how well the evening might go.

She was wrong. As soon as they'd ordered their food, he had launched into an hour monologue about his life, how he hated his job, how much he lived for the gym, and what his various friends (whom she'd never met) and he got up to in their spare time. She barely managed a word in edgeways, nor could care less about most of what he was saying.

Picking at her food and drinking more wine that she thought sensible, she twice tried to make her getaway (even the old trick of Izzy calling with an urgent reason to leave didn't work) and she resigned herself to sitting out the evening. When they did finally emerge from the bar, Sarah feeling shell shocked and a little tipsy, he'd then leaned in for a kiss.

She shook her head sweetly and whispered, as he drew nearer, "not a chance." She hailed a taxi and left him on the pavement.

Feeling bad the next morning she'd left a text message thanking him for a 'wonderful' night. Her niceties were wasted, when in response she'd received a message back telling her to 'sod off'. She guessed it could have been worse. Kate wasn't exactly pleased with Sarah when she'd heard what had happened, but at least hadn't tried to set her up again.

They giggled as they remembered that night and Sarah's vivid retelling of it the next morning to Izzy. Neither were unable to take another mouthful of curry for several minutes. Finally, Izzy calmed down and looked over at her best friend. She sent up a silent prayer, hoping Sarah would find the happiness she so deserved. If not with Dylan, or Dermot, or the postman, then someone. Anyone. And soon.

Chapter Ten

Two weeks had passed and Tessa was still sleeping on the sofa. Sarah had officially had enough. Each time she broached the subject she was given excuses and sob stories. Tessa would well up and cry over Kris, Sarah would feel bad and let her stay another night, and so the process went on. Enough was enough.

Flicking through her diary she found the contact she needed. She used to know this number off by heart, but hadn't had reason to call much the last couple of years. Dialling, she waited with baited breath and with a quickening of her pulse. It was picked up after just two rings.

"Hello, Miller's residence," came the voice the other end of the line. Sarah felt a rush of emotion.

"Hello Keith," her voice shook.

"Dear girl," he replied fondly. Sarah closed her eyes tightly to stop the prickle of tears. She realised in that instant how much she had missed them and how unfortunate it was to call in less than positive circumstances. Sensing that the topic of Tessa could wait, she found her wavering voice.

"Can I come and visit?" she asked in a whisper.

*   *   *

Keith and Lauren's house was a half hour drive away. The three-bed semi still looked as pristine as ever, with an overly neat garden and paintwork that looked like it was redone every year. Sarah remembered being brought here for the first time, just four months after she and Alex had started dating. She felt as nervous now as she did then.

Walking up the drive, with a bunch of pink tulips in her hand, she took a deep breath. It was nearly two years since she'd seen them. Phone calls and emails had continued for a while, but had eventually ceased.

Ringing the doorbell, she took a step back and waited, having first taken a deep steadying breath. The door clicked open and there stood Alex's mum. Lauren, in her mid sixties, had blonde hair with streaks of grey, pulled up into a loose bun. She wore a pale pink linen trouser suit and a pair of reading glasses perched on top of her head. She wore grey sequinned slippers and a mother of pearl watch.

Smiling at Sarah, she ignored the proffered tulips and embraced Sarah instead. "Come in child," she said huskily.

Sarah followed her through to the living area where nothing appeared to have changed. The curtains were still a soft yellow, the walls cream and wooden cabinets made of oak. It was simple, slightly old fashioned, loved and lived in. Sarah felt at home.

Keith came in from the kitchen and enveloped Sarah in a bear hug. He looked like an older version of Alex; dark hair, greying at the sides, with laughter lines in the corner of his eyes. The only difference was his build. Alex had had an athletic frame. Keith was built like a rugby player.

"The kettle's on," he said gruffly, his mild Yorkshire accent coming through.

"Thanks," she whispered and took a seat.

"Oh, aren't these lovely Keith?" Lauren remarked as she took the flowers to the kitchen. Sarah smiled after her and looked around the room as she waited their return. She noticed the photos on the mantelpiece and before she could think better of it, went over to look.

In centre place stood a large print of Alex and Sarah on their wedding day. They'd looked so young and carefree. She had longer hair then, swooped up into a bun with ringlets cascading down. She wore a unique fifties style dress, a tight bodice with a puffy skirt and a deep plum sash across her middle. The plum was mirrored in Alex's tie and he wore a silver-grey suit and white shirt to accompany it.

Their wedding had been simple yet elegant. A traditional church ceremony was offset with a tea party in the gardens of a stunning manor house. A marquee had been erected and Sarah had called in the skills of various friends and family to decorate. Mismatched china teapots, cups and saucers graced the circular tables and fresh wild flowers created the centre pieces. Still in her pottery phase, Izzy had made and donated small vases to decorate the marquee with further flowers. Sarah still had several vases she'd kept and pulled out of the cupboard on the rare occasion she received a bunch.

A local folk band played the music and a simple buffet of meats, salads, chutneys, jams and mini desserts adorned trellis tables. Fresh fruit platters and copious amounts of wine completed the menu.

It had been a stunning day and Sarah could still remember the joy and feeling of promise it gave. She had her future lined up. A new husband, good jobs, and no doubt babies within a few years. She had no reason to feel it would be any different. No reason to guess that not even eighteen months later she'd be picking out a headstone for the man she loved.

She looked at the photo intently and took in every minute detail of him. She couldn't remember much of how he looked. The only place she remembered were her dreams and she rarely looked at photographs any more. At one time it had been too painful. A photo could bring back too many memories and leave her in a downward spiral.

Now she simply felt wistful, a slight melancholy deep inside, but no longer the sharp pain it once was. The desire to pour over photo albums and relive the past was not there. It was like she had become numbed to it.

Keith and Lauren returned to the living room and stopped as they saw Sarah studying the photos. The next one along was of Alex at school, in his uniform, and looking at the camera proudly but with a glint of mischief in his eye. It was typical of his personality. Sarah smiled and turned away, seeing her parents-in-law in front of her.

"Sorry love, didn't mean to give you a fright," Lauren apologised. "Here's a pot of tea if you'd like?"

"Yes please. Milk, no..."

"Sugar. Yes, I remember." Sarah felt a pang of guilt for not having visited in so long, but she knew Lauren hadn't meant it in a malicious way.

Once they were all seated and sipping their tea, Keith cleared his voice. "We're so pleased to hear from you Sarah. We never knew if you wanted us to contact you. We hoped you were doing well enough in life to not need us so often."

Sarah was saddened by his words and tried to keep her voice under control. "Of course I wouldn't have minded you calling. I'm so sorry it's been so long. I should have called. I just... sometimes it felt better to just pretend certain things weren't happening and that everything was fine. I'm realising now that's not the best way to handle things. I was cruel not to contact you."

"Of course you weren't cruel," Keith interrupted with a wave of his hand. "You were widowed at twenty-seven Sarah. You're now in your thirties and you have a new life ahead of you. As much as we'll always love you, you are not obligated to keep us informed of your every move. We'd rather never have heard from you again, yet know you were happy."

"I'm afraid I can't say that I've really moved on all that much."

"Nonsense. Of course you have," Keith paused to drink his tea. "So, tell us what you've been up to then?"

"Well, I started a new job nearly six months ago. I'm still copywriting, but at a more senior level now. It's more stressful but it keeps me busy and I enjoy the challenge. Oh, and as you know, I moved out of Coronation Road last month," she concluded.

Keith and Lauren looked at one another, then back to Sarah. Coronation Road had been Sarah and Alex's first place together after they'd married. They guessed how much bravery it must have taken Sarah to move out to somewhere new with no memories of Alex attached.

73

"I'd say you've moved on very well," Lauren said smiling. "Alex always wanted you to succeed in your career and now you are. As for the new place, what an incredibly big step. We're proud of you."

Sarah sniffed back a tear and looked at the biscuit coloured carpet. She was touched and yet a little embarrassed by their praise. After nearly seven years she hadn't expected them to consider her steps as such a big deal.

She hadn't thought of her three-step plan in a while and now, amidst the conversation, it came flooding back. It seemed stage three was about to initiate and she still had no idea what it would consist of. All she knew was she needed to hang on with both hands and hope for the best.

"Thank you," she said after her contemplation. They drank their tea in companionable silence and looked over at the photographs on the mantle.

"That one was taken just a few weeks before he died," Lauren sniffed, as she pointed out the photo far left. Sarah recognised it as a trip to the beach they'd made. It had been a typical late summer's day, blustery with almost no promise of the sun pitching. They'd all laughed at the absurdity of it, as they lugged picnic blankets and deck chairs across the blowing sand. Keith, Lauren, Sarah, Alex, Tessa and her latest boyfriend eventually found a spot they'd hoped was sheltered. It wasn't and they soon gave up trying to eat the sand filled sandwiches and had gone for a brisk stroll instead.

Tessa moaned the whole way, having not had the foresight to bring a warmer layer of clothing and traipsing across the terrain in only a vest top and shorts. After an hour of her whining Alex, Sarah and his parents peeled off, leaving the boyfriend to handle it, and carried on walking on their own. The photo was of Alex striking a pose on a sand dune. Sarah had taken several similar photos herself.

Exactly two weekends later they were having the argument that Sarah now regretted. The following weekend and he was dead.

The impact it had had on all of them was great and indescribable. Steven had gone into a state of shock, from which he'd never really recovered. Pulling away from his family instead of drawing closer, he had eventually left the country to escape his grief. Tessa had become even more self-centred than usual, her grief demonstrating itself through tantrums. Keith and Lauren had cried more tears than they ever thought possible to cry and still the grief hadn't abated. And they had all since learned to live with it.

Sarah sipped her tea shyly. Alex had brought them all together, and although she never had the closeness with them as with her own parents, their relationship and his subsequent passing bonded them forever. Even with the long period of no communication, Sarah felt their affection for her was as a daughter. There would always be a fondness between them.

Pondering on wonderful and poignant shared memories, Sarah wondered how to turn the conversation back to the real reason for her visit. Tessa and her latest drama.

"How's Steven doing?" she asked, chickening out.

"We heard from him last night," Lauren brightened up instantly. "Skype is a wonderful thing, isn't it?"

"Yes, I guess it is."

"It'll never replace having him here face to face, but it goes some way. He's met a girl. Apparently, it's serious. An Aussie, obviously. And his job's going well. He's enjoying it," Lauren stated point by point. No mention of if and when he might come home, Sarah noted. She remembered how devastated Keith and Lauren had been when Steven left the country. It had been like losing two sons, not just one.

"And Tessa's doing okay too," Lauren nodded, as if trying to reassure herself. Having been given the perfect opportunity to raise the subject, Sarah took a deep breath and dove in.

"I know about Tessa. That's one reason I wanted to see you today."

Keith and Lauren both lifted their heads in interest. A slight flash of concern passed Lauren's features, whereas Keith simply looked amused. He obviously knew his daughter well.

"She turned up on my doorstep nearly three weeks ago. She said she needed a bed for the night and that she'd broken up with a guy called Kris. She was pretty upset, and despite not really having the room, I agreed she could stay the night. Well... she's still there and I wondered if you could perhaps... enlighten me on the situation or maybe even be willing to let her come back here?" There she had said it and she sat back on the chair awaiting their response.

Keith gave a snort and folded his arms in an attempt to be serious. Lauren threw him a glance, her worried expression firmly etched on her face. Sarah felt bad. She didn't want to be responsible for causing any more grief in this mother's life.

"We wondered where she'd ended up," Keith replied after what had seemed an age. "It certainly wasn't back with Kris. He was round here the other evening. He's a mess. Our darling girl has left another man crumpled and bruised in the dust. And we'd thought this one was different too."

It was all Sarah had feared and all Tessa had said. She had broken yet another man's heart for some reason unknown to all except Tessa.

"She's going to work as usual, but says she has nowhere else to stay. Her friends are all siding with Kris and she doesn't think she'd be welcome here."

"Well, she'd be right," Keith half laughed. Lauren tutted and shook her head at her husband, but he carried on.

"I love my daughter very much. If she hadn't done this so many times, I'd probably just shake my head and laugh. Which I have done before. But it's high time for a little tough love. Probably ten years too late mind, but better than never. She needs to learn to fend for herself, not use people and expect others to pick up the pieces. Especially with someone like Kris. He was finally a decent option as a son-in-law. She shot herself in the foot there."

"No wiggle room?" Sarah implored, her heart sinking. How she'd get Tessa out now, she had no idea. Her one alternative was gone.

"Sorry love," Keith stated and shuffled uncomfortably in his chair.

"We hate this too, Sarah, but we have to be strong here," Lauren spoke up. "I would like nothing more than to comfort my daughter through a break up. When she hurts, I hurt. But we've seen this pattern too often. We have to pull away rather than pick up the pieces. It's her job to sort it out, not ours."

Sarah sighed, "Then what do you suggest I do?"

Chapter Eleven

Dermot was in the back garden attending to his bike. He was fixing the burst inner tube that had abruptly stalled his morning cycle, when suddenly aware of another's presence, he lifted his gaze from the job in hand.

"Hello, doing something interesting?" Tessa asked, standing above him and looking down with an enquiring grin. She tucked a loose strand of hair behind her ear and turned her head on one side. She was wearing a burgundy coat with mismatched buttons and a fluffy silver scarf.

"Fixing the wheel," Dermot smiled in return. It was more out of politeness than anything else, but he sensed her increased interest at his reaction. He realised he'd have to be careful with this one. Usually oblivious to a woman's attraction to him, Tessa was giving off very strong signals that even he couldn't ignore. She had even started playing with her newly highlighted hair, winding it around her finger coquettishly.

He stood. "I don't have what I need. I'm going to have to pop down to the bicycle shop," he fibbed. "See you later." He made a fast exit, trying to ignore Tessa crestfallen expression.

He couldn't even understand his own reaction to her flirting. He was single, so was she. She was pretty and confident. But something held him back and prevented him from responding. With this one he decided to trust his instincts.

He waved as Sarah came out the shared back door and he left the garden via the side gate. She waved back looking distracted and concerned. He wondered about her. She was quiet, often serious, but with a grace about her that he found intriguing. For not the first time he wondered what her story was.

"Tessa, we need to chat," Sarah half mumbled, still emotional from her visit to Keith and Lauren.

Tessa looked like she was composing herself, her eyes a little puffy as she sniffed a few times. Suddenly wondering what conversation had been exchanged between Tessa and Dermot, Sarah then wondered why she should care. Because this girl is claiming of having a broken heart so she can continue sleeping on my sofa, Sarah reasoned to herself.

"We need to talk about our current living arrangements," she pushed on.

Tessa's eyes glazed over slightly and she gave a little cough. "Can we do this later?" she pleaded. "I'm not feeling all the best today."

"What is it this time?" Sarah struggled to keep her voice steady and controlled. She felt like she was babysitting a 6-year-old.

"I feel like I'm coming down with something. Not to mention that I feel depressed about my life and Kris and everything else right about now."

"Well firstly, is it a good idea to come out in the cold if you think you might be ill? It might be April, but it's freezing out here today. And secondly, you are not depressed, you are just needing to make some important decisions and sort yourself out and you're too scared to do it."

Sarah didn't know where all that had come from and even Tessa looked shocked by the uncharacteristic boldness.

"It's a bit more complicated than that," Tessa spat back and looked indignant. Dermot brushing her off had been the last straw. She wanted to feel attractive again, admired by others. Ending it with Kris had hit her harder than she'd imagined. If it had been any other guy, she'd have begun to feel normal again by now. But this time around, each day got harder. She had wanted to marry this one. But she'd messed it up.

"Complicated or not, you need to make a plan," Sarah reasoned. "Three weeks on my sofa is long enough Tessa. You either need to sort it out with Kris or sort it out with your friends. Or get your own place."

"On my salary?" Tessa laughed bitterly.

"Okay then, I'll buy you the newspaper and we'll find a decent house share for you," Sarah was on a roll now and not about to be deterred.

Tessa grimaced but said nothing. Sarah took that as a positive sign, at least one of compliance, and decided to grab it with both hands.

"Come on then. Let's get to the shops before all the good ads are taken."

"Have I been that awful?" Tessa said finally, in a small voice, as they walked swiftly down the street toward the corner shop.

"Challenging is the word I'd choose," Sarah smiled wryly. "I've a one-bedroom flat, it was never going to be easy squeezing you in. Besides, it was only meant to be one night, Tessa."

"I know. And I do appreciate it, honest. It was just the thought of facing them all again. I can't do it Sarah. You have no idea how hard it is to have your friends turn on you."

Sarah did know, all too well. And in her case, it wasn't her fault. Being a widow at twenty-seven turned formerly close friends into awkward strangers in a blink of an eye.

Thank God for Izzy and Will and the odd neighbour and work colleague who'd had the guts to stick with her. Nevertheless, Sarah was all too aware that her circle of friends was dramatically smaller than it once was, and fear of being hurt again had stopped her widening it on more than one occasion.

"What about Louise?" Sarah asked, vaguely remembering Tessa's best friend's name.

"Kris is her brother's mate," Tessa said grimly, shoving her hands in her pockets and staring at the pavement. "She's angrier at me than anyone. Apparently, she'd kept him from me for years, knowing I'd probably break his heart. When she told me that, I said she most likely fancied him herself. That's when she slammed the door in my face."

"Ah."

"None of my other friend's reactions were much better," Tessa sniffed as they entered the corner shop. Sarah grabbed the local paper, a couple of chocolate bars, and a cheap bottle of wine. They were going to spend the rest of the afternoon, and evening if necessary, looking for a place for Tessa to live. Sarah was more committed to the task than she'd been to anything else in a long time. She was far past worrying about Tessa being offended. Sarah needed her space back and as soon as possible.

*   *   *

Spring had finally settled over the city. Its streets were dappled in precious sun light with the occasional tree bursting with blossom. Easter had come and gone and the weather changed markedly. The nights continued to shorten, the early morning song of the birds and buzz of the rising sun hinting at the potential of a warm day to follow. Sarah had spent several evenings enjoying the roof terrace as she watched the dramatic skyline change in early evening. Pinks, oranges, piercing yellows, all mingled together across the sky as the evenings lengthened and ended in a dramatic chorus of colour.

Sat upon a cheap plastic patio chair, Sarah gave the early twilight sky a last glance and returned her attention to the journal. She was already halfway through the first and had endured a dozen or more entries on the various gripes and angst of a teenage girl.

Despite the difference in era, Sarah mused that teenage girls the world over were alike. Odd scribblings and attempts of poetry had adorned the last few pages, moans about her younger brothers and parents had become commonplace, and odd descriptions of the house (which Sarah was admittedly intrigued by) filled the various entries. Finally, something of interest caught her attention.

16th May 1907

I sit here exhausted beyond belief, my feet soaking in a tub of water Nanny kindly prepared for me. I am so weary, I am surprised I can concentrate enough to write this. I have been assigned the role of Nanny's assistant. Now my tutor has found other work, I am no longer required to complete my studies, and my fears of previous weeks have all been compounded upon this moment. I no longer have access to an education. My formal schooling years are over and there is nothing but a yawning chasm between now and when my parents see fit to have me 'out'. All I have heard all day long is an incessant call of 'Nor', 'Nor', from my brothers who insist on my full attention. I would have assumed Nanny's attention sufficient, but I fear I am the latest novelty, to which I hope will soon wear off.

Nanny first treated me with complete suspicion and disdain, no doubt fearful for her own job, worried that I'll be taking over her duties. A few days hence and I believe her fears subsided as she realised my very frustration and belligerence for the position I have been forced to hold. I have not one desire to remain in this situation for long.

I have noticed another few paintings have been removed from the drawing room. I doubt we will see them again.

Sarah mulled over the entry, her mind taking in the new information. A name had finally been mentioned, 'Nor'. It wasn't clear if this was a nickname, but she felt a stab of excitement to have found out a little morsel of information about the mysterious girl.

With the light finally fading Sarah made her way back inside the house and settled on the sofa. Tessa was out for the evening with some fellow waitresses from work. Still to find a house share, after a couple weeks of looking, Tessa felt it was time to let her hair down a little. Sarah had agreed, keen to have the flat to herself for once.

She had been pleased to see Tessa's apparent motivation in finding somewhere else to live and had come along for a few viewings. Unfortunately, there always seemed to be something genuinely wrong with them. Too far from work, snapped up before Tessa could get her application form in, a rat-infested hole, the list went on. Sarah sensed her frustration and was glad tomorrow was the start of the weekend, where they could cram in a new bunch of viewings.

She settled back down to the diary, ignoring the fleeting thought that she could be doing something better with her time on a Friday night, and read the next entry.

26th May 1907

I am not sleeping. The exhaustion of minding my brothers had proved a highly soporific tonic until these last few nights, upon which sleep now alludes me. My mind has conjured up a whole host of images of which I cannot displace and leaves me thoroughly worn out by morning.

It started just two evenings ago when I overheard the raised voices of my father and mother. They were attempting to keep their volume low, but the anger at which they conversed propelled them to be heard from the second floor. I am ashamed to admit I crept a little closer, down the staircase, with a curiosity my father has always said I am cursed with. To this I disagree. It is this curiosity that allows me access to knowledge of that which is going on around me. Without it, I would be clueless to the running of the household. Yet, no doubt, I would have a more dream filled and peaceable sleep.

"I will simply not hear of it," yelled my father, normally a firm man, but rarely one to shout with such passion. "I will not have the embarrassment of my wife earning in my place."

"Not in your place, Sir," my mother spoke compellingly. "But in addition to your ample provision."

I knew then she was attempting to placate him. There hadn't been ample provision in many a month. Even I knew this, curiosity or not.

"Your role is to run this household, I will not have my wife out there selling wears to goodness knows who," he thundered on.

My mother's own voice raised at that, no doubt indignant at how he described her exquisite paintings. "There are many reputable sellers who will act as an agent. I need not be selling myself. You know this Frederick and you know how even a little earned will assist us until this new business deal comes through."

"I do not need your charity, woman, and your fanciful ideas of how much your art is worth is laughable," Father erupted. I sat back on the stairs, my heart racing and tempted to run back up to my room.

"My business dealings are not of your concern and do not require any ill thought out rescue by your hands. No wonder Eleanor has acquired such fanciful thinking. I will not tolerate this in my household one moment longer."

I had departed at that statement, my heart full of sorrow and heavy at my father's words. I have not slept since. I am saddened by my family's dwindling resources. I am deeply saddened by my mother's missed opportunity to show the world her wonderful creations. But my heart cries for more than just that. I am filled with dread and sorrow for the future that lies before us all. This has kept me awake and no doubt will proceed to do so for a foreseeable period.

Eleanor's predicament resonated with Sarah and she wiped away a tear. Sleepless nights, an impossible situation, broken dreams and opportunities, all burrowed into Sarah's consciousness. Even the revelation of Eleanor's name could not lift Sarah's spirits as she sat contemplating what she'd just read.

The injustice of life never ceased to amaze her, and though it gave her a small amount of comfort to know she wasn't going through difficult circumstances alone, it never took that stab of anguish away. She sat in silence for a while, her mind constantly running over the words she'd read.

Suddenly feeling the urge for some fresh air and to escape the four walls around her, she flung on her thick duffel coat and headed out into the twilight.

Street lamps lit the way as she strode over to the common. Realising it was probably not the best place to hang out as it got dark, she kept to the outskirts, within a few feet of the pavement which ran parallel to the busy main road. She walked briskly and deeply breathed in the cool air.

Relieved to see she wasn't the only one about, Sarah took in the sight of others enjoying the park. A young couple walking hand in hand and giggling, several dog walkers throwing balls to their overexcited pets or trying to coax reluctant and straining canines along on their leads. A man holding a briefcase and wearing a suit was making his way home after a long day at the office. There was a family; a father, mother and two primary school aged children having a walk before the children's bedtime. It might not have been the most riveting of Friday nights, but she was out at least.

She thought back to the girl's night out she'd attend a couple of weeks back. Becca, Sadie, Verity, Allie the receptionist, and Sarah had ended up in some trendy new bar. Having come straight from work the bar was practically empty, much to Becca's chagrin who subsequently moaned for the next hour. The lack of crowds suited Sarah's mood, who hadn't much been looking forward to the night out anyway. But soon Becca's whining persuaded everyone to find a new venue. The night had improved from there. Even Sarah had enjoyed the food in the restaurant and later the music and dancing as they'd stumbled into a club.

Sarah had found herself relaxing, vaguely remembering the kind of venues she used to frequent with Alex, Will, Izzy and other friends. They'd had so much fun together and she'd forgotten what it was like. Although she realised that Becca and the other girls were unlikely to be her best buddies, she secretly hoped she'd be asked out again sometime.

Now another quiet Friday night had loomed and Sarah no longer felt content to just stay in and let the world go by outside. A spark of discontentment was settling in her gut and for the first time since Alex's death she no longer felt happy to let life pass her by. Something was shifting inside her and it scared and thrilled her at the same time.

Lost in her thoughts she barely noticed the bicycle stop in front of her.

"Hi stranger." She jumped at the words and looked up to see Dermot, appearing a little strange in all his racing getup.

"I haven't seen you much the last few weeks, all well?"

"Sure," she replied, slightly startled. Having been shaken from her reverie, it took a moment for her brain to connect to the conversation.

"Sorry, am I interrupting something?" he asked, a grin creeping across his features.

Sarah couldn't help noticing that he had a nice smile.

"Not at all. I'm just getting some fresh air. You're really getting into this bike thing, huh?" she added, matching his grin.

"I've a race on Sunday. Can't face looking like an unprepared ejit, can I? Why don't you come along and watch? Bring Tessa too. The more the merrier. It's early though. There'll be no lie in I'm afraid," his eyes did a twinkly thing that was quite distracting.

"Oh," was all she could manage and mentally kicked herself. When had she become such a terrible conversationalist? "I mean, sure. What time is it and where do we need to be?"

"I'll send you an email. I'm useless at directions. I do have your email address?"

"Unless Angel the letting agent gave it to you, then no."

"In which case I do," he laughed. "I'll message you tonight. By the way, is Tessa going to be at yours much longer? I don't like to be a stick in the mud, but it's not really allowed in the contract. I feel like such an ejit saying that."

"Don't, please. It's your flat and believe me I feel the same way. I'm helping Tessa find somewhere. Her budget is limited and rooms are being snapped up so quickly. But she'll be gone soon, I promise."

Dermot sighed with relief. "I'm sorry, I feel so pathetic even bringing it up. Personally, I'm fine with it, but the insurance company would have a fit."

Sarah nodded and smiled. "Your wish will be my command. Shortly. Hopefully."

She realised that Dermot had been walking alongside her while pushing his bike. They walked in companionable silence for a moment before he turned to her.

"Did you finish reading the journals? Find anything interesting?"

"Very," she admitted, relaxing a little. It was nice to talk to someone about it. "It's actually really compelling. But I'm not close to finishing them yet," she hastily added, in case he might ask her for them immediately.

Don't worry," he laughed, sensing her reticence. "There's no rush. I think tracking down the family could prove impossible, but I would like to the see the documents myself anyway. Could I come around sometime and check out them out?" Dermot asked.

Sarah nodded and grinned. She felt inexplicably happy all of a sudden.

Chapter Twelve

"I like it, I do," Tessa paused as Sarah held her breath. It was the third they'd viewed that morning and there seemed to be a problem with each one.

"It's a little way out for work," Tessa said eventually.

"It's barely a five-minute train journey," Sarah replied indignantly, highly suspecting that Tessa was delaying the inevitable move with excuses. "Take it Tessa," she implored firmly. "It's nicely decorated. The girl in the next room seems friendly enough. It'll be an adventure. A chance to make some more friends."

"I know..." Tessa hesitated again.

"What?" Sarah said impatiently.

"It just feels so final. Like I'm moving on with my life. Moving on from Kris. I know I dumped him, but this feels so... permanent."

"Do you want to get back together with him?"

"He won't take me back after what I did," Tessa stated simply.

"But you do want him back?"

Tessa fought her composure for a second, then shook her head. "No, it's over. I know that. You're right. Mum and Dad are right. I have to learn to stand on my own two feet now. I'll take it," Tessa gave a tight smile, having made up her mind.

Sarah felt a curious mixture of utter relief and concern that Tessa was making a mistake. Not in renting the room, but in casting aside any chance of reconciliation with Kris. She seemed resigned to her fate and Sarah worried that Tessa was punishing herself unnecessarily. However, a decision had finally been made on a house share and Sarah could breathe easy knowing her flat was her own again. There was a lot to be said for small mercies.

*   *   *

They stood on the sidelines, the metal fence barriers separating them from the cyclists, and waited with baited breath. Despite the ridiculously early start and copious amounts of strong coffee needed to wake them sufficiently, Sarah and her friends were quite excited by the unusual event. Neither Sarah, Tessa, Will, Izzy or Henry had attended a cycle race before and were amazed by the atmosphere around them.

The streets had been closed for the event and hundreds of people milled about excitedly awaiting the competing cyclists. There was a hum, not unlike that of a bee hive, as many voices carried across the air. Henry sat proudly on his father's shoulders and looked thoroughly alert of the first glance of an 'Ike'.

Izzy eyed up the portaloos with a mixed expression of disgust at the unhygienic facilities and relief at having found somewhere to ease the discomfort of her regularly squashed bladder. An impressive bump had popped out in recent weeks, casting no doubt that Izzy was with child.

"I wonder if we'll even recognise him? There must be hundreds of cyclists," Sarah mused, pointlessly blowing on her gloved hands in an automatic response to warm them. It was a chilly start to the morning, although the clear blue sky, with no visible cloud, hinted at a warmer temperature later on.

"Doubtful," said Will. "Unless he's wearing anything distinctive and even then, we still might miss him."

His number is 138. It'll be on his shirt," Sarah remembered. She wished she could recall any other details: the colour of his bike helmet, his outfit, even the colour of the bike itself. But it all alluded her.

"Well at least we can say we were here. I'm sure he'd appreciate that."

"I won't appreciate getting up this early if we can't even spot him," moaned Tessa.

Henry gabbled in response and excitedly pointed out the colourful banners and an aeroplane flying high above. Tessa looked up in spite of herself and huddled her hands deeper within her coat pockets.

Over a speaker system a male voice announced that the first batch of cyclists would be making their way through shortly. Sarah ignored Tessa's mumbled "thank God," and kept her eyes on the blind corner at the end of the street. Will and Izzy fussed over Henry briefly before turning their attention to the road, as two cyclists appeared into view.

The crowd began cheering as the leaders of the pack shot past at high speed. Sarah craned her neck to look, but couldn't tell if either had been Dermot. There was a pause before the next cyclists appeared and this time a group of half a dozen rode by.

Sarah and her friends cheered and clapped, Henry being the loudest of all. Sarah shrugged as they turned to her to see if she'd recognised Dermot in the group. She hadn't been able to catch all the numbers, but the ones she had didn't match his. Realising they might not spot him at all, Sarah decided to just relax and enjoy the experience, and look forward to a warming full English breakfast later on.

Twenty minutes and several dozen cyclists later and Tessa shrieked. They had all lost interest, chatting quietly amongst themselves and only giving a cursory glance toward each competitor. But Tessa had looked up at just the right moment.

"It's him, it's him! I'm sure of it." She jumped up and down excitedly and waved her hand toward the road. The number 138 stood out in bold black font across his shirt and Sarah recognised the shape of his nose and chin from beneath the helmet.

They all cheered harder and louder than before, hoping to gain his attention. But he was too preoccupied with the race and he rode past at a decent speed. Their excitement subsided and they stood in silence for a moment, watching the other cyclists pass through in a long line.

"Ike man," Henry quipped.

*   *   *

"Well that was fun, wasn't it?" Will addressed his offspring who was busy pulling Will's ear, still sitting high up upon his shoulders.

"Lots of ikes," Henry replied and wriggled, suddenly wanting to get down. The small group had arrived at the café, piling through the door and placing their orders of tea, coffee and cooked breakfasts. The warm atmosphere and the low buzz of patrons talking was comforting after the early and cold start to the day. Ten minutes later they were tucking in to full plates of steaming food and cups of caffeinated drinks.

"Well I'm glad we spotted Dermot after all. It makes the early start almost worth it," Tessa grinned behind her cup. "I wonder what place he came in?"

"It's a pity we couldn't get as far as the finish line, with the road already closed," Will added.

"We might have been able to if we hadn't been delayed." Izzy threw an accusing look at Tessa who shrugged nonchalantly.

"You can't expect me to function at such a ridiculous hour. Of course I was going to take a while getting out the house. Even my alarm clock was in shock. It's never been set at that time before."

Sarah smiled slightly at the humour, before catching Izzy's expression and returning her gaze to her plate.

Izzy bit her lip from retorting. She was almost always up at that time with Henry and managed to get out the house and organised, pregnant and with a toddler in tow, whereas Tessa had barely rolled out of bed by the time they'd arrived at Sarah's flat. Oh, how the other half lived.

"Well we did get to see him, so that's good enough," Sarah threw in her pennies worth. The stony silence she received prevented her saying anything more on the subject.

"It was a good morning out and a nice opportunity to do something different," Will said, always one to look on the bright side. "I'm sure he must be finished by now. Sarah do you want to try his mobile and see if you can get hold of him? Invite him to join us for breakfast. I think he deserves it."

Sarah felt a sudden shyness and a prickle of reluctance spread through her. Dermot belonged to her new building, to a place of one-woman piano concertos and mysterious journals in the attic. Mixing him with her life outside, amongst lifelong friends, was a surreal thought. Despite already knowing Tessa, who admittedly fluttered in and out of Sarah's friendship circle whenever she felt like it, Dermot was an almost separate entity and it was far too early for Sarah to contemplate mixing the two.

On the other hand, she had just invited her friends to come watch him race, despite having never met him. She'd reasoned it away as Dermot himself had asked her to invite people along, but she hadn't had to. And given the endurance and exhaustion of the race, it only seemed fair to shout him a good meal.

Izzy noticed her hesitate and nudged Sarah. "What's the problem?" she whispered, but Sarah shook her head.

"Nothing, I'll just go make the call outside. Less noise," she justified and made a quick exit. The ring tone echoed against her ear and she hoped it would go straight to voice mail.

"Hello?"

"Oh, Dermot? It's Sarah," she took a deep breath. "We came to watch you race this morning. We're in the café in Rhodes Street if you want to join us for some breakfast. On me."

"Sounds good. I was about to head home now, but I'll swing past. See you in a few minutes."

Sarah returned to the café and ordered another coffee. "He's on his way," she mumbled into the last few dregs of her drink. She felt nervous all of a sudden and had to stop herself drumming her fingers on the table.

"Hey relax," Izzy's voice soothed beside her. "Early morning jitters or too strong coffee?" she joked and Sarah smiled in return, making an effort to relax. She didn't like how anxious she was feeling or why that might be.

Dermot walked in, still in his racing attire and holding his bike helmet in one hand. He was grinning from ear to ear and looked exhausted. His hair stood in all directions and his green blue eyes sparkled from adrenalin and achievement. Sarah noticed Tessa shift in her chair and turn her body towards him. Sarah suppressed a stab of irritation and lifted her gaze to greet him.

"Well done," she exclaimed and beamed at him, ignoring her nerves. "What place did you come in the end?"

"Thanks," Dermot grinned, the look of utter contentment. "I came in forty eighth. Not bad for over three hundred cyclists, especially as it's been a while since my last race. My time was..."

"That's great Dermot!" Tessa said with an overenthusiastic tone. "Come and sit next to me and tell us all about it."

Sarah stared at her coffee and pursed her lips. Tessa's attitude and flippant change of emotions bothered her and she was glad Tessa was moving out. She was quick to cry of a broken heart, yet even quicker to flirt with the first man she set her eyes on. Sarah wondered if any of those tears had been genuine. She felt foolish for believing her.

"It's nice to meet you Dermot," Will enthused and held out his hand. "Sarah is really enjoying living in the flat. And you've done such a good job with the place." Izzy silenced him with a look. "Um... so what do you do?" Will redirected the inane conversation.

"I'm working as a surveyor at the moment for my brother-in-law's firm. I'm a property developer usually, but I needed a break and a more normal day job for a bit," Dermot explained. "Hold that thought; I'm just going to go order."

A minute later he was back and struck up the conversation again with Will and they happily chatted for a while. Sarah busied herself with finishing her second coffee and Izzy took Henry to the toilet for a nappy change, while Tessa sat poker straight, trying to look interested in a conversation which had turned to the finer points of the England cricket team.

"What's going on?" Izzy whispered in Sarah's ear as she returned to the table with Henry.

"Oh, something about wickets," Sarah replied absent-mindedly.

"Not that. Ever since you-know-who walked in you've been distracted. And what was with your reaction to Tessa?"

"What? Nothing. I don't know what you mean," Sarah tried to deflect.

Izzy stared at her best friend with her 'I'm not impressed' expression on her face. Sarah had seen her use it on Henry only that morning and it was scary.

"Don't pretend Sarah. You never tell me how you're really feeling. I'm asking you a direct question here, because I care about you and want to know the truth." This was all said in a firm whisper, but Sarah was still worried the others would hear.

"Izzy this isn't the place."

"Then I'm taking you out for a drink this afternoon and you can tell me everything."

There was no point resisting, not when Izzy had spoken in her strictest Mummy voice.

*   *   *

The wine bar was fairly quiet, given it was just past the opening hours and a

Sunday evening. A young couple sat on the tall bar stools sipping violent coloured cocktails, perusing their mobile phones and barely saying a word to one another. A single guy knocked balls around the pool table with the cue and looked thoroughly bored, while occasionally checking his watch. Izzy and Sarah were the only other patrons.

Izzy had ordered a pomegranate and cranberry juice and Sarah a white wine. Both surveyed the bar around them having neither been there before. Massive turquoise strips of glass hung vertically from floor to ceiling, interspersed with white and clear wavy stripes, giving the impression of an ocean. Deep mauve walls with pink lighting highlighted the entire back wall of the bar. A light blue dominated two of the other walls. A large glass window stretched across the fourth wall, not far from where they were sitting.

Izzy quite liked the decor and the lack of customers was a major plus. She intended to get Sarah to open up as much as possible. Sarah looked around her with a look of incredulity. What was designed to look tasteful simply looked tacky. She knew the atmosphere in the venue would be a very different one in a couple hours time. Not that she intended staying there that long.

"So, what happened this morning?" Izzy started, sipping her drink in an attempt to appear nonchalant.

"In what way?" Sarah knew she was being obtuse.

"Oh, don't give me that," Izzy threw her hands up. "Sarah, please," she leaned forward. "I've almost given up trying to find out how you are, what you're doing, how life is treating you. You never open up to me anymore. I feel like my best friend is slipping away and I'm fighting to keep you with me, but it's a fruitless battle and I'm tired. I'm tired and pregnant and worn out with the whole thing."

Alarmed and ashamed Sarah turned her face to the wine glass on the table in front of them. She had tried to protect her friendship by not opening up. Now it seemed that she was in danger of losing her friend because of it. She gave a deep sigh and looked Izzy in the eyes.

"I'm sorry Iz," she whispered. "I've been so scared to talk about deep things. I haven't wanted to lose you like I lost so many others."

"That's ridiculous," Izzy interjected. "They weren't real friends anyway. They never would have walked away if they were. I can't believe you'd think I'd do that too."

"That's not entirely true Izzy. Some were real friends, but they were Alex's friends too and they didn't handle their grief all that well. I can understand that. And the other ones? Well yes, my life is better without their insincerity, but that didn't stop me feeling scared that I might lose you too.

I know you're a proper friend, but fear is a powerful thing and I couldn't risk losing you. I just couldn't. The fear of it was stronger than the truth that you wouldn't abandon me. It might sound stupid, and I understand if you're offended, but that's what I've been fighting with every day. That's my reality."

"Oh, Sarah. I'm not offended. Not really," Izzy sighed. "I just wish you'd been able to tell me this. For the last year or two I've been so worried that I'd lose you too. You just seem to disappear into this space where I wasn't invited and couldn't penetrate. I've avoided so many topics and conversations because of it. I knew you'd withdraw and never share how you're feeling."

"Have I really been that bad?" Sarah tried to inflect some humour, but it fell flat.

"Quite simply, yes."

Sarah sighed again. "To be honest you haven't missed much. I go to work, barely talk to my colleagues, don't take a lunch break, come home and spend my evenings in solitude."

"Oh, come on, it's not that bad," Izzy waved her hand impatiently. "You've got two amazing friends with a cute as a button toddler, great family on both sides - well apart from Tessa maybe, but there's another one; you've had Tessa to keep you company for a month."

Sarah snorted. "And now you're making friends in your building," Izzy concluded, the hint in her voice unmistakeable.

"Ah, so we're back to that are we?" Sarah asked wryly.

"Well the tension was pretty noticeable."

"What tension?"

"As soon as Dermot walked in you tensed up," Izzy stated with a flourish, as if she'd just solved a murder mystery.

"I was annoyed because of Tessa, not Dermot," Sarah corrected. "Tessa's spent the last month on my sofa claiming to be broken hearted and yet you saw her; she couldn't stop flirting Dermot. I feel like I've been taken for a mug. I can't believe I fell for it."

Izzy sipped her drink and observed Sarah for a moment. "And that's all there is to it?" she asked eventually.

"Of course."

"Okay," sighed Izzy. "I'm only going to ask this once. Do you like Dermot? It's okay if you do," Izzy immediately added. "You are allowed to date."

"I know that," Sarah said impatiently. "And I have. It's not like it's an entirely foreign concept."

"Well it has been a while and no guy made it past the third date," Izzy teased.

"To answer your question, no, I don't think I like Dermot in that way. He's a friend, not to mention my landlord, which makes it complicated enough."

She believed her own answer on the most part, except that tiny flicker of doubt as his smile came to mind. She pushed the thought away. She knew she needed to start sharing her life with Izzy again, but she didn't plan to share that much. Not yet.

"As much as I hate to cut short this rare insight into your feelings, I need to pee rather desperately," Izzy declared. "I'll be back soon."

Izzy slipped off the chair with apparent difficulty and shuffled her way across the bar. Sarah suppressed a smile. Izzy looked like she was trying to walk cross legged.

While she awaited Izzy's return her thoughts slipped back to Dermot. She barely knew him. How could Izzy expect her to make a decision about him when their sum total of conversations had been about four. True, she had barely known Alex before agreeing on a date with him, but that was rare. It wasn't something she ever expected to happen twice. Especially not after losing Alex.

While she never deliberately compared guys to him, the truth was he'd be a hard act to follow. That's what had stopped her from dating beyond one or two dates.

Admittedly it had been a while since her last date and she could only guess if things had changed. She didn't think about Alex as much as she used to, and her sleepless nights tended to be through habit nowadays rather than grief. She rarely cried for him anymore. Life had moved on, cruelly not for him, but she had come to terms with that. The thought of a new relationship, however, was one element of life moving on that she didn't yet feel ready for.

"The toilets have seashells on the walls," Izzy returned with a whimsical smile on her face. "Do you think I can persuade Will to let me embellish our bathroom?"

Sarah let out a laugh. "Unlikely Izzy. Hasn't your creativity and unique flair been banned at home?" she joked and Izzy nudged her and stuck out her tongue. "Sorry, the effect of having a two-year-old for company all day long," she justified.

"And how's all that going?"

"Oh no, missy, you're not deflecting the conversation back to me. I brought you here to get you to open up. Not the other way around."

"I've told you everything you wanted to know," Sarah replied, finishing the rest of her wine.

Izzy contemplated her and Sarah knew she was scanning her face for any give away signs.

"Well thanks for sharing," Izzy eventually capitulated. "I do appreciate it. I miss you, you know?"

"I know Izzy. I'll try harder."

"It's not about trying harder. It's about trusting me. I'm not going anywhere Sarah. You can tell me all the ugly bits and I still won't run away. You can turn up at two in the morning in floods of tears and I still won't turn you away. I might be a bit cross, especially if you wake the kids, but I won't slam the door in your face." Sarah rolled her eyes.

"I'm serious Sarah," Izzy looked at her intently. "You're my best friend and

Will and I want to be a part of what's going on in your life. We knew Alex too. He was special to us too. Not in the same way of course, but when you hurt, we hurt. And sometimes we hurt all on our own. Trust us, that's all you have to do."

Sarah wiped her eyes as the tears began to fall, the first she'd shed in front of Izzy in two years. Izzy immediately removed a packet of tissues from her bag. Being a mum, she always had a myriad of items stowed away in there. Sarah took them gratefully and squeezed her best friend's hand.

Izzy wouldn't understand the significance of her words, but for the first time in a long time Sarah stopped feeling alone.

Chapter Thirteen

That evening, seven years before, Sarah had gone to bed chilled and relaxed. Despite the disappointment of not being able to attend the work do with Alex, she'd purposely decided to spend the evening on a positive note and spoil herself. A warm bubble bath, followed by a couple of glasses of wine and a box of chocolates and Sarah had climbed into bed with her favourite novel.

The clock had read 10:36 as she settled down to read a chapter or two before drifting off. The next thing she heard was a banging on the front door and flashing violent red lights. A lot after that was a blur. She still remembered the policemen coming in and sitting her down, while informing her there had been an accident. She'd known even before opening the door what they would tell her, yet the actual words still felt like she'd been hit in the ribs with a sledgehammer.

She remembered doubling up on the sofa in a deep unspeakable pain. It felt like waves were crashing over her, and she literally felt like she was drowning in her sobs, unable to catch her breath.

The journey to the hospital remained a mystery. She wasn't even sure she was entirely conscious at that point. At the hospital she remembered concerned voices, faces she didn't know mingled with faces she did. Izzy and Will sitting in the waiting room, looking up with sharp concern and sorrow as she entered the room, having just identified her husband's body. Her mum arriving in a flurry, yet bringing a moment of calm as Sarah childishly and briefly thought her mother being there would make everything all right.

The other hours that remained of the night were forgotten in a haze of grief and disbelief. As she was sat down by the doctor and given details of what had happened, she couldn't take them in. Only the next morning when her mother repeated the news had Sarah realised Alex wasn't coming home.

He had left the work do shortly after midnight. The alcohol in his bloodstream was minimal, whereas the car that hit his was driven by someone three times over the limit. In short, Alex was killed by a drunk driver.

By the time Sarah had been informed of the news, the clock had just struck 2 am. Alex had already been dead nearly two hours, his injuries killing him on impact.

The days that followed, the endless outpouring of grief from almost everyone who'd ever met him, the funeral arrangements which Sarah couldn't focus on and which the family had stepped in to help with, to Alex's own family and the grief they felt, yet at least could share with one another, to which Sarah had actually felt excluded from, culminated into one long nightmare.

All these memories, which had been painful and ugly and had tormented her for years after, now sat as a dull ache. Sarah could vaguely remember the grief she'd felt then, but thankfully the memory had taken pity on her and faded. She knew it was time to move on, to carve out a new life for herself. So far, the new year had propelled her into exciting and daunting steps, designed to push her out of her comfort zone and into the next phase of her life.

Opening up to Izzy had been a major part of that and Sarah, as she breathed in the fresh night air on top of the roof terrace, overlooking the darkened garden below, felt positive that she was headed in the right direction.

For the first time she felt a flicker of hope, burning like a minute ember hidden among extinguished coals. That ember had the power to reignite the fire that had laid dormant for years.

As she sat reflecting and looking out over the night sky she began to smile. It turned into a laugh which echoed through the quietness around her and sent a chill down her spine. Life was changing and she realised she was no longer scared but excited.

*   *   *

The day after Tessa finally moved out of Caledon Street, spring made way for a precious twenty-four hours of blissful heat. The first heat wave of the year brought people outside in droves, heading for the common, driving off to far flung places such as the coast, and chatting happily as they enjoyed the rare treat of sunshine.

Izzy, Will, Henry and Sarah sat on an old fashioned red and black checked picnic blanket and soaked in the atmosphere. The remnants of sandwiches, cake and fruit littered the disposable plates and Sarah sipped her paper cup of lemonade with a feeling of contentment.

Last night she'd enjoyed her first night alone in the flat for over a month. She was actually shocked to realise just how much she'd missed her own space. Perhaps Tessa's visit hadn't been so terrible, she thought. It seemed to have been the tonic needed in reassuring her that it had been right to step out on her own.

Moving day had started much how Sarah had expected. Tessa had a mad panic as she realised she'd left the majority of packing far too late. Clothes were thrown over every available surface. Sarah wondered how and when Tessa had managed to accumulate such a gross number of belongings, when she'd originally turned up with just a small overnight bag.

"I can't believe I've lost my hair dryer!" Tessa shrieked, throwing several tops into the air as she haphazardly searched the apartment. "It cost fifty quid and I've only used it twice."

She rummaged further with a look of utter frustration across her features. "You haven't seen it have you Sar?"

Sarah hated being called that and suppressed a cringe. "Not since Wednesday night, when you threw it on the sofa after getting ready to go out."

Tessa looked round at the sofa contemplatively. Her finger lingered across her lips as she tried to remember the incident. Shaking her head in defeat she began ripping her clothes in all directions again.

Sarah sighed and carried on piling Tessa's endless toiletries into a holdall. She was never going to get rid of her unless she was willing to pack up Tessa's things herself.

A ridiculous six hours later and Tessa was finally ready to go. Three holdalls and the original overnight bag stood in the entrance hall and Sarah leaned against the wall, arms folded, as Tessa knocked on Dermot's door.

"I just wanted to say bye, obviously not forever. I'll be round to visit Sarah lots of course," Tessa jabbered, the moment he'd opened the door. "And you must come around to mine too. I'll be having a house warming as soon as possible," she continued, barely drawing breath.

Dermot gave Sarah a side glance and raised his eyebrows. Sarah bit her lip, trying not to laugh out loud and managed a restrained smile back. Tessa, oblivious, gave Dermot a lingering hug goodbye and exited the building with the same flourish to which she'd arrived.

Sarah gave a little look back over her shoulder as she followed behind. Dermot still stood there and gave a little wave and nod. She returned it and a moment later unlocked her car and sat in the driver's seat with a lightness bubbling up inside.

*　　*　　*

The rest of the day passed in typical Tessa style, instantly flattering and charming her fellow housemates with her fun and flighty personality, and entrancing the male members of the household in a matter of seconds. Sarah felt like the uncool aunt all of a sudden and she kept her head down, taking through the bags into Tessa's nearly bare room, and avoiding too much conversation.

When Tessa finally joined her, having let Sarah do all the carrying, Sarah gestured around the bedroom. "There's no furniture except the bed. What are you going to do?"

"Oh, I'll be fine," Tessa waved away the concern.

"But you've nowhere to put your clothes. There's no cupboard, no wardrobe. You can't unpack without some storage space."

"I'll figure something out," Tessa's voice grew quiet.

"Where's the rest of your stuff Tessa?" Sarah asked gently, sensing Tessa's mood had shifted.

"At Kris'," she folded her arms and looked away toward the bags on the bed. "I'll just buy some new cupboards. You can help. We'll head to the shops and it won't take more than a few minutes to order something."

Realising it was a sensitive subject Sarah tried to tread carefully. "I'm sure he'll let you pick up your stuff Tess. If you don't want to face him, I understand, but we can get it picked up. You just need to organise a day and time with him."

"I can't speak with him!" Tessa replied, her voice shrill. "It's been over a month. I can't just phone up after that long and demand my stuff back."

"Well you can't afford to replace everything either," Sarah said firmly. "You're going to have to sort something out."

"It's fine," Tessa said high pitched and unconvincingly. "I'll manage fine Sarah. I just survived a month on your sofa after all. I think this will be just fine thank you."

"Well, I'm sorry my place was such a dive compared to this," Sarah blurted out uncharacteristically. She normally avoided conflict, retorts and general animosity, but she was feeling bolder these days.

Even Tessa looked shocked. "That's not what I meant," she replied, her voice lowering. "I do appreciate all you've done. I just thought you'd understand a bit better."

"Understand what?" Sarah asked, confused.

"I'm grieving Sarah, can't you see that?" she threw up her hands exasperated. "I can't face seeing him again. It hurts too much," she sank onto the bed and hung her head.

"But you've just spent the last month flirting with my landlord," Sarah exclaimed in disbelief.

Tessa looked up, her eyes swimming in tears and shook her head. "Kris was the best thing that ever happened to me and I messed it up. I was just trying to make myself feel better."

"By leading a friend on? That's the most selfish thing I've heard Tessa," Sarah raised her voice to head off Tessa's protests. "No, it's not fair. You've been nothing but persistent with Dermot and now you're telling me it was just a self esteem boost? You can't treat people like that!"

Tessa sat in shock before bursting into tears. Not knowing if it was genuine or another of Tessa's apparent manipulations, Sarah did the only thing she could think of. She went and made them both a cup of tea. Bringing the hot steaming mugs through to the bedroom, Sarah lowered herself onto the bed next to her sister-in-law.

"I'm sorry if I was harsh. I just fail to understand how flirting with one man is meant to make your heartbreak over another any better. It might be an ego boost, but can't you see how it just complicates things?"

"I know," Tessa sniffed miserably. "It's what I always do and it usually helps. But not this time. I just feel wretched and I miss him more each day."

Sarah put the tea on the floor, not trusting Tessa's shaky hands, and bit her lip. This was uncharted territory. The pattern Tessa had explained made sense, but Sarah had no personal experience, having never played childish relationship games herself. All she could do was put an arm around Tessa and let her cry it out.

*   *   *

The warming sunshine had a soporific effect on Sarah and she dozed on the picnic blanket. Henry and Will were playing with a ball and Izzy sat watching. Her two boys, the most important people in the world to her, were giggling and running around with great enthusiasm and hysterics. Izzy smiled and contently gazed in their direction, her hands resting on her growing abdomen.

Small movements stirred inside and Izzy couldn't help but beam. She'd only felt the baby moving a couple of weeks ago, but already the tiny fluttering had developed into small but definite motions. They were already strong enough to disturb her at night.

The fears of the previous months, which had dominated so many of her thoughts, had eased into a dull and less persistent worry. Already the maternal instincts she'd carved out upon the arrival of Henry two years ago were in full force. She felt at peace and ready for the new challenge.

Sarah had been right. Izzy was used to excelling at whatever life threw at her. It wasn't a boast, it was just the way she was. She focused on whatever subject got her attention and she gave it her all. Just because a career hadn't stuck didn't mean that she was lazy or inept. It simply meant that she hadn't found the right thing for her yet.

Sarah's observations that Izzy might be struggling with motherhood, a job role that required no training manual yet a CEO's level of responsibility, had struck a chord. Always a quick and efficient learner, Izzy had found motherhood unpredictable and a whole lot harder than she'd imagined. It wasn't easy. The fact that billions of other women were, or had been, in the same boat didn't make it better. It made it worse, because Izzy then felt like a failure.

Since her conversation with Sarah, now weeks ago, Izzy had tried to relax. It was okay to feel unsure. It was okay to be scared. She still longed for something of her own, her own business, or a gradually thriving career, but Izzy no longer felt that crushing panic she had before.

She took one day at a time, learning how to be mother to Henry and how to do the hardest 'job' she'd ever faced. The rest would come in time and she'd keep searching, but this time without the panic and desperation she'd been previously feeling.

Tipping her face to the sunshine and shutting her eyes, Izzy enjoyed the relative peace around her. Squeals of delight from Henry and guffaws from Will mingled with the distant chatter of others on the common. But it still felt like peace to her.

She sat like that for a while before eventually opening her eyes and looking over at her best friend. Sarah was fast asleep. Izzy wondered back to their conversation in the bar and mulled over the conversation. She wanted to believe Sarah. Nothing would have pleased her more than to believe that Sarah was doing fine and dealing with whatever life was throwing her way.

Izzy had noticed a massive change in her friend. Sarah was bolder than the timid woman she'd become. She possessed a small flicker of confidence which was growing with each week. Taking a step out of the static life she'd inhabited was having a dramatic effect. Sarah was healing, Izzy could see that.

And yet, Izzy still felt she wasn't getting the full story. Sarah's reluctance to discuss Dermot and the obvious attraction that Izzy had noticed straight away worried her. Perhaps Sarah hadn't figured it out for herself yet. But Izzy knew her friend better than that. Sarah was still hiding.

Since Alex died Sarah had dug herself a trench and had remained there. Every bullet and assault that came her way from insensitive comments and fake friends had had its impact. Sarah simply shut down, only allowing the people around her to get so close. Izzy missed Sarah, the real Sarah. She reasoned that love and devotion would be the only thing to bring her friend back to her.

The fear that might never happen was all too real and one Izzy rarely allowed herself to ponder on.

Chapter Fourteen

"I was wondering if I could come over and see the journals?" Dermot's voice carried down the phone line.

"Um, sure," Sarah looked over where the notebook lay on the coffee table, open to the latest entry. Nor, Eleanor's pet name, had just detailed a visit to the park, where she and Nanny had taken Alfie and Freddy out for the day. It had ended abruptly when Freddy, unsupervised for a matter of minutes, ended up hanging upside down out of a tree. His little adventure resulted in a sprained ankle and a hair full of mud. The simplicity of the incident amused Sarah.

"You're reading it now, aren't you?" She could hear the humour in his voice and she began to blush. "So, tell me what's happening. No wait, I don't even know the characters so go back to the beginning."

"Won't that defeat the point of you coming around and looking for yourself?" she teased.

"Ah, true. I'll definitely need to come over then. And soon."

"I might be free next Tuesday," she fibbed, knowing full well her evenings were free for the entire week. Her social life was still highly lacking.

"Only then?" he sounded a little disappointed.

"Yeah sorry," she stated. "I've plans this week. Tuesday's the earliest I can do."

It would also give her the time to read more of the journals. She still had a third of the first and the entirety of the second to wade through. She wasn't quite ready to share Nor with anyone else yet either.

"Okay then. Is 7pm all right?"

"Yes, absolutely fine," she said in a business-like tone. She jotted down the date and time and said her goodbyes, pleased that she'd managed to keep the small embers of a spark under control. She realised how much she enjoyed their conversations and each one left her feeling slightly ruffled after.

*   *   *

12th August 1907

The heat has become intolerable. I once enjoyed the summer months. I took much pleasure in participating in a game of croquet or watching an amusing Punch and Judy show, all the while basking in the glorious sunshine above. These days I am the one providing the entertainment, to my younger brothers whose appetite for such pursuits are relentless. I finally exit the heat of the day exhausted and beyond all recognisable form, drenched in sweat and uncomfortable in my clothing.

Oh, I feel I do little but moan these days. I long for the positivity I once felt and the joy which my peers seem to inhabit so easily. Margaret and Beatrice Harris paid a visit last week and informed me that they are now out in society, and attend frequent dances eagerly in their desire to make a fortunate acquaintance. They believe they will both be married within twelve months. I almost wished myself in their position, so keen to be free of this solitude that now grips me. This knowledge has affected me pitifully, despite marriage previously not being a desire of mine in the slightest.

Surely it cannot be for long now until Father permits me to be out. However, I fear his dwindling business attributes no longer determine a fortuitous marriage for his eldest.

*　　　*　　　*

The week went too quickly. Sarah battled to meet her deadlines at work, which added to the speed in which the week passed. Almost every evening was spent in the company of the journals and yet Sarah had not finished them, nor was she ready for Dermot's visit.

Eleanor had elegantly mapped out her life; one Sarah found intriguing, compelling and melancholy at times. Yet again she felt connected to this Edwardian teenager and wondered what had happened to her and her family.

Much of diary chronicled daily grievances, routine and the occasional anecdote. It seemed, over several months of entries, that Eleanor had accepted her situation, no matter how bleak a mood it sometimes gave her.

It was with a pang Sarah continued to read the girl's life story, in some minute hope that Eleanor would still achieve her heart's desire. However, the recent entries were giving little away, and as fascinating as the inner workings of an Edwardian household were (and startling at times), the subject that truly fascinated Sarah was often missing.

It was like Eleanor herself had deliberately stopped writing about personal things. Sarah could relate to that all too well. Nor had put up a wall, even in her own diary, which she couldn't have predicted would be read by anyone else. Least of all a young widow over a hundred years later. To save herself from perhaps disappointment, sorrow or despondency, Nor had stopped being honest even with herself.

Tuesday evening arrived and Sarah sat nervously on the sofa, one eye on the

Edwardian items laid out on the coffee table and another on the door. She heard movement on the stairs. Taking a deep glug of the white wine she'd poured to calm her nerves, she approached the door as he arrived.

"Evening," he said as she opened the door. "For inconveniencing you I have brought reinforcements, namely chocolate and the magnificence that is the jammy dodger," he waved the packet in front of her.

"Well in that case you're welcome," she smiled and let him in. He headed straight for the table and perused the contents for a few moments. Feeling apprehensive Sarah busied herself pouring him a glass of wine and topping up her own.

"Wow this jewellery is quite something," he mused, partly to himself. "I wonder why it was left behind. I mean these are special items, they must have meant something to someone. Or at the very least cost someone a good deal of money. This stuff can't have just been forgotten about, right?"

"I really don't know," Sarah said joining him around the table. He was holding the hair pin, turning it over in fascination. "It seems strange, I agree. I wonder if perhaps it was hidden." Knowing what she had learned about Eleanor, it was a distinct possibility.

"Hidden?" Dermot pricked his ears up. "What makes you think that? The journals?"

After weeks of keeping the information and the mystery to herself, Sarah decided to finally share what she knew. Giving Dermot a detailed overview of the content of the first journal, Sarah included her theories as to why they lay dusty and forgotten.

"Perhaps the family moved in a hurry," she talked fast and paced the living area. "And they got left behind in the confusion. Her father was in financial difficulty so it's likely they may have had to give up the house. Or my other thought was that Eleanor hid the diary.

We already know that her desire for a career was frowned upon and her own mother's talents had already been squandered and shut down by Nor's father. Maybe Eleanor hid her journals because they contained her fears and worries and that was never acceptable in her household."

"Maybe," Dermot didn't looked convinced. "I think you might be right about the sudden move though. I don't know much about the history of the house that far back, but it was once a grand home and if her father had no money, he might have been forced to give it up. Especially if they'd already let staff go and made Eleanor responsible for her brothers."

Sarah felt a thrill as they threw theories back and forth. Her worries about sharing Eleanor's story faded into obscurity. It was actually fun discussing it with Dermot, and his obvious excitement to solve the mystery spurred her own.

Refilling their glasses again, Sarah took a sip of her wine before posing the question she had been dying to ask all evening.

"What are you going to do with the journal and other items?"

He looked at her, studying her for a moment and she suddenly felt uncomfortable under his gaze. She shifted the glass from one hand to the other and tried to look nonchalant.

The urge to look away was strong but it was like the game where you stare each other out. She couldn't look away for fear of losing. She realised losing in this situation meant revealing more than she wished to let on. To either Dermot or herself.

A flush reached her cheeks and he looked away.

"Oh, I think we should try and find out what happened to the family, don't you?" he said.

A wave of relief hit her with the realisation that the journals weren't just going to be sold to the highest bidder. Her smile faltered however as the thought of the two of them searching for the family entered her consciousness. She worried spending too much time with this man could prove unsettling, for reasons she feared to explore.

"So, how do you think we should go about this then?" Dermot cut into her thoughts.

"What?" she struggled to shake herself back into the present.

"How do we start?" he asked, clearly at a loss.

"I'm not sure exactly," she admitted, then paused. "There must be house records, right? Either locally or nationally. I'm sure we could access it online. I would have thought you'd know something about this, seeing as you own the place."

"I've never needed to track down a previous owner before, at least not from so long ago. But what you're saying sounds familiar. I'm sure I've heard this elsewhere before. Probably just from TV though. I've never needed it in a professional capacity."

"Do you want me to look? Or are we doing this together? We need to figure out who does what and what responsibilities we can split."

Dermot looked amused.

"What?" she responded.

"You're pacing again. No, don't stop, it's nice to see you so excited. And organised. Definitely organised. Is this what you're like at work?"

Sarah instantly felt her heckles rise and she turned to face him. "What do you mean by that?"

Dermot put his hands up in defence. "Whoa, it was just a compliment. I barely know you. It's just... normally when I see you, you tend to have your head down and quietly go on your way. Not the times we've socialised; you're different with your friends. But in the house as you leave in the mornings and when you return in the evening."

Sarah felt deflated and sunk onto the sofa. "Really?" she asked in a small voice. Dermot cleared his throat beside her, "I'm sure I'm just mistaken," he quickly tried to backtrack.

"No, you're not. I just hadn't realised that anybody had noticed, even my landlord from downstairs," she attempted to inject some humour. "My life has... well... it's complicated."

Unable to elaborate she fell into silence. Her previous excitement had been vanquished and she was surprised to see Dermot still standing there and not running for the door.

"It's fine Sarah," he said gently. "It wasn't a criticism, just something I'd observed. For the record I'm a pretty quiet and private guy myself."

"Yeah right, you're out nearly every evening," Sarah blurted out before realising how much that made her sound like a stalker.

"Usually it's just training or exercising. But yeah, I enjoy a night or two out with my friends, or occasionally family. But my kind of night out tends to be a couple of pints, or if we're feeling particularly cultured a trip to the cinema or even, it has been known, to the theatre," his eyes twinkled as he joked and Sarah couldn't resist smiling in response.

"I have quite the social life myself, " she couldn't resist comparing. "Pilates which used to be with Izzy, but now she's pregnant I end up going myself. Izzy and I have switched out that night for wine, chocolate and a DVD instead. Obviously, I drink all the wine.

Then there's my parents, who usually cook for me once a fortnight, and then the odd night out with the aforementioned people, or simply a night out on my own, because I much prefer to enjoy an art exhibition, or a film, without others distracting me and trying to make small talk. Riveting, aren't I?"

"Actually, I can fully appreciate where you're coming from," Dermot sat down next to her. "Small talk is the worst."

Sarah couldn't help but smile. She didn't know if he was being genuine, or just trying to make her feel better, but she appreciated the effort anyway. "I have been known to frequent the odd bar too," she joked, then instantly worried how that made her sound.

"Yeah? Well I've been known to climb the odd tree. With my eight-year-old nephew, I hasten to add."

They sat in companionable silence for a moment and Sarah stared at the journals in front of them, trying to get her thoughts in line.

"So... you've never mentioned a boyfriend," Dermot enquired tentatively. Sarah almost audibly sighed. The connotation was clear and she instantly felt awkward.

"No, happily single," she hoped she sounded firm enough that that would be the end of it. Just in case it didn't she decided to change the subject. "I'm happy to look up the records of the house if you like. I'm quite keen to see the results myself, seeing as I've enjoyed the journals so much. I feel like I know these people."

"You're welcome to," Dermot agreed, not showing any obvious signs of being disappointed by the change of topic. "But I feel like I should be looking too. It's my house after all and I do feel a bit obliged, to be honest. Let's find out how to go about it and then we can delegate."

"I'm sure a quick Google search will tell us the basics. I can get my laptop out now."

"I actually have to rush off. Sorry," Dermot looked genuinely disappointed. "I wish I could stay a bit longer, but I have to meet my mates Jake and Al for some training. They signed me up for another race in three weeks." He lifted his eyebrows to the heavens and rolled his eyes. "I guess I'm committed to this thing."

He loved it really, but the thought of an evening investigating with Sarah suddenly seemed more appealing.

"You shouldn't have had the wine then," Sarah joked, hiding her own disappointment.

"Yeah, I might regret that. Anyway, thanks for showing me the items. I'm glad we agree on what to do next. Send me a text if you find anything out."

Sarah let him out, suppressing the despondency that followed. He hadn't asked her to call, just to text, and hadn't seemed unhappy by her deflection of her relationship status. It didn't seem that he liked her after all and instead of feeling relieved she just felt confused and more than a little fed up.

Chapter Fifteen

Pippa was on her knees, having long discarded the dibber, using her fingers instead to make the small holes needed to plant the coriander seeds. A dozen or more packets of seed lay on the ground next to her, from basil to rocket, oregano to thyme. It was the season for planting and Pippa was in her element.

She already kept a large volume of herbs growing, all year round, in the glass house at the end of the garden. But these seeds were for her own personal use, not for the local restaurants and cafés that she supplied herbs and salad items to.

Along the opposite garden bed seedlings of marigolds, forget-me-nots, purple veronicas and bright pink peonies awaited the compost, bone meal and sunshine needed to bloom into their full potential. Buds currently adorned the small plants and had yet to flower without the loving care of a permanent abode, in which they could spread their roots and grow strong.

Pippa tucked a strand of her auburn hair behind her ear as it attempted an escape from her ponytail.

She was wearing a khaki green body warmer over her cashmere lilac jumper and was wearing her comfortable outdoor trousers; grey sweats which had seen better days but Pippa could never bring herself to throw them out. It was a typical look for Pippa; the elegant mixed with the practical, depending on what job or errand she was involved in.

She heard the red garden gate open and she peeked over her shoulder. Seeing Sarah walking towards her, she grinned. Her daughter looked relaxed and more content than Pippa had seen her in a long time. She had noticed a change in her daughter in the last six months, and although she was sure Sarah couldn't see it herself, Pippa noted the signs were there.

Even on days when Sarah was stressed her countenance had changed. She held herself higher, no longer stooping as if carrying the world on her shoulders. She looked well rested and carefree. Well, as carefree as possible given the circumstances, Pippa mused.

"Hello Mum," Sarah smiled as she approached.

"Hello darling," Pippa stood up, holding onto her daughter for support, then embraced her in a tight hug.

"Wow," Sarah laughed into her mother's shoulder. "What did I do to deserve this?" Pippa just laughed and didn't elaborate. She had no desire to embarrass her daughter or make her feel self conscious. She had long learnt to just let her be, enjoying the positive changes in Sarah's life instead of drawing attention to them.

Sarah let go of the embrace and knelt down to inspect the small patch of soil that Pippa had cordoned off for her herbs.

"I'm going to put a little fence around them," Pippa explained. "I want to keep them contained and build up a herb garden, of sorts, in this area. I'll be planting the flowers over that side and your father will be digging up the old perennials in this corner, where I can then extend the existing veggie patch."

Sarah thought of the garden at Caledon Street and wondered if Dermot was planning on using the space himself. Currently just a bare patch of grass, Sarah was quite keen to get some advice from her mum on how it could be improved. Thinking of him she tried to turn her attention back to her mother's garden and admire the work going on around her. It wasn't working very well.

"Tea?" Pippa asked, sensing a shift of mood.

"Please."

They headed into the galley kitchen and Pippa flicked on the kettle, reaching into the cupboard for the teapot. It was white with faded pink roses and Sarah remembered it from her childhood. Her mother had always insisted on drinking tea from a tea pot.

"Your father is at the track again," Pippa explained his absence. "Sometimes I'd prefer he take up something a bit more sedate, like golf for instance."

"I couldn't imagine Dad being a golf enthusiast," laughed Sarah.

"No, that's a bit extreme isn't it?" Pippa pondered. "Maybe vintage car rallies then, rather than actually racing them."

She filled the teapot with freshly boiled water and allowed it to warm the pot. She fetched the milk out of the fridge and poured some into a small jug which matched the design of the teapot.

"How's work?" she asked as she busied herself with the tea preparations.

"Good," Sarah replied, sitting at the long rustic kitchen table. "We've just completed a major toothpaste campaign. You'll be seeing advertisements all over soon. TV, magazines, on the side of buses, train stations. You name it. I think it's the biggest client I've worked with."

"And are you making friends?" Sarah recognised the rather unsubtle hint in Pippa's question and decided, remembering her recent conversation with Izzy, to be honest for once.

"I guess so," she sighed. "Becca, she's the junior copywriter, invited me on a girl's night out with some others from the office. It was nice," she admitted. "A few probing questions, but nothing that made me feel uncomfortable. And we had fun. It was good. But there's been nothing since.

I can't help wondering if I made a bad impression, if they realised I wasn't fun enough. I know I've not been honest with them about my past, so maybe they just don't feel like they know me enough to invite me out again."

"Why haven't you told them Sarah?"

"Because they'll be like everyone else when they find out I'm a widow. They'll either give me a look of pity every time I walk in the room, else they'll ignore me because I make them feel awkward. It doesn't matter how many years pass, the response is still the same. I just can't tell them the truth. No one knows anything," Sarah had a fleeting thought of Dermot and she suppressed it again.

"I understand that, I do," Pippa said gently. "But by not telling them this, it seems like you're keeping a lot of yourself back. I'm sure you can allow people to know you without shouting 'I'm a widow' from the rooftops. And maybe you should organise the next night out rather than waiting for an invitation?"

Sarah mulled on her mother's advice. She guessed the answer could really be that simple. She needed to do the chasing a bit more and reveal more of herself as she did. It would be easier for Sarah to control exactly how much information she was comfortable to give and protect herself at the same time.

"So, tell me what you're really here about," Pippa said, pouring the tea into the teacups.

Sarah raised her eyebrows. "What do you mean? I wanted to see my lovely mum of course."

"You made a forty-minute drive without warning. What if I'd been out? You don't normally just turn up out of the blue. Not once since you left home, in fact."

"I guess I'm trying to live a little on the edge these days," Sarah joked. Seeing her mother's expression, she backtracked. "I actually didn't plan to come around," she admitted. "I've had such a busy week finishing this campaign at work and I took myself for a drive this morning just to think things through and... I realised I needed to run it past you first."

"Run what exactly?" Pippa asked, intrigued by what her daughter might be about to reveal.

Sarah took a deep breath. "A couple of months ago I found some items in the attic space above my flat. They belong to the original owners who lived there over a hundred years ago. I checked with my landlord who also wanted to see them, but was happy for me to go through everything too."

"That was nice of him," Pippa interjected absent-mindedly.

"I guess so. There were a couple of journals in with everything else and I started reading them. They're fascinating and mysterious and I haven't been able to get them out of my head since. The girl who wrote them is so feisty and sure of herself and has all these dreams that, because of the era, she couldn't seem to fulfil.

The short of it is I want to track down what happened to her. I haven't finished the journals yet, but Dermot, my landlord, is keen to start looking too. But for me it's so much more. I want to know what happened to Eleanor. I *need* to know what happened to her."

Sarah took a calming mouth full of tea and awaited Pippa's response.

"Well it sounds fascinating Sarah. You know how much I love history. I'm just struggling to see how I fit in?"

"Dermot and I discussed how to track down the family, but neither of us really knew. I've had to bring work home every evening this week to get the campaign finished, so my plan to just Google what to do hasn't yet materialised. I've just been too busy to look.

So firstly, I wondered if you knew how we'd go about finding a previous owner of the house? And secondly, what information can you tell me about the Edwardian period that might be useful? Dermot can reel off plenty about the décor of the time and house building techniques, but he knows nothing about the actual time period itself."

Pippa glossed over her daughter's frequent mention of Dermot's name, knowing it was neither the time nor place. A little glint of promise was all she needed. It had been a long time since Sarah had gushed a name like that. The fact that Sarah didn't seem to be aware kept Pippa from mentioning it.

Pippa was also intrigued by the journals Sarah described. Fascinated from an historical viewpoint, she briefly wondered at Sarah's motivations. Clearly it wasn't the history itself that had caught her daughter's imagination, but rather the story of the girl she'd mentioned.

"May I can take a look at the journals?" Pippa ventured. Sarah paused and visibly composed herself.

Pippa held her breath while she awaited an answer. She suspected Sarah had got herself emotionally involved and was reluctant to share what she'd found. Pippa's heart broke for her a little. It was a symptom she'd noticed in her daughter since her loss. Sarah found ways to distract herself, ways to suspend reality for a few weeks or even months at a time. It was a coping mechanism.

She hoped Sarah hadn't put too much of her energy into searching for the family. She didn't want her to be disappointed if she reached a dead end.

"It will help me ascertain the exact era," Pippa explained. "You mentioned the Edwardian period, but quite a lot happened during that time. There were many social changes, especially for women and even the class structure was beginning to loosen its chains. Heading into the First World War then changed our society completely. It was a fascinating period."

"Eleanor talks a lot about women's duties and roles and the opportunities that were opening up," Sarah replied eagerly, excited to hear something she recognised in what her mother was saying. "She mentioned the Suffragettes more than once."

"What year are the journals written in?"

"The first in 1907. The year is almost finished and there's a little reading left to do. I haven't looked in the second journal yet."

"Yes, well, there was definitely a lot happening with the Suffragettes at that time. Even more later on. Well Sarah, it seems you've stumbled on quite a find there. It must make for captivating reading."

"It does. I just find her story draws me in. I want her to succeed and achieve her dreams. So few of us get to do that...." Sarah tailed off and stared at her now cold tea.

Pippa reached out a hand and placed it over Sarah's. "You have new dreams now," she whispered gently. "You must try and track down Eleanor's life story if you can. But it's a big job, so don't feel disappointed if you can't. You have your own life to lead too, without getting entangled in someone else's."

The warning was clear and Sarah replied in acquiescence. "I'll promise to try Mum."

Pippa topped up her tea cup and offered to Sarah, who declined.

"I think the first thing you need to do is find the records of a census from that time. They'll be at the National Archives and you should be able to do it online. If not, you could always pay them a visit. You'd need to find out which is the right census though. It should be easy, given the dates in the journals."

"I'm glad to hear that. I was worried it was going to be a complicated process."

"It still might," Pippa warned again. "If the information isn't available you could hit a brick wall very quickly. At least you have the advantage of this Dermot helping you. Being the owner of the property, he might have more information at his disposal than you."

Sarah shrugged. "He didn't seem to know much when I asked. But thanks for that Mum, I'll definitely check the archives out."

"And I'll do a bit of digging into 1907 and find out as much as I can about life in that time period."

Pippa studied Sarah for a moment then put her head on one side. "Thanks for coming to me Sarah."

To feel included in her daughter's life again, even for something like this, meant more to her than Sarah would ever realise.

Despite the flicker of worry she had about Sarah getting too involved in the investigation, Pippa also felt glad that Sarah was directing her passions into something constructive.

It seemed finally, in a very small but meaningful way, Sarah's walls were starting to crack.

Chapter Sixteen

Dermot stared down at the details in front of him. The A4 pieces of paper were fastened together with a staple and contained photographs and information about a white washed cottage, complete with original wooden beams.

A thorough valuation and survey by his brother-in-law (Dermot hadn't seen it ethical to do it himself, considering his interest in the property) had found little wrong with the external shell, having been well maintained by its current owners.

The cottage was outdated and needed renovating as well as landscaping of its overgrown plot and the addition of a garage and perhaps even a workshop.

It wouldn't bring much of a return Dermot knew, but having taken on the massive project of the Edwardian town house the year before, he wasn't ready to take on anything else as potentially stressful. The last conversion had nearly put him off for life and saw him taking on work with Scott in his desperation for some normality.

"Are you going to go for it?" Scott looked amused and stood with his arms folded, leaning against his desk opposite. His dark wavy hair tickled his white and red checked collar and his crumpled khaki trousers hinted to the newborn he and Dermot's sister Rose had recently had. There was no time for ironing any more.

"I might do," Dermot replied, still staring at the plans.

"There'll be little return, nor a massive amount of excitement either."

"I need to ease myself back in slowly. I don't want a major project right now. Besides, if it was a big project, you'd be a surveyor down. I wouldn't be able to carry on here. Unless that's your plan all along Scott?" Dermot raised an eyebrow.

Scott laughed. "Rose would kill me if that was the truth. She adores her big brother."

Rose had always looked up to Dermot, four years her senior, who had protected his little blonde-haired sister from their older bully of a brother Kieran. Of course, they all got on well now, but as children Kieran ruled the roost and Rose, a slip of a girl, had often been the target for his practical jokes.

"This will suit me perfectly right now," Dermot gestured to the plans. "Small, but with enough work to keep me interested. Not to mention local. It's a small profit margin I know, but I haven't sold the place at Caledon Street so I doubt the bank will be too keen to hand out another large mortgage."

"I just never saw you as a cottage man myself."

"Believe me by the time I'm finished with it there'll be nothing twee about the place."

The rest of the day passed in a blur. All that consumed his thoughts were white washed walls and the potential conversion within.

The generous plot surrounding the property came alive with numerous possibilities presenting themselves for its use; a walled garden, perhaps a sun room off the back wall of the property, a deck leading to a barbeque area.

Knowing he was getting carried away he forcibly switched his thoughts to the cycle home.

He'd got used to making the seven-mile journey to work on his bike. It was good practise for the race coming up in a fortnight. Jake and Al had already surpassed him, each having covered at least twice the distance he had that week. The competition was on and Dermot was never one to turn down some friendly one-up-man-ship with his closest friends. Whoever lost the mile count for the week bought the drinks that weekend. Dermot was determined not to lose, especially with the possibility of a second mortgage on the horizon.

With that in mind he planned a long cycle home, a large semi-circular route out through the town, into the countryside, and around to the other side of town again. Rather than just riding right through the middle, facing the rush hour traffic, he was more than doubling his mile count for the day.

He knew he'd be exhausted come morning, when he'd be attempting the same loop again, but several rounds of drinks were at stake.

The cycle home proved cathartic. The exertion, coupled with the demands of the terrain, helped Dermot clear his thoughts.

Adrenalin pumped through his veins as nature, mud and fresh air whipped past him at increasing speed. There was nothing left to think of, except to enjoy the environment around him. It was exactly what he needed.

*   *   *

For the second time that evening there was no answer. Instead the phone call had diverted to voicemail and yet she was hesitant to just leave a message. Technically he had said to text, but the information her mother had given her was too long winded to fit into a couple hundred characters.

Sarah placed her phone back into the receiver and considered going and knocking on his door. But then she felt silly. She had nothing urgent to tell him.

She hadn't yet contacted the National Archives and had only briefly perused their website, but she felt like he needed to be kept in the loop. The sudden worry that she might prove herself a nuisance, should she interrupt his evening with a visit, only added to feeling pathetic. Not to mention embarrassed.

What if he got the wrong idea and wondered if she was interested in him? That would be beyond mortifying.

Deciding to leave it for another day, Sarah put her feet up and contemplated phoning Izzy instead. Guilt filled her as she realised how scarce she'd been recently.

Izzy was due for her twenty weeks scan any day now and Sarah couldn't even remember the exact date. She'd been so caught up in the drama with Tessa and the mystery surrounding the journals.

Ashamed with herself she dialled Izzy's number. It rang for a full minute before Sarah hung up. Either they were out or already sleeping. It seemed she wasn't meant to get through to anyone that evening.

The journals sat on the coffee table, where they'd been placed a fortnight ago as soon as Tessa had moved out. They looked tempting but Sarah resisted.

Right now, real life seemed more important than the admittedly fascinating history contained in its pages. Feeling the sudden urge to get out of the flat, somewhere, anywhere, Sarah picked up her jacket and bag and made her way out the door.

As she reached Greta's doorway, she heard the soft tinkling of the ivories. Sarah smiled as she recalled her visit, the day Tessa moved out. Embarrassed that she hadn't yet met her intrepid neighbour, Sarah had swung past her flat on the way home from Tessa's new place.

"Hello?" the glamorous elderly lady said as she opened her door. She must have been in her early seventies. She wore her hair up in a bun which was a curious and attractive mixture between blonde and grey. In fact, it was more grey than blonde, which gave the impression of flecks of gold weaving through the elegant bouffant.

She wore a purple satin smock with silver embroidery around the hems. Her skin was tanned and wrinkled, a combination of age and time spent in the sunshine. She must go abroad a lot, Sarah thought as she introduced herself.

"Come in my dear, you must be in need of a drink after the day you've had," Greta offered, as Sarah finished explaining where she'd just come from.

"Thanks, that's very kind." Sarah followed her through into the flat.

It was simply adorned with an old red sofa and potted plants dominating the living area. The piano stood in pride of place on the main wall where most others would have their television set. A small dining table with just two chairs was pushed up to the far corner, next to the breakfast bar that started the small but immaculate kitchen.

A hallway on the left led off to the bedroom and bathroom.

The decor was as impressive as her own flat, with similar luxurious wallpaper and panelling on the bottom half of the walls.

But most of the wall space was covered with weird and wonderful works of art, seemingly some of Greta's own designs. Bright swirls of acrylic paint filled the canvases, red, blue and green the favourite amongst dozens of other colours and shades. Odd shapes could be made out but none were definite or discernible as anything in particular.

"You have a lovely home," Sarah said not insincerely, admiring the mixture of artistic styles portrayed around her.

"How sweet dear," Greta handed Sarah a glass of orange juice and ushered her over to the sofa.

What followed was admittedly an awkward exchange; Sarah, keen to learn more about Greta's youth and her history with art and music, found her questions dismissed or unanswered in their entirety. It seemed Greta was either not much of a conversationalist, which Sarah highly doubted, or she kept herself and her life guarded.

Polite, albeit, stilted conversation passed a half hour, when Sarah finally felt it polite to leave. As she said goodbye to Greta, who had been entirely friendly throughout, she realised their topics of conversation had been restricted to how each enjoyed living in their flat, their favourite type of tea and of course, the great British classic, the weather.

It seemed that Greta would remain much of a mystery.

Sarah smiled now as she passed the pianist's flat and headed down the second flight of stairs to the front door. She had no idea where to go, she just needed to start walking.

Outside the fresh air hit her with intensity. The air had cooled dramatically from the daytime, which was now enjoying the hint of summer, and had shifted to a brisk cold that made her nose tingle.

Caledon Street was mainly residential with the common opposite and a 'open all hours' shop on the corner. Sarah stopped there and bought a bar of chocolate before carrying on her way. She wished she'd had the foresight to bring her thermos mug filled with warming tea or coffee.

Strolling on regardless she contemplated where to go. Main Road was a ten-minute walk away and offered far more in the way of options. Several pubs, a bar or two and at least a dozen popular restaurants adorned the stretch of road which passed through the middle of the bustling suburb.

Conscious of being on her own and with the darkening of the sky signalling twilight, she decided to find a late-night coffee shop and have a quick drink before heading home. Reaching Main Road, she began to peruse the perfect spot.

The streets were fairly busy as people made their choice between restaurants, bars and pubs. It would still be a while until the clubs opened.

Attractive lights lit the street and gave it a festive feel alongside the buzz of the crowds. Despite being on her own she was glad she came. The atmosphere was cheery and strangely comforting as she enjoyed strolling past the groups of friends, families and hen parties and observing them all.

She crossed the street halfway down in search of the café she and Alex used to frequent. She hadn't been there in a long time. Several of the shop fronts had changed and she was dismayed to realise that she no longer recognised where the café was situated.

After walking for ten minutes Sarah came to the conclusion that the favourite spot she used to enjoy with her husband had closed down. There were definitely no cafés in the vicinity and she was far past the route they'd used to walk.

Turning back Sarah noticed a side street across the road, lit up with fairy lights and buzzing with people. A sign above the alley read Drago's in scrawling black font. The name ran a bell and Sarah stood staring for a few moments, her forehead creased in thought. She vaguely remembered Tessa mentioning it. Something to do with Tessa's previous work colleague.

Then it came back to her. The poor unfortunate gallery owner who had taken Tessa's ill thought out advice and had been terrified of the gallery failing. A large the crowd of people milled around the doorway and it seemed full inside.

With no other nearby cafés to consider and the distinct urge to avoid restaurants and bars, where she would feel like a complete pariah sitting on her own, Sarah weighed up her only other option. Go home. Discounting it in a split second, Sarah crossed the street and entered the gallery.

Chapter Seventeen

Drago, or whatever his name was, flitted around the room in a semi state of panic. His bleached blonde hair clashed against his mustard coloured blazer, matching corduroys and red checked shirt underneath (with big silver buttons down the front). He rather reminded Sarah of Rupert the bear, in a strange and indeterminate way.

Sarah knew it was the gallery owner the second she walked in, seeing as he was literally the only one in a state of agitation, whereas everyone else was enjoying the art, drinks and nibbles.

Sarah picked up some complimentary sparkling wine and perused the paintings and sculptures. She was pleasantly surprised by what was on show. Impressive raiku vases stood as tall as she. Massive oil painted seascapes with dramatic waves threatening to spill out of the canvas, dominated the far wall. There was also a collection of whimsical sketches, intricate, delicate and fascinating.

Taking a sip of her sparkling wine her eye caught a glimpse of a man sitting in the corner. Initially she thought him an impressive sculpture, head in his hands, dressed in a leather jacket and dark denim jeans. Then he moved slightly and she nearly jumped out of her skin.

He ran his hands through his dark brown hair and gave a deep sigh which reverberated through his entire body. He didn't look up and Sarah, feeling uncomfortable, turned her face away, only to look directly into Drago's eyes, standing just a metre behind her. He was contemplating the seated man with disdain and more than a smidgen of panic. His eyes flickered from the man and rested on Sarah's and his shoulders seemed to slump.

"Oh, you noticed him," he said with a distinct wail. "This is what I feared. He's going to ruin my exhibit. Everyone's going to notice him and complain and no one's going to buy anything and leave. And I'll be ruined."

Sensing that Drago might be overreacting Sarah tried to placate him. "Or they might consider him part of an art installation? I did."

"Really?" his eyes lit up. "I didn't even consider that. And I call myself a gallery owner?" he began to wail again.

"Who is he anyway?" Sarah asked with a whisper. No one seemed to have noticed the man yet and she didn't want to add to Drago's problems by speaking too loudly and attracting attention.

"He came in at the start of the exhibition this afternoon. Refused to leave. I threatened to call the police, but I've been so rushed off my feet that I just let him stay."

"Why won't he leave? What does he want?"

"Oh, my friend dumped the guy the other month and he wanted me to ring her up and get her over here to talk. I told him it was impossible, I couldn't endanger my friend that way. Goodness knows if he's even *safe*. But he kept going on and on," Drago continued with an over dramatic sigh.

"So eventually I called her and she refused to come. So, I told him and now *he* refuses to go in case she turns up," he threw his hands into the air in exasperation.

Sarah's thoughts were in overdrive. Realising with a jolt who the man was, she needed to go talk to him.

"I'm going to go print up a card and place it next to him," Drago clapped his hands together in a eureka moment, as if the idea had solely been his. "Then everyone will think he's part of the exhibition."

Taking her cue, Sarah quickly approached the distressed man. Not quite sure on the best way to initiate conversation, she chose to dive right in. "Enjoying the exhibition?"

No reply. She shifted from one foot to the other and stared into her drink. "Can I get you a refreshment? These are really very nice," she added, signalling to her drink, which he couldn't even see with his head in his hands. Still no reply.

Feeling a little stupid now, she changed tack. "It's Kris, right?" He looked up sharply as if stung. She smiled at him, knowing she now had his full attention.

"How do know that?" his voice was hoarse. "Did Drago tell you?"

Sarah considered how to reply. If she said yes, it would exonerate her from any further questioning, but would also without a doubt end her conversation with him. Kris would just disappear into his hands again. If she replied no, she would have an intense evening ahead, possibly making the situation between him and Tessa worse, and possibly with another unwanted and unannounced lodger, if his stint at Drago's was anything to go by.

Alternatively, her evening, and her life if honest, was hardly proving to be thrilling right now. One more complication woven into the fabric of her tenancy at Caledon Street wouldn't hurt, surely?

"No," she replied simply. "I know Tessa."

*　　*　　*

The coffee was strong, but she guessed that he needed it. He looked like he hadn't slept well in weeks. He was an attractive guy; your typical tall, dark and handsome. He had an attractive amount of stubble and piercing blue eyes, with an angular jaw. He took the coffee gratefully and gave a muttered 'thank you'.

Sarah sat on the armchair opposite and wondered to the sanity of inviting an unknown man back to her flat. But Keith and Lauren seemed to think he was a good guy, and knowing how protective Keith had been of his daughter in years gone by, Sarah took this as good a sign as any that Kris wasn't a stranger to be concerned about.

Nevertheless, she kept the door to her flat open and she'd been firm in telling him that he could come for a warm drink and chat, and then leave. He'd nodded rather submissively, perhaps embarrassed by his display at the gallery.

"I must admit I'm vague on the details of why you and Tessa split up," she began. "And no, I'm not going to call her and tell her to come around. Just so you know," she tried to inject a humorous tone, to lighten the mood.

"I wouldn't ask you to do that," he said gruffly, the mug of coffee held between his two hands. "Today's the final straw. Enough people have called her on my behalf. I stopped trying myself weeks ago. She still won't listen to reason. I guess today I've realised that it's definitely over," he stared into the coffee mug intently, trying to steady his emotions.

No wonder he looked so distressed at the gallery, Sarah thought. He'd been holding out for reconciliation this long and Tessa's constant refusals had finally killed the last flicker of hope. Sarah felt sorry for him. She knew how difficult Tessa could be.

"So, this is where she was staying?" Kris looked around. Sarah had explained Tessa's unannounced visit while she walked Kris back from the gallery. "And how exactly do you fit in? I thought I knew all her friends."

Sarah paused then guessed that he would know the story. "I'm Alex's wife. Or technically, his widow."

"Ah, I see," he gave her a small sympathetic smile. "Now I feel guilty after the performance I gave today. My girlfriend walked out after three months. You lost your husband. No comparison really."

"Don't apologise. You love Tessa. It doesn't matter how long you've been together. Losing someone you love is hard, no matter how it happens. It sounds like you were serious about each other, right?"

"The night before she left, we were talking about marriage. So yeah, we were serious. At least I was. She did a bunk within hours of the conversation."

This was news to Sarah. She remembered Tessa mentioning that they'd discussed marriage, but failed to mention the part about dumping him the very next day. Sadly, Sarah wasn't surprised. Tessa had obviously been scared off

121

despite the strength of her feelings for Kris.

"How was she while she was staying?"

"Pretty miserable most of the time," she chose to reply truthfully, conveniently leaving out Tessa's flirtation with Dermot and hoping that Kris wouldn't decide that he still stood a chance. Tessa's stubbornness was legendary and Sarah highly doubted she'd back down, even if it meant losing the man who had meant so much to her.

"Really?" Kris perked up.

"Yes... but she was fairly determined that it was over," Sarah cautiously added emphasis.

"But if she was miserable there might still be a chance."

"Kris, with all respect, I don't think Tessa's about to change her mind. Hadn't you just come to that same conclusion yourself? I'm sorry if I got your hopes up there, but I honestly don't want you to think that you can just magic Tessa back into your life. I've known her a long time and this is unfortunately just something that she does."

He looked at her intently for a moment before shaking his head. "I know she has a history of this, but I also know she felt differently about me. Maybe I can't change her mind and I can't keep chasing her. But I know the truth and she's running because she's scared, not because she doesn't love me or doesn't want to commit," he ran his hands through his hair and expelled a frustrated grunt.

"She's infuriating! The most infuriating woman I've ever met. To waste what we had like this. She's too scared to let herself be happy. She's wasting the best thing that's ever happened to either of us."

Sarah nursed her coffee as he let out his pent-up frustrations.

"I've chased her for nearly two months. Can you believe that?! That's almost as long as we were together in the first place. Haven't I proved that this relationship isn't just a bit of fun for me? Haven't I proved that I'm serious about her and she needn't worry about being let down or hurt by me? Aargh!" he grunted loudly.

"I'm sorry Kris," she said with a whisper, once he'd quietened down and sat hunched on the sofa. "If I knew a way to persuade Tessa to change her mind, I'd tell you. After twelve years, she still remains a mystery to me."

He laughed wryly. "Me too. Even her mum and dad don't seem to know what to say to talk sense into her. I guess I am now at a dead end. I've tried. She can't accuse me of not trying."

"I'm sorry I've not been more helpful."

"Ha, I don't expect you to be. I appreciate the coffee though," he smiled a crooked smile and Sarah could see why Tessa had fallen for him, with his handsomeness and hint of charm beneath his pain. What Sarah couldn't understand is why Tessa had allowed fear get in the way of the relationship.

"I guess I better go and leave you in peace," he looked reluctantly at the open door, as if aware that he was about to walk away and have the door shut behind him; the metaphorical dead end he'd referred to becoming literal.

Sarah sensed his reluctance and hesitated about whether to let him stay longer. But the hour was late and she'd done all she could. He stood, gathered his jacket and nodded his thanks.

"I'll see you out," she offered and walked him to the flat door. "It was nice meeting you. I wish it was under better circumstances."

"Thanks Sarah. You too. Tessa talked about Alex a lot. She really misses him and it sounds like he was a great guy."

"He was. He definitely left a big gap in our lives," she said, wrapping her arms around her to keep the chill of night away. She led him down the second flight of stairs and heard the front door click below her.

"Oh hi," Dermot came into view, walking towards his flat with key at the ready. "How's your evening been?"

"Good," Sarah began, before Kris became visible on the stairs behind her. Dermot looked from her to Kris and back again. "I actually need to talk to you about the journals," she said. "I spoke to my mum and she recommended the National Archives website as a good starting place."

"Great," he said, his eyes sliding towards Kris again in distraction. He brought his gaze back to Sarah. "Have you had a look yet?"

"No, I wanted to let you know first."

"I'd like to take a look with you if that's okay? I've been mulling on it for a while and it's actually quite exciting. I'd hate to miss out on any important information."

Kris hovered between them looking perplexed. Sarah turned to him. "Sorry, just house stuff. We're trying to track the original owners," she didn't feel uncomfortable telling him. He was a stranger and unlikely to set foot in her flat again.

"Oh," he looked interested, but didn't pry further.

"Night then," Sarah gave Dermot a smile and showed Kris to the front door. "Night."

*   *   *

Dermot entered his flat with a squirm in his gut which he could only attribute to irritation. Seeing a strange guy walking downstairs with Sarah had irked him. For all he knew he was Sarah's brother. Or maybe he was her boyfriend and why that should bother Dermot he didn't like to think on too deeply.

Hearing the brief goodbye on the doorstep he began to relax a little. It was short, perfunctory and certainly not the goodbye he'd have expected from a boyfriend and girlfriend. He exhaled in relief, then gave a little laugh and shake of the head.

What did it matter who she was dating? The thought that it might was a new development and Dermot later went to bed, wondering all the while what it might mean.

Chapter Eighteen

Izzy and Will sat in the peach coloured waiting room. Outdated magazines haphazardly covered the coffee table in the middle, threatening to spill over the sides onto the grey coarse carpet below.

Another couple sat opposite, the dark-haired woman absentmindedly stroking her bulging stomach and staring past the white blinds and out the window. Her partner perused a well-worn car magazine, seemingly enthralled by the articles within.

Will fidgeted nervously with his tie. Having come straight from work he hadn't had time to change. Izzy also felt anxious. As excited as she was to see the baby again a sliver of fear always attached itself to the appointments.

What if something was wrong? Something they hadn't picked up last time? Now Izzy was halfway through her pregnancy she felt bonded to the baby and dreaded the minute possibility of a complication.

Deciding to distract herself from morbid thoughts she grabbed at the nearest magazine. The action brought Will's gaze to hers and he gave a tight smile. He was terrified too. She gave his hand a quick squeeze in reassurance and opened the publication. The page she landed on was an article about a water birth. Inspiring no doubt, but not what she needed to read about right now. She put it back down quickly.

"Mr and Mrs Horsley?" The receptionist called from behind her high desk. "You can go in now."

They walked into the examination room and both took an audible deep breath.

*   *   *

"Everything looks perfect," the Sonographer commented and Izzy felt like crying in relief. "Your tests have all come back from your last check up and they too are fine. Looks like you have yourself a textbook pregnancy."

"Fantastic," boomed Will, his voice hoarse from keeping deathly silent while staring intently at the ultrasound screen. "And... can you tell what it is? Or is it too soon still?"

"I'm happy to look for you. We should be able to see quite clearly at this stage, but there's always a chance we could be wrong. Now let's see...." she moved the transducer round the bottom of Izzy's belly to the other side and pressed slightly deeper into the skin.

The picture on the screen was fairly indeterminate to the untrained eye. Gone was the solid outline of the skull and the waving digits at the end of the still skinny limbs. What filled the screen looked static and fuzzy, but the Sonographer said 'ah-ha' with definite recognition.

"What is it?" Izzy squeaked, her voice restricted with excitement and anticipation.

"It looks like a... yep, looks like a girl!" The Sonographer grinned as she turned to Izzy and Will who both beamed back at her.

"A son and a daughter," Will breathed in awe. Izzy grinned up at him and took his hand. He squeezed it while not taking his eyes off the screen. "So how do you know it's a girl and doesn't have, you know... bits," he asked inelegantly.

The Sonographer laughed and pointed out more vague shapes on the scan, while Izzy lay back and sighed with happiness.

*   *   *

Sarah sat at her work desk mulling over the brochure in front of her. She was meant to be proofreading it for a team building company, advertising their package deals. It was littered with mistakes, bad grammar and punctuation, with a dull, uninteresting tone running throughout. It should have been an easy job, anything would have been an improvement compared to the original, but Sarah's mind just couldn't focus.

She was awaiting a phone call from Izzy, whom she knew was at her hospital appointment. Having received a text message that morning from Izzy, apologising for not picking up the phone (Henry had been up all evening with a poorly tummy and had clung like a limpet to Mummy) and with the time of the appointment.

Coupled with her previous evening with Kris, Sarah's mind was buzzing with everything other than work. She hadn't slept well last night, the first time in weeks that she'd had a disturbed sleep. She didn't know whether she should call Tessa and tell her of her ex's visit, or to leave it well alone.

On top of that was the pressing memory of her conversation with her mum. She was about to follow her mother's advice and take life into her own hands.

"Becca, have you got a minute?" Sarah asked as she hovered over Becca's desk, mobile phone firmly shoved in her pocket awaiting the call.

"Sure," Becca looked up from her computer and smiled.

I can do this, thought Sarah. I'm a grown woman and I'm perfectly capable of organising a girl's night out.

"I really enjoyed the night out last month. I was thinking we could all do it again. I noticed there's a new bar opening up on Main Road next Friday. They've got a whole evening of specials, so I'm going to book a table for whoever wants to join me," Sarah explained, pleased with how confident she sounded.

"Sounds great," Becca enthused. "You hear that Verity?" she called behind her. Verity, who had obviously been eavesdropping nodded excitedly. "I'll be there. I'll bring my sister too. She's in town next weekend."

"Great. I'll email you all the details. Invite who you want, the more the merrier," and with that Sarah turned and walked back to her desk.

She wondered if the pull of the bar had more to do with their resounding 'yes' than Sarah's company itself, but she didn't care. For the first time in several years, she'd taken the initiative and allowed herself to step out of her comfort zone in order to make new friends. It seemed there was a glimmer of her former self starting to peek through the thick grey clouds.

She returned to her struggle with the brochure for a few more minutes, then slipped out the office and into the kitchenette. Turning on the kettle she checked her phone for the eighteenth time. Still no message or missed call.

She busied herself making coffee and allowed her thoughts to swing back to Tessa and her inability to commit. Sarah certainly didn't see herself as a matchmaker, nor was about to offer her services as one, but she wished she could help Tessa see sense. Neither could she comprehend why Tessa had chosen to run from her relationship. Sarah didn't know Kris, but if Tessa's friends, not to mention her parents, had all taken his side in the break up, she could hazard a guess that he was a good guy.

Sarah's phone rang, shocking her from her reverie. She grabbed it clumsily and excitedly with both hands and pressed the answer button.

"Hello?"

"Hi love. Sorry to ring you at work. I just thought you ought to know I've been doing some research for you about the Edwardian period. A fascinating time in British history, I must say," Pippa's voice rang out. "Come around for dinner this weekend and I'll show you what I've got. How did the National Archives pan out?"

"Hi Mum." Sarah fiddled with the handle of the coffee mug. "I'd love to come over. I'm having lunch with Izzy on Saturday, but I'm free all Sunday."

"That's great. Come for Sunday lunch then, about one o'clock."

"Will do. Oh, and I've not yet checked the National Archives. Dermot wants to be involved, so he's coming around Friday night after work. I think he might need to do some digging around to find out some more background on the house."

"Yes, the more information he knows the better. These searches can be tricky."

"Okay Mum, I'd better go. See you Sunday."

"Bye love."

Sarah made her way back to her desk and the dreaded brochure. Taking a sip of coffee, she sat down and tried to focus her mind on the task ahead. Within seconds her phone rang again. Bolting back into the kitchenette Sarah answered on the third ring.

"Hello?"

"It's a girl!" came the shriek of an ecstatic Izzy.

Sarah narrowly avoided shrieking back, given the close proximity of the office beyond. "That's great!" she gave as upbeat a whisper as possible.

"Will's beside himself, can't stop jabbering on about it. One of each, Sarah. How lucky are we?!"

Sarah smiled, equally for her best friend's news as for the unconscious joy in which Izzy had shared it. Too many times Sarah's friends had skirted around their good news, and certainly would never have used the phrase 'how lucky am I' through fear of upsetting Sarah. In reality she would have been delighted for them, but was often still treated like the victim.

"Very lucky Iz, I'm so thrilled for you. We'll have to celebrate with some non-alcoholic sparkling wine on Saturday."

"Urgh! I can't wait to have a glass of proper wine again. Where are we going?"

"It's a restaurant deli called Amber's. The menu looks amazing."

That was the advantage of her jaunt down Main Road the other night. She had memorised several venues that she hadn't previously known about and that looked like nice places to try.

"I'm going to dress up!" Izzy enthused. "I think I might still have one dress that fits me. All my maternity dresses are comfortable, but hardly glamorous."

"What about the pretty white wrap around with forget me nots?"

"I've worn that about a dozen times since Easter. Uh uh, I want to wear something more special. Something that makes me feel attractive."

"In that case, I'll put your hair up in the messy bun you like."

"Yes please! Can I borrow that gorgeous lipstick of yours too? The bright red one you wore at our Christmas party."

Sarah grinned. It was wonderful to chat with Izzy like this again. Both women had become caught up with the seriousness of life of late, and Sarah found it thrilling to just enjoy the relative banality of discussing their day out.

"Sure, I remember the one. I'll keep it out for you. Congratulations again on the good news. Pass on my love and congratulations to Will."

"Will do. See you Saturday Sarah. I can't wait."

Chapter Nineteen

It was the random text message from Tessa that made up Sarah's mind. It had come through on Thursday evening, as Sarah sat at the dining room table trying to catch up on work, she'd missed with all the distractions during the previous work day.

Hey gal, did I leave my Jo Malone candles in your bathroom cupboard? Can't find them anywhere. Panicking.

The text message had sparked a 'how are you' conversation, during which Sarah dug out the candles from the bathroom and filled Tessa in on Will and Izzy's news.

Having a house warming next Saturday. Bring Dermot.

Sarah suppressed the niggle of irritation at Tessa's flippancy. Having been witness to Kris' heartbreak just a few days ago, she wondered if Tessa really realised the destruction left behind her. Most likely not. Either that or she didn't care.

Going against her natural tendency to not interfere, Sarah decided she needed to do some stirring. If Tessa wasn't going to choose to see sense on her own accord, maybe some gentle nudging would help.

I'll be there. Will ask Dermot. Might be busy though.

She'd attend the house warming quite happily. And while she was there, she intended to get the truth out of Tessa, once and for all.

*   *   *

Dermot stared at the email in his inbox. He reread it for the eighth time and gave a small satisfactory smile. Following on from the phone call earlier that morning, the agent had been quick to email the confirmation. Dermot's offer on the cottage had been accepted.

The excitement that had been missing from his life the last six months was reignited. The regular job hours hadn't done it. The cycling and racing hadn't even sparked the same reaction. He was a property developer through and through and he was finally done denying it. The exhaustion of the Edwardian project had faded into a vague memory and he was ready to get out there and conquer the next challenge.

Perusing the contents of the email again and imagining the possible development in detail, he gave a cursory glance at the clock to see if it was time. It was. Shutting his laptop, he tucked it under his arm and made his way up to Sarah's flat.

Sarah was enjoying the sanctuary of the roof terrace. With the warmer and lighter evenings, she had taken herself up there almost every day after work. It was peaceful, even with the slight hum of traffic and commuters below the building.

Today she needed the peace more than ever. With the sudden busy direction her life was taking, her thoughts inevitably backtracked to Alex. It happened every time. It was as if her sub-conscious tried to punish her every time she seemed to make any positive social steps forward. There was a lingering guilt that she could be starting to enjoy life. That she could be considering enjoying other's company. That she could be making a new life away from the one she'd shared with her husband.

She'd spent the whole day trying to bury her thoughts in work, but as soon as she'd returned home the guilt arrived with a vengeance. She knew it was fear speaking, it's crippling icy fingers trying to ensnare her back to a life half-lived. She fought it with every fibre of her being and knew from bitter experience that the fear would eventually retreat again. It no longer scared her like it had to begin with. She now knew its limits and that gave her a sense of power over it. But it had become a nuisance, a distraction, and one she could certainly live without.

Hearing the faint knock of her door Sarah broke her reverie and returned to the flat.

"Evening," Dermot said in welcome.

"Come in," Sarah waved him through.

"Thanks for agreeing to see me on a Friday night. I'm sure you had more exciting offers than this?"

She gave him a look. "I'd put off any night out for this. A chance to find the girl behind the diaries? Far more exciting than a loud club and cheap nasty tasting drinks."

"My kind of girl," Dermot joked and turned to place his laptop on the kitchen counter. Sarah's cheeks blushed at his comment and was glad he couldn't see her face. He had obviously meant it light heartedly and in jest, but Sarah wasn't used to being complemented in that way.

"Hmm," she cleared her throat. "A drink?"

"Sure, what have you got?"

"Coffee, tea, a bottle of white and a few dregs of Pimms. But no lemonade."

"Ah, then a glass of wine please."

"Make yourself at home," she pulled the bottle out of the fridge and poured the contents into two wine glasses. Dermot sat down on the sofa and drew the coffee table closer to rest his feet on. It was an oddly intimate gesture, as if he belonged in the flat. In a way he did. He owned the building.

"Oops, you don't mind, do you?" he asked, noticing her glance.

"Normally I'd take offence, yes. But not with you," she pondered. "I think it's either because you can be quite inoffensive and charming, or that you're my landlord and I don't want to get on the wrong side of you."

Dermot laughed, the same rich laugh she'd heard before. She liked it. "No excuses. Tell me to get my damn feet down if you want to. I won't put a strike against your name, honest."

"It's fine really," she handed him his glass and powered up her own laptop, resting on the other end of the coffee table. "I'm really hoping we can find out some information tonight. I feel so connected to this family. I just have to try to track them down. I'll regret it if I don't."

"Any hint in the journals?"

"Not really. Nor's life seems so confined to the house or the local area. There's really little to pinpoint. For instance, she never really mentions what her father does, which would be a great help to us. I'm not sure she even knew. Maybe it wasn't acceptable then, for a child to know their father's profession? Certainly not a girl. And yet Nor is so curious and feisty and sure of her own mind. I can't imagine her being ignorant of that information. Perhaps she omitted it for a reason?"

"These journals sound very intriguing. Have you finished with them yet?"

"I've only just finished the first, I'm afraid. I've jotted down anything of interest, but like I said there's little, if anything, that'll help us with our search. My notes are more made up from information about the layout of the house, that kind of thing. Did you know my flat used to house her bedroom, the boy's nursery and staff quarters?"

Dermot thought for a moment then nodded with recollection. "I do remember Barbara, the previous owner, mentioning something about the conversion her father had done all those years ago. Something about the children and staff being confined to the top floor. Before these bay windows and the open plan layout the rooms up here would have been poky and dark. Hardly a nice environment for children."

"Did she mention anything else?" Sarah asked, feeling excited. She was finally getting a picture in her mind, after weeks of pure imagination.

"She talked a lot about the state of the place when her father bought it. Peeling wallpaper, bad plumbing, that kind of thing. But it had been empty a while and she was young herself, so couldn't remember too much. She was in her early sixties when she sold to me two years ago. She'd inherited it from her parents."

"Did her father ever mention the previous owners to her?"

"I don't think so. Remember her family only bought it in the early fifties. It must have belonged to someone else before then, and was empty a good few years during the war. I don't know if it would have been your family. It seems they were a while before then."

"Yes, the early twentieth century. Unless the house stayed in the family when the children grew up. But knowing the family's financial difficulties I'm not sure if that was even possible."

"Let's start this search then," Dermot jumped up to get his own laptop. "Hopefully all the information will be on this website."

They sat down together and each opened a browser on their respective computers. Typing in the right website address they spent a good half hour searching through the National Archives menus. After dead ends searching for a person they didn't know the surname of, nor the exact age of the house (Dermot had left his household documents at work, having perused them during the day in preparation for this evening), they stumbled across the 1901 census.

A redirection took them to a new site, whereupon entry of the address, parish and area, they could pay to access the results online. Fortunately, Dermot had remembered the details of the parish from his documents, and heaving a sigh of relief, they were let through to the payment section of the site.

"That was lucky. The parishes change over time. It wouldn't have recognised the address if that had differed," Dermot explained. Sarah, not keen to miss a thing, but wanting to give Dermot his privacy while he entered his credit card details, returned to the kitchen to top up their glasses.

Her pulse was racing. The previous half hour had been tense. Uncertainty of what to look for, while trying to navigate an unfamiliar website, mixed with trepidation of the possible search results, was a gut twisting experience.

She took a deep gulp of wine to steady her nerves.

"Okay, here we go," Dermot announced and she felt her heart constrict. Tentatively approaching the back of the sofa, she peeked over his shoulder. The webpage had opened a document, filled with spidery scrawled script, in a font that was too small for her to view from that distance. She moved closer, taking her seat beside Dermot.

They scanned the document for a few minutes, before Dermot almost made her jump out of her skin by pointing and exclaiming, "There!"

Before her were several of the names that her life had become entwined with. Frederick, Margaret and Eleanor. Neither sons, Alfred or Frederick Junior seemed to have yet been born. The addition of a fourth name surprised Sarah. Another girl, two years younger than Eleanor was documented. Her name was

Beatrice.

Sarah swallowed as she realised that this daughter, and sister to Eleanor, had never been mentioned in the journals. Sarah knew that childhood mortality was far higher in those days and she choked back the sudden sense of loss. She realised it also explained the large age gap between Nor and her brothers. It began to make sense.

She scanned the document again and took in the limited, but valuable, information. Apart from the discovery of another sibling, what really stood out was the missing detail that would hopefully assist their search further.

Alongside Frederick Senior's Christian name was the surname that Sarah had been wondering on for weeks. The scrawling font revealed the family name. Bartley. Mr and Mrs Frederick Bartley.

Chapter Twenty

Sarah felt numb and excited all at the same time. She finally had a family name. It was a small victory, but tangible and was something concrete. The next part of the search was an alien unknown, but for that evening she could rest knowing that she was a step closer.

"How do we go about finding more information?" Dermot asked.

"I don't really know. I guess we could look in the local records office for any more information. Or look at local news archives for obituaries. I get the feeling this is just the beginning. It could be a long search."

Contemplating the depth of research they would have to do, Sarah sank into the sofa with a heavy sigh. She hoped it would be easier than she feared.

Dermot sat back with a pensive look on his face. "I agree, we'll head down to the local archives and see what they've got. They might not have anything, but there could be lots of information. Especially if the father was an influential figure in the local community."

Sarah stood and began to pace. "Okay. We'll do that. There must be newspaper articles. Deaths, marriages, perhaps even births. Hopefully it'll give us a better picture of their lives and what might have happened to them."

Dermot smiled. "Sarah sit; you'll wear a trail in my expensive carpet." Sarah blushed at the joke, suddenly remembering that Dermot was in fact her landlord and not just a friend. Were lines getting blurred here?

She sat down and took hold of her glass of wine. She sipped it contemplatively.

"Right. We've had a successful evening. We might not have much else right now, but we do have a surname," Dermot continued. "I suggest we leave it here for now and relax for the rest of the evening. We can ramp up the search next week."

She looked at him incredulously. "I've spent the last two months letting this family into my head. I wish I could let go of it so easily," she gave a sigh. "But you're right, I do need to relax. Otherwise I'll be up all night, unable to sleep."

She already suspected she would be. Her thoughts were currently processing at light speed.

"You really care about this don't you?" Dermot asked, a gentle amusement across his features.

Sarah tried to spit out a witty reply, but no retort came to mind. She supposed the avid interest of a fourteen-year-old Edwardian's journal was a strange thing to understand. She didn't entirely understand it herself. She just hated Dermot calling her out on it. She didn't want him thinking her weird.

"It's a mystery," she tried to explain. "I need to know what happened to them if possible. Knowing that they slept under this same roof, going through the tragedies and hardships that they did, with Eleanor facing such an unknown future. Wouldn't you want to find out what had happened to them? Or at least try?

It's like a great novel half finished. It just ends when you're getting to a really good bit, and you're desperate to discover what happens to the characters and how the story develops. Except this is real life, with real consequences and broken dreams. Real choices that have led their subsequent family members to where they are today. I simply can't throw in the towel yet. It's not even an option."

"Well, I'm glad I've got you on the team then," Dermot grinned. "Determination. Passion. Drive. There's little chance we *won't* find what we're looking for with those attributes on board."

Sarah would never have naturally thought herself any of those things. "You're teasing me."

"Not at all. I don't think you realise you've got it in you. But you do; in bucket loads. You're a lot stronger than you give yourself credit for."

If only he knew, she thought wryly. If only he knew what she had learned to be strong about.

"Top up?" she asked instead.

$*$ $*$ $*$

The evening was late and Sarah had spent two hours enjoying Dermot's easy-going nature and a shared sense of humour. In all reality she didn't want the evening to end. He was funny, easy to talk to and seemed genuinely interested in what she had to say.

They'd swapped anecdotes about work, laughed about Dermot's various cycling mishaps and shared basic history about their families. She was enjoying their evening so much that she hadn't noticed the time and was only alert to the late hour by Dermot's attempt to hide a yawn.

"Sorry," he apologised. "I know it's only eleven, but I was up early this morning training. I'm going to have to crash soon."

"Sure," Sarah practically leapt up, not because she wanted him to go, but because she didn't want to impose.

"Thanks for the great evening," Dermot smiled warmly, standing up and facing her as he reached for his coat.

She returned his smile in reply and reluctantly showed him to the door. The thought of spending more time with him, during their investigation into the Bartley family, was a rather nice one.

"Oh, by the way," he stopped in the doorway suddenly. "The council accounts have arrived. I'll email you the bill tomorrow morning. If you wouldn't mind paying it promptly please, that would be great."

Sarah felt her euphoria plummet to earth with a bump. Here was the second reminder of the evening that Dermot was in fact her landlord, first and foremost. The relaxed atmosphere had instantly switched to a business like one and she said goodbye rather flatly.

Powering down her laptop, she headed to the bedroom and grabbed the second journal waiting on the bedside table.

*   *   *

09th March 1908

The loss of Housekeeper's departure at Christmas still resounds through the household. Nanny spent a full week in bed with grief and I was forced to step into her well worn shoes. I had never imagined the full drudgery of life below stairs before this last year. I had of course observed the comings and goings with avid interest. But it was with a detached air of someone who had never worked a day in their life, observing yet not appreciating the scenes before me.

Now it is with great respect that I hold my opinion of all those who have served my family. Mundane conversations at social events no longer entertain my interest. The triviality of my peers' lives and what they consider of great import now irritates me. I find it increasingly difficult to stay captured by the joviality and opulence I have at times been cocooned within.

Father's work situation is as dire as ever. Imports are slacking and money is drying up, according to minute snippets of conversation I have overheard. He pretends in high society that all is well. But his countenance at home tells the truth of our situation.

Dinner parties are few. I am still not out, having turned fifteen already. This is despite my mother's best attempts to persuade father. She sees it a fortunate time now. Her reasoning is to marry me off before the truth of my father's financial affairs can be made public. He has so far refused, his denial proving my respite for now.

Nanny and I spend our days preparing food for the household, keeping the fires burning in this long and cold winter and tutoring the boys until they reach school age later this year. I do not know if father will be able to send them away for their education, or even afford a professional tutor. I suspect he will make every effort to achieve one option of the two,

137

otherwise all society will know of our circumstances before long.

Sarah looked up at her bedside clock. It was nearing midnight. Despite the tiredness nagging at her mind, she was alert enough to note the new snippets of information in Eleanor's first entry. She had mentioned her father's company and how it related somehow to imports. It certainly wasn't a lot to go on, but was the first hint to what Frederick's profession was.

She felt as if she was slowly putting together the pieces of a gigantic puzzle. Each piece was crucial but there were still so many more to go.

Turning off the lamp and lying down she let out a huge sigh of someone having had an exhausting but exhilarating experience. Despite her earlier concerns she now had no doubt she would sleep soundly that night.

*   *   *

Izzy spent a full hour in front of the mirror, getting ready for her lunch with Sarah. She honestly couldn't remember the last time she'd had a day off to herself, to spend how she chose with whom she chose. It felt like a holiday.

She was back in the dress she'd been so desperate to wear. Navy blue with a sequinned neckline, the knee length dress still managing to create the illusion of a waistline. However, she had become self conscious by the amount of leg showing. Her ankles already felt swollen and her legs developed varicose veins in her first pregnancy and had never gone away.

She had pulled it off hastily and thrown on some black linen trousers and a sparkly silver top. However, the top had strained across her increased bust and the trousers adorned a suspicious stain, which looked a lot like a toddler's snotty smear.

Several changes later and she still wasn't happy. Reaching for the original dress of choice she reasoned she could just hide her legs under the restaurant table. It was by far the easiest option.

Having nearly ran out of time for her makeup, she quickly applied some smoky eye shadow, mascara and tinted moisturiser. Sarah was bringing the bright red lipstick and had offered to do Izzy's hair.

"You look lovely," Will admired from the doorway.

She started. "I didn't know you were there."

"Only just now. I've got Henry down for his nap. Now you go and have some fun and don't worry about us."

The doorbell ran downstairs. Sarah had arrived.

*   *   *

"And then he puts his favourite car in my tea, bursts into tears and won't take it back, even when I've cleaned it and reassured him that the 'engine' still works!" Izzy laughed, snorting slightly. "He was so cute. I think the car dripping from the tea was all a bit too much for him. He's such a sweetheart."

Sarah laughed and took a satisfying sip of Rosé. "That's my Godson!"

"Oh..." Izzy smacked herself on the forehead. "I promised myself I wouldn't talk about Mum things today. Sorry Sarah."

Sarah waved it off. "I love hearing about him. I don't see Henry often enough. It's my own fault. I get so busy and then... well I'm not always a great friend at that point. I forget there's a whole world out there and before I know it Henry's grown another inch taller."

"Pah! You've got a fast-paced job, glamorous new flat, cute landlord; you don't want to be hanging out with a tired and pregnant best friend any more than you have to," Izzy joked.

Sarah decided to ignore the 'cute landlord' comment and focus on her wine glass for a moment. "But you are feeling better about being home with Henry though?"

"Yeah," Izzy sighed. "I am. I've realised that I have plenty of time to get stuck into my career again after this one arrives. I've actually found some possible options for when the baby's past the newborn stage. There's a couple of sales companies; cosmetics, high end products, that kind of thing. I can go in as a rep, work from home, drum up sales on social media and networking sites, train and train up others. It's something I can do with small children. I can choose my own hours and how much I earn is up to how much effort I put in. It's actually ideal. I've always known I'm good at selling things."

"It's not a pyramid scheme, right?" Sarah ventured cautiously.

"Oh no," Izzy shook her head vehemently. "Loads of cosmetic companies sell online these days. They make full use of social media, blogging, videos, all that kind of thing. It's the new way of selling. Door to door just doesn't work anymore. People want 'instant', they want to be able to order without the inconvenience of a sales spiel or to have to go to a shop. It'll be my own little business and we'll see where it goes from there."

"You've obviously done a lot of research."

"I just want to be prepared Sarah. I'm finally happy with the idea of being at home for now. You were right. The challenge of being a mum was more an issue than even having a job. I felt like I was drowning. I thought it was lack of direction making me feel like that. But I've realised that uncertainty in my ability as a mum was causing most of my frustration.

But I have also realised that I do need something eventually. I'm not made to hide inside four walls, away from people and the big wide world. When the time is right, when I feel able to attempt it, I at least now have options," Izzy stopped and took a large sip of her virgin margarita.

"Well I'm pleased for you Izzy. And you'll be great in sales. It definitely is one of your strengths," Sarah said as she contemplated Izzy's words. She too recognised how she had been hiding away from the world at large.

"I've organised another work night out," she blurted out self consciously.

"That's good. You've been there long enough. You need to start mingling a bit more."

"I'm not sure if anything is going to come of it."

"No matter. The important thing is you're putting yourself out there."

"Have I really become so dull and boring?" Sarah asked morosely.

"No, not at all. But here is your chance to develop friends without all the history and awkwardness you had after Alex died. Let's face it, many of our friends just didn't know how to handle the situation and you were the victim of it. It's understandable that you've wanted to protect yourself from all that crap. But here's an opportunity to make friends on your terms. They don't have to know your past and if you do decide to tell them, sure they'll sympathise, but they won't have that emotional trauma that our friends had. Your past is your past and your work colleagues aren't part of that."

Their food arrived and Izzy clapped her hands in delight. "I can't believe they had my favourite on the menu."

She looked down at the plate of arancini balls and dipping sauce, with a grin of delight. Just what she'd been craving.

Sarah admired her bowl of carrot and fennel soup, with a crusty artisan roll on a side plate. She wasted no time tucking in. Deciding that a lighter tone of conversation was needed, Sarah wiped her mouth with the napkin and looked Izzy in the eye.

"So, tell me more about your attempts at potty training Henry...."

Chapter Twenty One

"Searching the local archives is certainly the best place to start," Pippa concurred, as Sarah filled her mum in on the details of the search so far. "There's websites too that could help find out records about a person. Also, consider posting on forums."

Sarah never failed to be amazed by her mother's vast knowledge. They were sharing a big bowl of homemade chocolate mousse Pippa had made in preparation for her daughter's visit. David had already taken a large portion and escaped to his workshop as soon as the dinner plates were cleared from the table.

"It was a fascinating era. Victorian and then Edwardian Britain really ushered in a new age for England," Pippa mused, as she lifted another full spoonful to her lips. "The Suffragette movement, compulsory education and then the First World War were instrumental in changing societies perceptions and ways of living."

"Eleanor talked about the Suffragettes and how she admired them."

"No doubt she did. For the first time women of all ages and class structures came together to fight for their right to vote. Not only that, but for the right to proper education and jobs. There were very little opportunities for women before. Either a life as a servant to someone, especially if you were lower class, or a life of marriage and children, with no aspirations or expectations beyond that.

Of course, in my generation we couldn't wait to marry and have children either, nothing wrong with that. Raising children is one of the hardest jobs going, let alone a career on top. But at least we had the choice, and like many of my friends, we all enjoyed careers outside the home as well as being wives and mothers."

"It was what Eleanor wanted more than anything," Sarah reflected. "She was so scared that her father's failing business would hinder that. She didn't want to just get married off like her friends."

"There were many women starting to feel the same way as Eleanor, at least from what I've seen from my research," Pippa agreed. She paused in thought.

"You mentioned a while back about a photograph of a woman. You said it looked more like a newspaper cutting. I wonder if it's connected to the Suffragettes, or perhaps someone else Eleanor admired?"

"Could be. Do you think we could track down the original article?"

"It'll be a long shot. Unless there's a convenient date printed on it. Or if it's a famous suffragette... that'll certainly make it easier."

Sarah dipped her own spoon back into the bowl and glanced out the kitchen window to the garden beyond. Hints of summer were beginning to show, with many of the trees and bushes in full flower already. There was a lazy warmth to the air that remind Sarah strongly of beaches and picnics in the countryside.

"I just want to know what happened to Eleanor. Whether she ever realised her dreams," she said, almost idly. She swayed her spoon from side to side.

"I'm sure she did in one way or another. Sometimes dreams have to change," Pippa said shrugging.

Sarah looked at her mum and nodded slowly. "Yes, sometimes they do," and helped herself to another huge scoop of chocolate mousse.

*   *   *

"Hey, it's Dermot. Apologies in advance. I'm going to be a bit scarce this week. Work related. So, I'm not going to be able to check out the local archives with you. Feel free to go by yourself, I know how much it means to you, so don't feel like you need to wait for me. Otherwise, we'll discuss it next week, when things calm down. Thanks."

Sarah listened to the answer machine message for the third time and sighed. She knew Dermot wasn't as enthusiastic as she was about the Bartley family, but she had hoped he'd make their search a priority. Although, she reasoned, work was a valid excuse. She herself had struggled to reach her deadlines this week and had put in a few extra hours.

Still she was disappointed.

At least Dermot had had the decency to let her know and hadn't left her hanging. She contemplated going without him, but realised she quite enjoyed his company. It was fun to spend time with him, especially when the search was so enthralling.

Picking up a mug of Horlicks (sleep had evaded her the night before and she was pre-empting any further attempt of insomnia), she headed up to the roof terrace, journal tucked under her arm.

The evening was mild and remnants of sunshine clung to the horizon. Within minutes twilight would start descending and the gradual transformation from day to the inky black of night would be complete.

Sarah opened the journal and continued her journey back into the

Edwardian world.

19th April 1908

Margaret Hewson is engaged. The official announcement was displayed in the local newspaper last evening and announced by my father over dinner. Father says her parents are delighted and an indulgent wedding is being planned for the summer months. She is but six months older than I.

Father showed a certain consternation as dinner progressed and I sensed my father's current thinking towards my own marital status begin to alter. I disappeared to the kitchen as soon as my absence was granted and busied myself in the soap suds, hiding a few betraying tears in the process.

22nd April 1908

I sit here on my bed, my fingers encrusted with the fat of the cooking pans, my nails chipped and my hair lank across my brow. I feel an utter exhaustion I had never thought possible. The thought, nay the idea, that I could be seen fit to be 'out' is almost laughable. If I had enough energy left to laugh.

My dear mother has visited this afternoon in the kitchen. I do not believe she has ever ventured there, but I envision a future where she may have to get used to it. Considering her news, if truth indeed, that father is considering me to be declared 'out' and actively attending social functions, the kitchen may well have need of another helper.

I am entirely aware that my social standing is a means to attract a suitable husband. My father has perhaps had a change of heart, or in the recent news of Margaret Hewson's engagement, perhaps my father's peers are asking questions of my own standing. I would think that was a higher likelihood.

Father will need me to marry quickly before his financial difficulties have been made public. I imagine I am still considered an advantageous proposition at this present time, but Father will have to act in haste. I am full of fear and doubt and trepidation.

Sarah shut the journal and took a deep breath. The thought of fifteen-year-old Eleanor sat on her bed, just metres below where Sarah now sat, depressed and facing an uncertain and frightening future, was too much for Sarah to bear.

Despite the warm evening she felt a chill. Suddenly the journals she'd found therapeutic had become like a blade piercing her skin. Sorrow mixed with fear flooded through her, before she'd had time to employ any of her coping methods.

She stood up, looked out over the violent pink sunset and sobbed. Raw pain coursed through her body and she doubled over. Her throat throbbed as the sobs came in quick succession.

"Alex," she shouted through her tears at the sky above. "Alex," she whispered hoarsely a second time.

It had been a long while since she'd allowed herself to cry and she stayed on the roof terrace until it was fully dark and every last tear had dried.

Chapter Twenty Two

"This place is great!" shouted Becca over the din. The bar was thriving, with crowds of patrons squeezed into the small building, and a long line of people waiting outside to get through the doors. Music pumped through the speaker systems and a few brave souls were already bobbing about on the dance floor.

The surrounding tables were a buzz of activity. Couples out on date nights sipped cocktails and enjoyed the ambience. Groups of friends laughed raucously amongst themselves, raising the average noise pollution levels to just bearable.

Quite a few patrons still wore their work clothes, suited up and letting their hair down after a long week at the office.

Becca, Sarah, Verity and her sister Anna, and Becca's housemate Amber had arrived an hour before and quickly settled at the reserved table. They'd wasted no time ordering tapas and drinks with crazy names.

Now, food finished along with several drinks each, and Becca was trying to drag her unfortunate colleagues onto the dance floor.

"Come on," she wailed. "No one will dance unless we kick things off."

Amber rolled her eyes and allowed herself to be dragged out of her seat. Sarah shook her head emphatically as Becca turned her attention in Sarah's direction.

"Uh uh," Sarah said, "I'm still eating," gesturing to the tiniest morsel left on her plate and the inch of drink in the glass. Becca shook her head in dismay.

"Poor excuse," she scowled. "Can't you dance or something?"

"I'll be there soon. I promise," Sarah couldn't really come up with any excuse, beyond the truth of simply not wanting to dance. A tense meeting at work with the corporate paying them ridiculous amounts of money for a campaign they kept moving the goal posts on, to the sleepless nights she'd endured most of the week, was a fair enough basis for how she feeling.

However, knowing she'd been the one to organise the evening, she felt guilty and didn't want to appear antisocial. She sighed. "One more drink, then I'll come."

Becca pulled Amber off to the dance floor looking as if she didn't trust Sarah one bit. Sarah was left alone at the table. Verity and Anna had bumped into some friends at the bar and had been chatting for ages.

Planning to be true to her word, Sarah approached the bar to order one more drink. She'd finish it and go dance for a few songs to placate Becca. As she waited to be served, a guy with blonde hair and stubble sat on a bar stool next to her and lifted a beer to his lips. He was wearing a grey work suit with a pale blue shirt underneath.

"You'll be waiting ages. I've not seen anyone served this end in at least five minutes," he said suddenly.

"Oh," Sarah answered, surprised by his attention.

"Yeah, there's a group of girls hanging out down there. I think one's from that trashy reality show that started last week. Seems to have caught everyone's attention, including the bar staff," he flashed a smile in amusement and Sarah found herself grinning back.

"Well in that case, I guess I'm far too unglamorous to be served."

"If it gets that desperate, I can take you to my local pub down the road and buy you a drink. No problems ordering there. Especially for an attractive woman like yourself."

Sarah was taken aback. His directness reminded her strongly of another. Images flooded her mind of the first time she'd met Alex. He had struck up conversation with her at a bar, again while waiting to be served. He'd asked her out immediately.

She felt uncomfortable, yet a strange mixture of excitement and nostalgia shot through her. Maybe this was a sign, perhaps just a bizarre coincidence; either way she seriously considered taking him up on his offer of a drink.

"What do you want luv?" the barman interrupted.

"Oh," she startled back to reality. "Um, just another house white please."

The stranger beside her had his eyebrow raised in amusement. "I guess I miss out on that drink then?"

"Well," she said, sounding bolder than she felt. "I could always join you here?" She took her drink from the barman and signalled toward the bar seat next to the stranger.

He nodded and lifted his drink in salute. "Absolutely. You won't hear a 'no' from me."

She grinned and pulled out the stool.

*   *   *

His name was Joe, he worked for the council (in a role he insisted wasn't dull or boring, and that he actually got to make some pretty important decisions) and now Sarah had his phone number. Having been dragged back to her table

146

by some overexcited work colleagues, she'd been forced to say goodbye.

"Who *is* that?" Becca shrieked with an equally hyped up Verity beside her.

"Yeah, I thought this was a girl only night out," Verity chirped with a look of mischievousness.

"He spoke to me first," Sarah shrugged, playing down her own excitement. "We chatted, that's all."

"Yeah?" Anna joined in. "What about the phone number on that piece of paper?"

"We swapped numbers, so what?" The girls squealed despite Sarah's monotone attempts to keep cool.

"You dark horse," Becca giggled. "I always assumed you were married or something, given that your... you know... a little... older than us," suddenly Becca looked horrified, matching the expressions of the other girls around the table.

She looked so mortified that Sarah decided to respond graciously. "No, I'm single," she smiled.

"Me too," Anna held up her drink in declaration.

"Long live the single life," Amber joined in. "Although not for you, you've met someone," she mused.

"He just gave me his number, it probably won't even get to a date."

She remembered the first date she had gone on after Alex's death. It was only eleven months later and she'd known she wasn't ready. But a misplaced determination to prove that she was fine led her to accepting the offer of a drink with a guy from the gym.

She'd spent the evening fighting back tears having realised her mistake and awkwardly trying to come up with interesting conversation. Gareth, her date, soon cut the evening short after seventeen minutes of absolute silence, with not one word spoken across the table.

Sarah had taken a taxi home, her relief complete as she unlocked her front door, only to then face a sleepless night. She hadn't called Gareth and hadn't heard anything else from him. It was another year before she felt brave enough to attempt a date with anyone else.

She had had dates since. Equally disastrous ones, some pleasant enough but with no real spark, and the odd one which had hinted heavily at promise.

But none had turned into a relationship. Usually by the third date it would fizzle out, any attraction on Sarah's behalf fading fast. In the earlier days it was easier to see why; comparisons to Alex, a memory that would trigger an overwhelming sense of grief. But after a while she no longer felt she had justification for the lack of success.

Only on the one occasion had she liked a guy enough to get past the two-week mark. His name was Edward, he was funny, self deprecating and intelligent. She enjoyed their conversations and felt comfortable around him, as if she'd known him for years. She had honestly thought this one might be different. And then he'd told her he was still in love with his ex.

She did the kind thing and let him go. But it had left a wound that stopped her from dating again in a hurry.

Now, with the first phone number for months in her hand, she wondered what, if anything, might come of it. It was only Joe's spontaneity, not unlike Alex's, that had caught her attention, otherwise she'd have ordered her drink and carried on her evening unaware.

But maybe now was the right time to take a risk. To call the number and see what may come. Sarah was tired of living in the past. The last few months of deliberately forcing herself to move forward proved that. She needed to make some things happen, things that perhaps were nestled in the elusive and alarming step three, the one she'd been avoiding.

She couldn't avoid it forever and she was beginning to suspect that she no longer wanted to.

Chapter Twenty Three

"Ahh, you came!" shrieked Tessa and threw her arms around Sarah, practically dragging her through the front door, before she'd had a chance to admire Tessa's bright red a-line dress and matching heels. "It's been ages since we spoke and I wasn't sure you'd get my message. You know what? I've actually missed you! I really have."

"Um, thanks?" Sarah tried to not be offended. Although, she thought, that was fairly generous of Tessa to say so, seeing as Sarah couldn't say the same in return. Nothing against Tessa as such, Sarah was just relieved to have her own space again.

"Come through. It's still a bit quiet. I do hope more people turn up," Tessa mused and led Sarah into the kitchen. As with most parties a crowd had formed in the room, hanging out as close to the drink and snacks as possible.

"You've met my housemates already," Tessa waved at them briefly.

"Hi, I'm Brett." An Aussie guy stepped forward and offered his hand in a shake. Slightly scruffy, in a mustard yellow shirt that had seen better days, he smiled warmly.

The others simply nodded, each holding half finished drinks and looking warily at the strangers beginning to invade their home.

"Sarah," she offered her name and helped herself to a glass of wine.

"Ollie," grunted a guy in the corner with thick afro hair sticking up in all directions and wearing purple thick rimmed glass.

"Yasmine," said a short attractive and freckled red head, standing with her arm through Ollie's as if daring anyone to try claim him for themselves.

"You remember Catherine from the deli, right?" Tessa's voice was over bright as if glossing over the fact that most of her friends still weren't talking to her. Perhaps Catherine, who Sarah couldn't ever remember hearing of before, was an invite out of desperation.

"Hi," waved Catherine with a smile. She had short bleach blonde hair and was wearing a nineteen fifties style prom dress. "This is Pete my husband."

The guy next to her nodded, exposing the start of a long tattoo from the

149

base of his neck.

Sarah smiled and nodded back at them.

"And this is our neighbour Andy," Tessa continued. A rather bashful looking man stood in the far corner, nursing a drink, with an expression of someone wondering if accepting the invite was such a good idea.

"Of course, there's someone here you do all ready know," Tessa eyes twinkled with mischief.

"Oh?"

"Well, I had asked you to invite him, which is why I wasn't sure you'd got my message, so I invited him myself," Tessa tutted. "He went to take a phone call, he'll be back soon."

Knowing who she was referring to, Sarah's stomach took a dive. It startled her. She hadn't seen him in days and wasn't prepared for that reaction. She had swapped numbers with another man just the evening before, for goodness sake. It made no sense.

"Hi Sarah," said a familiar easy-going voice, from the door behind her.

"Oh hi," she forced herself to sound casual as she peeked around and gave him a nonchalant but friendly nod. Suddenly what she had come to the party to do seemed low on her list of priorities and she fought to get her thoughts back in gear.

Dermot entered the kitchen and helped himself to a drink. He was wearing a red checked shirt and blue jeans and looked, Sarah couldn't help notice, rather good.

She smoothed a hand self consciously down her emerald green Grecian style dress and lifted a glass of wine to her lips with her other hand. She mentally shook herself. She hadn't had this reaction to Dermot before and it unnerved her.

Tessa, not noticing any tension, strode over to Dermot and began to enthusiastically engage in conversation with him. Sarah suppressed her irritation over Tessa's confident display and used it as an opportunity to pull herself together.

The guests began to show up over the next half hour. Despite Tessa's recent falling out with many of her friends, Sarah couldn't help but be impressed by the turnout. Tessa had no problem attracting new acquaintances and soon the house was packed.

"Hey," Dermot sidled up to Sarah in the living room. "Sorry I've been scarce this week."

"Oh, no problem," she said, keeping up the nonchalance. "It's been a really busy time for me too."

"So, you didn't get down to the local record offices then?" Sarah couldn't tell if he was irritated or not, but the abruptness in which he asked surprised her.

"No. I thought you'd have wanted to come," she replied, a hint of annoyance creeping into her voice.

"I do, but I've a lot going on and you shouldn't feel like you need to wait for me."

This was news to her. She knew he wasn't as passionate about the search as she was, but she'd thought her enthusiasm had been infectious and he had certainly shown plenty of interest previously.

"Amazingly enough I've had a lot on too. It was only out of courtesy that I waited for you," she replied, knowing that wasn't quite true. "I'll make my own plans, then shall I?" Sarah knew she was being uncharacteristically catty, but her defences were down.

Dermot frowned slightly. "I don't mind coming with you Sarah. But I thought you'd understand after my phone message the other day."

"Well, if you still want to that's fine," she found herself back peddling, realising the conversation was getting out of control. "I just didn't want you to feel under pressure."

He frowned again. Clearly Sarah's retaliations had thrown him off.

"What are you two chatting about?" Tessa swung into view, looking very much like the cat who got the cream. She always had loved being the hostess and centre of a party.

"Nothing much," Sarah mumbled and decided now was her chance. "Tess, I need a word in private please."

"Oh?"

"Yes, this way," Sarah beckoned, leading Tessa to her bedroom and leaving a confused Dermot in their wake.

Tessa's room had barely improved. Most of her clothes were thrown over the backs of two chairs and stuffed into her bags which lay underneath. A small chest of drawers contained the rest of her belongings, with a cluttered surface of toiletries and make up.

"I'm still settling in," Tessa hastily explained. Sarah raised her eyebrows. "You didn't get any further with the furniture then? Look Tessa, I can shout you the money to go down to the High Street and get yourself a cheap wardrobe. They're not expensive. You really can pick up a reasonable quality one for very little."

"You've already done so much for me," Tessa waved off the offer, yet her eyes lit up, suggesting it had piqued her interest.

"Or maybe you could go and fetch the furniture that is rightfully yours," Sarah dove in.

Tessa's eyes narrowed and her eyes flickered to the chairs serving as a temporary wardrobe. "It's fine as it is. I'm managing," her voice was dull and resigned, an opposite to the jovial and carefree hostess she'd portrayed during the evening.

Deciding to jump right in and get the painful bit over with Sarah said, "I saw him a few weeks ago Tessa."

"Who?"

"You know who. Kris. He told me how you left the day after you'd spoken about marriage. Why did you do that Tessa? Are you afraid?"

"What? How? How did you see him Sarah?" her tone was accusing.

"I bumped into him. It wasn't on purpose."

Tessa snorted. "How did you manage it then?"

"He was at your friend's gallery. I happened to be there for an exhibition and Kris was there hoping you'd show up. He's a wreck Tessa. He can't understand what happened and why you won't even talk to him about it. Even I can't understand why you've given up something which seemed so good, even by your own admission," Sarah said in exasperation.

"So, you thought you'd come to my party and ruin my evening, did you?" Tessa pouted. Her defensiveness was back and Sarah knew how impenetrable that could be.

"I'm not trying to ruin your evening. I'm trying to understand what went wrong and how I can help," Sarah replied, her voice softening.

Tessa threw her arms up in frustration. "Help? I ended a relationship. It happens every day. Why my relationship ending is such a big deal to you is the real question that needs answering."

"Tessa, you turned up at mine with no notice and with nowhere to go. You were clearly distraught, despite pretending otherwise, and you stayed with me a full month, never once giving satisfactory answers to my questions. I let it go. I let you stay in my home hoping you'd trust me and eventually explain. You didn't. Then I had a chance to meet Kris and hear his side.

And I'm sorry," Sarah sighed. "But I can't help but feel you're throwing away possibly the best thing that's ever happened to you."

"Why don't you get your own life sorted before you start telling me what to do?!" Tessa yelled.

"Tess, I'm not...."

"I came to you because I thought you'd understand. You've been through loss. I thought you wouldn't ask too many questions because you knew what it's like. I came to you because I never for a second thought you'd try and tell me what to do. That you'd just let me be. What an idiot I was."

"Tessa, come on. I did let you be. I let you into my life with very few questions. Many wouldn't have done that."

"Well, aren't you the martyr?" Sarah shook her head in exasperation, but Tessa wasn't done. "Poor old Sarah. The widow. The one we all tiptoe around so we don't upset you. You want to tell me what to do? Well let me tell you something. Alex isn't coming back. It's been seven years. Move on Sarah. Stop playing to the same tune and move on. Alex is dead!"

The fury in Tessa's eyes shocked Sarah more than her hurtful and cruel words. Sarah wanted to hit Tessa for her thoughtless attack, but the pain swimming in Tessa's tears calmed her down.

"We're not that much different Tess," Sarah said carefully, methodically. "You're hiding your own pain as much as I've been. Alex, now Kris. You won't let yourself be happy because you're hurting, just as I've done since the night I lost him. The difference is I've now made a choice. A choice to move forward with my life and reclaim what's been stolen from me. I'm not running away any more. When are you going to face how you're feeling and do the same?

I'm sorry if I've spoilt your party. That was not my intention. But I love you and I want to see you happy. If Kris can't do that, fair enough. But at least give him five minutes of your time to explain why. And then... well the rest is up to you," Sarah looked at Tessa saddened.

"I'll see myself out and I hope you can enjoy the rest of the evening."

She left Tessa's bedroom and walked to the front door, where she'd left her coat and bag. She slipped out without saying goodbye to anyone, not even noticing a confused and concerned Dermot watching her silently.

Chapter Twenty Four

Sarah arrived home at the flat with a weariness clinging to her. She'd fought against tears the whole way home, and now she'd arrived she just wanted to collapse in bed and sleep her emotions away. She hadn't expected her confrontation with Tessa to go well, but had hoped she'd at least listen to Sarah's reasoning.

Chucking her coat and bag on to the floor Sarah made her way to the bedroom, planning to just throw herself under her covers and worry about clothes and make up in the morning.

But in her peripheral vision she noticed a dark wet patch snaking out across the carpet in front of her, coming from the kitchen. She stopped, lifted her leg over it and peeked around the kitchen counter in trepidation. The entire kitchen lino was covered in a film of water and seemed to be coming from beneath the sink.

Sighing, she reached for her bag and phoned the letting agent. Given the time of night it went straight to voicemail, so she left a short message explaining the situation. Heading back into the kitchen, she waded across the small lake forming and reached the cupboard under the sink.

Inside the water pipe dripped steadily. She fumbled around trying to find the stopcock, located it and turned with all her might. It didn't move to begin with and she wrapped a dry tea towel around her palm to gain some friction. Trying again, the valve gradually turned and she managed to slowly turn it until the water stopped flowing.

Standing up she looked round in dismay at the carnage. The lino shimmered under a layer of water which led to the thoroughly sodden carpet beyond. Her weaved storage boxes, which housed numerous CDs and magazines glistened like dew under the lights. The bottom inch of the sofa was a darker shade where the water had seeped through the material.

The thought of phone calls to insurance companies and replacement furniture made her head spin. She sat down in the puddle on the lino floor, no longer caring if she got wet. Tessa's words still hurt and had numbed her to the discomfort of a wet backside.

The other phone call she feared to make was to Dermot. After their altercation at the party she wasn't looking forward to their first conversation since. It wasn't the kind of conversation she longed to have with any landlord but especially this one.

Well, she thought to herself, I've ruined one person's evening already. I might as well ruin another's.

She stood up and grimaced at the sodden feeling at the back of her clothing. Making her way to the counter she picked up her phone again and made the call.

"Hello?"

"Hi, Dermot. It's Sarah. Are you free to talk?"

"Sarah?" she could hear the confusion in his voice. "Sure. Where are you? I saw you leave. Are you back home already?"

He sounded concerned and she felt instantly reassured that they could recover from their falling out. "Yeah, I'm home. That's why I'm calling. Dermot, I've some bad news."

"What's happened?"

"There's been a leak in my flat. I've managed to get the water turned off, but I'm going to need a plumber in the morning and there's quite a lot of water damage."

"Crap!" he exclaimed and there was silence down the phone, apart from the distant hum of music, no doubt from Tessa's party. "I'll have to come home."

"No, don't do that," she said hastily. "I just wanted you to know. I've stopped it for now."

"But what if the water has seeped down to Greta's? She could have water damage too."

"Good point," Sarah conceded.

"Right," he gave a deep world-weary sigh. "I'll be home as soon as I can. Maybe you can check on Greta while you wait."

"Sure," she replied sheepishly. His brusque tone reminded that he was first and foremost her landlord. Any sense of friendship they shared took second place. The thought dismayed her.

Heading downstairs she knocked on Greta's door and surreptitiously checked out the ceiling above the hallway for telltale signs of water. Thankfully there was nothing.

"Oh, hello dear," Greta said, swinging the door open to reveal bright leopard print pyjamas. The flat was dark behind her.

"Oh, I am sorry. I didn't wake you, did I?" Sarah apologised.

"No dear, just a doing a bit of light reading in bed. I was out all evening last night for a concert recital and I've simply no energy left for anything this evening but an early night."

"Well, it's not that early any more. I'm sorry to bother you at this hour...."

Greta shook her head. "It only half past ten. I'm usually up until midnight. I've never needed much sleep. Tonight's an exception."

"Right. Well, I'm afraid to have to tell you, but I've had a water leak in my flat and I need to check if it's come through your ceiling or not. Dermot's on his way."

"Oh dear, well in that case you'd better come on through."

Greta switched on the living room light and beckoned Sarah in. There were no obvious stains or drips on the ceiling, but Sarah checked each room twice and stood staring at the living room ceiling directly below her own for some time.

She was still staring when Dermot arrived.

"Evening ladies," he addressed Greta more than Sarah and gave her only the briefest glance. Sarah felt too sheepish by her attitude toward him at the party to be offended by his now.

She stood hovering while Dermot checked over Greta's flat first and gave the all clear. Then she followed him up to hers. He swore as he pushed open the door and saw the dark stretch of water across the carpet.

"I know," she whispered, in what she hoped was a sympathetic way.

He shook his head. "I'll have to get on the phone first thing in the morning. I doubt a plumber will be able to help us out until Monday, but at least we can get things rolling on the insurance front."

"I phoned the letting agent...."

"Well they won't do anything until Monday either. Best I get on with it," Sarah felt chastised by his tone. She felt small and didn't like it, especially after the exhausting evening she'd had.

"Okay, I was just letting you know Dermot," she said abruptly, feeling very tired all a sudden. He lifted his head at her tone and looked her in the eye for the first time since arriving at the house.

"Annoyed with me again?" he said, folding his arms.

"Look, I'm sorry for how I was at the party. But you've been tense with me all evening too. I feel like I've done something wrong, but I'm not sure what."

"You haven't done anything wrong Sarah, but I'm exhausted and I feel like I'm being punished for it. I've had a hectic few weeks and yet I'm made to feel bad because I've not been around to search for the Bartleys. So yes, I've been a little tense perhaps, but you don't seem to understand that I haven't got time to just drop everything."

"And I have, is that what you're saying?" Sarah was apoplectic. How many more insults was she expected to endure that evening?

"For your information, I also have a very trying job and while I may not have the social life you seem to enjoy, I am a busy person too. I'm searching for this family because it means something to me. If it doesn't to you, then that's fine. But it wasn't long ago that you seemed interested in it too and then all of a sudden you go cold on it. Excuse me for being confused and a bit pissed off at you!"

They stared at each other in angry silence. For once Sarah was not going to back down for want of an easier life. Dermot had his own explaining to do and behaving as he was now was not helping matters. Sarah wasn't about to accept all the blame for their altercations.

"Fine," he said eventually. "I'm sorry for suddenly going quiet on you. You're right, this search is not a priority for me as it is for you. But I am interested. I had every intention of going to the records office with you, but work... and life, had just become too hectic right now."

"Then I'll do it on my own," Sarah said, sounding confident but secretly feeling disappointed that he wouldn't be joining the search. She decided not to pull on that thread.

"As long as you're happy about that?"

"Dermot, really, it's fine," she sighed, lying. "I'm sorry I snapped at you at the party. It was uncalled for."

He seemed satisfied with that and carried on assessing the flat. "Don't use any plug points or electricity until it's dried out. Oh, and keep the water off, obviously." He paused, "where are you going to stay?"

"What do you mean? Here of course."

"You can't stay here with the place like this. No electricity, no water. Not until Monday at least."

Sarah sighed. "I'm too exhausted to worry about that tonight. I'll sleep here. My bedroom is fine. I'll make a plan tomorrow."

Half an hour later Dermot finally left, satisfied that there was no imminent damage that would send the ceiling crashing down. Sarah saw him out and made her way to the bedroom.

Collapsing onto her bed, still dressed and with remnants of the evenings make up, she fell asleep in a matter of seconds.

*   *   *

Annoyed didn't seem a strong enough word. A water leak was the last thing he needed. What with the new house about to go through and drawing up plans for it, as well as his day job and training for another upcoming bike race, life was suddenly overwhelmingly busy and this was one stress he could do without.

However, he felt guilty about his reaction to Sarah. He didn't fully understand where their fight had come from, but he hated that he'd made her feel bad. He shook off those feelings. He was her landlord. He didn't need any further complications in his life, personal or otherwise. Whatever the fight had been about he needed to forget about it.

But as he sat in his flat, his mind mulling over the phone calls he'd be making in the morning, nursing a beer in one hand, he felt a minute tinge of regret. Regret that he was Sarah's landlord, that he was working alongside her in a professional capacity and simultaneously wondering if it actually really mattered at all.

Chapter Twenty Five

"What exactly are you looking for?" Izzy asked, as she flicked through the gigantic tome in front of her.

Her hair was plaited to one side and she was wearing her favourite purple jacket with sheep skin fleece inside. Despite the temperature pushing twenty-two outside, Izzy had insisted she was cold and blamed the pregnancy.

"My body temperature is erratic," she had said in way of explanation. "First I'm burning up and then I'm shaking from head to toe."

"Are you sure you're not ill?" Sarah had asked, pushing aside her cereal bowl.

She'd been staying with Will and Izzy while her flat got fixed up. She hadn't heard from Tessa since their falling out and the subsequent water leak. She hadn't expected Tessa to initiate an apology, and for once she wasn't about to take the first step.

"No!" Izzy almost spat. "I'm six months pregnant. That's what's wrong with me."

Sarah hastily changed the subject.

Now they were casually strolling through the local archive office, Sarah having finally explained to Izzy about the journals, with the intention of searching copious folders and newspaper files to track down the Bartley's.

"Any mention of a family member really," Sarah said, realising she was being too vague. This could take them hours and Izzy's mum was only able to babysit Henry until lunchtime. Time was against them and while Sarah could stay on, she knew two people searching would speed things up compared to one.

"Don't they have computers for that kind of search?" asked Izzy reasonably.

"Yes, but the lady at the desk warned that a computer search could be just as vast. There could be quite a few Bartley's on the system. She said to try the books too and she'd help us if we get stuck." Sarah sat down at a desk with a computer monitor on top and typed Frederick Bartley into the search bar.

Izzy sat down beside her and looked perplexed. "You're going to a lot of trouble over this."

"Not really. Once I knew where and how to look it's actually been quite easy."

"But why? I understand that you want to know what happened to this girl. We'd all be curious. But to actually spend time and energy searching, I don't really understand that."

"What's not to understand?" Sarah replied shortly. "I want to know the 'end of the story', so to speak."

She didn't elaborate on how Eleanor's situation resonated deeply and how Sarah could relate to the fifteen-year-old in a way that people with twice the life experience couldn't. Hadn't they both faced loss? A different kind perhaps, but loss nevertheless.

Sarah rarely came across anyone in her walk of life who'd experienced what she had. Sure, meeting an older more mature person and she might have some life stories to share, but her own age? Everyone she knew were getting married, having families and living out their dreams.

She had no one she could talk to. No one she could share her life, dreams and doubts with. Past or current. Eleanor was the closest thing she could relate to, and that was the sad truth.

The search engine scanned through thousands of possible documents (mostly newspaper articles) before stopping with a halt. Over one hundred entries were listed in front of her and frustratingly she could see that all the Bartley's shared the same initials as Frederick, but not necessarily the same man. She'd have to scroll down one by one.

"Hmm, this might take a while," Izzy stated the obvious. "Shall I go and look up some more info about the house?"

"Please," Sarah nodded and gave her friend a warm smile. Izzy might not understand the urgency of the search, but she was loyal to the end.

Sarah sat looking through the entries, trying to find some detail or other to narrow it down. Eventually, after about twenty minutes, she came across an entry with the right Christian name. Not wanting to place all her hope on it, she tentatively clicked with the mouse and the entry extended.

It was a newspaper article, fairly short, and dated back to 1899. No photo accompanied the three-paragraphed article, but the name matched and so seemed the subject matter.

The article mentioned a Frederick Bartley and his fortune at the take over and improvement of a local import and export company. It praised Mr Bartley for the gross profit seen in the previous financial year and the forecast for the current. The article concluded that the local and successful businessman had a promising future, both personally and for the City's economy.

This little morsel of information felt like a golden nugget. Finally, Sarah had a minute insight into Frederick's profession. She wondered what had happened in less than ten years to turn such a promising start into a massive financial slump. She didn't know enough about the era to know if the economy had played a part or whether Frederick wasn't quite the savvy businessman the newspaper made him out to be.

She scanned through the rest of the entries, but saw no more mention of the most senior Bartley. She took a deep breath and began to type a new name into the search bar. This was the name that meant the most to her and she almost dreaded what results she might find.

Pressing enter on the new search, Sarah sat back and waited with bated breath. If Eleanor's name did appear, the anticipation of what might be revealed was almost too much.

Sarah felt a pang as she wished Dermot was here to share in the moment. For the support, for the shared knowledge, for the feeling of having achieved something together. This surprised her and her mind slipped to the phone number still sitting on her night stand. She'd yet to phone Joe, or hear from him either, and she felt a sudden conflict of emotions.

It was an effective distraction from the computer screen in front of her, but eventually the search screen came to a halt and she was faced with dozens of results. Again, the entries were mostly initials, instead of full Christian names, so she began to scroll down.

"Well, the house was built in 1887," came Izzy's voice behind her. "And your family lived in it until 1912."

"Really?" Sarah's head snapped to attention. The second journal had so far chronicled life in 1908. It wasn't many years after that that Eleanor and her family had moved away. But where to and why?

"Yeah, it got sold to another family, the Kilroy's or something, and then sat empty a while following the second world war. That's as far as I got. I thought it was time for a break. Fancy a coffee?" Izzy stared longingly at the entrance door, knowing beyond was a coffee shop almost opposite.

"I would but I've just started a new search," Sarah didn't elaborate on how she was itching to get started and how this particular search enthralled her.

Izzy hovered impatiently for a moment. "Go!" Sarah laughed. "I'll join you if I don't find anything soon."

Izzy muttered her thanks and sped off. Sarah turned her attention back to the computer. She quickly skimmed past mentions of Edward Bartley a local greengrocer from the 1820's and Ernest Bartley a family Doctor.

She finally stopped at a couple of small and warming mentions of Eleanor. The first was her birth announcement in the local newspaper, the eldest child of Mr and Mrs Frederick Bartley. The second was a photograph of a fete held on the same common opposite 6 Caledon Street. Several young girls smiled formerly at the photographer, in their straw hats, gingham dresses and stockings. It was clearly a warm summer day, despite the black and white background giving little away about the season.

The caption underneath mentioned the girl's names and their enjoyment of the annual fete and its various stalls. The second girl from the left was identified as Eleanor Bartley and Sarah zoomed into the picture to get a better look.

She couldn't have been more than seven years old, with dark hair beneath the straw hat and a glint behind the eyes. A cute and upturned nose was decorated lightly with freckles and her heart shaped face was finished off with a rounded chin. She looked like a typically mischievous and fun little girl.

Sarah couldn't stop staring at the photograph. Even though it was grainy, especially up close, it was still enchanting. To finally see the face behind all the journal entries, albeit a face a few years younger than the one writing, was a joy.

She sat back with a smile. This was Eleanor. Nor, the feisty girl whose opinions seemed far advantaged for the era she was born into. The teenager she would become, surrounded by the adult issues of her father's financial difficulties and the uncertainty of even a roof over their heads. Tutors dismissed, dreams downgraded and a future with seemingly little promise, except for an arranged marriage and a lifetime of running her own household.

Perhaps Eleanor had settled into those roles. Perhaps she had mellowed with her age and circumstances. But an enormous part of Sarah hoped that was not the case. Sarah also hoped there was more to discover and her search wouldn't come to an abrupt end, just as it was getting interesting.

Composing herself, Sarah continued scrolling down the screen. More mundane and arbitrary entries were glossed over. Eventually, toward the end of the page Sarah came across a newspaper article. This one was of another announcement.

In the society news section of a local paper was a short paragraph under the heading 'Engaged'. A small photograph accompanied the announcement and there within its frame posed a couple. Formerly dressed and looking off camera in the same direction was a sandy haired gentleman and a woman who was no doubt Eleanor. Sarah didn't even need to read the caption to know that.

Eleanor facial features had barely changed, with just a maturing to the natural angles of her face. Her dark hair was pinned into a neat chignon and held a slight wave. Her formal expression matched her Fiancé's. However, a small smile was evident in the corner of her lips. Sarah hoped that boded well.

The announcement read:

Mr and Mrs Frederick Bartley are delighted to announce the engagement of their daughter Eleanor Evelyn Bartley (18) to one Tobias Gordon Wyatt (24), a junior attorney based in Clapham. They are betrothed to be married on the seventeenth of May, 1911 at St Mary's church.

*   *   *

Sarah left the records office with her head buzzing with information. She'd been sorely tempted to carry on the search under Eleanor's married name, but she needed time to process what she'd found out. She also realised that with Eleanor's new husband based in London, Sarah's search could draw a sudden blank. Or she would have to visit London to find out more.

Izzy had parted ways and headed back to fetch Henry and Sarah was glad of the time to mull over her thoughts. It hadn't shocked her that Eleanor was married off at a young age, certainly not after the strong hints in the journals. She just hoped that the teenager had married for love. Sarah equally hoped that Eleanor was able to have some sort of career, one that she had so desperately wanted.

Sarah returned to Caledon Street to check on the progress in the flat. The carpets were being replaced, the plumber had fixed the pipes, and she'd received a brief message from Dermot on her phone letting her know the job would be finished by the end of the day.

She entered the flat to chaos. Three guys were busy laying the new carpet and she stood and watched as they nosily laughed and joked as they worked. Realising she wasn't about to get into her home any time soon (she'd been hoping to pick up a few extra supplies), Sarah hovered a moment then found her way back downstairs.

Her phone began to ring. Pulling it out of her pocket she registered an unknown number and pressed the answer button.

"Hello, Sarah speaking."

"Hi Sarah. I don't know if you remember me from the bar?" said a familiar voice. "It's Joe, the guy who'd like to take you for that drink down the pub, if you're still interested."

"Oh," she said surprised. She hadn't actually thought she'd hear from him again.

"Or somewhere a bit more sophisticated, if you prefer," he added hastily.

Sarah laughed. "No, the pub is fine. Although I guess it depends which one."

"I only frequent the very best," came the reply and Sarah laughed again.

"How's this Friday work for you? I could meet you there at seven?"

"Okay," Sarah agreed, feeling a sudden thrill of excitement.

"Great, it's the Hammer and Tongs off Main Street. It's better than it sounds," he added reassuringly.

"Oh, I'm sure it is," she said with a smile.

They said their goodbyes and Sarah walked down the last flight of stairs with a sudden a lift of her mood. She liked Joe. He was fun to talk to, attractive and confident. A date with him wouldn't be a hardship and it was about time she went on a date again.

"Oh hi," Dermot's voice cut into her reverie and she started. His sudden appearance instantly made her uncertain about her date with Joe. Which of course was ridiculous, she told herself. Dermot had never shown any interest other than as a friend and landlord and Sarah herself had never examined what she might, if anything, feel for him.

"Hi Dermot," she said as breezily as possible. "The carpet is coming along nicely."

"Oh good," he appeared distracted and glanced at the phone in her hand. She wondered if he'd overheard the conversation and felt uncomfortable.

"Um," she fought to get her thoughts back on track. "I went to the records office this morning. I found out a few things you might find interesting."

"Sure. Maybe we can make a plan to meet up again. Sorry you had to go on your own."

"I had Izzy with me."

He nodded. "Well count me in for an update. When were you thinking?"

His light-hearted tone was reassuring. The tension between them the week before seemed to have dissipated. He also seemed genuinely interested in the Bartley search again. She felt a small sliver of relief by his renewed involvement.

"It'll have to be early this week, or next," she said. "I've got plans later this week."

"Sure," he said nodding curtly, and she knew then that he had definitely overheard her phone call.

"Wednesday then?"

"That should be fine," he thought a second. "I've got a long afternoon at work, so might not get back here early. Shall we meet in town? A coffee shop perhaps?"

"Okay," she said, feeling a little self conscious about the arrangement. It almost felt like pre-empting her date with Joe, which was ridiculous. This was strictly business.

Dermot's eyebrow was raised, as if he'd had the same thought, and she began to blush. Mentally shaking herself she made a quick goodbye and exited the house to the street beyond.

All of a sudden life seemed to be getting more complicated and she didn't quite know what to make of it. She was out of practice with the nuances of relationships, whether a guy was truly interested or not, and even how she was meant to feel towards someone. That angle of her life had laid dormant and untapped for so long, she barely knew the rules any more.

All she did know was that her life at Caledon Street was filling up more by the day and stage three of her plan had definitely commenced.

Chapter Twenty Six

Henry crawled across the floor with impressive speed, barking and panting like a dog. Izzy bent down and scooped him up.

"Right, you little doggy, it's bath time."

"Let me carry him Iz," Sarah offered. "You shouldn't be lifting him."

"Please, tell me how I'm supposed to avoid carrying and lifting my toddler? It's impossible, he clings to my ankles most of the day."

"Well, you could accept people's offers of help for a start," Will laughed, before falling silent at Izzy's expression.

"Sure, that'll work. Just quit your jobs and be here all day and then I can avoid lifting him around."

"We're here to help right now, so stop being a martyr and let us step in," Will responded, his tone a little short.

Izzy's mood swings had caused a certain amount of tension in the few days Sarah had been staying. She was glad Will was starting to stand up for himself. It certainly wasn't pleasant being in Izzy's firing line.

Sarah looked over wistfully at her packed bags by the door. She was looking forward to going home and not just to escape Izzy's outbursts. Caledon Street had become more of a home than her and Alex's previous place ever had. It was strange to think that, but she'd hung onto their flat for the sake of retaining memories, rather than because of any loyalty to the place. Caledon Street was comfortable and she enjoyed being there.

She just hoped the strange atmosphere that threatened to descend between her and Dermot wouldn't rear its head again. She finally acknowledged she might be a little attracted to him, inconvenient with him being both landlord and neighbour. Add on top of that her impending date with Joe and she felt more confused than ever.

She wanted to remain at Caledon Street and didn't want anything to overshadow that. She hoped meeting with Dermot the following evening would get things back on track between them. Joe was another matter entirely.

"Fine!" Izzy snapped. "You take him then!" She threw up her arms

167

exasperated and stalked out the room, leaving Will holding their son who was still barking like a dog.

"Excuse me," Will whispered apologetically. He left the room, carrying Henry upstairs to the waiting bath.

It was definitely the right time for Sarah to head home.

*   *   *

Dermot gazed over the panoramic views in awe. Wild grass swayed alongside the curvature of the fields, leading down to the woodland surrounding their perimeters. The fresh air that had struck him the moment he stepped out his car still did, minutes later, and he breathed in it deeply and greedily.

The cottage he'd bought, and would hold the keys of in just a couple of months, stood to his left, a little up the lane. The fact that the bedrooms would share the fantastic view he now gazed upon, filled him with enthusiasm.

This was a great investment. Out in the quiet of the countryside, with only a dozen other dwellings down the lane, but still just a five-minute drive from the outskirts of town, it would appeal to a lot of people.

Dermot felt that familiar thrill of a new house, and of a new project, bubbling up inside. After Caledon Street he'd been spent. He'd just wanted to have a normal existence again. To have a regular day job. To be able to finish work and join his friends in the pub without putting in a late night renovating.

But life had slowly faded into a dull ache. He'd thought the cycling and racing would help. It did, to begin with. But it couldn't quite fill the gap that property developing had left. Dermot realised it was inevitable that he'd crave it again and it now finally felt like the right time.

He reluctantly tore his gaze from the incredible view and walked a little further down the lane.

The fresh air also helped him clear his head from other thoughts. Thoughts that had begun to swim insistently through his mind. Having overheard Sarah on her mobile the day before, confirming a date with some guy, Dermot had felt a niggle which hadn't gone away.

He realised that it bothered him that she was dating. Throw into the mix the recent water leak, where he'd for the first time actually felt like her landlord, and he couldn't help feel confused. What was his role here? And did it really matter? He could still be professional in his capacity as a landlord, yet show interest in Sarah as a friend. Perhaps even as more. Although now she was dating, he wouldn't interfere.

He felt a sudden stab of irritation that he might have had this revelation too late. Okay, so she was only just starting to see a guy, but his integrity knew better than to chase someone already interested in someone else. Why couldn't he have realised his feelings a week ago? He could kick himself.

He pulled his attention back to the new house. This was a situation he could control, providing all the finances went through. The previous owners had already left for their comfortable new life in a retirement village on the south coast, so the property was almost already his.

He walked back to the car, hand in pockets, and gave the view a last longing glance. He couldn't wait to be spending more time here, despite a niggle at the thought that he wouldn't be spending so much time at Caledon Street. Nor that he would see Sarah as often.

"Shake it off," he muttered to himself, and got into the car, slamming the door shut a little harder than intended.

*   *   *

"Evening," Sarah grinned as she made her way through the bustling coffee shop. Dermot had arrived half an hour earlier and after a long day at work, hadn't been able to resist ordering a gourmet burger.

"Evening," he replied, wiping his mouth self consciously with the napkin.

"Wow, that looks good. I might treat myself," she looked at the food wolfishly and grinned again apologetically. "Sorry, I only had a quick sandwich for lunch. I had an important meeting with a client and didn't have time for a proper lunch break."

"Go ahead, they've got a limited but good menu here. I recommend the pasta dish too. I had it last week."

"Eat out a lot then?"

"Just when I've had a long day. I actually enjoy cooking, but I seem to lack the time these days."

"Me too. When did life suddenly get so busy?"

He smiled, enjoying the easy atmosphere between them. It certainly seemed that the previous tension had dissipated. He wished she would stop grinning so much though, it was distracting.

"I'll go up and order then," she excused herself and headed to the counter. She liked the setting and was glad Dermot had chosen it. While it was busy and noisy and perhaps not the best environment for a detailed chat about the Bartley's, it was warm and vibrant, with a young crowd.

She placed her order, having scanned the menu and deciding on an anti-pasti platter and side salad, made her way back to their table.

She was aware of Dermot watching her as she squeezed past the other patrons and she felt self-conscious, but strangely pleased by his perusal. She mentally scolded herself, her date with Joe was only two evenings away.

"So, you've been having fun with the Bartley's?" Dermot joked.

Sarah felt a slight pang at his obvious desire to talk business so soon.

169

Perhaps she had misinterpreted his look.

"Yes," she answered as breezily as she could. "I've found out quite a bit actually. Including who Eleanor eventually married, not long after she wrote her journals."

She showed him the information she'd copied and he looked through it, clearly interested and nodding along. "This is great stuff. And well done for being so dedicated to wade through it all. I wouldn't have had the patience."

"Well we both know how obsessed I am with it," she joked, referencing their previous argument and rolling her eyes to show she wasn't offended.

"No just dedicated, there's a difference," Dermot said sagely.

Sarah's food arrived and she tucked in quietly for a moment. Thinking as she ate, she didn't really consider what she was saying until it had already rolled off her tongue.

"I just think Eleanor's story resonates with me because we've both had broken dreams and lost things we care about. I can understand her loss and not knowing what direction her life is going to end up in. After losing Alex I couldn't imagine even having a future, something Eleanor also faced with losing her education. I guess I can relate to her, which I never thought I'd say about a fifteen-year-old!"

"Alex?" Dermot asked, his brow furrowed in question.

Realising what she'd said, she felt her cheeks redden and a prickly heat creep up her neck. She was partly horrified and partly impressed that she had mentioned Alex so easily, after years of purposely avoiding talking about him. She wondered if her walls were slowly coming down.

"Alex was my husband. He died seven years ago in a car accident. We'd been married a year," she said it as casually as possible, her tried and tested way to avoid making the recipient of the news uncomfortable.

Dermot shifted in his seat as he considered her reply. She could tell he was deciding how to react, but found she wasn't nervous. Firstly, she'd seen every reaction; sadness, tears, anger, disbelief and pity. She realised she was no longer fearful of those reactions.

Secondly, she also realised that she trusted Dermot, and whatever his reaction, he wouldn't intend to hurt her.

"Wow, Sarah. That must have been hectic," he knew it was an understatement and smiled apologetically.

"It was a long time ago. I've learnt to deal with it on the most part," she took a mouthful of food and chewed thoughtfully. "I've got good family and friends, who've been a massive support too. That definitely has helped."

"Even Tessa?" Dermot grinned. Sarah shook her head in admonishment. "She's Alex's sister. I'm kind of stuck with her. Although, really, I wouldn't want my life to be without her either."

"That explains a lot. I couldn't understand why she was staying with you.

You seem so different. I could tell she tested your patience."

"Was I that obvious?" Sarah looked so horrified that Dermot laughed. "No, maybe I'm just very perceptive," he joked.

"Oh, is that what that is?" she joked back, her eyebrow raised.

Dermot watched her eat another mouthful of food and thought about all she'd said. He could hardly begrudge her date now, could he?

But he couldn't help wishing it was him taking her out and not this other guy. He swallowed that thought quickly and focused his attention on the already cold coffee dregs in his cup.

"So, what's the next stage with the Bartley search?" he asked, bringing their conversation to safer ground. She looked relieved, perhaps keen to move on from talking about Alex.

"I want to look her up under her married name. But it seems she moved to London after getting wed, so I might need to go there to search."

"They don't have the information on the National Archives website?"

"I think maybe the death certificates. And maybe a census or birth certificates for any children. But I'm hoping the records office in their borough will have more detailed information. I just want to know that she was happy. That she either fulfilled her dreams; although she was only fifteen so I realise dreams change, or that she at least led a full life. That would make me happy."

Dermot smiled and nodded. "I'll take you up to London if you like. I just need to figure out a few logistics first."

"Oh?"

"I'm buying a new property to fix up. It might be a while yet before I can get in, but I've loads to plan and budget for. I've got to draw up plans, source materials and visit scrap yards, that kind of thing. I'm already pushed for time and it'll be a thirty-minute drive across town, in busy traffic, to get there every day. Even longer if I go directly from work.

So, I'm considering moving in during the renovation and letting out my flat. I might even decide to keep the cottage, I'm already falling in love with it. I know that's the major rule for a developer; don't fall in love with the property, but this is a project. I'm not really reliant on the money straight away. I can keep it if I really want to, although I do plan to sell as it'll be a financial push."

Sarah felt like she'd been punched in the stomach. She tried to nod encouragingly, all the while thinking 'Dermot's moving out, I won't get to see him any more'.

The stark revelation of her feelings was shocking enough, on top of processing all the information he'd just thrown at her.

Sarah took a deep breath and a sip from her glass of water. She was going on a date with Joe in two evenings time. What was she doing worrying over Dermot like that? Surely that strength of reaction went beyond just friendship? And would he really move out? The thought of him no longer living downstairs was a horrifying one.

Suddenly she felt the need to just leave the coffee shop and hide out in her flat. She forced herself to stay seated where she was and nodded along as Dermot enthusiastically explained his plans for the cottage. All the while her heart sank a little lower with each sentence.

How could she go on this date now? Realising the reaction Dermot had caused, she could not ignore her feelings. But it might never be reciprocated, so could she really go on a date with another man knowing she liked someone else?

And more importantly, was she really ready to contemplate a new relationship with anyone? It was still such an unknown and unanswered question that it became too big to attempt to answer.

No longer hungry, she pushed aside her plate and tried to concentrate on what Dermot was saying. But every inflection in his voice, every crooked smile as he spoke, every hair on his head she suddenly became aware of. Holding his gaze was a challenge, her beating heart wanting her to look away.

The next half an hour was pure torture. As they finally parted company, bill paid and goodbyes at the coffee shop door, Sarah felt exhausted. Not only that, she felt thoroughly confused and bereft. What was she going to do about Joe? What was she going to do about Dermot? Could she stop him leaving the flat, and did she want to? Did she want *anything* to happen with either of them?

She just didn't know the answer to any of these questions and she headed home with a lump in her throat.

Chapter Twenty Seven

11th June 1908

I am officially 'out'. My father has wasted no more time lingering upon his decision and I am to attend two balls with my parents within the month. I am under no illusion that Father has shared this news amongst his friends in high society. I have yet to receive an offer of course, I will need to show my face among the crowds first.

My one saving grace amidst the uncertain torrent surrounding me, is the relinquishment of my household duties. It has been granted by upstairs. I am to engage in activities more aligned to the running of a home and what shall be expected of a new bride. I am learning how to organise social events, manage the staff (although we have but one left) and basic skills such as darning and sewing.

My mother has found herself in her element, teaching what she has waited years to share. I find it endearing to a degree and have found the bond between us strengthened a little through our joint endeavours.

I am still to assist Nanny in the education of the boys, which mercifully will come to an end at the commencement of their schooling in a few months time. Nanny is yet again taking strain and Father relented in allowing a friend of Nanny's to assist her in the kitchen. I know not how Father can afford this, yet she is young and sleeps in the kitchen itself, so cannot have cost him too dear.

My heart is full of trepidation as to how my life may change now such measures have been put in place. I can only hope with all my being and pray nightly that my future happiness is guaranteed and not at stake.

19th June 1908

I have partaken in my first ball. I was quite caught up in the excitement and thrill of my new dress and my hair being tousled into an elegant style, which instantly made me looked older than my years. Leaving the house into the night and being transported to the venue added to the mystery and awe of it all.

Upon our arrival my nerves somewhat let me down, the volume of people to the room, the incessant chatter and confidence of my fellow attendees, all served to remind me of my age and my previously sheltered existence. Fortunately, I was not obliged to make conversation, merely to stand graciously beside Mother and Father while they engaged in social niceties.

I was invited to dance by a young gentleman, perhaps only a few years my senior. My father permitted the interaction and we danced alongside others, my feet and mind becoming confused on several an occasion. My dance partner seemed not to mind, but his weak smile began to irritate and I found myself keen for the dance to end. His second invitation, later during the evening, was met with a polite decline.

My first social event was both thrilling and overwhelming. I am not sure I am ready for such a responsibility as to soon become a wife. My mother seems most encouraging, but I am not at all convinced.

4th July 1908

Father has organised a dinner party, the first my family have engaged in many a month. Two balls have passed with no interest between myself and any prospective candidate. I suspect this dinner party is Father's attempt to take matters into his own hands. No doubt suitors will be present.

I almost long for the days where my biggest worry was chasing after my brothers in the park. It seems so much simpler and less stressful than this. My fear of not being a good enough bride is driving my low mood.

I have accepted I am to marry. But I am struggling to find the fortitude for it. I no longer dream of the education I always desired, but my hope still remains to marry well and into a loving environment and one where my freedom will not be compromised.

16th July 1908

The dinner party was hailed a great success. I assisted Mother in organising the event and as such was able to address everyone by name and hold conversation with all. I am beginning to feel more confident with each social occasion I attend and while no suitors yet, much to my father's dismay, I am embracing my new role with a spark of enthusiasm.

During the dinner party I was introduced to two gentlemen, both business contacts of my father's, young but still much older than I. They held good conversation and both seemed pleasant and amiable. The one seemed keener than the other and I feared he might make my father an offer before the evening was out. As pleasant as he was, I had no doubt that I did not want to marry him.

Nothing has been said since and knowing my father's keenness, I highly doubt an offer is being kept hidden for any reason.

I can breathe easy for the time being as Father has some potentially exciting business matters to attend to in London. There'll be no more social occasions for a month or more.

Sarah placed the journal on her bedside table and took off her reading glasses. Knowing that Eleanor had gone on to marry shortly after the journals were written, she felt a twinge of anxiety.

Would Eleanor like her husband to be? How did they meet and was it orchestrated by her father? Did her life change for the better, the way Sarah's had when she met Alex, or was it purely out of a sense of duty and lack of options?

Sarah picked the journal back up and thumbed through the remaining pages. There weren't many left. As tempted as she was, she didn't flick to the end or read snippets from pages ahead. She wanted the story to unravel in order, no matter what the end result. It seemed only fitting to treat Nor with respect and allow her to reveal her life story in the way it had been written.

Sarah sunk back on to her pillow. She was exhausted. After her meeting with Dermot on Wednesday night, she hadn't sleep well.

Tomorrow night was her date with Joe. Unable to make a decision whether to cancel or not, reasoning that the alternatives were too unknown and complicated (she had no idea if there was anything between her or Dermot), she had decided to go ahead.

It was just a first date anyway. A drink. If it felt wrong, she could easily leave without too much fuss. If she felt guilty... well she still hadn't figured out why she needed feel guilty at all, but she could handle it if the date was kept short and informal.

She closed her eyes and tried to block out the confusing thoughts jostling in her mind. How had she gone from a widow without having had a date in over a year, to a date with one guy and a worrying burst of feelings for another? Life certainly seemed to have got more complicated all of a sudden.

*   *   *

Yawning behind her hand, Sarah made her way to the pub where she'd be meeting Joe. She still hadn't slept well the previous night, though that wasn't unexpected. She'd spend most of the night and day that had followed wondering if she was doing the right thing.

Despite her mind protesting that she had nothing to feel guilty about, she couldn't avoid the prickle of uncertainty running through her.

As she reached the pub door she almost turned around and ran away. She mentally shook herself. She was not allowing herself to slip back into a life of loneliness. Even if nothing happened with Joe, it was a step forward in the right direction and she wouldn't waste the opportunity.

And Dermot? He hadn't shown any interest in her, that she could see. He was her landlord, neighbour and hopefully a friend too. But he was also busy, focused and hadn't shown even the slightest hint of feeling anything for her. Besides their search for the Bartley's he hadn't demonstrated any desire to

175

spend additional time with her.

It was time for her date with Joe and time to put any doubts behind her. With a deep breath for confidence she opened the pub door and stepped inside.

*   *   *

"You look fantastic," Joe enthused. "What can I get you?"

"Oh, a glass of white wine please," she smiled back and he went to order at the bar.

Pleased by his comment she assessed her outfit. She had wanted to remain casual but smart and had chosen a dark pair of denims and a white blouse with gold sequins around the neckline. Her short hair was pulled into a tiny ponytail and she wore delicate gold tear drop earrings. A smattering of makeup, tinted moisturiser, and swipe of mascara and lip tint completed the look.

She was pleased. It didn't look as if she was trying too hard.

Joe returned with their drinks and she appraised him for the first time. He was still casually suited, just like when she'd met him in the bar, but this time with a deep purple shirt and subtle silver stitching. She wondered briefly if maybe she should have dressed up a bit more, but remembered his compliment and relaxed.

Taking a sip of her wine she met his gaze and smiled self consciously. She hadn't been on a date in so long she wasn't sure she could recall how to start.

"So... have you had a good week at work?" she inwardly cringed at her inane question and took another sip of wine to disguise it.

"Stressful. We've got multiple projects on the go and I'm leading a team that needs a little more encouragement than usual. But knowing I had this evening to look forward to helped me get through it," he flashed a confident grin, showing off his perfectly white teeth.

Sarah shrugged in a modest way and matched his smile. "What about you? You're in advertising, right?" he asked.

"Yes. Well I'm a Senior Copywriter. It's my job to help put together campaigns and slogans and branding and write the content for it," she said. "It's very stressful at times, especially when you've got companies spending a lot of money on you and relying on your skills to propel their product into the stratosphere. But I have a good team, so it's not all on me."

"Maybe we could swap teams then," he laughed, but Sarah could sense the tension behind his words. Time to change the subject, she thought.

"So, do you live nearby?"

"Just a five-minute walk actually. I'm a bit of a regular in here. I'm from Hull originally, but left as soon as I could. I've been here two years. London for a few years before that. I move where the work is. And you?"

"I've been here my whole life. I even studied here. I travelled a lot to make

176

up for it, but I have my family and friends here and a good job, so never found reason to leave."

"I don't know if I could settle in any one place," Joe mused. "I guess I'm a wanderer at heart. I'm always looking for new opportunities, especially career wise."

Sarah took a deep gulp of wine and nodded in what she hoped was an understanding way. She got his passion to travel, the desire of ambition, but she wondered if he was searching for something other than that, with his constant need to move on. She also wondered if he could be serious in pursuing a relationship if he got bored so quickly.

"So where have you travelled?" she asked, realising she was asking all the questions.

He reeled off a list of countries and she enjoyed relaying her own travelling experiences. Feeling a bit more at ease she happily accepted a second drink and settled back into the conversation.

Joe had a good sense of humour and cheeky smile. He was interesting to listen to, especially as he recalled some of the hairier experiences of both travelling and office life. She laughed along heartedly and put aside her earlier concerns. He was fun and attractive and pleasant.

What's more Sarah was actually enjoying a date. It had been a long time since she could say that.

As the evening due to a close and after she'd completely lost track of time, she found herself hoping they'd meet up again.

"Thanks for a great evening," she said. They stood outside the pub doors, the darkening summer sky giving way to a slight chill. She hovered from foot to foot to keep warm.

Joe looked down at her with intense eyes and a grin full of mischief. "It was the best. I'm hoping you'll agree to a repeat evening soon, this time with dinner included. My treat."

"No, I'll go Dutch," Sarah waved away the offer. Alex had often paid for any meals out they'd had as a couple, especially when she was a penniless aspiring writer. But these days she was independent and determined to stay that way.

"Fine by me, as long as you agree to that second date," he replied, a cockiness and confidence in his crooked grin.

"Yes," she almost whispered. "Next Friday night okay with you?"

"Perfect," he kissed her cheek goodnight.

She left with a skip in her step and sighed happily. The date wasn't perfect, certainly at the beginning, but there was potential there. The ease of their conversation was a major plus and Sarah certainly felt an attraction to Joe too.

It was a short walk home and Sarah mulled over the evening as she made her way. Her mobile phone began to trill in her pocket, breaking her train of thought.

"Hello?" she answered.

"I hope you realise how much you've ruined my life?!" screeched a high-pitched voice on the other end. The unmistakable sound of sobbing followed and Sarah stopped walking in shock.

"Tessa?"

"You couldn't just leave your nose out of my business, could you? You just had to ruin my party and my life, didn't you?" the sobbing started again in earnest.

Rather than be offended, Sarah knew she had to be patient. Tessa needed time. The fact that she'd called was a miracle in itself, and suggested that Tessa wasn't quite as furious as she was making out.

It had been nearly a week since their falling out. The fact that Tessa had said some very hurtful things hadn't been forgotten. Sarah had forced herself not to dwell on the painful words. But during the two recent bad nights their conversation had trickled back into her consciousness. Tessa's words were said in anger, but that didn't make them completely untrue.

"Tessa," she began, holding her spare hand to her forehead in frustration. "We both said things that perhaps we shouldn't. Can we not talk this through?"

"What?" Tessa spat through her tears. She spluttered as if to say something else, but collapsed into hysterics again.

"Okay, Tessa. Do you want me to come around? I'm free the rest of the evening. We need to talk."

"Don't do me any more of your favours Sarah," Tessa shouted, suddenly managing to break free of the tears. "I just want you to know what you've done."

"And what have I done?" Sarah felt her patience slipping. Her euphoria after the date with Joe had now faded. A prickle of annoyance at Tessa's timing, not to mention her self-centredness, flickered through her.

"I encouraged you to stop running away from your problems. I've learned that lesson the hard way and all I wanted was to help you."

"Help me!" Tessa exclaimed, yet her tone of voice had softened and the sobbing had finally stopped.

"Yes, help you. I'm sorry if it was unwanted, but I had the best intentions," this was met with silence which Sarah took as a good sign. She waited a moment. "Can we meet to chat this through? I'm free tomorrow night if now is not a good time."

"I don't know," Tessa hiccupped.

"Well, think about it. Just send me a text, or call if you prefer. I'll be up for a while yet," Sarah said, her voice as soft and encouraging as she could manage. "I love you Tess."

Tessa sniffed and ended the call. Sarah sighed and put the phone back in her pocket. At least Tessa had called, even if it was to shout and rant. This was a major breakthrough. Perhaps something Sarah had said had impacted Tessa after all. Maybe her kid sister was finally showing signs of maturity and responsibility, no matter how poor her execution on the phone.

Feeling her evening might not have been completely ruined, Sarah lighter mood returned. She had just finished getting dressed for bed when her phone beeped, indicating an incoming message. Checking her mobile, wondering if it might be Joe, she read the message with a small smile.

Come over tomorrow night, if you want. T

It was a step forward.

Chapter Twenty Eight

The consistent drizzle of summer rain seemed fitting as Sarah arrived at Tessa's house. When the front door opened, she was greeted with the sight of puffy red eyes and dishevelled hair. Tessa sniffed some form of welcome and let Sarah through.

The grey skies outside were mirrored in Tessa's bedroom. Her curtains drawn, the room was still sparse of furniture or any of her personality. Clearly Tessa hadn't settled here which no doubt was not helping her mood.

"Cup of tea?" Tessa's voice was hoarse from crying.

"Please," Sarah replied. She hadn't expected any hospitality. Tessa's lack of eye contact was enough of a hint that she still had yet to forgive and forget. Sarah knew she needed to tread carefully. She hovered in the kitchen as Tessa made the tea in silence. The tension was almost unbearable.

"Where are all your housemates tonight?" Sarah asked tentatively.

"They've gone down the pub. They do that together a lot. I didn't get invited," she left it hanging in the air and Sarah had a sinking feeling she'd asked the wrong thing. But everything she said to Tessa felt like walking on egg shells anyway.

Sarah sat down at the kitchen table and tried to relax. She was not here to tiptoe around her, nor to fall on her knees and beg forgiveness. Tessa had to learn to be responsible for her own choices, including the words she threw out in haste.

Tessa shoved the cup of tea in front of Sarah, tea bag still floating in the anaemic looking beverage. Sarah sipped it quietly as she watched Tessa pace up and down the kitchen, before leaning against the fridge door in utter despondency.

"I haven't stopped crying all week. I've barely slept," she spat accusingly. "My housemates are avoiding me because they are so fed up with me moping around."

"I didn't say it to hurt you Tessa. I wanted to help you."

"And that makes it all right?!" Tessa threw her hands up in disbelief.

"Whether you agree with it or not, it was done from a good place. Sometimes it's not easy to hear the truth, but rather from me, someone who loves you, than from a stranger who doesn't care."

Tessa shook her head vehemently and started pacing again. "So, you think that you're off the hook then?"

Sarah sighed and pushed her unappealing tea aside. "Tessa, I'm not here to apologise. I've done that already. I'm here to explain my motives. I'm here to reassure you that it was said for the best. Perhaps it's a good thing you're feeling like this..."

Tessa snorted, but Sarah ignored her.

"My point is that you are running from something. Whether it's Kris, or for some other reason, I don't know. But you can't go through life hiding from your responsibilities. And neither can I, before you turn it back round on me again. I'm working on it. Maybe you need to as well."

Tessa stood in silence, her face fighting a mixture of fury and disbelief. But her eyes began to water and she twisted her mouth as she fought the rising flood.

"Tessa," Sarah said softly. "Come and sit down. You're my sister and I love you. Please let's talk this through."

"I don't have a sister," Tessa whispered her voice shaking.

Sarah tried to ignore the stabbing pain of the obvious slight. Tessa was hurting and was yet again using her sharp tongue in defence. Sarah wondered how many barbs she'd have to take before Tessa calmed and saw sense.

"When I married Alex, I married into the family. I'm the closest thing you have to a sister."

"Well, I never wanted your advice. If I wanted it, I'd have asked."

"Fair enough," Sarah conceded. Tessa hovered near the table but didn't sit down. She'd got her tears under control and threw Sarah the odd glance.

"You're not happy Tessa. I realise that has a lot to do with me, but even before last week it was obvious. When you stayed with me you were barely keeping it together, despite acting like you were fine. Your flirting with Dermot, avoiding all questions about Kris, pretending the break up hadn't happened. None of that was normal behaviour."

"Of course, I wasn't happy," Tessa screamed. "You really expect me to be fine when I've just ended a relationship? Were you okay just after Alex died? Of course not!"

"But I didn't avoid the situation Tessa!" Sarah said in exasperation. "Kris is in bits. He doesn't know what went wrong and you won't even talk to him, or me, or anyone, about it. You can't run away and just expect things to be fine. That was my point!"

Feeling they were getting nowhere, Sarah contemplating calling it a day. Tessa hung her head in silence.

"He hasn't left a message in two weeks," she whispered. "He called every day. I ignored them, but still he'd call. He's stopped now."

"Why are you doing this to yourself Tessa?" asked Sarah gently.

Another pause followed and Tessa took a deep sigh. Reaching out with one hand she took the back of the chair and sat down, joining Sarah at the table.

"I know I have a history of this," she admitted. "But Kris *was* different. The others... they felt wrong, even at the beginning. But he... well he was the one."

"Then why run away?" Sarah asked, with a hint of frustration.

Tessa made eye contact for the first time. "Because I'm scared he'll die and I'll be on my own. Like you and Alex. I couldn't bear losing him."

Sarah was shocked into silence for a moment, then shook her head vehemently. "That makes no sense. If you're scared of losing him, why dump him?!"

"It might make no sense to you, but I'd rather walk away before we get too deep. The pain of losing him later on is so much worse."

"Well, the pain I've seen you in, in the last couple of months hasn't been a walk in the park either," she reasoned. "In fact, you're not one step closer to being over him today than you were back then. Look at you Tessa. You can't tell me this is really for the best. You love him and you're in pain being apart from him. No fear of the future is worth losing the love of your life over."

Sarah lent over conspiratorially, "If I had known Alex was going to die, I'd still have married him. In fact, I'd marry him ten times over, knowing the end result would be the same. Why? Because the years we spent together were precious, and no matter the pain of losing him, I'm glad I had that time.

Tessa the chances that Kris is going to die young are slim, you do realise that? Don't waste your chance of happiness on a what if. Especially not on a what if which is unlikely to happen anyway."

Tessa contemplated Sarah through her tears and said nothing for a while. "You'd really go through all that knowing Alex would die?" Her tone sounded sceptical, but the slight hint of hope was obvious.

"Yes. It hurt like hell. But I would."

"You're so brave."

"No," Sarah sighed. "I'm just a normal woman taking each day at a time and remembering to breathe. I don't get it right all the time. I've pushed people away. I've hidden my thoughts and feelings. I've run, just like you. You were right."

Tessa groaned. "I'm so sorry I said those things. I was so cruel. I didn't mean it."

"But you were right. I've done the same things you have. The difference is I've started to deal with it, and that's why I said what I did. I wanted to see you overcome those issues too. But I've realised only you can do that. It's not my job."

"Maybe it was your job to point it out. If you hadn't said all that, I'd have carried on as normal."

"Eventually you'd have been miserable enough to face it."

"Oh, I've been miserable enough for weeks, Sarah. I miss him."

"Then call him. Talk it through. It doesn't mean you have to get back with him. But he does deserve to know the truth. And you deserve to get over your fears and move on, with or without him. Do it Tessa," Sarah let the suggestion hang in the air between them.

Tessa squirmed uncomfortably on her chair and made a pained face. She suddenly looked so much like the teenager Sarah had met all those years ago, that she had to stifle a laugh. This definitely wasn't the moment for humour.

"Okay," Tessa whispered eventually, once several emotions had crossed her features. "But in my own time," she added hastily.

"Fine," Sarah agreed. "When you're ready. Only you will know when. Believe me, I've plenty of experience there too. Some days you wonder if you'll ever be ready. Just take it from me, sometimes it's best to just step out and take the risk. It's hardly ever as bad as you think it'll be."

"Thanks Sarah," Tessa gave her first smile. "And thanks for coming. I've been so beastly towards you. Treating you and your flat like a dumping ground, saying those things to you, flirting with Dermot. I don't even know why I acted like that. Especially when I knew you liked him. It's unforgiveable."

"What?!" Sarah asked stunned. "What do you mean 'liked him'? Who, Dermot?" She gave a little self-conscious laugh.

Tessa looked shocked then composed herself. "Oh, no of course not. Sorry, I just assumed... well that's okay then. No harm done. Sorry...." she said again.

Sarah took her now lukewarm tea into her hands to distract herself. Taking a sip, she realised the irony of coming to persuade Tessa to stop hiding from the truth, and here she was ending up doing exactly the same thing.

Chapter Twenty Nine

The rest of the summer was quiet and mostly restful. With so many staff away on their holidays Sarah found the office environment more relaxed than usual. Their current deadlines were only to come into force at the end of August and Sarah could get home from the office, work all done, at a pleasingly early hour.

Having taken a week off herself, she'd spent the time relaxing in the flat, drinking good coffee, listening to Greta's symphonies, and catching up on time with friends. A couple of days had been spent at her parent's house, where she'd enjoyed her mother's hospitality and plenty of sunbathing in the garden with a good book.

Her second date with Joe had passed. It was pleasant. She still found him great company and was certainly attracted to him, but she awaited that bolt of electricity to jolt her spine, as it had with Alex, and still as yet nothing had come. A second tentative good night kiss had been lovely, but it wasn't setting her world alight.

They had agreed to meet again, but with a holiday looming for Joe, it would be a few weeks before they could next go out. He'd text her a few times since their meal out and she'd initiated a couple herself, but they hadn't spoken on the phone. Part of her missed their conversation, the other part of her was relieved to just have space and time to herself.

It surprised her to think that. So many years she'd feared being on her own, yet inevitably she had ended up alone, trying to hide her hurts and feelings. Now she realised, the need to have space resulted from actually wanting to spend time with herself. She enjoyed her own company again. It was now through choice and not because of a lack of other options.

Izzy, Will and Henry had also enjoyed a family holiday down in Cornwall and had come back brown as berries and full of beach anecdotes. Burying Daddy up to his neck in sand was Henry's favourite. Not to mention the almost endless ice creams.

Izzy's bump continued to expand at an alarming rate, but finally the pregnancy looked like it was starting to suit her. She was relaxed and happy and carefree. Just like the Izzy Sarah had known for years.

Sarah had joined them in the park for several picnics and lazy weekend afternoons. On the odd occasion they'd bumped into Dermot, either training on his bike, or making his way out or back from somewhere. But once again he'd fallen off the radar. Sarah hardly saw him. She hardly heard him in his flat either.

She wondered if the sale had gone through and he'd already moved over to the new house. It was a sobering thought and she realised how much she missed him being around. It was the only downside to the summer, but a rather big one at that.

She'd had to put it out her mind and focus on the long balmy evenings on the roof terrace and the seemingly endless summer sunshine. It wouldn't be long before the familiar autumnal chill crept back into the atmosphere and she wanted to lap the warmth up as long as she could.

As the mornings and evenings grew crisper, she found herself tucked up into bed finishing off the last pages of the journal. Eleanor had also seemed to have a respite, her socialising minimal amongst the new business dealings occupying her father's attention. Sarah was pleased the Edwardian teenager hadn't found herself married off to the first suitor and she felt a spark of hope that Tobias had been a good match after all.

As August drew to a close Sarah found her working day heat up again. Leaving early the one morning, with another impending deadline she was determined to reach, she bumped into Dermot also sneaking quietly out the house.

"Hi," he said, his eyebrows raised in surprise. "I didn't know you were such an early riser."

"Just this morning," she replied with a tight smile. She was still waiting for her hastily sipped coffee to kick in and lift the shadows of sleep that hung over her. "Are you off out for a bike ride?"

"No, off to the cottage. I got the keys last week. There's no time to waste now. I've got at least a couple of months work ahead, doing the place up."

"So, you'll be pretty busy then?" she felt stupid even asking the obvious question.

"Yeah, you could say that. I won't be around much. If you need anything, you'll have to contact the letting agent."

The formality of their conversation depressed her. Where had that ease gone? The humour that so often accompanied their exchanges?

She fiddled with her handbag self consciously, only looking briefly in his direction. "I'd better go then," she said.

"Sure," Dermot replied, his hands in his pockets looking just as uncomfortable. "Well, see you around."

"Yeah, see you," she inwardly cringed as she headed out the door. A sinking feeling hit her in the stomach and she wished she could rewind the last few minutes. Hoping that she hadn't just burnt her bridges with someone she considered a friend, she walked down the street feeling decidedly glum.

*　　*　　*

"How about this weekend, are you free?" Joe's voice was tinny down the mobile phone.

"Possibly. I might have to work from home to reach this deadline though," Sarah warned.

They'd already been on the call over ten minutes and hadn't reached an agreed date to meet. Even ten minutes was time she could ill afford. With the summer holidays now a distant memory, the staff were rushed off their feet with several new projects.

Joe sighed. "I've seen you just an hour in the last month. Surely we can do a quick lunch again like last time?"

They'd met briefly the previous week, once Joe was back from his holiday, and grabbed a quick sandwich from the deli. It was good to see him again, Sarah had decided, and she was keen, if a little restricted for time, to meet again.

"Okay, but not this week. I have important meetings over the lunch hours. We're ordering in. Maybe Monday?"

"Cool," he sounded decidedly happier. "I'll come to you again, shall I?"

"That's great. I'll text you to confirm. I really have to go now," she cut him short and gave a quick goodbye. She felt a little bad, but couldn't risk falling behind because of a personal call.

Her earlier conversation with Dermot played through her mind. They had both sounded so detached. Perhaps it was because of their shared busyness, or perhaps there was something not quite gelling. Part of her felt relieved she had Joe still interested in her, but another part felt a little downhearted about it.

Shaking off her thoughts, which were equally as distracting as Joe's phone call, she returned her attention to the storyboards and copious notes piled upon her desk. She needed to make sense of them quick and get back to the job in hand.

*　　*　　*

"I bought takeaway!" shrieked Tessa in excitement, as Sarah, weary from her long day, opened the door.

As tired as she was, Tessa was a welcome surprise. The fact that she'd bought food (Sarah hadn't even rustled up the energy to make a piece of toast)

187

was a massive bonus.

"Come in," Sarah said enthusiastically. It was good to see Tessa. She'd been scarce after their heart to heart, only sending occasional text messages reassuring Sarah that she would talk to Kris, at least at some point.

Seeing her now, she looked brighter, her hair freshly coloured and wearing brand new clothes. She looked more rested and her skin was glowing. Yet the strain behind her eyes was clear to see. A makeover couldn't hide that.

Tessa unpacked the Chinese and scooped spoonfuls onto two plates that she snatched off of the drier. Chucking a fork in Sarah's direction, Tessa used her own to shovel a massive amount of food into her mouth.

"I haven't eaten all day, I'm starving," she managed to sputter. Also hungry, Sarah dived in too.

Ten minutes later they lay reclined on the sofa, the cartons of food empty and plates dumped in the sink. Tessa sighed happily and closed her eyes. Sarah joined her and they sat in companionable silence for a while.

"Do you have any wine?" Tessa asked eventually.

Sarah smiled without opening her eyes. "In the cupboard next to the sink. There's only red left."

"Hmm, wine's wine. The colour doesn't matter," Tessa sniffed and Sarah heard her approach the kitchen. She heard the cork pop and the satisfying sound of wine being poured into glasses.

"I phoned Kris," Tessa said suddenly out of nowhere. Sarah opened her eyes and sat upright.

"You did?"

"He didn't answer. I left a message. That was two days ago. He hasn't replied," she said matter of a fact, but Sarah recognised the anguish underneath.

"Maybe he hasn't checked his messages yet?" Sarah said reassuringly, but knew it sounded weak.

"That phone is attached to him, of course he's checked them," Tessa said with a bite. She handed a glass of wine to Sarah and sat down heavily on the sofa. "I can't exactly expect him to reply, can I? We broke up months ago. He's probably dating someone else by now."

Sarah heard the pain in her voice, yet Tessa hid her expression behind her glass of wine.

"What are you going to do?"

Tessa paused for a moment, "What can I do?" she shrugged. "I've tried. I told you I'd call him and I did. Maybe if I'd called him straight away, he'd have answered. I have to live with that. I've missed my opportunity," her voice broke before she composed herself.

"Oh Tess."

"It's my own fault. This whole thing has been," she said in defeat. It was true but Sarah's heart still broke for her.

The sudden makeover now made complete sense. Tessa was hiding her heartbreak behind new hair, makeup and clothes. Her happy demeanour was hiding the truth. Sarah no longer knew what to say. Tessa had to find her own path. Sarah had no more advice to offer. All she could do was be there for her.

They sat together and finished their wine. Sarah moved closer to Tessa and put her arm around her, not speaking a word. Sarah simply held her sister in law as Tessa sobbed tears she'd held back for days.

Chapter Thirty

"I'm so sick of being pregnant!" Izzy fumed, brandishing the bottle of washing up liquid in one hand and dishcloth in the other.

Sarah raised her eyebrows in amusement and glanced at Will. His face contorted between wanting to smile and keeping a straight and serious face in support of his wife.

"I know sweetheart," he soothed. "Only a few weeks left to go."

"Four!" she spat. "And that's only the due date. I could go six. SIX!"

The relaxed and happy Izzy that Sarah had encountered during the summer months had long since disappeared. Now she was tired, worn out, heavy and sore. Add to that the frantic attempt to potty train Henry before the baby arrived (going against everyone's advice) and she was frayed to the edge.

"I'll make you a cup of tea," Sarah said, moving away from the little nook where Henry's toy box lived. He played happily on the floor with his toys, ignoring his mother's sudden outburst. Obviously, he was used to it.

"No, I don't want tea," Izzy sighed. "I want a nice cold beer. And to sleep. Just one night. Without waking up to pee, or to see to Henry or to just lie wide awake unable to sleep... just because."

"Go nap, Will and I can take Henry out for a walk."

Izzy sighed and nodded. "Thanks. I know I'm being such a pain. You must be so sick of me by now. Almost as much as I'm sick of being pregnant."

"It's almost time now, Izzy. You're almost through it. And we're here to support you, whatever you need," Will said.

"You don't disagree that you're sick of me then?" Izzy eyed him suspiciously. Sensing another domestic brewing, Sarah took the initiative and whisked Henry up in her arms.

"Come on, let's go for this walk. Then Mummy can have a nice rest."

Will smiled at Sarah in gratitude and grabbed his shoes by the back door. "Sleep well honey," he kissed Izzy's cheek.

Izzy watched them go and felt terrible. Lately she'd found herself snapping at every little thing. She knew it was the hormones but she hated making her family feel on edge. Especially as of late she'd been enjoying their company so much, embracing her role at home with Henry and looking forward to the new arrival.

Now she felt terrible, looked terrible (in her opinion) and acted terrible. She'd always vowed to not allow the emotions to control her and with her pregnancy with Henry she'd managed that fairly well. But this time round she was extra grouchy and extra large. She'd had enough and couldn't wait for the last month to end.

Lying down in bed she waited to feel comfortable. It didn't happen. Knowing her time was short, an hour at the max, made matters worse. Her ribs ached and not even a pillow could ease the discomfort of her hips and swollen abdomen.

She lay for a few minutes before contemplating giving up and making the cup of tea Sarah had promised and then forgotten about. Izzy wasn't stupid, she knew Sarah's sudden exit was to escape the unpredictability of Izzy's moods. This made Izzy feel even more guilty.

She closed her eyes and decided to try again. She had so little opportunity to rest these days, she wasn't about to waste it on depressing thoughts. She needed to sleep and that was the bottom line. Screwing her eyes tight she focused on relaxing breaths and gradually felt herself drifting away.

*   *   *

The park was awash with early autumnal splendour. Summer was still clinging on for its final weeks, with long wild grasses along the banks of the pond and late flowers just starting to wilt amongst the brush.

But along the tree lined paths the tell-tale colouring of the leaves gave away the coming season. Leaves were altering to yellow and bronze and still hung precariously within their branches. The odd leaf had given up and had fallen to the ground below. Henry giggled as he kicked the few leaves around.

Will was busy regaling Sarah with stories about Henry's recent first day at playgroup, when Sarah heard her name shouted from afar. She turned to look and could just make out Joe approaching from the other side of the pond.

"Hey!" she said with a smile, as he reached them. He looked from Sarah to Will to Henry and back again. A frown worried his forehead. "And who is he?" he asked gruffly.

Sarah was shocked by his rudeness and immediately felt embarrassed. "This is my friend Will," she answered, her tone implying that she was not impressed. "And his son Henry."

Joe looked between the two other males again, still frowning and clearly trying to work out how they fitted in to Sarah's life. She wasn't about to enlighten him. She was still too rankled by his rudeness to throw him a lifeline.

"Hi," Will held out his hand and Joe shook it reluctantly. "You must be Joe. We're taking my son for a walk, so my heavily pregnant wife can rest."

Sarah wished he hadn't felt justified in explaining his presence, but that was Will all over. He hated conflict of any kind.

"Oh," Joe's eyebrows raised in relief and recognition. "Sarah's best friend, right? Amy?"

"Um, no, Izzy," Will coughed uncomfortably.

The awkwardness was palpable and Sarah longed to break it. "So," she asked as breezily as she could manage. "What are you up to?"

"I'm meeting a friend. Why?" his suspicion riled her, especially after his reaction to Will.

"Well, we're going to go and get an ice cream. Have you time to join us?" asked Will.

Joe looked at Will as if he was insane. Feeling more embarrassed than ever, Sarah had had enough.

"I'll see you on Monday Joe," she said firmly and took Henry's hand, steering him away from where Joe stood.

"Sure," Joe replied, the frown still present.

As they walked away Will coughed again. "So that is Joe? He seems pleasant."

Sarah couldn't help burst out laughing. "Oh Will, you really do see the best in every situation."

They said no more about the incident, but it had left a sour taste in her mouth and further niggling doubts whether she should be dating Joe at all.

*   *   *

6th January 1909

The festivities of Christmas and ushering in the brand-new year has brought a joviality to the household. As well as the formalities of my parent's entertaining, I joined the excitement of the staff celebration. Although just four of us (my father has insisted on the employ of a groomsman now he is conducting business again), we took full opportunity to celebrate as well as those upstairs. My months of hard graft in the kitchen has gained me respect from the other staff and I find myself relating better and enjoying their company far more than my own family.

Freddy and Alfie have been home for the holidays, having completed their first term away at school. Their countenance is much improved and their behaviour more in line with what is expected of life upstairs. They were permitted to join us for meals for the first occasion and I was impressed by their understanding and application of etiquette. They are no longer the little rambunctious boys they were under my charge, barely two years since.

193

I tentatively look forward to the year ahead, aware still of my father's lingering desire to marry me off. My furtive attempts to persuade Father to allow me to attend a women's college to study a typewriting course have been met with derision. Even Margaret attended this course, shortly before her nuptials last year. Father deems it unnecessary and has resisted any attempt to discuss it further.

I dare not even read the newspaper any more. Stories of the suffragettes litter the daily rags and while in the past I have found it inspiring, their lives no longer share any relation to mine. I am too entrenched in the lifestyle of the Edwardian upper middle class. I have no future to look forward to other than the satisfaction of my husband and children.

Of this I am no longer fearful. I simply wish my desire for a little more had been respected and allowed by the Master of this house, to whom I am still under submission. Perhaps marriage will be my saving grace after all.

18th February 1909

Life has quietened here. The boys have returned to school. Father has been away for business and Mother and I are completing a patchwork quilt we began at the eve of winter. My remaining duties downstairs have halted upon the increase of staff. I have spent my extra time, of which there seems an abundance, perfecting my sewing, learning basic dress making and under my mother's tutelage, painting. She is really very talented and has confided her own paintings to my viewing.

Upon this there is a small spark of hope inside. My mother has skill beyond her duties at home and while she has not the freedom to explore them, it is a comfort to know. I hope I am able to go further than she has. I will not allow that spark to die, not yet.

*   *   *

"Dermot, this is a call to let you know that I'll be heading to London on Saturday to the local archives there. If you can make it, please call back and confirm. If not, I'll pass on any details I find out," Sarah left the perfunctory message on Dermot's voicemail and made her way to lunch with Joe.

Truth be told she hadn't been looking forward to their date since Joe's rude remarks in the park. She'd almost phoned to cancel, but decided she'd rather see him face to face and try to work out what his attitude had been about.

They were meeting in the deli across the road from Sarah's work. It was her favourite place to pick up a quick lunch. They served a range of artisan breads stuffed full of fresh meats, hummus, olives, heirloom tomatoes and rocket. They also sold crisp salads with an abundance of homegrown herbs and salty delicious feta cheese.

Sarah entered the deli and looked around. There was no sign of Joe, which annoyed her, as she'd warned him she wouldn't have long to spare. Quickly ordering a sandwich of rye bread, goats' cheese, prosciutto ham and pepper dews, as well as a coffee, she chose a table and sat down.

She thought about her plans for the weekend. Choosing to head down to London was a two-fold decision. Firstly, she was desperate to fill in the remaining puzzle pieces of Eleanor's young life and secondly, she needed the change of scenery. Work was getting her down, with its endless pressure and deadlines and clients moving goal posts. She needed something to look forward to and something to take her mind off the daily grind.

Busying herself with a hectic job had been a coping strategy after losing Alex. Now it seemed more a pain than anything satisfying. She wondered fleetingly if working for such a corporate company had been a good move. She felt a temptation to take a salary dip for a calmer role.

Her coffee arrived and she sipped it eagerly. She seemed to survive on caffeine these days. The exhaustion of the working day was at least providing a decent night's sleep. But she needed coffee during the day, mostly to cope with the stress.

"Hey," Joe slipped into the chair opposite.

"Hey Joe," Sarah replied, suppressing a sigh.

Suddenly the thought of their date was draining, even though it was only for an hour and for a bite to eat.

His expression gave nothing away to the incident in the park and she wondered if he'd even been aware of his rudeness. Instead he grinned and proceeded to launch into a monologue of the productive work week he was expecting.

The waitress brought over Sarah's sandwich and Joe leaned over to take a look. "So, what you recommend I eat?" he asked.

"They do great sandwiches and salads, but they've specials on the board too."

"I think I need something more than just a sandwich," he mused and got up to study the board.

Sarah found herself irritated at his every word and scolded herself. This was not going very well.

Her phone beeped with a text message and she surreptitiously gave the phone a glance. It was a reply from Dermot. She ignored the sudden soar of her stomach as she opened the message folder.

Saturday might be difficult. I might have to give it a miss sadly. I'll let you know during the week. D

Feeling an overwhelming disappointment, and an alarming prickle of tears behind her eyes, Sarah put the phone away and composed herself.

Taking a bite of the sandwich she tried to relax. Joe was at the counter ordering, and although she'd usually wait to eat until his food had arrived, he was late and she needed to get back soon.

"Eating without me?" his eyebrow raised as he sat down.

"Sorry Joe, I've got about twenty minutes before I have to head to the office."

"Not meeting any more strange men then?" he said with a grin.

She was too shocked to reply at first. No apologies. Just humour which seemed to direct the blame at her and away from himself.

"About that," she began cautiously. "You were quite rude to Will, not to mention me."

"Really?" he said quizzically and she fought the temptation to just walk out. "Well forgive me for getting annoyed when I see the woman I'm dating with a guy, walking in the park, as if you'd known each other years."

"Well, we have known each other for years," she shrugged belligerently. "The point is you were confrontational and when we did explain, your attitude didn't improve."

He paused a moment, then laughed. "What… about the ice cream? I'm not five years old Sarah."

"Well, Henry is two and even adults can enjoy ice cream, Joe," she finished her coffee with a last swig and began to wrap her sandwich in her paper napkin. "I have to go."

"You've at least another ten minutes," he said, an impatience creeping into his voice.

"No, Joe, not even one minute." She stood. "You were rude to my friend. A friend who I have known in years, who is very dear to me, helped me through the death of my husband, and supported me through God knows what else, and you can't even humble yourself to apologise for your behaviour.

I get the misunderstanding, but your handling of it was unacceptable, as is your denial now."

She grabbed her bag from the chair and swallowed, trying to dislodge the sudden lump in her throat.

"Your dead husband?" came the disbelieving reply. She stood up straight. She hadn't realised what she'd said.

"Yes, I was married a long time ago. He died." She didn't wish to elaborate.

She had already decided she saw no future with this man and wasn't about to waste any more of her time.

"It was nice meeting you Joe, but I won't be going out with you again. I wish you all the best." She left the deli without a backward glance and fighting the tears that inexplicably began to flow.

Chapter Thirty One

The train journey to London was cathartic. The gentle clacking of the train against the tracks lulled Sarah into a welcome, relaxed state. The week had been intense. Work, Joe and then Dermot's unavailability to accompany her to London had taken its toll.

Sat in a relatively quiet carriage, having chosen the earliest train to make her way into the City, she placed her head back against the headrest and closed her eyes.

Reaching London, she'd have a day of searching in a sea of records and information. It would be exhilarating, exciting, tiring and possibly stressful. Here in the train carriage she could focus on just one emotion, that wonderful feeling of calm.

As the train slowed upon its arrival on the outskirts of London, Sarah stirred and stared out the window.

The grey, dirty streets of the big city assaulted her vision. Numerous houses connected to each other, stretching as far as the eye could see. Traffic moved like ants below the elevated tracks and traffic lights added a vivid dash of colour as they changed from red to amber to green.

It had been a couple of years since she'd been to London and she hoped it was still familiar enough to remember her way around. She had spent a lot of time visiting the city with Alex.

It had always been a treat to jump on the train and a couple of hours later experience the bright lights, theatres, museums, galleries and restaurants in abundance. Her last jaunt there had been for a work colleagues hen do and she admittedly missed the buzz of the big city.

Watching the train snake its way through the last ten minutes of its journey, she admired the red sunrise piercing through the grey smog. It captured her attention until the train finally pulled into the large, imposing station.

Exiting the carriage and blinking in the artificial bright lights, Sarah made her way to the barriers which separated her from the tube platforms below. She vaguely remembered the right tube stops from the map she'd studied before she left home.

In her hurry to get to the train on time, she'd forgotten the A-Z that had sat on the dining table in preparation. She'd mentally kicked herself the first ten minutes of the train journey upon realising her mistake, before the relaxing sway of the train had convinced her it wasn't worth the stress. She could easily buy another copy in London.

Rushing down the concrete stairs to reach the first tube platform she looked forward to seeing fresh air again and finding a nice coffee shop, while she waited for the Archives office to open.

Hating the squash of the tube, people pressing up against her and the roar of the train through the darkened tunnels, she quickly exited at the second stop.

Following the crowds, she found the next platform and within thirty seconds jumped onto the next tube train. Managing to get a seat, she took a deep breath and waited for the tube to reach her destination.

After what seemed an age, she exited the tube station for the blast of air above ground. The buzz on the streets was intense. Pedestrians moved quickly in all directions, a cacophony of voices reached her ears, and vehicles lined the street not going anywhere quickly.

Pausing to get her bearing, she realised she didn't know which direction to go next. Noticing a board with a street map not far in the distance, she walked towards it. Detailing the tourist attractions within the area, she got a quick grasp of where she was and crossed over the street, in what she hoped was the right way.

Just a few minutes later she could see the records office ahead. Relaxing she wandered up the street a little in search of a coffee shop.

Disappointed that a local market wasn't open she retraced her steps and entered the doors of a nearby Starbucks. Ordering her favourite hot beverage, a Cinnamon Dolce Latte, she sunk into the leather sofa by the window and took a deep satisfying sip.

As she contemplated her search for the morning and her strategy for finding out more information about Eleanor, her phone began to ring. Tempted to ignore it, old habits die hard and she reluctantly answered.

"Hi," Dermot's voice call out. "Are you on your way yet?"

"Um. I'm already here," Sarah said, momentarily confused.

"Great! I'll be with you in about forty minutes. Where can I meet you?"

"But I thought you couldn't come?"

"I moved a few things around. I'll explain when I see you." He held the hint of humour in his tone and Sarah found herself smiling in response.

She gave him directions. "Let me know when you're in and I'll order you a coffee."

"Deal. See you soon." He rang off and Sarah sat back in the sofa and exhaled.

Stunned, shocked and more than a little delighted, she processed her feelings. She hadn't seen him in nearly two weeks, and despite her own denials, she had missed him. The thought he'd be joining her shortly and they'd be searching for the Bartley's together filled her with nerves and elation.

This was originally their search, their secret even, and she realised how hollow she felt doing it all on her own. She drank the rest of her coffee to calm her nerves and threw the odd look at the clock on the wall.

She felt touched that he'd thought it was important enough to change his plans. She knew how busy he was. Sarah checked her phone with frequency, but each time the screen was blank, indicating no new message from Dermot.

Coffee dregs cold and her nerves tripling as the minutes elapsed, she finally heard the ping of a text message. Grabbing her phone in haste she read that Dermot had just arrived at the station. Standing, while straightening her clothing to calm her nerves, she ordered two coffees.

Within a few minutes Dermot was walking through the door. He looked relaxed, with a few days' worth of stubble across his chin, and wearing a blue checked shirt and faded denims.

As he turned to grin at her, Sarah felt a bolt of electricity shoot through her and took a deep breath. It had been a long time since she'd had that reaction to anyone.

"You're here," she said, mentally kicking herself for saying something so stupid.

"Thanks for ordering for me," he said good naturedly. He took the beverage gratefully and took a gulp. "I so need this coffee," he grinned.

Sarah smiled back self-consciously and felt a shyness sweep over her. She needed to get on top of her feelings quickly if she was going to cope with his presence today.

"No problem," she managed.

"I only crawled into bed at one this morning," Dermot explained. "I feel I need a bucket of coffee this morning."

"You shouldn't have come then, Dermot," she said, feeling guilty.

"That was my choice. I let the ball drop with our investigation and I've felt bad about it. You shouldn't have had to do it on your own. I promised to help, then I didn't. I need to make that up to you. Besides I need to prioritise sometimes. The cottage will still be here tomorrow."

"I understand that though Dermot. You've a huge project on your hands...."

"No, I should have been there. Remember that excitement when you first discovered the journals? Well, it was infectious. I couldn't wait to join you in the search, but I got distracted. The house is important, but so is friendship and honouring promises."

"I don't think you ever actually promised..." Sarah said, despite being pleased and touched.

"Well, regardless, I left it to you and that was wrong. I said I'd help, I'm sure I did, and that's what I'm here to do," he grinned again.

She'd missed that grin. It was so easy, so sure. Unlike Joe's which was designed to be cheeky and impish, Dermot's grin was just part of who he was. And it made her feel a little nervous.

He drank his coffee with more than a hint of satisfaction. The late night and early start had taken its toll. The beverage was like strong medicine at the onset of flu. It hit the spot almost immediately.

He surreptitiously glanced towards Sarah over the rim of the mug.

She looked well. Her cheeks were flushed by the autumnal chill in the early morning air. Her hair was a little longer than he'd last remembered, even though it had only been weeks since their last encounter. It held a slight wave in the ends, which flicked against her shoulders.

While working on the cottage Dermot had had plenty of time to think. Sarah came into his thoughts often. Knowing she was dating, he had decided not to pursue anything, yet the sneaking suspicion that what he felt for her was beyond friendship grew. The more distance apart, the worse it actually got. He still mentally kicked himself for missing an opportunity.

The last couple of times he'd bumped into her, he had tried to keep it professional. He didn't believe it was appropriate to flirt with someone already dating another. But in doing that they'd lost the ease at which they normally conversed. He missed the banter they'd had together. Not only that, he'd missed her too.

It wasn't long before they'd finished their drinks and started the walk towards the Archives. The sun was finally high in the sky, but the grey above, indiscernible between cloud and smog, hid it for most of their journey.

Sarah reminded him of what she had found out so far. Dermot asked lots of questions and seemed excited by the progression of the search. Their conversation then deviated as Dermot asked after Will, Izzy and Tessa. Sarah filled him in, pleased that not only did he show interest in her friends, but also in their ease of conversation. She hated how stilted things had become between them.

Entering the archive offices, Sarah and Dermot immediately quietened. Both had a sense of excitement and trepidation and the enormous task ahead was not lost on either of them.

Dermot took charge, leading Sarah to the monitors and desks where they could peruse the archives on the computer. It wouldn't hold all the information available, but was the best place to start.

Just like the previous archives office, Sarah had several screen pages to scroll through. She was looking up Eleanor's married name as well as looking up Tobias, while Dermot searched Eleanor's maiden name just in case any additional information was available.

After half an hour Dermot shook his head and sighed. "Nothing here," he said. "I'm wondering if I should ask at the information desk directly. They might be able to direct me to archives not stored on the database."

"Good idea," Sarah nodded enthusiastically. She was beginning to get neck ache from being hunched over the screen and stretched her arms out widely. She watched him for a moment as he approached the desk and instantly charmed the older lady behind her desk. Sarah smiled.

Turning her attention back to the monitor she narrowed her eyes, focusing on the list of names. Suddenly Tobias' name jumped out at her. Clicking on the link, Sarah felt a buzz of excitement.

A file containing a birth certificate opened up. Tobias and Eleanor's names were recorded as the parents. A daughter called April was registered as born on the 11th of March, 1913. Eleanor was just twenty-one when she became a mother. Sarah was aware that was normal for society at the time, but couldn't imagine becoming a parent at that age. Not long after she discovered a second birth certificate for a son, named Charles, born the 19th of November, 1914.

Pleased for Eleanor, Sarah continued her search. She wondered how, and if, the First World War had impacted the young family and looked intently at any entries that appeared to be from newspaper articles.

There was nothing, but given the age of Tobias, Sarah was under no doubt that he would have been drafted into the army in some form. She had a sudden compulsion to silently pray that he hadn't been killed in action. Her heart would break for Eleanor.

She was then relieved to find an entry further down the page. It was a register dated 7th of February, 1926. Sarah was thrilled to read Eleanor and Tobias' named as local business owners, running a shop selling fresh groceries, homemade cakes and pastries.

It reminded Sarah of her own parent's catering company and it warmed her inside. Eleanor finally had the career, out of the home, that she'd wanted. Maybe it wasn't quite the job she'd envisioned, and had perhaps been borne out of difficult financial circumstances, given the economy at the time. It seemed her upper-class lifestyle had become obsolete as a result of the war and Sarah wondered what Eleanor's parents would have thought of their daughter running a shop.

Sarah was also pleased that Tobias had survived the war. With running a family business together, Sarah hoped that was a strong hint that they'd had a happy, or at least workable, marriage.

The next hour of searching provided no more clues and she sat back, frustrated. The last mention of them seemed to be in 1926.

Sarah hadn't expected much more in the way of newspaper articles, but she'd hoped for something. Some little titbit. But there was nothing. It was like they'd disappeared off the face of the earth.

Needing to stretch her legs, she walked over to where Dermot was studying some massive tome. He'd long finished talking to the lady behind the desk, had busied himself at a computer for a while, and then had searched the shelves themselves. Sarah was both impressed and appreciative by his effort.

"I need a break," she moaned, massaging her neck with one hand. Her neck and shoulders were stiff all over from sitting so long. "And I've hit a bit of a brick wall."

"Then let's go and find something to eat. I'm sure we've been here all morning." A brief glance at his watch confirmed it.

"By the way, the lady I was talking to earlier? Her name is Gwyneth. I asked her to look up some records for me. She'll have the results in a little while."

"What kind of records?" Sarah asked.

"Death certificates. I think perhaps it's best to start from the end and work our way back."

"That kind of makes sense," Sarah agreed. "I've found out some good stuff, but only up until the mid-1920s. Beyond that I can't find any mention. Either nothing happened in their lives after that, or they moved out of the area."

"Which poses a bit of a problem for us. And a possible dead end."

"I hope not," said Sarah grimly. She was desperate to have some form of conclusion. She didn't want to end up on a wild goose chase. However, she was willing to keep digging, for Eleanor's sake. She just didn't know how tangled and confusing it might become. She couldn't keep searching indefinitely.

They headed out into the open air and made their way to the nearest coffee shop, as Sarah filled him in on what she'd discovered so far.

Ordering a sandwich Sarah realised how ravenous she was. Her head full of new information and her stomach empty, she eagerly tucked into the food as soon as it arrived. Dermot sat across from her, tucking into a bowl of chips. He looked as exhausted as she felt.

"This is exhausting stuff, right?" he pressed. "I can't believe you did this on your own last time."

"Well, I had Izzy. Although she didn't really discover anything, but she was great emotional support."

"I don't feel like I've done much," Dermot shook his head. "My search drew blanks."

"But Gwyneth is looking up death certificates for us," Sarah replied. "That could be huge. And, I never would have thought to ask. I would have kept going all on my own."

"It doesn't seem to be doing any harm. You've found out a lot."

"Except for the ninety odd years of nothing," Sarah muttered.

"Ach, we'll fill in the gaps, don't you worry."

The mention of 'we' sparked a chain reaction inside her. There was a sense of comfort, a thrill and a nervousness flowing through her. She tried to suppress it, but on a day of emotional discoveries she knew it was a losing game. She attempted distraction instead.

"So, how's renovating the cottage going?" she asked.

"Good actually," Dermot sounded enthused by his favourite topic. "I didn't realise how much I've needed this. I love bringing a rundown property back to life. That thrill and excitement makes all the long hours and back breaking work worth it," he grinned, only half joking.

"And you're still carrying on with your day job?"

"At this stage, yes. I stopped working for a year to fix up Caledon Street. It ended up taking longer than that in the end, but I couldn't have completed such a huge project with a day job too. The cottage is much smaller and less daunting, but equally as exhausting, as I'm finding out. But I want to keep the job. Not selling Caledon Street means I don't have the luxury to quit yet."

"Why didn't you sell?"

"I fell in love with the property. I planned to sell the other two flats at least, but the thought of permanent residents put me off. I'll sell eventually. The first rule of property developing is not to fall in love with the house. I failed that miserably, but I've so much money tied up in it, I'll have to sell one day."

"Well, perhaps you could persuade Greta and I to buy our flats," Sarah teased. "At least then you'd know you have good residents in the building. And of course, you can give us a really low price for them!"

Dermot grinned. "Tempting."

They smiled at each other across the table and Sarah felt a twinge of self consciousness as she held their gaze.

"Why don't you come and see the cottage?" Dermot offered, after a minute of silence between them. "I'd love to show you around. Developing can be a lonely job sometimes and no one's seen my progress yet."

"Okay, I'd like that," she replied, hiding a huge smile behind her coffee cup.

Chapter Thirty Two

Returning to the Records Office, Sarah headed back to the computer to enter any information she hoped would highlight another entry. Dermot discovered that Gwyneth was at lunch, so busied himself at the computer too while he waited.

Half an hour later Sarah admitted defeat. There were no more entries regarding Eleanor, Tobias, nor either of their children. Her head was spinning and in truth, she just wanted to head on home.

She saw Dermot move in her peripheral vision and turned her head to look. Gwyneth was back at her desk and quickly engaged in conversation with him. Sarah interest piqued, she joined them.

"I've had a good search through. I found copies of two death certificates that I can show you," Gwyneth explained. She held out the certificates almost reverently as Sarah and Dermot poured over the desk.

The certificates belonged to Tobias and Eleanor. Tobias had died in 1972, aged 82. Eleanor had died four years later, aged 84. Despite the long lives they'd had, Sarah still felt a lump in her throat as she viewed the certificates.

"We have an obituary section," Gwyneth cut into Sarah's thoughts. "There might be some extra information there. Would you like to order a copy of these?" she addressed the question to Dermot, who held the corner of Eleanor's certificate and still studied it.

"That won't be necessary," Sarah answered for him in a whisper. She had already memorised the few details on the certificates.

"The obituary section is in the next room, if you'd like to investigate further. Just let me know if you need any more help," Gwyneth took the copies from them and smiled.

"Thanks Gwyneth, you've been a great help," Dermot said. He turned to Sarah who was still processing the emotion of the moment.

Of course Eleanor was dead. If she'd still been alive, she would have been one hundred and twenty-three. It was simply the jolting reality that her search was drawing to a close. Sure, she could keep looking for additional information, but that might prove either fruitless, or endless, one of the two. She had her own life to live too.

"Do you want to check out the obituaries?" Dermot asked, his question penetrating her thoughts.

She contemplated saying no. Part of her was exhausted and ready to head home. But the other part of her wanted to at least see if there was something, anything, to explain the course of Eleanor's life. Had she been happy? Had she achieved her goals? Had she had a full life? The snippets Sarah had found out told nothing except cold hard facts. Perhaps an obituary would give a hint to what kind of person Eleanor was, and had become.

"Yes, I'd like to look. Then we can head home," she decided. They moved toward the room Gwyneth had indicated and began their last search.

With the help of another member of staff, this time a bubbly student called Kitty, they found what they were looking for. An archived newspaper article detailed Eleanor's death over thirty years prior.

Mrs Eleanor Wyatt (84) of Henley Road has died after a short illness. Survived by her daughter, April Turner (63), three grandchildren and seven great grandchildren, Eleanor was a much-loved matriarch of her family. Born in 1892 in the South East, Eleanor lived her formative years there before moving to London upon her marriage to Tobias Wyatt in 1911. Together they had two children and partnered in business together, running a successful fresh food store. Upon the death of their son serving in WW2 and the destruction of the blitz, the family relocated to the West of England. There they resided for two decades, building their family business with daughter April, to include six successful outlets.

It was in the 1960's the family returned to London and restored and re-launched their flagship store. April took over the family business as Tobias and Eleanor retired and enjoyed a slower pace of life. This continued upon the death of her husband four years ago.

Eleanor's interests included an active role in the local community, through various activities such as charity work and visiting the elderly and infirm. She had a love of nature and despite residing in London for much of her life, she took the opportunity to explore Britain's countryside at any given chance.

She was a much-loved wife, mother and grandmother and will be sorely missed by friends and family alike.

"Wow," Dermot exhaled. "She lived quite a life."

Sarah reread the information slowly, taking it all in. Suddenly the young girl in the journals seemed evident in the woman she'd become. She hadn't withdrawn into a shrinking violet. Whatever the state her marriage may have been, whether she was happy or not, she had taken control of her life and made it work. That strong characteristic of the young Eleanor had never been lost or suppressed.

Reflecting on the paragraph about Eleanor's son, Sarah felt a brief jolt of grief. Having lost a husband, she could only imagine the absolute sorrow of losing a child. He wouldn't have been much older than Alex, and Sarah remembered the almost gasping grief in which his parents had coped with the news.

Sensing the emotion Sarah was battling with, Dermot placed a hand on her shoulder. "Are you okay?"

Sarah looked up at him and saw the concern in his eyes. If it had come from anyone else it would have annoyed her. She might even have returned to that well-worn shell of hers. But with Dermot she felt comforted. She had a fleeting desire to melt into his arms.

"Yeah," she whispered, controlling her emotions. "I guess this is the end. It's finished, done. I can't go anywhere else with this."

"You didn't want the search to end?"

"No, it's time it did. I know that. Just seeing it all in writing is so final, I guess."

"Shall we go? Or do you need more time?"

"Let's go," she thought only momentarily. "It's time to get back to the present."

*   *   *

The journey home was a sobering one. Sarah spent much of the time staring out the window thinking about the information they'd found. Dermot hadn't minded. He was busy sending emails on his smart phone, trying to organise the week ahead with various contractors he had coming in to work on the cottage. Sarah was grateful for the time to contemplate.

Her main concern, the one thing understandably missing from the search, was whether Eleanor had been happy. She might never know and that played on her mind. But there was nothing else she could do, or was willing to, to find out. Ten years of searching might never answer that question, and besides Sarah believed she'd discovered what she could.

Tired, Sarah stretched out her limbs toward the empty seat opposite. Tearing her thoughts off Eleanor, she listened in to Dermot's conversation. He was instructing his plumber on a job needing doing on Monday. She didn't mean to pry, but hearing Dermot talk with such passion, even just in regards to a plumbing job, had caught her attention. She wished she felt the same passion over her own career, and thought not for the first time if she was in the right job.

No longer needing the job as a distraction, Sarah wondered if it was time to look for a slightly different role. As she contemplated the ramifications of leaving a job she'd only been in for a year, she barely registered Dermot ending his phone call.

"How about dinner?" his voice permeated her thoughts.

"Mmm?" Sarah answered without really hearing the question.

"Dinner," Dermot repeated. "Do you want to join me for dinner? We're going to be hungry by the time we arrive back."

"Oh," Sarah replied inelegantly. Suddenly the thought of dinner with Dermot seemed a little overwhelming. Not to mention nerve wracking. Yet at the same time she couldn't think of anything else she wanted to do. "That sounds great," she finally managed with a self-conscious smile.

He smiled back and Sarah simultaneously felt at ease and felt a wallop of electricity. Deliberately turning her attention back to the window, Sarah used the time to calm herself down. She wondered if this is how Eleanor had felt meeting Tobias. She sure hoped so. It was how she'd felt meeting Alex and now she couldn't deny the replication of feelings for Dermot.

What she wanted to do about it was what she couldn't decide. Not knowing his feelings, nor having the confidence to investigate too deeply, she was reluctant to do anything too soon. This was a decision she wouldn't rush. Her third step was becoming all too real and as scary as she had feared.

Chapter Thirty Three

The train pulled into the station and they made their way towards the high street. Deciding on Chinese, they entered the restaurant and were soon seated at a table. Dermot swiftly ordered crispy Peking duck and pancakes alongside a glass of red.

"Tuck in," Dermot said, once the dish had arrived.

"Are you sure?" Sarah asked, still perusing the menu herself.

"Absolutely. Peking duck was meant to be shared. I always order it, although usually I end up finishing most of it on my own."

Sarah happily filled her pancake with the duck and accompaniments, lathering on the plum sauce and folding it tightly. The sweet and zingy flavours burst in her mouth at the first bite and she sighed happily. Peking duck was also one of her favourites, but she usually ordered a cheaper dish.

She sipped her white wine while choosing from the menu. Gaining the attention of a waiter, she placed her order. Minutes later it arrived, steaming hot from the kitchen and looking inviting.

"Help yourself," she offered. Her Kung Pao chicken looked delicious as did the seafood noodle soup starter she'd ordered. A basket of prawn crackers was added to the table.

"Suddenly I feel like a cheap skate," Dermot laughed, looking at his own dish.

"Hardly, crispy duck is the most expensive on the menu," Sarah said in return. "And, these portions are plenty big enough to share, so seriously, help yourself."

Dermot took a handful of prawn crackers and a discreet spoonful of Sarah's Kung Pao chicken. Munching happily, they sat in silence, exhausted from the intense day.

"More pancakes?" Dermot offered.

"No. I'd love to, but this food is filling me up already."

"Then, I'll save you one and get it doggy bagged."

Sarah smiled at the gesture and sat back in her chair. She contemplated

Dermot for a moment. Initially his role of a landlord had concerned her, especially once she realised her attraction for him. But as they got on so well and enjoyed each other's company, that was ceasing to be a problem. Besides she could always move out.

The thought entertained her a moment, before she realised just how much she loved living at Caledon Street. Her flat matched her personality and she loved every quirk of the building. Greta's music was a complimentary addition and Dermot downstairs, albeit rarely these days, was a comfort and at times a thrill.

She didn't want to move and if there were any chance of anything happening with Dermot, she hoped she wouldn't have to. She swallowed down her concerns with the remainder of her white wine.

"Big day, hey?" Dermot cut into her thoughts.

"Yeah," she looked longingly at the wine glass, wishing she hadn't finished it so quickly. "My mind still needs to process all the information. I just hope that thinking about it won't keep me up all night."

"It's been pretty intense, hasn't it? If you want, we could have coffee tomorrow morning and talk it through then. It might help you relax a little this evening."

"That's a good idea. Come to mine at ten. Greta will be playing the piano by then, so she'll add to the ambience!"

Dermot laughed. "I have some incredible neighbours." He looked highly amused and Sarah returned his laughter.

"We are amazing. You'll be very sorry to lose us."

"Is that likely to happen?" he asked, looking slightly alarmed.

"No plans," Sarah said simply. "Just reminding you how awesome we are."

"And, am I a great landlord? Or am I letting you down there?"

"You've been very discreet. I like that in a landlord."

"That's probably because I'm not any more. Not really. I handed over full responsibility to the letting agent when I started on the cottage. I don't have time for any extras, no matter how small and piffling they might be. So now I'm just the guy downstairs who happens to own the building."

"I think I prefer that," Sarah admitted. "You've become a friend. Your role of a landlord always made me feel a little awkward, to be honest."

"Me too," Dermot smiled self consciously. Sarah felt herself blush. "Another glass of wine? My shout," Dermot asked. She nodded gratefully and lapsed into silence.

Still in the dark as to how Dermot might feel, she concentrated her attention on the remainder of her food. Dermot excused himself to go to the toilet and Sarah used the time to compose herself. She needed to get back on track and get the conversation going again. She hated those moments when they became awkward around each other.

"You really love property developing, don't you?" Sarah asked upon his return. His passion for his career intrigued her.

"After Caledon Street I didn't," he admitted, sipping his red wine. "It wore me out. But it was by far the biggest project I'd ever attempted. Perhaps it was too big, but I've always been ambitious. But after a year and a half, I needed the challenge again. For me there's nothing quite like property developing. Buying a house in desperate need of TLC and nursing it back to health is a fulfilling process. I've never been in it for the money and I'd never rip the heart out of a place. My passion is to restore and rejuvenate a property that has become run down and a ghost of its former self."

"I used to feel that way about my writing," Sarah interjected. "Transforming a piece of writing from something dull and uninspiring to something punchy, exciting and full of life. Or taking a spark of an idea and igniting it into a successful marketing campaign."

"But now?"

"The high pressure of the job was always a good distraction from Alex's death. But nowadays... I still want to write, and in essence I still enjoy the role, but I wonder if I need to diversify. Or even if I need to do something new entirely. I'm just not sure."

"I know it's easy to say, but I really think you should follow your passion, whatever that might be. I spent many years avoiding what I really wanted to do. I had a whole bunch of reasons, financial, family expectations, expectations from society. But ultimately, I couldn't fool myself anymore." Dermot confessed.

Sarah sighed heavily. "I just feel like I've already stepped out of my comfort zone enough this year."

"That's the way it happens though, right? It's never one thing at a time and it's often painful. But it's worth it."

Sarah loved the ease at which they conversed. She had no problem sharing with Dermot. Things she hadn't even confided in Izzy, she now found herself telling Dermot with no hesitation.

She met his gaze across the table and he held it a few seconds. A jolt of electricity passed through her, but for once she didn't withdraw and shy away. She liked the feeling and was finally comfortable enough to admit it.

He ran his fingers through his hair, leaving it ruffled. Suddenly he seemed unsure and for once Sarah felt confident in return. Was this a slight hint as to how he might feel?

After a loaded pause, he spoke again. "Well before you make any decisions, would you like to come and view the cottage?" Dermot asked tentatively. "You can see what I do and whether it's worth your while stepping out into what you want to do. Besides, I've been desperate to show the property off to someone," he grinned nervously.

She thought briefly, but had already decided her answer. "Yes, I'd love to," she grinned in response.

Chapter Thirty Four

"Mummy, Henry have a biscuit?" the doe eyed toddler pulled at her skirt. Izzy looked down and found herself unable to resist. Henry seemed so adorable of late.

Aware that her time with him as an only child was now short, she'd been making an effort to spend quality time together. They enjoyed trips out to the swings, messy afternoons painting and rainy mornings curled up under a blanket watching children's films.

She'd resisted the strong urge to rush around getting jobs done and generally 'nesting' before the baby arrived. Instead she waited until Henry was in bed, having spent the day with him, before attempting to get through her increasingly long 'to do' list.

Aware she still needed to pack the hospital bag, Izzy suppressed the temptation to panic. She'd have time and right now Henry was her priority.

"Sure honey," Izzy answered Henry and reached for the biscuit tin on the kitchen counter. She didn't mind indulging him on occasion. Especially as she now worried about the lack of time she'd have to give him once the new baby arrived.

Uncomfortable and not sleeping well, Izzy couldn't wait for the little girl's appearance. Yet she also knew life would change completely. She hoped her relationship with her first born wouldn't change completely too.

Taking a biscuit for herself, she led Henry over to the play mat, where his toys were haphazardly strewn around. He gasped in delight as he saw his beloved teddy bear and grabbed it up with sticky, biscuity fingers.

Izzy sat down on the nearby sofa and smiled. The simple pleasures of a toddler had been a source of comfort for her. It was the small things she tried to remember and appreciate. So much so that she had felt inspired to journal down the previous week and the adventures they'd enjoyed together.

Trips out in the autumnal sunshine, picking crisp red leaves for a collage, feeding the ducks with stale bread, Henry's fascination with the prickly casing of a conker... She'd had fun journaling their escapades and her thoughts surrounding them.

She remembered reading an article from a blog about doing just that, and then it hit her. That's what she should do! She sat bolt upright on the sofa, her thoughts suddenly racing at a hundred miles an hour. She should turn her journal into her own blog. A Mummy blog, just like the one she'd read the other day.

Her frustration at a lack of career, although long since resolved, was based (she knew) on needing something for herself. She gave so much of who she was to Henry, Will and even the bricks and mortar around her, that she'd longed for something to call her own. And here it was.

Better yet, it was something she could start now and not have to wait for until after the baby was born. While it wouldn't necessarily produce an income (she'd read somewhere how blogs could be turned into successful businesses), it was of her own creation and a way of channelling her creativity. In addition, it could be used to help others, teaching new skills, parental advice; the list was endless.

Thrilled by the sudden opportunity before her, Izzy quickly grabbed up a pen and pad and made notes. Henry played happily with his bear and a pile of Lego blocks while she sketched out her ideas, possible themes and content of her blog.

She resisted the urge to call Sarah right away, knowing with her profession she would have advice to offer. She couldn't wait to confide in her best friend, but she also wanted to start this on her own. There would be time to strategise with Sarah later. Besides, with the baby due in a couple of weeks, Izzy hardly had time to lose. She needed to get started as soon as possible.

With a satisfied smile on her face she sat back on the sofa and watched her son contently. Yes, it was certain. Life was certainly about to change, completely and utterly.

214

Chapter Thirty Five

Sarah woke to the sun streaming through the bedroom curtain. Given the recent chill in the mornings, the sun was becoming a rare sight. She basked in its warmth for a few minutes, before hauling herself out of bed. She had a busy day ahead at work and was paying Dermot's cottage a visit early evening.

They'd spent a nice Sunday morning together, with a pot of strong coffee keeping warm and Greta's music creating a subtle ambience, discussing their visit to London the previous day.

Neither had mentioned their meal the previous evening. She still felt embarrassed by her feelings and didn't want to draw attention to it. She wasn't ready to figure out what to do.

Three days later the work week had proved a good distraction, but now, with the visit to the cottage ahead, her nerves were back. Dressing quickly, before grabbing a quick breakfast of strong coffee and a slice of toast, she headed out the door. At least she had the busy work day to try focus her thoughts.

At her desk the stress of the day ahead was evident. Her email inbox was cluttered beyond a joke. The desk itself was covered with files of half completed work, placed there by her juniors who needed it checked before they could continue.

What Dermot had said at the restaurant about following dreams resonated in her brain. Looking down at the scattered documents in front of her she had a sinking feeling in her gut. He was right and she knew this job was not.

Leaping from her chair she headed to the kitchen. Another hit of caffeine was in order if she was to overcome her worrying thoughts and get on with the day. Whether the job was right or not, she had things to do. No decision was going to have an immediate effect anyhow. She'd have to work her notice and she'd never leave a project unfinished. It just wasn't in her nature.

Half a cup of coffee later and Sarah felt more prepared for the task ahead. It was time to get on with the day and stop obsessing over her thoughts.

The morning progressed steadily and the mess upon her desk began to look more orderly. Becca assisted her, taking the files that had been checked and approved and handing them out to the team. With them all working efficiently Sarah began to relax. Her mobile phone started to ring and she picked up.

"Hello?"

"Sarah. Are you at work?" Tessa's voice crackled on the other end.

"Of course. But I can talk," Sarah moved away from her desk and took the call in the relative quiet of the corridor. "I tried calling you over the weekend. I kept getting your voicemail. Are you doing okay?"

"Better, I guess," came the unconvincing reply. "I'm just a bit confused right now," Tessa's voice broke slightly and sounded more like a twelve-year girl than a confident woman.

"Why, what's happened?"

"I'm not sure," was the unsatisfactory reply.

Sarah looked back toward her office and thought of all she still needed to do. She wished she had more time to talk it through, but today was just not going to work.

"Can I call you after work? We can chat it through in more detail then. It's just a bit hectic at the office today."

"Oh. Okay."

"I want to talk through this Tessa, I do. I'd just rather do it without distractions."

"Yes, that's fine," Tessa's voice had reduced to barely a squeak. Sarah felt instantly guilty, but running out on her team was not an option and there was nothing more she could offer.

Concerned by Tessa's manner, Sarah headed back into the office. The incident played on her mind the remainder of the day. It was a major distraction she could have done without.

After finishing the work day Sarah headed to Dermot's cottage, via the sushi section of the local supermarket. There wouldn't be time to cook tonight. As if her day hadn't been crazy enough, it seemed her evening would push her out of her comfort zone too.

Arriving down the country lane in her car, the darkening sky added to the feeling of isolation around her. But it wasn't a horrid feeling. Instead the simplicity of nature and the quietness accompanying it was a welcome change from the day she'd endured. She parked up outside the right address and took in a deep breath of the fresh air that greeted her as she opened the car door.

Birdsong had reached a frantic crescendo against the failing light. The odd call of a larger bird reached her ears. Wondering if it was still too early in the evening to be an owl, Sarah made her way over to the front door.

The cottage was pretty from the outside. There were windows on both sides of the door and three smaller windows faced the garden on the first floor. An old trail of roses above the door was still visible, even though the trellis had seen better days and the roses were long past their best. A blue door stood bold against the whitewash of the walls. The paint was peeling off and the knocker and door knob were both rusty.

The small front garden was overgrown with a bird bath in the centre, now hanging at a strange angle. A collection of chipped flower pots was placed under the window on the right of the property, their contents uncertain. A light shone from the same window and the odd glimpse of cupboards hinted that the room inside was the kitchen.

Sarah knocked on the door. Her head was still full of thoughts of her conversation with Tessa. While known for her over dramatics, Sarah was nevertheless worried about her. Something had happened. Something wasn't right and Tessa was not giving the game away.

The front door opened wide and Dermot stood before her. His hair and clothes were dusty. He'd clearly been hard at work on some DIY project or another.

"Come in," he said with an extravagant hand gesture, waving her into the hallway. It was dark and smelled musty. Sage green wallpaper peeled off the walls and the white wallpaper below the faded dado rail had yellowed over time. Dermot clearly had his work cut out for him and this was just the entrance hall.

She followed him into the first room on the right and into the kitchen. It was far better than the hallway had been. New cupboards and doors had been recently installed and the counter tops were in the process of being cut and fixed into place.

A small dining table in the corner of the room was where Dermot had set up his office. His laptop was on the one side while the rest of table looked not unlike Sarah's desk had that morning. Plans, blueprints, and invoices all made up the barely organised chaos upon the surface. Several empty mugs added to the scene.

"Sorry about the mess. It'll be another couple of months before the place looks tidy."

"Fair enough. You've got a lot to do."

"Hey, I've done a lot already, you know," Dermot said in mock protest.

"I'm sure," Sarah grinned at his teasing. "I'm keen to see what you've achieved."

Dermot looked a little sheepish. "Now the pressure's on. You're right, there's more to do than what's been done. Hopefully you'll see all the small things, otherwise you might be disappointed."

"The kitchen looks good already," Sarah threw him a lifeline.

"Thanks," he scanned the room briefly and stepped closer to the kettle. "Cup of anything?"

"A tea would be nice," Sarah sighed. It felt like the world and all its problems were on her shoulders.

"Bad day?" Dermot asked. She felt touched by his obvious concern.

217

"You could say that," she replied, without elaborating. She had still to process all that was going on in her mind, before she could share the half of it. She, of course, wouldn't mention her confusing feelings for Dermot, but even Tessa's issues and work problems were too much to share at that moment. She needed a holiday.

Dermot busied himself making the drinks and didn't push the subject. Her expression must have put him off, she thought ruefully.

"Show me around then," she announced as he handed her the drink. She needed the distraction.

"Follow me," Dermot said good naturedly, and they headed back out into the hallway.

Opposite the kitchen was the door to the living room. Dermot opened it, flicked on the light and showed Sarah through. Exposed floor boards were in the process of being sanded and polished. The wallpaper had been stripped and the walls were awaiting a new lick of paint.

The fireplace was in good nick, the tile surround an original, and the mantle above surprisingly simple and chic. It was made of thick oak and Sarah like the rustic nature of it. A rusty sliding door gave access to the garden, although she seriously doubted in its current condition that it would even open.

Next to the living room door was the staircase, which was in good need of a coat of paint and a new carpet. Under the stairs a small cupboard smelled rather musty. Beyond that was a small cloak room, fairly inoffensive in design, and the back door to the garden.

Dermot led her upstairs. Three bedrooms and a family bathroom filled the space. The master bedroom was already decorated, a simple off white with natural wood furnishings and matching fitted wardrobes. It was plain but a good blank canvas for whoever bought the place. A second bedroom was a small double, with a drab single fitted wardrobe and a mottled green carpet.

The third bedroom was a single room. A small cupboard provided a few shelves for clothes with the boiler squeezed in on the one side. The wallpaper had given up the fight, massive swathes of it hung in pieces across all four walls. The carpet had patches and stains and was an offensive shade of pink.

The bathroom, the last room to be shown, was an avocado suite with matching tiles. It was hideous. Boxes of new tiles, in pebble shades, were stacked neatly against the wall. A shower door was propped up next to a bath, which obviously hadn't been used in a long while.

"I'm planning to take out the bath, it's too large and has the wrong angle to be comfortable. Not to mention that it's past its prime. I'm going to replace it with a smaller but better designed bath and add a shower unit in the corner. And of course, change the tiling and dreadful lino."

He shared a little of what he wanted to do with the other rooms as they headed back downstairs.

"And the front and back gardens need some landscaping too," he concluded.

The passion in which he spoke about the place made Sarah feel both uncomfortable and with a sense of longing. Surely there was a job out there that would replicate the same feelings in her?

"So, what do you think?" Dermot asked.

"Well there's clearly a long way to go, but you've achieved a lot for sure," she hoped she sounded encouraging.

"It's been four weeks of stripping, sanding, plastering, painting, you name it. I've had electricians and plumbers traipsing through the house and a new kitchen installed. But that's just the start of it."

"What you've done is huge in such a short time," she replied, genuinely impressed.

"But it's about time and money. I can't risk falling behind. That's why you've seen so little of me. I've had to sleep here to guarantee a full evenings worth of work. Not to mention weekends too. I've squeezed the surveying into three days a week, so I've extra time here. I need to flip this place over within twelve weeks."

"Wow, that's not long."

"It'll take another three plus months to sell and get the money transferred, then I'll need to buy the next one. Every week I go over delays the entire process."

Sarah couldn't get her head around the pressure he must be feeling. And yet, his enthusiasm for the task overruled any negative elements. She pondered this for a moment and sipped the remainder of her tea.

Dermot, now sitting at the kitchen table and powering down his laptop, shot her a quizzical look. Sarah looked stressed and tired. Something was nagging at her thoughts and she'd withdrawn behind her wall again.

He'd found himself thinking about her more and more. Even the distractions of developing a house were no match. While painting he was thinking of her. While installing the kitchen he couldn't take his mind off her. Since their trip to London and subsequent dinner she'd even crept into his dreams.

A woman was definitely not a distraction or complication he was needing. He had too much going on without adding to his plate. And yet, he would be disappointed if she wasn't a factor in his life.

Seeing her withdrawn and concerned bothered him. He wanted to solve whatever the issue was. He wanted to break through her self-imposed walls. He wanted to hold her in his arms and comfort her.

He watched her battling her emotions and had a horrible feeling he might be the reason for it. Had he said or done something wrong? Nothing in her expression was giving anything away. She fiddled with her tea cup. He noticed that she did that a lot when nervous or unsure. Deciding against asking her

219

what was wrong, he simply observed her inner battle.

She placed the cup upon the table and pulled her handbag closer to her. "Thanks for showing me around Dermot. This place is incredible. But I really have to go. It's been a long day." She wasn't looking forward to phoning Tessa when she got home.

Dermot stood to see her to the door. He was worrying his lip and seemed suddenly serious. She hoped she hadn't offended him with her abrupt manner. The last thing she wanted was to create tension between them again.

They said a stilted goodbye and she headed to her car with her heart sinking. Somewhere in the evening something had gone terribly wrong and she suspected she was the cause of it.

Chapter Thirty Six

"Tessa speaking."

"Hey, it's Sarah. I'm parked up and just wondered if you'd rather I pop in this evening? I can be with you in ten minutes."

"Oh, okay. Where have you been then?"

"Just visiting a friend," Sarah replied vaguely. She didn't want the third degree from anyone, least of all Tessa. "I'll be with you soon."

Not long later Sarah pulled into the small cul-de-sac where Tessa lived. Tessa answered the door, already in her pyjamas and her hair freshly washed. She looked better than Sarah feared she would, and wondered what was going on.

"Tea?"

"No, I've just had one."

Tessa led Sarah into her bedroom. It was looking marginally better than last time. A cheap wardrobe was a new addition to the room and hid the clothes that had previously been thrown over the chair. The room was also a little neater than before and an old photograph of Tessa with her family, including Alex, stood in a frame on the bedside table. Sarah felt a pang looking at it and turned her gaze away.

Tessa sat down on the bed and picked at her nails. "I've had a confusing few days," she said blandly.

"What's that mean Tessa?" Sarah asked, refusing the chair which Tessa had pulled out for her and pacing the room instead. "I've been worried about you all day."

"I had a call from Kris," she replied. Sarah stopped pacing and stared at her. "I wasn't expecting it. I'd accepted that I'd never hear from him again. And then, he just called."

"Well, what did he say?"

"He was angry. He called me a few names. I started to cry which seemed to make him angrier," Tessa admitted, her gaze fixated on the carpet.

"Then he calmed down and apologised and I got tongue tied. I didn't know what to say. I've spent weeks imagining how to explain myself, but I couldn't find one word," she paused and fell into silence.

Sarah froze and waited for Tessa to continue. When she didn't Sarah grunted in frustration. "Tessa, what happened? Why are you confused? What did he say next? Tell me!"

"I asked if I could call him back," Tessa half laughed. "He wasn't amused, but I was so choked up he agreed. I phoned him an hour later and explained everything. All I told you, I told him."

"And then?"

"He said he needed time to think through what I'd said. He only phoned me again this morning. I'd given up hope. He said he wanted to see me face to face. He wasn't sure whether I was just making excuses. He said he needed to see my eyes, as I can never lie by my eyes."

"Wow," Sarah managed.

"I know," Tessa said, her eyes swimming in tears. "He must hate me right now."

"But he wants to see you. Maybe you've got a chance to bring him round."

"But I don't deserve him!" Tessa wailed. "He hates me. I hate me. How can I ask him to come back when we both feel that way?"

"He doesn't hate you. He's just angry. If he hated you, he never would have listened to your reasons, let alone call you back. He just wants to be sure."

"You think?"

"Look, I'm not saying he's going to take you back," Sarah tried to reassure Tessa at the sudden alarm on her face. "However, it is positive that he wants to meet you. You never know what could come from that."

"The thought of seeing him freaks me out. How can I face him?" Tessa's eyes were wide and Sarah took pity on her.

"Why don't you plan to meet him at mine? I can be there if you need me. I can hide in the other room or act as mediator between you? Besides, if he's in my house he'll be on his best behaviour, right? He can't get too angry with me there."

"I'd love that. Do you think he'll agree to it?"

"You can only ask."

Tessa thought a moment. "What should I wear?"

Sarah laughed in relief and shook her head. "We'll figure all that out. We'll have an evening to dress up and choose if you like?"

"Thanks Sarah," Tessa said. "You're the best. You're... you are like a sister. Better than a sister actually. I'm sorry for what I said before."

Sarah was touched.

"Thanks Tess," she whispered.

They smiled at each other. Sarah wasn't sure it was wise to ask the next question, but she ventured forth anyway. "If it came to it, would you get back with him?"

Tessa closed her eyes. Sarah wondered if she'd gone too far. Tessa's emotions were so delicate right now and she didn't want to tip her over the edge.

"I don't feel I deserve him, but yes I would," she finally answered. Opening her eyes again she looked at Sarah with a brave smile.

"But I don't think it'll come to that. How can I expect him to give me another chance when I broke his heart?"

"Stranger things have happened. I think you just need to focus on the meeting and not beyond that. Explaining your actions and gaining his forgiveness might be the best you can hope for," Sarah said sympathetically.

Personally, she wouldn't like to be in Tessa's shoes. Her hasty and ill thought out actions may have cost her a wonderful relationship and man. But Tessa was irresponsible, not malicious, and Sarah still felt sorry for her. It was going to be a painful lesson to learn, but maybe she needed to learn it. She wasn't a child anymore and had to learn to deal with circumstances appropriately. Not for the first time Sarah felt more like a mother to Tessa than a sister.

Only an hour later, as the moon hung high in the inky black sky and Sarah could no longer stifle her yawns, did she finally head home. It had been a long day and once again her mind was packed with information.

Once home in bed, unable to sleep, Sarah mulled over the comings and goings of the day. She had a lot to think about, decisions to make and emotions to overcome. Only as the early birds began to twitter in the still dark sky, not far off from dawn, did Sarah finally manage to fall asleep.

Chapter Thirty Seven

"Oh, this is so nice," Izzy sighed in ecstasy and replaced the cup back in the saucer. Sarah had taken her out to a traditional tea rooms, where they'd ordered afternoon tea as a last hooray before the baby's arrival.

"Couldn't agree more. I think we both need this," Sarah said enigmatically, having not yet explained the stress of her week.

Today was about Izzy though and Sarah had had enough time to worry over what else was going in her life. She now just wanted to treat her best friend and gloss over the finer details of her own problems.

"Hmm," Izzy replied, only half listening. She was munching her way through a salmon and cucumber sandwich, having already polished off a scone with raspberry jam and clotted cream. An array of cakes and sandwiches remained and Sarah took a jam tart with fresh glazed strawberries on top.

"I've something to tell you," Izzy managed eventually, finally swallowing the last morsel of triangular bread.

"Oh yeah?" was all Sarah could emit amongst the flaky pastry and rich filling clogging up her teeth.

"I've started a blog," Izzy stated proudly. "I'm officially a mummy blogger."

"Really? That's great Iz. When did this happen?"

"Just a couple of weeks ago. Obviously, I'm not making any money from it. I'm still trying to figure all that out to be honest. But I'm networking with all these other mums and I'm loving it. To know that there are so many out there who feel the same way I felt a few months ago; Mums who get frustrated at home and are desperate for something of their own. I honestly thought I was the only one. And now I can share my own journey with them through the blogging. It's so much fun," Izzy finally took a breath. "I'll send you the link."

"That's great news. You're so creative, that you're bound to be good at that kind of thing. Yes, send me the link. There's a couple of mums at work that I can email the details to. And if I can help in anyway... just give me a bell."

"I was hoping you could give me some tips. I know you've got a few staff who work on the social media side of things. And of course, your own knowledge of effective marketing. Oh, I feel like I'm just begging here."

"I'd be happy to give you some tips. It's not easy starting out on your own. If you don't know how to make your blog a success it will most likely fail. But..." Sarah hastened to add at Izzy's crestfallen expression. "if you're prepared then you've got a good chance to really make a go of it. I'll coach you. Let's set aside an evening or two and I'll fill you in on what I know."

"Thanks Sarah," Izzy looked relieved. "I feel so clueless. I'm loving the interaction with others, but I want to make the blog successful too. I'd hate to be wasting my time."

"Then I'll help you so you won't be," Sarah grinned. They both helped themselves to a sandwich and munched happily for a minute.

"So, what's going on with you?" Izzy asked as soon as her mouth was empty.

"Too much to get into right now," Sarah admitted.

"Sounds interesting," Izzy raised an eyebrow. "Come on. You can't bring me out for afternoon tea and then not give me all the gossip. That's what these things are for."

"Look, it's nothing too exciting. I'm stressed out and overworked and Tessa's still involving me in her tangled love life and..." Sarah stopped short of mentioning Dermot.

"And?" Izzy didn't miss a thing.

Sarah sighed. "I stopped dating Joe," she attempted, hoping that would throw Izzy off.

"Yeah, you told me that already. But I thought you were happy about that. Or is there something else you're not telling me?"

Knowing she was not going to get a moments peace unless she confessed, Sarah reluctantly explained.

"I'm... I've been missing Dermot since he started work on his new property," Sarah spilled. "At first, I thought it was just his friendship I was missing, but, well we've seen each other a couple of times recently, just as friends mind you, and I'm beginning to wonder if it's more than that."

"But of course it is Sarah," Izzy laughed good naturedly.

"What?"

"I've known you a long time. I know when you're interested in someone, even if you try to hide it from everyone. Including yourself, by the way. Dermot's a great guy. If he likes you back then I say you should go for it."

"But I don't think he does," Sarah sighed. "We get on well. He's certainly a friend. But I have no clue whether he likes me more than that. And don't suggest I ask him."

"Okay," Izzy held up her hands in mock surrender. "It just seems a pity if you don't push on that door a bit. Sometimes it's not always obvious until you just say the actual words."

Sarah shook her head. "I'm not about to wreck the friendship based on an assumption. Especially when I'm not sure I want a relationship anyway."

"But you dated Joe," Izzy pointed out.

"I guess because it was easy," Sarah shrugged. "He was nice at first and made me laugh. He wasn't a threat. But Dermot is."

"Because you like him so much more?"

"Perhaps. Probably," she admitted. She sat back on her chair and took a deep breath. "Anyway, I didn't want to talk about this today. This is your treat. Let's change the subject."

"Oh no!" Izzy exclaimed. "You can't do that to me. This is major Sarah. You met a guy you like. Really like. You can't tell me to change the subject now!"

"I don't *really* like him," Sarah protested weakly. Izzy smiled and finished off her dregs of tea.

*   *   *

"I'm so scared," Tessa wailed, clutching the purple dress to her and looking in the full-length mirror. Sarah stood behind her holding the large bag of cosmetics Tessa had handed her upon arrival.

"You'll feel much better once you're dressed. You know he loves you in it and it makes you feel great. You'll feel indestructible once it's on," Sarah had rehearsed most of what she was saying, knowing it would come in handy at the first sign of Tessa losing her nerves.

"Oh!" Tessa wailed again, placing her forehead against the cool glass of mirror and closing her eyes. "I feel sick."

Sarah rubbed her back. "You'll be okay. I'm in the next room. Let's get you dressed and you'll feel a bit better."

"No, I won't," Tessa mumbled almost inaudibly.

A lot of coaxing later and Sarah finally persuaded her to put on the dress and start paying attention to her hair and makeup. Tessa had been the one insistent on dressing up, but Sarah had got her to agree to toning it down slightly. Looking gorgeous and glamorous could actually backfire if Kris was as angry as Tessa claimed. Looking a mess probably wouldn't help either, simply because Tessa never looked a mess and was unlikely to convince him. A happy medium was needed.

This was why the purple dress was being toned down with natural flowing locks (with just the slight teasing of a curling iron) and, despite the massive bag of makeup, just a dash of foundation and only a smear of lip gloss. The dress itself was pretty and feminine and not too sexy, and apparently Kris' favourite of all Tessa's dresses.

Having achieved the so called 'natural' look, they stepped back to assess the end result in the mirror. A glass of wine to steady her nerves, Tessa surveyed herself with a look as close to satisfaction as she was going to get.

The doorbell rang downstairs for Sarah's flat and Tessa whimpered. "You'll be fine. Remember I am here," Sarah said as reassuringly as she could and went to buzz Kris in.

A minute later he entered the flat looking intensely angry; thunderous even. Nodding aggressively at Sarah in greeting, Kris searched behind her, before his eyes rested on Tessa who was hovering timidly near the dining table. They narrowed as they zoned in on her and Sarah fleetingly wondered if Tessa and Kris' meeting was such a good idea after all. He was clearly furious.

"Come in Kris," she said eventually, deciding to get it over with. She was here after all. He surely wouldn't try anything with Sarah present?

He grunted in reply and came into the room. Sarah turned to view Tessa and her heart went out to her. Tessa was grey with fear and bit at her lip intensely. Her posture was diminished compared to usual. She was almost bent forward at the waist, hanging onto a chair for support.

Her timidity didn't seem to abate Kris' anger one bit. He stood glaring at her while keeping his distance and Sarah deliberately stayed in between them.

Eventually after several awkward minutes had passed, Sarah now happy that Kris wasn't about to do anything dangerous, she moved from her strategic position in the living room and entered the kitchen.

"Can I get anyone a drink? I've the usual; tea, coffee, juice, some white wine?" she kept her voice as breezy as possible, hoping to cut through the tension hanging in the room.

"No," Kris said abruptly turning his gaze back to Tessa. She was now sitting at the table, still nervous and avoiding too much eye contact. Sarah really didn't want to abandon her, but couldn't see the evening progressing from this point unless she left the room. Kris clearly wasn't going to talk with Sarah there.

Pouring herself a glass of wine Sarah moved back towards the sofa.

"Um," she cleared her voice. "I really think you guys need some space to talk. I'll be in my bedroom if you need anything."

Tessa looked panicked and Sarah mouthed a "don't worry, I'm right next door," to her. Tessa didn't look reassured.

Shutting the bedroom door behind her Sarah took a deep breath and a large gulp of wine. She wasn't planning to deliberately eavesdrop but wished she could have kept the bedroom door open a fraction. Then at least if she was needed, she could act quickly.

The silence that followed was deafening. Sarah sat behind the door, sipped her wine and waited.

"I can't believe I agreed to come here," Kris said eventually. Sarah could hear his words clearly and hoped he wasn't about to exit the flat in a fury. "You have no idea what you've put me through these last few months."

Tessa responded with what sounded little more than a squeak. "Come on girl," Sarah whispered.

"Thank you for agreeing to come. I know I don't deserve it," Tessa finally managed, her voice struggling under the emotion.

Kris responded with a grunt and they both fell into silence again. Sarah sighed. This was going to be a long night.

Chapter Thirty Eight

Sarah must have drifted off briefly, because she stirred abruptly at the sound of raised voices. Her cricked neck, having been resting awkwardly against the door pained her, but she ignored it to focus on what was being said in the other room.

"I spent weeks phoning everyone I could think of. No one knew where you were, or they wouldn't tell me. You weren't answering your phone. I could only guess why you left. You didn't even have the decency to tell me," Kris shouted.

His anger and frustration was overwhelmingly evident. Once again Sarah was reminded how far Tessa had pushed him.

"I know! I'm sorry. I hated myself. I wanted to put it right, but each day made it harder," Tessa cried in return. Sarah could hear her quiet sobs from the other room.

"And to use your brother as an excuse," Kris spat, interrupting Tessa's tears and shocking Sarah.

Silence followed a second before Tessa, in amazingly controlled tones, spoke carefully. "I would never use the death of my brother as an excuse for my behaviour. I've apologised for that. My behaviour was shocking. I hated myself for weeks after for treating you like that. But I would never have lied or embellished the reasons I did what I did. And to do what? Get a sympathy vote? Is that what you think? You must think I'm evil if you believe I'd use his death like that."

"Not evil. Just incredibly selfish," Kris said matter of fact. His voice was no longer shouting but the anger within was still evident.

"Yes, I'm selfish," Tessa sighed and Sarah heard her sit down heavily on the table chair. "But not devoid of emotion. And not cruel."

"What you did *was* cruel Tess. We had just decided to become husband and wife. Okay, so we hadn't dated long, but I was sure and I thought you were too. Walking out the next day, it was as if you had died. Let alone your brother."

"I was scared..."

"So, you say. But we could have talked it through. You wouldn't give us the chance."

"You're right. I avoided your calls. I thought running, like I've done before, was the only way. I couldn't cope with how I was feeling. You've got to believe me Kris, I loved you and it was the fear of losing you that sent me running."

"But as you said, you've done it before. You could do it again. How could I ever trust you? Are you going to run out on our Wedding Day? Or perhaps if I was ever ill, seeing as you're so scared of something happening to me?"

Tessa began to sob. Heavy, noisy sobs of years of heartbreak. Sarah, still behind the door, began to cry too. She'd never realised quite how much Alex's death had affected Tessa. She'd always been difficult, immature at times and had never really shared her emotions, but clearly losing her brother had caused more damage than Sarah had ever credited her with.

All the pain of Sarah's own grief found its way to the surface. Seven years without Alex had been long, hard and at times unbearable. Life of late had improved, but the grief never completely went away. Seeing how his death still affected all their lives, all these years later, proved to Sarah that Tessa was telling the truth. She hoped Kris would realise it too.

Kris grunted in frustration. "Stop crying Tessa," he sounded annoyed, yet his tone had softened. Sarah heard her make a conscious effort to halt the tears, snorting as she did so.

"I don't expect you to ever trust me again," Tessa said in a whisper. "I'm not asking you to. I just ask that you consider forgiving me."

"So, you don't want to get back together then?" he sounded incredulous.

"I don't expect you'd want to," Tessa sounded so resigned that Sarah wanted to hug her.

"I don't know what I want," Kris growled. Sarah's heart leaped at the small spark of hope laced within his words.

"You've caused a lot of chaos. Not to mention unnecessary pain," he paused briefly. "But if it's only forgiveness you want, then I guess I can work towards it. It won't be easy."

"Kris," Tessa began and then stopped. "I... I love you. I want you to know that. I don't expect anything to come of it. But I want you to know that I didn't run out because of any lies or pretence. I loved you very much. I still do."

Sarah stood from behind the door and made her way over to the bed. She suspected now had come a time for a heart to heart and she didn't want to eavesdrop on it. She quietly got ready for bed, the evening already late. She'd head out to the living room in her dressing gown if she was needed.

She could only hear muffled talking now, but resisted the urge to head back to the door.

Instead she turned her attention to the last of Eleanor's journal, now on its second to last page. Just a few more short entries remained and Sarah was almost reluctant to finish them.

But with all going on in her life and around her, it seemed fitting that she did. Life moved on. It was time for her to move with it.

* * *

14th December 1909

It has been a while since I last wrote in my journal. The circumstances under which I now write have changed entirely compared to this same date just twelve months hence. Last Christmas was one of much joy, my father in high spirits upon his new business endeavours and my brother's joviality at being home for the festive season. My brothers cut more solemn figures now, despite their endearing youth. Life has grown hard in a way incomprehensible on the most part.

Just a few months ago my Father's business dealings took on a sudden shift, much like their arrival in the first place. What had seemed an advantageous opportunity turned into a financial bog and although I am unclear of all the details, it seems that my father's reputation took a terrible plummet.

I have overheard my parents discussing selling the house, for which my heart is still sore. My brother's seasonal visitation has not lifted the spirits of any of us. Christmas will be a dire one this year and next year's uncertainty is fearful and draining of optimism.

9th February 1910

I have nothing but praise and admiration for father's tenacious attitude. Many a lesser man would have the found the last months a depressing fare and not risen above their circumstances. Father certainly had his weeks of worry, but has risen out of it with a determination I can only hope that I inherit in some part.

Despite many associates refusing to discuss business with him, he has not sunk into depths of despair. Rather he has made new contacts, pursuing them and proving himself a man true to his word and of strong fortitude. It is small strides towards restoring our wealth, but there is promise there.

27th July 1910

We are now without staff. Nanny has finally had to leave us, despite my father's small turn around in fortune. It is simply not enough to continue her employ. I am used to hard work and have no concern of what looking after a household will require. My mother is of a greater sensitivity and has not had her hands dirty in washing up water before. It will be an education.

My father is working. I know not the details, but the talk of my marriage has once more entered his vocabulary and I fear he wants me married off before folk realise the dire straits he is been in. He cannot be earning a lot and furthermore cannot risk my hand becoming an unexciting prospect. I have not had to worry about this for over a year, but now the familiar dread has returned.

19ᵗʰ August 1910

My father hosted a small dinner gathering this evening. For the occasion my mother and I enlisted the help of a local lady to help prepare and cook the meal. My mother has grown into her new role and almost knows the way around her kitchen. She is becoming confident in the basics, but a formal meal to accommodate eight people was beyond her abilities.

I was permitted attendance to the meal. I am now considered a grown up in my own standing, being eighteen and ripe for marriage. This however was strictly a business dinner and no such opportunity to marry me off was present in my father's mind.

How astounding it was then to be faced with a predicament of my own. A young man, a junior business acquaintance of my father's was also in attendance. Although the opportunity to converse was too few an occasion, I enjoyed his company very much. He seemed at ease with me as I was with him.

His name is Tobias Wyatt and I feel compelled to share this encounter with my precious journal, which has kept me company through some of the darkest times. I know not if I shall encounter him again. If he should grace me with his presence at a later date. But my mind and dare I say, my heart, is full of the potential and promise of what could be. I shall have to content myself in believing that what will be will be.

Sarah smoothed the journal between her hands, caressing its faded and aged cover.

She'd reached the end, had read the very last entry and was left with a sensation not far off heart palpations. Having a sneak insight into Eleanor and Tobias' first meeting was more than she had expected.

To read that there was indeed a chemistry between them was more than she could ever have hoped.

Whispering a silent prayer of thanks Sarah smiled at the little book resting in her palm. Finally, she felt her question had been answered. No more would she worry about Eleanor's happiness. She had her answer and she was unbelievably relieved.

"Good on you Eleanor," Sarah grinned. She laughed with nervous energy.

The emotion she'd invested into the journal and the characters within was intense. In a way it had taken over her own life. But it had also enhanced her own dreams and at that moment gave her a sudden passion to not waste opportunities. Eleanor had created her own destiny against all odds. Despite social difficulties, prejudices and financial constraints, she'd made her life work and had been happy. Sarah wanted to be happy too.

As her thoughts inevitably lead her to Dermot, she blushed and felt an instant determination to resolve that issue. One way or another she needed to know how he felt. Whether they had a future was uncertain. Anything could happen, but for once Sarah wasn't scared of the result.

She sat and mulled over her thoughts. It was a while before her mind quietened enough to notice what else was going on around her. The living room was silent. She could no longer hear any talking between Tessa and Kris.

Curious she made her way out of bed and cautiously opened the bedroom door. The lights were bright yet Tessa was lying fast asleep on the sofa. She looked exhausted, the strain still apparent on her face. Sarah grabbed a blanket from the bedroom and draped it carefully over Tessa, not wanting to wake her.

She'd have to wait for morning to find out how Tessa's evening had gone. She wasn't full of hope considering Tessa's tense and worn out expression, but she'd been surprised more than once that evening and decided to reserve judgement until morning.

Chapter Thirty Nine

As the coffee pot stirred to life, Greta's melodic tinkling of the ivories drifted up to the flat on cue. It was Sarah's favourite time of day, especially at the weekend. No matter how stressed her week, how little sleep she might have had, this was the time when she felt most at peace and completely content.

Tessa lay sleeping on the sofa. She looked as if she hadn't stirred all night. Sarah, still in her dressing gown, prepared two mugs in the kitchen. She didn't want to wake Tessa unnecessarily, but wanted to make sure there was a strong beverage waiting should Tessa need it.

Amazingly, despite the crazy thoughts going through her mind the night before, Sarah had slept well. Now her mind was alert with the scenarios and possibilities running through it. She wanted to talk to Dermot, but as yet she hadn't worked out exactly what she wanted to say.

As Sarah poured the coffee Tessa began to stir.

"Morning honey," she said as she passed her the drink. "How are you feeling?"

Tessa groaned and pushed her hair back from her eyes. She barely registered Sarah as she had her first gulp.

"Hmm," she managed eventually and Sarah took a seat opposite.

"I didn't hear Kris leave last night?" Sarah ventured carefully. She didn't want to be insensitive if things hadn't gone well. But there were few ways of asking the necessary questions without risking it.

"He didn't stay much longer after you left the room," Tessa croaked and took another sip of coffee. She looked up for the first time and Sarah could see the tears swimming in her eyes. Her heart sank. "It didn't go well?"

Tessa shrugged and sniffed. "He heard me out at least."

"Well, that's something. Maybe he needs a bit of time to think it all through."

"I don't think he'll be taking me back, if that's what you mean?"

"Sorry Tess."

She shrugged again and tried to look nonchalant, but she wasn't fooling anyone.

"Only my own fault," she sounded pitiful. "He said we could meet sometime to finish talking, but I don't see any point. He won't change his mind."

"He said you could meet up? But that's great Tessa! If he hated you, he would never have suggested it," Sarah exclaimed.

"No, he only said it because I was crying and he was tired. I wasn't in any state to carry on. There's a reason I fell asleep on the sofa," she said ruefully and gave a weak smile.

"He could have just finished it there and then though," Sarah said reassuringly. "But he didn't. He wants to talk it through further."

"I suppose so," Tessa said, still in her solemn mood. Determined to shake her out of it and find out more details, Sarah pushed on.

"So, what did you say to each other after I left?"

Tessa contemplated the evening before and Sarah noticed another small smile, this time in recognition.

"I talked a lot. Apologised a million times. He just glared at me for a long while. But then... well, he said although he struggled to trust me... he admitted he still loved me," at this Tessa gave her first genuine grin and almost immediately her scrunched shoulders straightened and she sat upright.

"Do you really think him wanting to meet is a positive sign?" her face transformed into one of hope.

"I'm not Kris," Sarah threw her disclaimer out there. She knew Tessa could get away with herself. "But I wouldn't be depressed yet. See what he has to say first. When did he suggest meeting?"

"This morning," Tessa glanced at the clock and practically jumped out of the sofa. "I'd better get home and get showered and dressed. He mentioned brunch."

Sarah rolled her eyes fondly. If he was talking brunch then he certainly wasn't beyond forgiving his ex. Tessa's own self doubt was the main cause for her depressive slump, rather than for anything Kris had said or done.

Ten minutes later and Tessa dashed out of the flat with a heartfelt thank you and a bear hug. Sarah waved her off and returned to the kitchen area, where she prepared French toast for breakfast. Her mind was back on all the changes going on around her and she smiled as she fried the gooey bread mixture.

Kris had shown his true colours, even if Tessa hadn't picked up on it. Despite Tessa's failings and tendency to run from anything good in her life, he still loved her. The fact that he wanted to see her again proved the strength of his feelings.

Touched and moved by their story, Sarah wondered at her own. Finally, she could admit to herself that she was tired. Tired of going through life alone. Tired of fighting to hide from the emotions that seven years ago had threatened to engulf her. Tired of running from her own opportunities, just like Tessa had.

Eleanor, against social stigma, had reached above her circumstances and had made a go of her life. Fortunate to have met a husband she actually loved, she was ahead of the curve, but nevertheless tragedy and hardship still came her way. That was life, all the ugly and crazy of it. For once Sarah wanted to be part of that tangled mess, instead of observing from the side.

So, it was with that thought that she picked up the phone and asked a slightly startled Dermot if he wanted to come around for dinner that night.

Chapter Forty

The dinner table was set out as casually as she could manage, without appearing to have made an effort. She had put out her favourite crockery: simple white plates with slim gold bands around the perimeter, placed in between knives, forks and spoons. Wine glasses stood beside water tumblers and she'd resisted the urge to bring out the serviettes. It all looked elegant but understated.

Dinner was also kept on the simplistic side. Wanting to impress, but nervous enough already, she'd opted for the easy solution. A shop bought prepared salad stood in a bowl in the middle of the table and feta stuffed chicken breasts and crispy roast potatoes sizzled in the oven.

A simple chocolate sponge cake mixture (which her mother had taught her to whip up in a hurry) was due to go into the oven once the mains were served, and a packet of instant custard leaned against the kettle in anticipation.

Sarah stood looking over the dinner table and felt her remaining level of excitement tip over into sheer nerves. Wondering, not for the first time, if she was doing the right thing, she took a deep breath and glanced again at the clock. He was due in less than five minutes.

She'd pinned her hair back for cooking and liking the result when she'd peered in the mirror later, had kept the style as it was. She wore a long black maxi skirt and a cream chiffon top. A dozen outfits remained scattered on her bed, including a deep blue dress which she felt was too showy and her comfiest jogging bottoms which were definitely not trying hard enough.

The complexities of keeping the evening casual had detracted Sarah from the nerves of what she was planning to do. Never before had she broached the topic of whether a guy liked her or not, with the guy himself. Never had she prepared herself to ask a guy out on a date even if the answer was favourable.

She was anxious and already doubting the wisdom of her plan. She had no concrete proof he liked her. For all she knew he just saw her as a friend and she'd end up embarrassed and mortified.

But, she reasoned, that was the topsy-turvy element of life that she'd decided to embrace. If she never stepped out and took a risk she'd never get anywhere. And certainly, nowhere she wanted to be.

When Dermot arrived at the flat Sarah's nerves showed no sign of abating. She took the proffered bottle of wine and welcomed him in, reminding herself to remember to breathe as she did so. He looked tired, but happy, and regaled her for a few minutes with the DIY tasks he'd completed since they last spoke.

"Thanks for organising this evening," he said gratefully. "The thought of another soggy burger and chips on my own, in a half-finished kitchen, wasn't a welcome one. I was surprised you invited me though."

"Really?" Sarah squeaked, wondering if he knew her intentions.

"Well we've not done this before have we?"

"We did have Chinese, which you ended up treating me to," Sarah reminded him, recovering her nerves at the same time.

"Ah, so you owe me then?"

Sarah offered him a glass of wine. She wasn't ready for the real reason to be revealed yet. They made small talk while she dished up the food and grinned at Dermot's appreciative glances at the roast potatoes.

"Gravy?" he ventured tentatively.

"Of course, Mr Matthews. What kind of a hostess do you think I am?" Sarah laughed and produced a jug from the cupboard beneath her. "Instant I'm afraid."

"Perfect," he grinned and took his plate over to the table. "Seriously Sarah, thanks for this. I can't tell you how much I appreciate a decent meal."

Her heart sinking, she hoped he wasn't purely here for the food. Whisking the boiling water into the gravy powder she took a reassuring deep breath. Even if he was here for the food, and hopefully her friendship too, it was better than nothing. She was determined not to lose him as a friend no matter what happened.

She joined him at the table and sat opposite. Pouring another glass of wine each, she tucked into the food in front of her.

"You seemed a bit tense the other night," Dermot commented, after finishing a mouthful of roast potato. "I was worried I said something wrong."

"Oh," Sarah said in surprise. "I'm sorry, I was stressed about a few things. Tessa was having some relationship issues and work was pushing all the wrong buttons."

"Well I'm relieved it wasn't me," he admitted. "But work? Have you made any decisions about that yet?"

Sarah played with her food. "I don't think there's any short-term solution. I haven't been in the job a year yet. I'm not planning to be there forever, but I don't honestly know that I can leave for a while."

She looked stressed and Dermot felt for her. The urge to hug her was overwhelming. He wondered if, in her current state, she'd be averse to it. He cleared his throat and pushed his thoughts aside.

"I'm here for you if you need any advice. I've been in similar situations myself," he offered. It felt inadequate, but it was something at least.

Sarah smiled and cut into her chicken. "Thanks Dermot," she looked up at him then and contemplated him a moment.

He wondered what was going through her mind. She blinked and looked away and Dermot was left none the wiser.

"More gravy?" she ventured and inwardly sighed. She'd copped out and wondered if she'd have another chance to ask him what she wanted.

They reverted back to small talk, discussing the week ahead, Tessa's relationship woes and the state of the local housing market. The main course was quickly consumed and Dermot helped her clear the table.

She stirred the pot containing the custard as Dermot dished up portions of the sponge cake. It felt companionable and suddenly she felt her seeping confidence step back into play. She could actually imagine them doing this every weekend. Cooking together in the kitchen, sharing stories from their week, the laughter and ease of conversation flowing between them. What's more, she realised she wanted that very thing. She missed that.

Her own company was fine, she actually enjoyed being by herself and yet she wanted something more. She wanted a relationship and not just with anybody. She wanted a relationship with Dermot.

Thinking over Eleanor's story and even more of Tessa's recent bravery she decided enough was enough. She needed to get over her fear and at least ask. If nothing else, to have an answer. Whatever that answer might be.

They sat down to dessert, Sarah having flicked on the kettle for coffee, and enjoyed the cake in companionable silence. She waited until the kettle stopped boiling and then decided to broach the subject.

"Um," she began inadequately and then ground to a halt. How could she bring up the subject cold? If there had been a little look, a suggestive remark, then she'd know. But she was having to completely guess.

"Yeah?" Dermot asked, his mouth full of chocolate sponge and custard. It wasn't the most romantic look and Sarah stifled a giggle. This certainly wasn't going the way she'd planned, but at least her nerves had abated again.

"I... invited you here... well, it wasn't a payback for the Chinese," she admitted.

He looked curious but didn't press her. She paused and struggled to maintain eye contact with him. It was the longest they'd looked at each other and she realised how attracted to him she was.

"I..." she choked with the nerves that had come back with full vengeance. "I wondered if maybe you'd want to consider... perhaps... going for a drink or a meal out sometime?" she sputtered.

"Isn't that what we're doing?" Dermot asked with an exaggerated expression of confusion, but with a betraying smile hiding behind it.

"Yes," she said, flustered. She couldn't think what else to say, despite the hours she'd spent imagining each scenario and possible conversation in her head.

"So, what you're wanting to know is?" he asked, the smile playing on his lips and lifting her spirits a little. Whether he knew what she was indicating or not, she was reassured he wouldn't be offended by the suggestion. It bolstered her.

"I guess, what I'm wanting to know is whether an official date would be a possibility?" she said quickly and with a slight air of defiance. Her defences were alert in case of a rejection, but she wasn't about to back down from her offer. What would be would be.

He contemplated her for a minute, the smile still on his face and a noticeable glimmer in his eyes but he began to shake his head. Her heart beating painfully in her chest she felt the plummeting of her stomach like a sudden punch.

Her mobile phone punctuated the heady atmosphere with a shrill shout. Keen to avoid the inevitable rejection coming, she jumped up to answer it. She couldn't look Dermot's direction as she pressed the green button.

"Hi Will," her voice wavered, briefly noticing his name on the screen.

"Sarah, I'm so glad I got you," his voice boomed from the other side. "We're at the hospital. Izzy's contractions started this afternoon. It looks like it won't be long."

"Really?" Sarah felt breathless with anticipation. "That's amazing Will, thanks for letting me know."

"Well, the thing is," Will continued and pause in his voice. "Izzy has asked if you could come down. She wants you here at the hospital."

"What?"

"I know..." Will said quickly. "I said it wouldn't be convenient. It won't be long, but it still might mean a late night and we can't do that to you with work tomorrow morning."

"No," Sarah said hastily. "Of course, I want to come! I can go into work late if I need to. I'll be there as soon as possible."

"Are you sure?" Will didn't sound it.

Sarah nodded vehemently as she practically yelled "yes!" down the phone.

"We'll see you soon then," Will said in relief and rang off.

Sarah turned around to Dermot, who was still sat at the table, and smiled tightly.

"Izzy's having the baby. They want me there. I need to head off."

She was partly relieved to get away from the topic of a date, but also disappointed to not have an answer one way or another.

"I'll take you down," Dermot said instantly. Sarah was surprised.

"No, that makes no sense. I could be there for hours. It'll be better if you head home and get an early night," she replied.

He shook his head and stood from the table. "You invited me here for the evening. It's only right that we complete that evening, don't you think?"

She laughed nervously. "I'll let you off the hook. It's exceptional circumstances after all. Besides they may not allow you in the hospital."

"Then we'll take our own cars and I'll drive home from the hospital if that's the case. They're my friends too," he added, noticing her reticence. "And besides, I'm not asking to be there in the delivery room, just in support of you. We've an unfinished conversation to complete as well, in case you've forgotten."

She blushed and mumbled under her breath something to do with it being ridiculous. He smiled.

"I'll make myself scarce if I'm not wanted, don't worry."

He followed her out the door and wondered if they'd have a chance to finish talking where they'd left off. He didn't want to miss the opportunity.

Sarah left the flat thoroughly confused and not understanding Dermot's reasoning at all. If he'd been so put off by her suggestion, as the shake of the head indicated, why was he so keen to complete the embarrassing thread of conversation?

The only thing she could think of was that he wanted to let her down gently. He was a gentleman after all. The thought made her heart sink into her boots.

Chapter Forty One

Four hours later little Arabella Iris was born.

Sarah and Dermot had arrived separately at the hospital and straight into the chaos of a busy maternity ward. It seemed Izzy's baby had decided to arrive on the busiest night of the year. Midwife's flitted between delivery rooms and the odd groan and cry could be heard in the distance.

Dermot looked faintly grey but pulled himself together and headed toward the waiting room, away from the where the action was. Sarah approached the desk and waited over twenty minutes until someone was free to assist her.

Soon after she was ushered into Izzy's delivery room and she tearfully greeted her best friend.

Izzy was sitting on the edge of the bed, with Will rubbing her back intensely. The midwife rechecked Izzy's vitals before leaving her in peace.

"How's it going?" Sarah asked gently.

Izzy looked up at her with a half smile. It was clearly an effort.

"It's hurting now," she said simply and grabbed at the gas and air mask lying beside her. She took a few deep and steadying breaths and placed it reverently back on the bed.

"The midwife said it is progressing quickly. We just hope not too quickly, as it could lead to complications," confessed Will.

"Do you want me in here with you, or would you prefer I wait outside?" Sarah asked, not wanting to impose or add any unnecessary pressure.

"Please stay a bit," Izzy breathed through the discomfort.

"And I could really do with a coffee, if you wouldn't mind heading down to the canteen later?" Will asked hopefully.

"Of course," Sarah smiled.

Will handed her a flannel and she mopped Izzy's brow for a few minutes.

"Dermot is here too," she said eventually.

"Really?" asked Will, sounding surprised. "How did that happen?"

"We were having dinner together when you called," she admitted self consciously.

Izzy's eyes lit up, despite her obvious pain, and Sarah laughed at the ridiculousness of it all.

"Don't worry, we're not dating. But I was planning to maybe ask him out on a date."

"That's so amazing!" Izzy managed before diving behind the mask again.

"Listen, I'm going to go and get Will's coffee. Don't get your hopes too high for Dermot and me. It wasn't going all that well when Will called. But you need to concentrate right now, so don't worry about me. We'll talk when it's more appropriate."

She left the room and headed to the canteen, via the waiting room to get Dermot's order. He decided to accompany her and they proceeded down the lift together. It took a further twenty minutes to find the canteen and they ordered coffees and bought a few snack bars for Will and Izzy, if she wanted them.

By the time they returned to the delivery rooms, Izzy's labour had progressed quite dramatically. Will had a few gulps of coffee before it was discarded, as he turned his attention back to his wife.

The midwife soon confirmed that Izzy was transitioning into the final stages of labour and Sarah decided to leave them to welcome their new baby as a family.

She kissed Izzy's clammy brow and wished them the best.

"I'll be in the waiting room," she whispered and backed out of the room.

She joined Dermot in the waiting room and they sat quietly anxious for a while. Eventually, with nothing better to do and nerves at their peak, Dermot decided to raise the issue of their prior conversation.

"Dinner was great," he began, innocently enough.

Sarah thanked him.

"But we never finished our discussion."

"No," Sarah began slowly. "But it was just a suggestion," she added hastily.

"It was a good one though," Dermot shrugged nonchalantly.

"But you shook your head..." she said, confused.

"Only because I wished I'd asked you the same question sooner," Dermot replied, his gaze steady and not taking his eyes off of her.

"I feel like an ejit for not being braver and waiting so long that you had to ask me."

Sarah raised her eyebrows in surprise and her heart began to beat faster.

"I'm a modern woman you know," she teased, as she felt a burst of excitement inside. "We can do that kind of thing these days."

He grinned widely. She found herself grinning back.

"So when would you be available for our date?" she asked.

"Breakfast time?" Dermot suggested. "I know a great canteen nearby.

Actually, scratch that, I know a great little bistro down the road. I'm sure Izzy won't mind if I steal you away for an hour or so in the morning."

"I'm sure she won't," Sarah let it hang in the air and they smiled at each other for quite a long time.

*   *   *

Less than an hour later, Will came out to announce the arrival of his brand-new little girl. He couldn't have looked prouder. Izzy and the baby were fine and were about to be transported to the maternity ward. Sarah was allowed to visit briefly once mother and baby were settled.

Quietly ushered in to the ward by a hesitant midwife, Sarah kissed Izzy and Arabella in turn.

"She's beautiful, Iz," Sarah smiled.

Izzy looked tired but content and Sarah felt a sudden pang for her own future. She knew she wanted children but hadn't dared to dream it could happen after Alex's death. Now, seeing her best friend holding her daughter in arms, Sarah couldn't deny her own feelings.

"Do you want to hold her?" Izzy whispered, proffering her sleeping child.

"I'd love to," Sarah glanced at the midwife who was still hovering. "But I need to be quick. I've been told we are well out of visiting hours," she giggled, nodding towards the ward clock which read 2.00 am.

"I'm so sorry you've been here so long," Izzy instantly looked guilty.

"Not at all. I'm glad I was here. I'd have only worried, waiting for news at home."

Sarah took baby Arabella and nestled her in her arms. She didn't stir, but breathed gently and made odd mewing noises. Her skin was silky soft and little tufts of caramel coloured hair poked up in disarray. She was adorable.

"Oh Izzy, she's simply perfect."

Izzy shifted her weight in the bed and smiled doggedly. She looked exhausted.

"I need to go and let you rest," Sarah said, gently handing the baby back. "I'll come visit tomorrow after work. Will said he'd let me know if you'll be at home or still at hospital."

"Thank you for coming Sarah. I felt bad asking, but I just felt like I wanted you to be near."

She gave Izzy a kiss on the cheek and shook her head. "Please don't worry. I wouldn't have wanted to be anywhere else. I'll see you tomorrow. Try to rest."

Ten minutes later Sarah was driving home, the darkness of the night sky heavy around her and no sign of the morning, which would inevitably come in just a few hours time. She was worn out but happy. Dermot had said goodbye in the car park and had reminded her of their breakfast plans.

Even just a couple of hours sleep would be worth waking up early for that.

Chapter Forty Two

Barely three hours later Sarah awoke to the dawn chorus. The familiar crash of tiredness engulfed her, having been used to so little sleep in such a long time.

But the dread that usually accompanied it was missing. In its place was a keenness to start the day. Anticipation was building, especially after she'd viewed the plates from the night before, still on the dining table and containing scraps of the food she'd prepared.

So much had happened since the dinner, where so unsure and self conscious she almost hadn't asked the question she'd been wanting to ask. How glad she was that she had taken the risk. Now she was meeting Dermot for breakfast amid a heavy hint that he was interested in her.

There was no guarantee their relationship would even go beyond that very morning, but the possibility contained more excitement within it than Sarah had felt in a long time.

Showering quickly and choosing her favourite work clothes, she gathered up her belongings and headed out the flat.

Outside 6 Caledon Street the air was brisk, fresh and with a hint of the winter ahead. The trees lining the streets were losing their leaves, which were an array of colours: gold, amber and honey.

The myriad of commuters walking along the street were all wrapped up in scarves and hats. Sarah enjoyed the icy coolness of the breeze. After the lack of sleep, it invigorated her. It gave her an alertness that even a full night's sleep would have struggled to give.

She strode on trying to remember the bistro Dermot had mentioned. She vaguely recalled its location and headed in that direction. As she saw the signage ahead, she took a deep breath and broke out in a wide grin.

Today signified the beginning of something new. Even the fresh air reminded her of the change in seasons and how when one stage of life dies, another is inevitably born.

Encouraged by Eleanor's apparent rise from the ashes, Tessa's bravery to try and grab hold of what she might have lost, and Izzy's embrace of her role as a mother, powered Sarah on towards those cafe doors.

It was new. It was real. It was a start. And she'd never felt more excited in her life.

Epilogue

The following six months brought many changes in the friend's lives.

Dermot and Sarah's breakfast had been a resounding success and they'd gone on to date, become boyfriend and girlfriend and at the completion of the cottage's sale, Dermot had whisked Sarah away for a weekend and proposed.

She said yes.

During those six months, Sarah had found herself gaining an interest in the cottage's many DIY projects and had discovered a love for property developing that Dermot was thrilled by.

Deciding to take the leap from an unhappy job situation, Sarah decided to go freelance and work part time alongside Dermot on their next property. They'd split the profits fifty/fifty.

Now engaged, Sarah found they had a big decision to make. Both wanting to keep their flats, they had yet to work out which one to settle into as a newly married couple.

Greta's beautiful music didn't travel so well downstairs, so Sarah is resisting moving into Dermot's, and instead pushes for him to move upstairs. It has yet to be resolved.

Not long after they started dating Sarah had, rather ceremoniously, handed the journals to Dermot. Handing them over had felt symbolic. It was time. It was now up to Dermot to decide what to do with them. Whether to track down the family and return the items from the attic; it was now his decision. Sarah was happy to step back.

Izzy thrived as she grew her mummy blog from strength to strength and looked after her two precious children from home. When the newborn months were over and Henry was settled into preschool, Izzy took an online sales job, where she could work from home. Needless to say, she thrived at that too.

And Tessa? After her second tentative meeting with Kris they'd agreed to take things slowly, simply meeting for coffee and then lots of talking for weeks on end.

Finally deciding to trust Tessa again Kris took her back. She returned the favour by agreeing to marry him a few months later and threw herself into the wedding plans with gusto. They married shortly before Dermot and Sarah's engagement. Sarah was chief bridesmaid.

Printed in Great Britain
by Amazon